Cynthia Harrod-Eagles stu[...]
the Universities of Edinbu[...]
THE WAITING GAME won [...]
in 1972. She lives in London, and will be taking the
story of the Morland family up to the present day.

Also in the *Dynasty* series:

The Victory

Cynthia Harrod-Eagles

Futura

A Futura Book

First published in Great Britain in 1989 by
Macdonald & Co (Publishers) Ltd
London & Sydney

This edition published by Futura in 1989

ISBN 0 7088 4296 8

Reproduced, printed and bound in Great Britain by
Hazell Watson & Viney Limited
Member of BPCC Limited
Aylesbury, Bucks, England

Futura Publications
A Division of
Macdonald & Co (Publishers) Ltd
66–73 Shoe Lane
London EC4P 4AB
A member of Maxwell Pergamon Publishing Corporation plc

To Lesley, Cathy, and Sid,
without whose support many a book
would be started, but few finished.

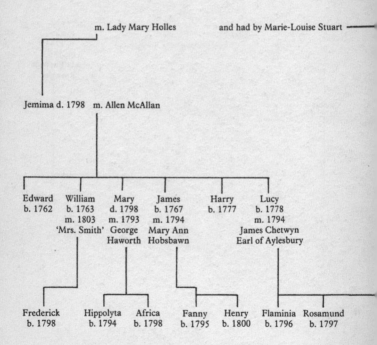

THE MORLAND FAMILY

James Edward Morland — — — — — — — — — — — — — —

m. Lady Mary Holles   and had by Marie-Louise Stuart — — —

Jemima d. 1798   m. Allen McAllan

Edward | William | Mary | James | Harry | Lucy
b. 1762 | b. 1763 | d. 1798 | b. 1767 | b. 1777 | b. 1778
| m. 1803 | m. 1793 | m. 1794 | | m. 1794
| 'Mrs. Smith' | George | Mary Ann | | James Chetwyn
| | Haworth | Hobsbawn | | Earl of Aylesbury

Frederick | Hippolyta | Africa | Fanny | Henry | Flaminia | Rosamund
b. 1798 | b. 1794 | b. 1798 | b. 1795 | b. 1800 | b. 1796 | b. 1797

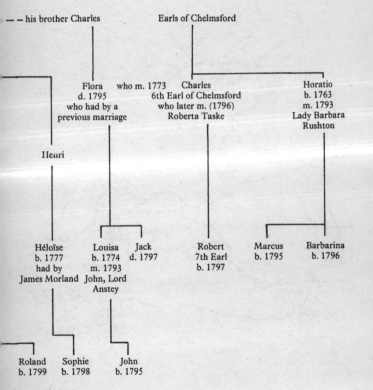

— — his brother Charles

Earls of Chelmsford

Flora
d. 1795
who had by a
previous marriage

who m. 1773

Charles
6th Earl of Chelmsford
who later m. (1796)
Roberta Taske

Horatio
b. 1763
m. 1793
Lady Barbara
Rushton

Henri

Héloïse
b. 1777
had by
James Morland

Louisa
b. 1774
m. 1793
John, Lord
Anstey

Jack
d. 1797

Robert
7th Earl
b. 1797

Marcus
b. 1795

Barbarina
b. 1796

Roland
b. 1799

Sophie
b. 1798

John
b. 1795

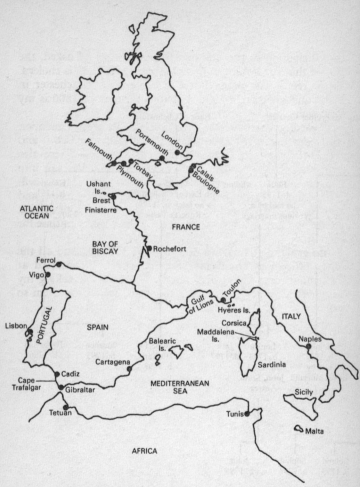

Plan of the principal seaports of the Trafalgar Campaign

FOREWORD

In anticipation of the question I know I shall be asked, the plague that breaks out in Manchester in this book is cholera. There really was an epidemic of cholera in Manchester in 1796, and another in 1832, but the outbreak of 1806 is my invention.

Regarding the battle of Trafalgar, all the ships I mention really did take part, except for the *Nemesis*, the *Cetus*, and the *Furieux*, which I invented for my purposes. There also really was a King's ship *York*, and she really did sail into oblivion on Boxing Day 1803. I hope the Royal Navy will forgive me for giving her a new captain for the occasion; and also for the truly dreadful things I did to the poor *Africa*, before handing her over to the real Captain Digby in time for the battle.

My grateful thanks are due to Steve Howick, and all the other officers of the Senior Service whom I consulted at Portsmouth and Greenwich, for their courtesy in taking my enquiries seriously, and their patience in answering them so fully.

SELECT BIBLIOGRAPHY

Edward Baines	*History of the Cotton Manufacture of Great Britain*
R. Bayne-Powell	*The English Child in the Eighteenth Century*
Geoffrey Bennett	*The Battle of Trafalgar*
	Memoirs of Lady Bessborough
G.D.H. Cole & R. Postgate	*The Common People 1746-1946*
	Letters of Cuthbert, Viscount Collingwood
John Ferriar	*Proceedings of the Board of Health in Manchester 1805*
Christopher Hibbert	*George IV Prince of Wales*
E.J. Hobsbawm	*Industry and Empire*
William Howitt	*The Rural Life of England*
William Jesse	*Life of Beau Brummell*
Michael Lewis	*England's Sea Officers*
Rene Maine	*Trafalgar*
J.H. Plumb	*The First Four Georges*
R.E. Prothero	*English Farming Past and Present*
E.S. Turner	*The Court of St James*
J.S. Watson	*The Reign of George III*
R.K. Webb	*Modern England*
	Memoirs of Harriette Wilson
	Diary and Correspondence of William Windham

*Contemporary sources

BOOK ONE

The Dolphin

Baby, baby, naughty baby,
Hush, you squalling thing, I say;
Hush your squalling, or it may be,
Bonaparte may pass this way.

Baby, baby, he's a giant,
Tall and black as Rouen steeple;
And he sups and dines, rely on't,
Every day on naughty people.

Anon (Nurse's song)

Chapter One

Old Sam'l, the village hornblower, walking up from his out-
lying cottage at his accustomed time one morning in April
1803, was mildly surprised to hear a horseman coming up
behind him. From the lightness of the tread he could tell it
was a gentleman's riding-horse, and it was an early hour for a
gentleman to be abroad. He stepped off the path to let the
rider by, and then smiled to himself in sudden understanding
as he recognised the distinctive long ears and square muzzle
of Nez Carré, the bay gelding belonging to Master James
Morland of Morland Place.

'Morning, master!' Old Sam'l cried, baring his naked gums
and tugging the disreputable brim of his ancient hat.

'Morning, Sam'l!' James replied. 'I have the start of you
this morning, you see!'

Sam'l gave him a sly look. 'Ah, but then I'd lay a shillin'
you've not been to bed yet.'

'Quite right,' James confessed. He was on his way home
from the Maccabbees Club in York, where he had spent the
whole night playing whist and drinking brandy, as he did
from time to time when the inner voice of his discontent grew
too clamorous. Drink and lack of sleep blunted his percep-
tions, and the unreliable light of an April morning only
emphasised the strange, detached feeling of unreality. 'How's
your daughter?' he asked with an effort. He knew Old Sam'l
lived with an unmarried daughter, but he couldn't recall her
name. His mother would have remembered, he thought: she
remembered everything about every one of her people, which
was one of the reasons she had been so beloved.

'Main well, thankee, master,' Sam'l replied, pleased with the
attention, 'though troubled with the rheumatics, this damp
weather.'

'It doesn't seem to bother you, at any rate,' James said.
'You look as fit as ever.'

'I keep myself busy, master, and the Lord keeps me well,'

13

Sam'l nodded, touching his hat again as James rode on. With a further effort, James recalled that Sam'l's only son had been killed at Malta in the late conflict with the French. His father and grandfather had each been hornblower before him, and James spared a thought to wonder who would call the villagers to their labours when old Sam'l was dead.

Well, that would be brother Ned's problem, not his. Edward was the local squire, magistrate, Justice of the Peace, and guardian of Morland Place into the bargain, for all that it was James's daughter Fanny who would inherit the estate. James had not been considered, in her grandparents' opinion, responsible enough to be his daughter's trustee; and perhaps, he reflected, yawning, they had not been far wrong. Here he was, after all, coming home like an alley-cat in the early hours after a night of debauchery. He would be going to bed just as dear old reliable Ned was getting up, and he would not rise again until half his brother's day's work was done.

Nez Carré put in a little dancing step here and there, flicking his long ears back and forth with interest at every movement and sound in the waking world around him. He was as fresh as his master was frowsy, having spent the night in what was becoming his accustomed stall in the Bunch of Grapes.

'Deep doings I had, too, my boy, while you were asleep,' James said aloud, reaching forward to turn Nez Carré's one wayward lock of mane back to the proper side. 'But I came out of it rather well — a hundred guineas up on the week's play.' Nez Carré knuckered in response to the voice, and took it as permission to break into a trot, and James checked him gently with a smile at the old horse's sudden skittishness. 'Must be spring,' he remarked.

He turned into the village street, where already the houses were astir. Doors and windows were thrown open on the fine morning; the smell of cooking issued from some of the houses, while at others the menfolk had brought out wooden stools to sit in the early sunshine and break their fast with bread and beer. Hens and geese, just let out, were everywhere, ruffling their feathers and stretching their necks in raucous contention as they re-established social order. A family of ducks crossed the road in single file, heading flat-footed for the stream; a grey cat on a sunny window-ledge blinked and paused in the first serious wash of the day as Nez Carré's shadow crossed her; a dog ran out and barked at him, and then grinned foolishly and wagged its tail in self-congratulation.

Stone, the tailor, was already at his work, sitting on a stool in the doorway of his cottage, one foot up on the door-frame to support the cloth he was stitching. His two little girls, identical twins, sat on a mounting stone outside eating cold porrage with their fingers out of wooden bowls, the rhythm of their hands never faltering while their round eyes followed James's progress. At another house, weaver Batty's young wife, suckling her baby, came to the door to shake out a cloth with her free hand. She smiled and blushed as James passed, turning her shoulder not with embarrassment, but with the grace of a simple modesty.

Most of the village folk worked for the Morland family in one way or another, some on the land, others in the various processes of the manufacture of Morland Fancy. Half the houses he passed had a loom in the attic or in a back room, and most of the women spun wool in between their other tasks, either on a wheel, or, increasingly, on a hand jenny.

There was no sign here of the poverty that one heard about farther south. The enclosures carried out in his father's time had created not less but more — and more regular — work in the fields; the demand for woollen cloth had grown slowly but steadily; and nearby York, a wealthy and sociable city, provided plenty of work for domestic servants, and a steady market for meat and milk, bread and vegetables, shoes, clothes, furniture, and artifacts of all kinds.

It was a prosperous area, and the Morlands were well-respected landlords. Edward was esteemed as a fair master and a knowing one with stock, and James's indiscretions were forgiven him partly for the sake of his good looks and personal charm, but mostly because he was considered the best horseman in the Ridings. James's wife Mary Ann, who was nominally mistress of Morland Place, had not the knack of making herself liked, but their daughter Fanny would inherit all when she was twenty-one, and those folk who mourned the old mistress, James's mother Jemima, told themselves that Fanny would be just like her.

James wondered if they deceived themselves. He could not help knowing that Fanny was horribly spoiled — Edward pointed it out to him daily, and his own judgement could not deny that she did behave very badly sometimes. But she was not yet eight years old, after all, and he trusted that she would grow out of it. James adored her, and found it impossible to deny her anything. In his better moments he realised that it might well be his indulgence which made her so ungovernable.

James had a son, too, though he often forgot the fact, for Henry, two years old and unbreeched, was still the property of nursery maids. Besides, as the boy owed his existence to purely financial considerations — the necessity for a male heir to inherit Mary Ann's father's cotton mills — James found it difficult to think about him as part of his family. He seemed as exclusively a Hobsbawn as Fanny was a Morland.

Thinking about his wife depressed James. He had married her for family reasons, and would have found it difficult to love her even had her existence not separated him from the woman of his heart, his cousin Héloïse. Once, when his mother was still alive, James had run away from wife, home and family to live with Héloïse for a few painfully ecstatic months, until conscience and social pressure had driven him to return, leaving Héloïse pregnant — that was Sophie, the child he had never seen. The wrong he had done his wife, the suffering he had caused her, only made it harder for him to like her. We must all, he thought wryly, hate those we hurt, because the shame of their suffering wounds our self-esteem.

At the end of the village street was Abley's, the baker's shop, and the delicious smell of hot bread drifted out to him and made him realise how hungry he was. Abley himself came red-faced to the door for a breath of air, and nodded to James civilly.

'Now then, Maister Morland.'

'Fine day, Abley.' James reined Nez Carré, who stretched his nose with interest towards the source of the agreeable smell.

'Too bright,' Abley dissented succinctly, peering up at the sky. 'Too bright in April likes to turn off, you mark my words. We s'l have a storm before day's out. Now then, 'oss, keep thy nose to thyself! Any news from London, maister? Shall we have war soon, dosta think?'

'I've heard nothing certain,' James replied, 'though my sister in London says it's only a matter of time. If Boney won't give us satisfaction, we shall have to fight him.'

'The sooner the better, to my mind,' Abley said severely. 'By, if I were ten years younger, I'd tek the shillin' maself, for the sake of givin' yon Boney Party a right good drubbin'.' His expression softened. 'But how is Miss Lucy — her ladyship, I should say?'

'Just exactly as she always was. She never changes,' James said.

'By, she were a right plucked one when she were a little lass, and that clever wi' animals an' doctorin' an' such! I'll never forget how she 'tended a sore on ma prize pig Caesar's back, an' cushed an' petted him so soft, he nigh on fell asleep while she did it — an' him that fierce i' the normal way, I never went into his pen wi'out a pitchfork.'

James had no desire to spoil Abley's image of Lucy by telling him that she was at present scandalising London by living openly with her lover, Captain Weston, while her husband, James Chetwyn, Earl of Aylesbury, lived a bachelor life in an apartment in Ryder Street. Instead he said, 'They say the Prince of Wales always asks her advice before buying a horse.'

Abley shook his head admiringly. 'To think of our Miss Lucy hob-nobbin' wi' the Prince himself! Well, to my mind, it's the Prince as gets the honour by it, for there's not another like her i' th' world, since your sainted mother passed away. Maister James. Willta tek a bit o' ma fresh bread, now, an' a sup of ale? Likely tha's had nowt sin' supper?'

'I should love some of your fresh rolls to take home and share with Miss Fanny for breakfast,' James said. 'You know she always says your rolls are better than ours at home.'

Abley looked pleased. 'Well, I won't say she's wrong! Tek 'em, an' welcome, maister. She went past ma door yesterday, on her little pony, an' called out to me, right friendly. Rides like a cyclops an' all! Near as good as Miss Lucy when she were that age.'

As James dismounted in the yard at Morland Place, Edward appeared from the stable.

'Hullo, Ned. You're out early!' James called.

Edward came across to him. 'One of the carriage-horses is lame,' he said, fending off Nez Carré as the old horse shoved him affectionately in the chest.

'Oh — which one?'

'One of the greys, Sparta. A touch of thrush. Hoskins *will* over-feed 'em when they're not working.' Edward looked more closely at his brother. 'Have you been out all night?'

'Guilty! But don't 'rate me — it means I can have breakfast with you before I go to bed. Look,' said James, holding up the bag of rolls as a peace-offering.

'A rare pleasure,' Edward said, but his frown dissolved before his brother's charming smile. James handed Nez Carré to his groom and linked arms with Edward as they turned towards the house.

'I suppose,' Edward went on, 'from this display of affection that you've outrun your allowance again. I wish you wouldn't gamble, Jamie. Not that you aren't entitled to your share of the estate's income — you work hard enough — but I hate to see good Morland money passing into other men's pockets for no return.'

'Don't be such a puritan, old dry-bones,' James said affectionately. 'I must have my little bit of pleasure now and then. Besides, you're wrong on this occasion: I've come home with my pockets freighted with gold — a hundred guineas to the good, dear brother, so I'm in a clinking good humour! Fortunately,' he added with a chuckle, 'Arthur Fussell is as rich as he is fatuous. He plays cards even worse than he rides.'

They crossed the great hall, heading for the steward's room, where Ned always took his early bite to stave off the pangs of hunger until breakfast proper at nine o'clock. A tray was waiting for him, with new bread and cold beef, and a jug of home-brewed, since Edward did not care for coffee so early in the day.

'The thing is,' he reverted when they were sitting either side of the fireplace with the tray between them, 'I don't believe you do enjoy it. You'd get far more pleasure out of a day's hunting, which costs nothing.'

18

'I can't hunt at night, can I? Come, Ned, leave me be. I only go to the Maccabbees once a week now. A fellow must have something to keep his mind occupied,' Edward looked as though he would continue the argument, so James added quickly, 'Besides, how else would we get the news so quickly? Crosby Shawe was in the club last night, just down from London, and he says the Government's told Lord Whitworth that if Boney don't agree to our terms within seven days he's to leave Paris. An you know that if the British Ambassador leaves Paris, it can only be war.'

'Seven days?' Edward said, brightening. 'Come, that's more like it! I don't know why we've shilly-shallied so long, anyway. It's as plain as bread that Bonaparte doesn't mean to give up Malta —'

'Or to withdraw his troops from Switzerland and Holland.'

'— and the longer we wait, the more time it gives him to raise troops and make his preparations.'

'It gives us the same time for the same purpose,' James pointed out.

'If we used the time properly,' Edward said, 'but what has our Government done? Brother William says the Frogs have got better than fifty ships in Santo Domingo, all ready to sail home, while most of ours are still laid up, and our best captains are sitting around in Fladong's waiting to be commissioned. And the army's no better off. The Government's done nothing there.'

'Fifty thousand militiamen balloted back in March is hardly nothing,' James reminded him.

'Militiamen aren't the same as a trained army,' Edward said with a harassed frown. 'Besides, who's to clothe them? Where are the guns and ammunition to come from? The Government leaves it all for us to do, as usual. Enrolling the men was a nightmare: I swear nine out of every ten claimed exemption. Substitutes are asking twenty, even twenty-five pounds now — aye, and getting it! And how do you think that's going to affect the recruitment of regulars, when their bounty's only seven pound twelve-and-six? Rustics armed with pikes is all we shall have to fight with — against French veterans, *and* the best artillery in Europe.'

James patted his arm. 'Eat your bread and meat, old

fellow. You'll feel better when your belly's full. Have one of Abley's rolls. I perjured myself to get them.'

'You don't take anything seriously,' Ned complained. 'But you'll change your tune when the French come marching up the Dover road and hoist the tricolor over St James's Palace.'

James grinned. 'Oh yes, I'll start worrying then, I promise you. It's about as likely as my becoming the next king of England! We'll beat 'em when the time comes, Ned, never fear.'

'It can't come too soon for me,' Edward said, cutting another slice of beef and dabbing it with mustard. 'Damn Addington and his conciliation! We need a Pitt to bring this cursed peace to an end.'

'How bloodthirsty you are,' James remarked mildly, breaking a roll and reaching for the butter.

'Nothing to do with being bloodthirsty,' Ned answered quickly. 'Don't you realise what a good thing the war is for us? The price of wool is bound to go up, with the demand for cloth for uniforms. And don't tell me you've forgotten how many more horses we sold up until that wretched Peace? I don't see,' he went on, warming to his subject, 'why we shouldn't get a government contract for horses this time. After all, it isn't as though we haven't got influential friends. There's John Anstey a Member of Parliament to begin with, and cousin Horatio a bosom-bow of the Prince; and Chetwyn's always been well-liked in Court circles, if he'd stir himself.'

'The name of Morland is much better known at the Admiralty than at the War Office,' James reminded him lazily.

'Well then,' Ned countered, 'what about a contract for supplying provisions for the fleet?'

'Surely the commissioners at Portsmouth must get all their beef and mutton from the southern counties? I can't see them wanting our cattle, all skin and bone after a two-hundred-mile drive.'

'I wasn't talking about cattle,' Ned said impatiently, 'I was talking about corn. They're going to need tons of it, for ship's bread. We could turn over all our arable fields to it, and then there's that piece of land on the edge of the moor that only wants draining ...'

James yawned. 'Whatever you say, old fellow. You don't need to ask my permission. It's no concern of mine.'

'The estate is held in trust for Fanny,' Edward pointed out. 'Of course it's your concern. You're her father.'

'The merest accident,' James said, taking a bite of buttered roll. 'The more I think of it, the more I feel it would have been better all round if *you* had married Mary Ann, rather than me — inherited her from Chetwyn, you might say, when he decided to marry Lucy instead. You and he being so close, it would have kept it in the family, so to speak.'

Edward reddened a little. James's assumed carelessness always irritated him. 'I don't suppose I could have made a worse husband than you, anyway,' he retorted. 'I wouldn't have run off and broken Mother's heart.'

'But then your sense of duty to the family wasn't strong enough to persuade you to marry at all, was it?' James said, nettled into retaliation. 'It was left to me to provide an heir, since you wouldn't.'

There was a tap at the door at that moment, and Father Aislaby, the chaplain, came in most timely. 'Ah, I thought I heard your voice,' he said to James. 'I thought perhaps you ought to know that Fanny has gone out.'

'Gone out where?' Edward asked before James could speak.

'That I can't tell you,' Aislaby said. 'But she's taken her pony and that young stable-lad, the red-haired one —'

'Foster,' James supplied with a smile. 'Yes, she would — he's a thorough reprobate. Fanny's taste is consistent, at least. I suspect they've gone off to steal pheasant's eggs. She did seem to take an unusual interest in the clutches yesterday, when we were riding in Harewood Whin.'

'How can you take it so lightly?' Edward exclaimed. 'Really, Jamie, that child goes beyond all bounds! You should never have given her a pony. She careers about the country-side like a little savage, completely unrestrained — and as ignorant, as far as I can see, as the day she was born. I doubt whether she can even read and write.'

'That's an aspersion on you, Father,' James said. 'What have you been teaching my daughter all these years?'

'Precious little, I'm afraid,' Aislaby admitted, unperturbed. 'If I can keep her in the schoolroom at all, it's as much as I compound for. As for teaching her anything, I fear it's beyond me.'

'How poor-spirited of you,' James murmured.

'The lessons I teach the choristers are not suitable for a girl, in any case,' the chaplain went on. 'I've said before, many times, that Fanny ought to have a governess; but even that will do no good unless you, her father, discipline her. As long as she knows she can appeal to you to countermand anyone else's orders, there will be no doing anything with her.'

'Just what I've always said,' Edward exclaimed triumphantly. 'If you go on like this, Jamie —'

'Yes, yes, spare me the reiteration,' James cried, ruffled. 'Lord, what a pair of Methodists you are! Let the poor child have a little fun! She's only seven years old. There'll be time enough for simpering and sitting when she's older. She likes to romp and play, and what harm can there be in that? Lucy was just the same at her age, and she grew up to marry an earl.'

'Lucy was never as wild as Fanny, and she was very good at her lessons,' Ned said. 'She was a romp, true enough, but Mother saw to it that she kept within bounds. Even so, I doubt whether any earl but Chetwyn, who was practically a brother to her, would have taken her, after she ran away to sea.'

'Well, Fanny won't run away to sea, anyway,' James said, tired of the argument.

'She's run away this morning,' Edward pointed out, 'and not for the first time. Someone ought to be sent after her. How you can just sit there, while —'

Aislaby interposed himself between the brothers soothingly. 'I expect she'll be back by breakfast time. Hunger is a stern imperative at that age. And now I must get ready for the early celebration,' he added, and withdrew.

Mary Ann, only daughter of Joseph Hobsbawn of Hobsbawn Mills, wife of James Morland and mother of Fanny and Henry, led a well-regulated life divided, though unequally, between duty and pleasure. Duty, that morning as every morning, was represented by her private and public devotions before breakfast, her presiding over the coffee-pot at breakfast, and a long interview with the housekeeper and the cook immediately afterwards. Pleasure then had its turn, as she mounted the stairs to the nursery to visit her son.

'How is he this morning?' she asked Sarah, the under-nurserymaid, who tweaked Henry's lace petticoats into position and propelled him gently towards his mother. 'Has he coughed much?'

'Not so much, today,' Sarah replied nervously. She evidently had something on her mind, and began, 'I beg your pardon, madam —'

Mary Ann was not listening. She lifted Henry in her arms and set him against her shoulder. 'My little dear,' she murmured. 'My pigeon!'

Henry's solemn face regarded her for a moment consideringly, and then broke into a smile, and Mary Ann felt the rush of love like hot blood through her heart. 'That's my little man,' she said. 'Has the nasty cough gone away, then?' Henry, though healthy enough upon the whole, had never been quite as robust as Fanny, who had never ailed a thing since the moment she was born. It was Mary Ann's deep and unspoken fear that something would happen to her son, who was the one joy of her life. She turned to Sarah again. 'I think we had better continue with the syrup, at least for a day or two.'

'Madam,' Sarah tried again, 'if you please —'

'Has he had his pap?'

'No, madam. But —'

'Then I shall give it to him. Run and fetch it, Sarah. Quickly, girl, don't stand and gawp like that. God loves those who do their duty with a light tread and a glad heart.'

'Yes, madam,' Sarah said resignedly, and trotted away. Mary Ann took her child to the window-seat and sat with him. The window looked out over the orchard towards the track which branched one way to York and the other to the moors and the open country. In the nine years, almost, that she had lived here, she had never managed to grow used to the views from the windows. Born and brought up, as she was, on the edge of a town, with streets and gardens and noises all about her, the country around Morland Place still often seemed very desolate and lonely to her.

'Though perhaps,' she said aloud to the baby, with a short sigh, 'it may be in me, and not in the place.' Henry had nothing to dissent to the proposition. He had hold of her hand, and was engaged in the pleasant game of folding and unfolding her fingers. A movement took her attention, and she turned her head to watch a groom with a pair of horses, riding one and leading one along the track at the slow trot thought proper for a gentleman's carriage-horses. She had given no orders for the carriage that day, so of course the horses must be led out for exercise.

'Routine,' she said aloud, 'is a beautiful thing.' A saving thing, that kept man from the chaos all around him. And woman, of course.

Henry examined her forefinger carefully and then carried it experimentally to his mouth, in the way of very young creatures.

But there were good routines and bad routines. Her husband, for instance, had developed a routine of visiting his club and staying all night. From her window she had seen his return early that morning; and that was all she was likely to see of him until dinner. It wasn't even, she thought with another sigh, that he avoided her. 'He doesn't know we exist, you and I,' she said, gathering Henry into her arms again. Henry smiled and put a fat hand up to tug her ear, and she pressed him to her in a sudden and painful access of love which startled him enough to make him cry.

'There now, madam, let me take him!' It was Jenny the senior nurserymaid, entering as if on cue, with Sarah behind her carrying the tray with Henry's bowl of pap. 'Hush now, my dear.'

'No,' said Mary Ann to the reaching hands. 'I wish to feed him myself.'

'Of course, madam,' Jenny said, too good a servant to argue, though her eye was rebellious. 'Sarah, the bowl and spoon.' She waited until her mistress was settled and Henry's wails had ceased in favour of a more contented sound, and then said, 'One of the gardeners was in the kitchen just a while back, madam. He'd been talking to a chap from the village, seemingly.'

'Yes,' Mary Ann said with a lack of encouragement which would have quelled a lesser mortal.

'It's about Miss Fanny, madam,' Jenny went on. 'This chap was out in the north field this morning, and saw Miss Fanny go by with young Forster and the carpenter's lad from Hessay, heading for the Lord knows where.'

Mary Ann raised her eyes from Henry's face and regarded Jenny blankly. 'What of it?'

'Well, madam, it isn't right. Really it isn't. It's not so much that she might come to harm, for God knows everyone here-abouts would lie down and die sooner than let anything hurt a hair of Miss Fanny's head, but —'

'Enough, Jenny.'

'But it's the scandal, madam,' Jenny continued stubbornly, 'and the talk. It reflects on us to have her wander about so unseemly, and without so much as a kitchen-maid to attend her. And then, she's a girl, when all's said and done, for all that she's only a child; and when girls are suffered to grow wild, the trouble they get into is always worse than anything anyone expects, and that's the truth, madam, if I was to die for it.'

Mary Ann's eye was flinty. 'I really cannot listen to any more nonsense about Miss Fanny,' she said coolly.

'It isn't nonsense, madam,' Jenny protested.

'Miss Fanny's behaviour is none of my concern,' Mary Ann went on. 'I won't be troubled with it, do you understand?'

'Someone's got to be troubled with it,' Jenny muttered angrily.

'If you have any complaints about her, you must speak to the chaplain or her father,' said Mary Ann, looking away to signify the end of the matter. 'She is nothing to do with me, and if you haven't learnt that by now, then you have been wasting your time here. Now leave me. I wish to be alone with my son.'

Jenny stared red-faced a moment longer, and then turned away abruptly, ushering Sarah out before her. The door was not closed quickly enough to keep her underling's comment from Mary Ann's ears. 'The truth of it is she's jealous of Miss Fanny, because Mr James loves her more.'

Mary Ann's lips moved in a little spasm of wry humour as

she loaded the spoon once more and conveyed it to Henry's mouth. 'Love!' she said aloud. Henry looked up at her. It was a very long time since she had expected or even wanted love from her husband. 'But servants are always so vulgarly sentimental.'

'Spoon!' said Henry, waving both hands in approval.

The hour for morning visitors found Mary Ann seated correctly in the drawing-room with her work basket and her embroidery frame to hand. It was also the hour for the chapel boys to practise their singing, and with the chapel door and the drawing-room both left open, she could just hear them. She loved music, and it soothed her.

Ottershaw the butler soon announced Lady Fussell, who as Lizzie Anstey had once been in love with James and hoped to marry him. She had been married now for six years to Sir Arthur Fussell, an experience which had produced in her a deep sympathy for all women who were married to uncongenial men. She visited Mary Ann more often than any of the other York ladies of their circle, and defended her vigorously when they abused her for being repulsively cold or stupidly silent.

'Who would not be reserved, in her situation?' Lady Fussell would say, and they would stare at her in amazement. Most of her contemporaries had been violently in love with the elusive James Morland at some time in their youth, and he still held for them all the charm of the eternally unattainable. Many a private tear had been shed when he brought back a bride from Manchester, and many had been the private smiles when he had abandoned her in that scandalous way and run off to live openly with another woman. Mr James Morland's former admirers, with their respectable but dull husbands, could safely assert to themselves in their most secret thoughts that he would not have run away if he had been married to *them*.

'What lovely music,' Lady Fussell remarked when the initial commonplaces had been exchanged. 'What is it?'

'The chapel choir is practising the anthem for Sunday,' said Mary Ann briefly.

'It sounds familiar,' Lady Fussell pursued. She was used to having to try hard with Mrs James Morland. 'Can I have heard it before?'

'It was written by William Morland, who I believe was an ancestor of my husband,' Mary Ann said unwillingly.

'Oh yes, of course! Everyone in York has heard of William Morland. He is quite famous, I assure you,' Lady Fussell smiled.

'It has been arranged for the boys by Father Aislaby,' said Mary Ann.

'How lucky you are in your chaplain,' Lady Fussell changed tack. 'So talented as he is, in so many ways.' She was about to add, and so handsome, but stopped herself in time. 'He will make a fine tutor for your son in a few years' time.'

'Indeed,' was all that Mary Ann said, but she almost smiled. She was aware that Sir Arthur Fussell was both stupid and profligate, and was frequently unkind to his wife. Mary Ann felt very sorry for Lady Fussell, and almost welcomed her visits.

'You have heard the news from London, I suppose?' Lady Fussell went on. She was sure that no-one else troubled to tell poor Mrs James Morland anything, and that without her own visits she would have gone on in ignorance, since she was too proud to ask for news. 'Buonaparte is given an ultimatum, and Crosby Shawe believes we shall have war within the month. He dined with Sir Arthur yesterday.' Crosby Shawe was her brother-in-law, married to Sir Arthur Fussell's sister Valentina. 'The men are all very excited about it. Valentina says she does not know who could have arranged the Peace, since every man in the country now claims to have been against it from the first.'

'My brother Edward mentioned it at breakfast,' Mary Ann admitted. 'He seems to think war will be a good thing for us.'

'Oh, certainly! And an excellent thing for your father, ma'am, I believe,' Lady Fussell added. 'The demand for cloth of all sorts is bound to increase.'

Mary Ann only bowed, and Lady Fussell passed on to a more interesting subject. 'I suppose you must have heard that Lady Anstey's child was born yesterday?'

Mary Ann had not, and said nothing.

27

'A girl this time,' Lady Fussell went on obligingly, 'and they are to call her Mary. And Valentina has announced that she is increasing again. All the world seems to be burgeoning,' she added with a smile and a little sigh. Her only pregnancy had ended in a stillborn child three years ago. 'Your children must be such a comfort to you, Mrs Morland. I do envy you them.'

A certain light in Lady Fussell's eye suggested to Mary Ann that some unwelcome communication about Fanny was about to be introduced, and it was necessary to say something to ward it off. She hastily broke in: 'Lady Anstey is quite well, I hope? She has a large family. How many are there now?'

'The new baby is the sixth surviving. It is fortunate that John — Lord Anstey — is so well-to-do, with such a brood to provide for! His eldest, little John, can think of nothing but the navy, and longs so to go to sea, you can't imagine. He is so excited about the war, it quite made me laugh to hear him talking.'

'He is very young to be thinking about such things,' Mary Ann said.

'Indeed,' Lady Fussell said, 'but Lord Anstey said yesterday, when I called, that if the boy was still of the same mind next year, he would try whether he could get him aboard some ship or other. If he wants a naval career, he must start it as early as possible, so Lady Anstey says.'

'I should think Lady Anstey would be against it,' Mary Ann remarked.

'You mean, because her brother was killed in a naval battle? Oh no, you mistake. She is very proud of her brother, and would like nothing better than for little John to follow in his footsteps. She resolves to ask your sister Lady Aylesbury's advice about a suitable patron.'

Mary Ann eyed her visitor cautiously. Lucy had a large and perfectly respectable acquaintance amongst the navy, apart from her disreputable connection with Captain Weston, so it was hard to know whether or not to be offended by the reference. 'I believe Admiral Collingwood thought highly of Lady Anstey's brother,' she said at last.

'Quite so,' said Lady Fussell quickly, 'and he is so very fond of Lady Aylesbury that the connection must be useful to the Ansteys.'

Mary Ann did not in the least want to talk about her sister-in-law Lucy, and she was quite sure that Lady Fussell was bursting with some information about Fanny's whereabouts that she did not want to hear either. In desperation she stood up and said, 'You spoke so appreciatively about the music just now. Perhaps you would like to step into the chapel for a few minutes, to hear it better?'

Lady Fussell could only accept. 'Thank you, I should like it extremely,' she said.

The rules of social intercourse had their advantages sometimes, Mary Ann reflected, leading the way out.

Chapter Two

The hour for morning visits was very different at Lady Aylesbury's house in Upper Grosvenor Street, where the butler Hicks had developed a very sinewy leg from the superfluity of daily visitors to a tall, narrow house with many stairs. Despite the scandal of her relationship with Captain Weston and nominal separation from her husband — matters which Hicks found very hard to bear, his heart being a great deal less tough than the sinews of his legs — Lady Aylesbury was an extremely popular hostess, had a large acquaintance in the *ton*, and an even larger acquaintance amongst sea-officers, whose obsessive sociability while on land was proverbial.

At whatever hour her ladyship had retired, she was always up early the next day to take her horses into the Park, for she liked to ride when there were none but grooms about, so that she could exercise properly without tripping over 'fashionable ladies dawdling on one-pace slugs', as she called them in what Hicks thought of as her colourful way. Later in the day, at the afternoon hour of promenade, she would ride or drive again, attired to swooning-point in the very apogee of fashion, to see and be seen in the correct way like other ladies of the *ton*; but her mornings were her own, and precious to her.

Captain Weston had been again to the Admiralty that morning, and on his return was told that her ladyship had retired to her chamber to be dressed. At the Captain's entrance, the maid Docwra withdrew without further instruction, and Weston walked across to kiss Lucy's upturned face tenderly, and to sit beside her at the dressing-table.

'Well, what news?' Lucy asked.

'War is certain,' Weston said. 'It's only a matter of time. Days, weeks at the most.'

'But what news of you? Have you got your ship?' Lucy asked anxiously.

Weston shook his head. 'I'm afraid they must be giving out the commissions in alphabetical order,' he said, trying for lightness. 'They've got as far as the aitches, at all events. I saw your brother Haworth there, and he told me they've recommissioned the *Africa*.'

'Oh, I am glad for him! I know it's of all ships the one he would most have wanted.'

'I think he'd have taken any ship offered, like the rest of us,' Weston said wryly, 'but I daresay he is fond of her, for all that she's given the dockyard a great deal of trouble.'

'But how can that be?' Lucy asked with a frown. 'She was a new ship in — what was it? — '96 or '97.'

'That's the heart of it, my love. She was built partly with new timbers, not properly seasoned, and they have warped badly. But Haworth says they had her in dry-dock until last week, and so he hopes they have solved the problem. He intends to walk up and see you this morning, so you can ask him all the technical details yourself.'

She made a face, aware that she was being teased. 'I shall also ask him what he means to do with his children,' she said. 'They can hardly stay in that tiny house at Southsea with only servants to look after them. He had probably better send them to me. They can perfectly well live down at Wolvercote with my three. They'll be in nobody's way there.'

Weston smiled and kissed her hand. 'I love the way you collect children, so carelessly, as though they were snuffboxes or Sèvres vases.'

To his surprise she looked a little upset and confused for a moment, and when she did reply, it was with a forced laugh. 'I should much prefer Sèvres vases, I assure you,' she said lightly. 'Who else did you see this morning?'

He knew that it was of no use to press her; that if anything was wrong, she would tell him in her own time, or not at all. 'Let me see, now,' he mused. 'Old Admiral Scorton was there, of course. He said he saw you in the Park this morning, on Mimosa, and waved to you.'

'That's right. He hailed me as if I were at the foretop, and told me there were more gales on the way! I love that old man,' she added inconsequentially. 'Who else?'

'None of your particular friends. I heard some news, however. Collingwood is in Town. I didn't see him — he was closeted with Lord St Vincent — but he's sure to call on you

31

later. Everyone says he's bound to be promoted to vice this time, which will cheer a few northern hearts. Scorton thinks he'll get *Victory*. She's lying at Portsmouth, newly refitted.'

'She's a good ship, isn't she? And what command?'

'Second in command to Cornwallis, Scorton thinks.'

'Is Blue Billy to have the Channel Fleet again?'

'It seems likely. St Vincent likes him, and he thinks he did well there before the Peace; and Pellew is to have the western approaches, almost certainly.'

'And Nelson?'

Weston made a comical face. 'He and Lady Hamilton are out of mourning for poor old Sir William, at all events. He's busy making himself unpopular by demanding a pension for Lady Hamilton for her services to the country —'

'What, as his mistress?' Lucy put in, in astonishment.

Weston roared. 'Oh Lucy, you are such a joy to me! No, no, you simpleton, for her diplomatic services in Naples! He's also put a petition before Addington for an increase to his own pension, on the grounds that both St Vincent and Duncan get more than he does, and that since he has a wife *and* a mistress to support, he simply can't manage on two thousand a year.'

'I can't see even Addington acceeding to that,' Lucy smiled. 'Has he his command yet?'

'Not yet. He'll probably get the Toulon station again, but I think Their Lordships will delay as long as possible in appointing him, in order to shew their disapproval of his private life.'

She stared at him in sudden concern. 'Oh Weston —!'

'What is it, my love?'

She gripped his hand tighter. 'It has just come to me,' she said reluctantly. 'Do you suppose ... could it be that it is our relationship which has prevented you from getting your ship?'

Weston hesitated, and shrugged. He never lied to her: their relationship was not built along those lines. 'It is possible.'

'Oh Weston —!'

'Now, Lucy, don't look so tragic. There'll be ships for all the active officers as soon as war is formally declared. I've never blotted my service record, don't forget. Disapproval of my private life may delay matters, but I shan't be left on the beach, never fear.'

'I don't know how any of them dares to point a finger,' she said indignantly. 'As if they were above reproach! Why, I dare say if one enquired —'

'Precisely so — if one enquired. Their Lordships don't like officers to be involved in public scandals. That's where Nelson goes wrong — he and his Emma do make such a noise about their love! If they would but sin quietly, no-one at the Admiralty would care two straws. And you and I, until last year, were discreet enough. It's only since I came to live here that we have become the object of gossip.'

'They can't bear openness and honesty, that's what it is. Hypocrisy and show is all they care about.' She looked at him anxiously, her face a little pale. 'Perhaps you ought to have a place of your own again, like before, when you had rooms in Ebury Street. If you lived apart from me, perhaps the scandal would die down, and you would get your ship.'

'My love,' he said tenderly, 'you refine too much on it. We only became a scandal because the Season was so quiet. As soon as war is declared, everyone will have too much to talk about to be interested in us. I shall have my ship, don't worry. And . . .' He hesitated.

'Yes?'

He lifted her hand to his lips again. 'Only this — that since war must come, and I must go away from you, for God knows how long, I had rather be with you, properly with you, for every moment I can.' He smiled faintly. 'I must be the only red-blooded man in England at this moment who is actually glad Addington has kept the peace so long.'

Lucy bit her lip, and understanding much of what she felt, he released her hand to consult his pocket-watch, and stood up with a lighter smile. 'I had better let Docwra back in, or you won't be dressed in time for your visitors. Is this what you are to wear?' He touched a lilac-coloured muslin which was lying over the back of a chair. 'You'll look charmingly, as always.'

He bowed, and had his hand to the door knob when Lucy called him.

'Weston!'

He turned back enquiringly, and watched as she struggled to find words for what she felt too deeply for speech. 'I have

33

been so happy this past year,' she said at last, awkwardly. 'Thank you for it.'

He had no answer for her, could only bow again, and leave.

Captain Haworth was the first to lift the great knocker on the front door. He arrived with naval promptness exactly at noon, and, as a family connection, took the liberty of advising Hicks to save his legs. 'I can find my own way up. I know her ladyship is expecting me to call, because I told Captain Weston so this morning.'

George Haworth had astonished the fashionable world ten years ago by marrying Lucy's older sister Mary, who had been famed as one of the three most beautiful women in England, and who had turned down so many offers for her hand, even from such eligible *partis* as the Earl of Tonbridge, that everyone had decided she meant to go a maiden to her grave. Why she should have accepted Haworth's offer, when he had neither fame, fortune, rank, nor even particularly distinguished looks, was something that no-one in the *ton* could determine.

The fact of the matter, as Lucy could have told anyone who was interested, was that Mary fell in love with the obscure and shabby sea-captain the very instant she saw him, and had lived in blissful happiness with him until she died of childbed fever on board the *Africa* off the Egyptian coast five years ago. Lucy could perfectly well understand it. She liked George Haworth very well; he reminded her of her father.

'Congratulations, Captain, on your appointment,' she greeted him. 'You must be pleased it is the *Africa.* Do you know where you are bound?'

'I'm meant for the Channel Fleet,' Haworth said, 'but not for a few weeks yet. *Africa*'s only just out of dry-dock. They'll be warping her up to Spithead tomorrow, and as soon as I join her I have to take her out for sea trials.'

'I told Lucy about her troubles,' Weston said. 'Sea trials suggest that she's in a bad way.'

'I'm afraid so,' Haworth said with a rueful smile. 'You were congratulating me on an early appointment, but if *Africa* has to go back into dock, you may well be at sea before me.'

'Have you got your old crew back?' Weston wanted to know.

'A large number of them. As soon as the word went round that *Africa* was commissioning, they started to volunteer. It was most touching.'

'It's a tribute to you,' Lucy said, 'that they should be so loyal.'

Haworth smiled. 'You mustn't make too much of it. They know they will be pressed anyway, sooner or later. By volunteering they get the bounty, and the choice of ship.'

'Well, at all events, you are spared the problem of manning,' Lucy said.

'I shall still have to take my share of quota-men, but I'll probably sail short-handed at first. It won't matter for the trials, and Their Lordships are anxious to have them completed as soon as possible.'

'I'm astonished they are granting you time for trials at all,' Weston grinned. 'They don't usually flinch from sending men to sea in sinking ships. Remember the poor old *Rochester*, that fell to pieces in calm weather off Martinique in '91?'

'That reminds me,' Haworth said to Lucy. 'I was talking to Nepean just before I walked up here, and he said that a report has come in from Santo Domingo which will be of interest to you.'

'My brother William?'

Haworth bowed. 'The *Argus* was in a successful single-ship action with a French seventy-four, the *Glorieux*. The Frenchman struck after a spirited defence, but both ships were badly damaged, and Captain Morland had much to do to get them to Kingston to refit.'

'He won't be sorry to stay there a while, I imagine,' Weston said. 'I hear the Yellow Jack is raging all through Hispaniola.'

'William's had it, years ago,' Lucy said. 'But his wife and child are in Kingston, so I expect he'll be glad to be there for that reason. And talking of children —'

'Yes, I had meant to bring up the subject,' Haworth said apologetically. 'The thing is, you see —'

'No need to explain,' Lucy said firmly. 'Your girls can go to Wolvercote and stay as long as you wish. Miss Trotton is an excellent governess, and it can make no difference to anyone

35

there how many children they have to look after. They have nothing else to do for three-fourths of the year.'

'It is more than generous of you, ma'am,' Haworth said, 'and I do believe it's what Hippolyta wants more than anything. She misses your daughter Flaminia very much.'

'I always told you she would,' Lucy said, 'though I suppose Farleigh has enjoyed having her back. How is old Farleigh?'

'She has not been at all well recently, and though she loves the children dearly, I think she finds them wearing. She wants to retire. She has family in Devon, and her savings, and I don't feel I ought to stand in her way.'

'I never thought of Farleigh's having family,' Lucy said in surprise. 'In all the years she was Mary's personal maid, I never once heard her mention a relative.'

'Commonly the lot of servants, I imagine,' Weston murmured, lifting his hands from his knees so that his cat Jeffrey could jump up. Jeffrey turned round three times and settled, his claws clenching and unclenching in delight, his rusty purr throbbing like an engine as he flattened his head up under Weston's hand.

'Well, it doesn't matter,' Lucy had continued. 'Let her go as soon as she likes. I can send a servant down to collect the girls, if you can't bring them yourself.'

'It would be helpful if you could send someone for Polly,' Haworth began, and Lucy interrupted him.

'Polly? You don't mention Africa.'

'I've seen it coming these ten minutes,' Weston said. 'Look at that guilty expression! Let me save you the trouble of explaining, Haworth. You want to take your younger brat to sea with you again. How old is she now?'

'Nearly five. We've never been parted, you see, and the idea upsets her dreadfully; and she's lived most of her life on shipboard. She doesn't like living on shore a bit.'

'But if Farleigh doesn't go with you, who will look after her?'

'The carpenter's wife is a very good sort of woman, and she's willing to do what's necessary. But Africa's such an independent child, she hardly needs looking after, and on board ship all the men keep an eye on her.'

'I've heard it works both ways,' Weston said. 'She keeps an eye on them, too.'

'She's more useful to me in keeping discipline than the cat,' Haworth agreed with a smile. 'The men don't even cuss when she's around.'

'Well, I've nothing to say to it,' Lucy said. 'You must do as you think fit. But I should like to know that you had plans to attend properly to her education.'

Before Haworth could reply, the door opened and Hicks announced Admiral Collingwood. He was preceded into the room by his little white terrier, Bounce, who rushed forward to greet Lucy with such enthusiasm that Jeffrey, who had drawn himself up warily at the first sight of him, jumped from Weston's lap in affront and made a rapid ascent to the top of the nearest bookcase.

Collingwood bowed over Lucy's hand and received the cordial greetings of the other two officers. He was a slender, handsome man, with finely-chiselled features and gravely beautiful eyes which a woman might have envied. He had been at sea since he was eleven, and out of the last forty-two years had spent no more than six or seven on shore. He was a consummate seaman, a superb tactician, and from having spent most of his life fighting the French one way and another, he had developed an almost uncanny way of knowing what they were about to do next. He was also one of the few captains who could keep order entirely without the use of the cat; it was said a look of censure from him hurt his jacks a great deal more than the lash.

'What was it you were discussing when I came in?' Collingwood asked Lucy as he took the seat opposite her. 'I thought I heard you mention the education of females? It's of all subjects the dearest to my heart.'

'I was enjoining Captain Haworth to make sure that both his girls were properly taught,' Lucy said. 'Too many men seem to think that education doesn't matter for girls, and let them scramble into whatever learning they can get for themselves without troubling anyone. But that's not our way — not the Morland way.'

'Dear Lucy, don't you think Haworth knows that?' Weston laughed. 'Didn't he marry your sister Mary?'

'I was taught Latin, Greek, mathematics, astronomy, history, and the natural sciences,' Lucy went on, 'and I am determined my girls will learn them too. Not,' she added frankly, 'that Flaminia shews much promise in anything but drawing. But that isn't the point.'

'I do so agree with you,' Collingwood said. 'It is quite a hobby-horse of mine. I am at pains to have my own dear girls learn the same subjects as are taught to boys. I wish I could be more often at home to supervise their education,' he added sadly, 'but I have been so little ashore since they were born ...'

'Well, sir, you will find no contrary argument in this room,' Weston said, 'but I think the majority of people would claim that too much education for females does not conduce to a proper delicacy of mind.'

'And I would say to them,' the admiral rejoined firmly, 'that ignorance can never be conducive to delicacy. How can you instruct a girl to love God, when you give her no means of understanding the astonishing miracle of His creation?'

Weston bowed. 'As I said, sir, none of us would disagree with you. Haworth and I have both had the honour of loving educated women.'

'Morland women,' Haworth added with a smile. 'There's something special about them. If my daughters grow up like their mother, I shall have nothing to regret except, like you, Admiral, that I have not been able to spend more time with them.'

'You have your ship, I understand, Captain Haworth?' Collingwood said.

'I have, sir, though I don't know for how long. But if she doesn't sink under me, I can look forward to a leisurely cruise off Brest this summer.'

Everyone smiled at this reference to the most treacherous stretch of water in Europe, and Collingwood said, 'We shall all have our work cut out, soon enough. It's no secret that Buonaparte has sworn to invade England, and only by continuous vigilance will we be able to hold him. Blockade duty is hard and tedious, but essential.'

Haworth nodded gravely, having done his share of it before the peace, and Collingwood looked enquiringly at Weston and went on, 'But you, Captain? I understand you're still waiting for your commission.'

'Their Lordships haven't found a use for me yet, sir,' Weston assented.

'I suppose a dashing young officer like yourself must be longing for a frigate,' Collingwood said with a smile and a glance at Lucy, who lifted her hands in an involuntary gesture which did not escape the admiral's eye. 'But I don't think there's any harm in telling you that there's some doubt in Admiralty circles as to what is best to be done with you.'

'Sir?' said Weston, a little anxiously.

'Intelligent officers are always needed at the Admiralty itself. I understand you had a shore appointment during the late conflict, and acquitted yourself very creditably.'

Weston and Lucy both stared at him, straining their senses to understand. Was he saying, then, that it was not moral disapproval which had kept Weston from being given a ship, but a doubt as to whether he might not be better employed on the Admiralty staff? And if that were so, could he, ought he to resist? It was a great honour to be considered in that special capacity; and to be on shore was to be with Lucy. But for a sailor the first longing is always to be at sea. Weston was torn, and his face shewed it.

'I am Their Lordships' to command,' he said at last in as neutral a tone as he could manage. 'Wherever I will be most useful —'

'Of course,' Collingwood said, but he was looking at Lucy, and his soft Northumberland burr was softer than ever as he said, 'but every young officer wants a frigate, doesn't he?'

Lucy, still fondling Bounce's ridiculous ears, met the admiral's eyes in a moment of complete sympathy; and then the door was opened again to admit Hicks and a new influx of visitors, whose arrival must change the subject.

'Major Wiske, my lady, and Mr Brummell.'

The following morning Lucy was seated in the breakfast parlour, a smaller, sunny apartment which was very pleasant early in the day, when the door opened and her husband, the earl, walked in.

'Pardon me for not having myself announced,' was the first thing he said, and Lucy frowned a little.

'Don't be silly,' she said, but awkwardly. The status of an estranged husband in his own house was a delicate one. 'Hicks would have a fit if you asked him to.'

The earl fixed his eye on Jeffrey, curled up on the window-seat, and then looked pointedly at Lucy and raised an eyebrow enquiringly.

'No, he's not here,' she said. 'He's down at the Admiralty. I wanted to see you alone.'

'So I gathered from your note. You see with what promptness I hurried round here,' he said. 'I inferred it must be something urgent, for you to have gone to so much trouble.'

Lucy grew impatient. 'Oh, do sit down, Chetwyn, and stop talking nonsense.' He obeyed her with a faint smile, taking a chair on the other side of the table at which she sat, and folding his hands with an air of composure. His eye, however, was wary, and the muscles of his jaw were tense.

A silence ensued which Lucy found hard to break. 'I wanted to see you,' she began at last, hesitantly. The earl looked at her blankly, giving her no help. 'There is something I have to tell you.' She bit her lip, but there was no help for it, no way to say it, but simply to say it. 'I am with child again.'

As soon as the words were out, she knew that she should not have said 'again'. Chetwyn said nothing at first. She hardly knew what she had expected from him — shock, perhaps; anger certainly — but what she saw was something she had not bargained for. His face seemed to grow suddenly older, and set into its lines in a grey and exhausted way that filled her with fear. He *minds*, she thought in sudden bewilderment. She waited, her mouth dry.

'Does he know?' was what he said at last.

'I haven't told him.'

He raised an eyebrow, 'Why such restraint?' he asked cynically.

'He — I didn't want to say anything until he has his commission. There's some question of a shore appointment. I didn't want to influence his decision.'

A wry and bitter smile touched Chetwyn's lips. 'Dear Lucy, you do like to play fair, don't you?' he said ironically.

Fear and guilt stung her. 'I wanted to tell you first, in any case,' she said quickly, putting up her chin. 'It's only right.'

Chetwyn shrugged, a lazy gesture which imperfectly concealed the brittleness of his shoulders. 'It has nothing whatever to do with me,' he said.

Lucy paled a little. 'Why — what do you mean?' she stammered. 'You mean — you won't —?'

Now the anger came. 'Oh no, Lucy, not again. What do you take me for?' He stood up abruptly and walked a few steps away and back. 'For God's sake, the whole world knows we have been living apart these eighteen months! You have taken your *lover*' — his lips curled bitterly over the word — 'to live with you in the most public way, and made yourself a talking point all over London. I said nothing. I left you alone —'

'Because you didn't care one way or the other!' she cried out. 'It suited you to live as a bachelor.'

He stopped, and looked surprised. 'Is that what you thought? No, even you could not be such a fool. To have protested about what you were doing would only have made me ridiculous, so I pretended you had my blessing. What else could I do? But now you ask me to acknowledge his child, which no one, no-one, could believe for an instant is mine! Oh no, Lucy, I won't do it. *Damn* you,' he said with sudden venom, 'I won't do it.'

She looked at him in silence, filled with all manner of unhappy speculations. Her hands crept for comfort over her belly, a gesture not lost on her husband. 'What, then, is to become of me?' she asked at last in a small voice.

'I really have not the slightest interest,' he said, turning away and walking to the window at the other end of the room. Her heart contracted at the words; but he did not leave, and after a while she tried again.

'Will you divorce me?'

He answered without turning round — a single, neutral word. 'No.'

'Then — what shall I do?'

He said nothing for a long time, and then she saw his shoulders rise and fall in a deep sigh, and he turned back to her, reluctantly, wearily, as if taking up again a burden he had long wished to walk away from.

'You are my wife,' he said. 'I will keep and protect you, whatever happens, but I will not acknowledge your child. You must go out of London, to some secluded place in the country where your condition will not cause talk, and stay until the baby is born. You may choose where to go — I will see to it that you are comfortable. If the child lives, it must be sent away somewhere to foster parents. Then you may resume your usual pursuits.'

He had spoken in her direction, but without looking at her; now his eyes focused on hers and he saw that she was pale and that her lips trembled. This was not like Lucy, who was always so strong, so practical; yet, he thought bitterly, she does not feel it as I feel it. He was forty-six, but he felt old, so old. 'All I ask is a little discretion,' he went on, but more gently. 'Is that so much to ask? Have I not the right to a little loyalty from you?'

'Yes — yes, of course,' she said faintly. She rose from her seat, and put out a hesitant hand to him. 'I didn't understand. I didn't know. Chetwyn, I'm sorry.'

'Sorry?' he said harshly.

'I didn't think you really cared about it,' she said helplessly.

He looked at her in silence for a long time, thoughts and memories passing in swift succession through his mind. He remembered with sudden, vivid painfulness a happy time, long ago, when he and Edward and Lucy had romped together at a picnic on the bank of the Ouse; the sun glittered on the water, and there was no shadow anywhere in the world. How could they have come so far from that careless place in so short a time?

'Oh Lucy,' he said, 'you're such a child.' He walked past her to the door, and her hand faltered and dropped again to her side. 'Let me know when you have made your arrangements,' he said, and left.

Lady Aylesbury was not at home to callers that morning. Hicks and the footman Ollett took it in turns to deny the stream of visitors and to accept the calling-cards and scribbled notes that were left in their place. When the Captain came home at two o'clock, Hicks admitted him and replied to his query with the information that her ladyship was above, and alone.

Weston ran up the stairs two at a time, and burst into the bedchamber with such excitement that he did not remark upon the unusual sight of Lucy lying on the daybed with a handkerchief clutched in her fingers.

'I have it! I have my ship!' he cried out, crossing to her, flinging himself on his knees beside her and seizing her hands to kiss them. 'They have given me a frigate! And not just any frigate, my love, but the *Nemesis* — a thirty-six, and the fastest in the service! She sails like a dream, and everyone knows she's a lucky ship, too! She took a Spanish specie ship singlehanded in the West Indies in '98 without a life lost, and made her captain's fortune. That was Blackwell, of course — you must have heard the story.'

He sat back on his heels, grinning with delight. 'When they said they were giving me a frigate, I thought it was going to be the poor old *Java*, and my heart was in my mouth, because you know she was a Dutch prize, and she sails like a haystack, apart from being so worn out she's only held together with prayers. But I heard the secretaries talking about her just before I went in, and I thought that was that. I even wondered whether they were going to give me the *Java* as a punishment! But the *Nemesis*! Any frigate-captain in the fleet would give his eye-teeth for her. And Moore was in the outer office, too. You know, Graham Moore, the general's brother. I told him when I came out that they'd given me *Nemesis*, and he was wild, though of course he said everything proper. But I could see he must have known she was commissioning, and with his connections he'd have made sure he would get her himself!'

It was necessary to say something. Lucy roused herself, and if her smile was forced, Weston did not at once notice it. 'I'm so very pleased for you,' she said. 'It's an honour to be preferred over Captain Moore.'

'Well, I think it is, and do you know what, Lucy — I'm sure it was Collingwood spoke for me, to Lord St Vincent. Melville hinted as much, that someone important had my interests at heart. Isn't that like him? God bless him — he's a true friend!

I am so lucky that you have such a connection.'

'I'm sure you would have done as well on your own merits,' Lucy said, and now at last Weston noticed that she was not as enthusiastic as she ought to be.

He sat down on the edge of the daybed and took her hand, and asked gently, 'What is it, my love? Were you hoping I would get a shore appointment?'

'I'm very happy for you,' she said. 'I know you wanted a frigate.'

'Well, I did,' he admitted. 'It isn't that I want to go away from you — God knows, I have been happier this last year than ever in my life — but we've got to beat this man Buonaparte. I'm a sea-officer, and it's only natural that I should want to be out there in the thick of it. The sooner it's done, the sooner I can come back to you,' he added uncertainly.

She forced a smile, and said, 'I am glad for you, truly. I know what you are, and I wouldn't want you any different. Do you think it would please me to have you stay at home for my sake? I only wish I were a man and could go too.'

He leaned forward to brush the curls from her brow and kiss it. 'Do you? I don't. I much prefer you as a woman, my Lucy.'

'Being a woman has grave disadvantages,' she said in a low voice. He regarded her with his head a little tilted.

'What is it, my love? Something's wrong. Has something happened while I was out?'

'My husband came to see me,' Lucy said.

He sat back. 'Ah,' he said, 'I see.'

'No, you don't,' she said quickly. 'I *asked* him to come and see me. I had something — something to tell him. Something —' She stopped and swallowed. 'Weston, I am with child.' He said nothing, nothing at all, and in terror she seized his hand and cried, 'Weston do you hear me? I am with child! I am going to have your child!'

His breath left him in a long sigh. 'Oh, Lucy,' he said, and reaching forward he took her in his arms and held her against him, and laid his cheek on the top of her head. She clung to him, wondering if he were glad or sorry, knowing only that he was offering her comfort. But when she released herself and pushed him back so that she could look at him, she saw in his face such an expression of wonder and joy that made her breathless.

'You're not angry?' she said.

'Oh, my darling,' was all he said, but it was enough.

'I didn't want to tell you until you had your ship,' she went on, 'because I thought you might refuse if you knew. And I had to tell Chetwyn first. He is my husband, after all.'

Weston grimaced. 'Yes, I know that. You don't need to remind me. But Lucy, this changes everything. You must see that. I can't go away and leave you now. I'll go to the Admiralty tomorrow and tell them that I decline the commission. They may still give me a staff appointment, and if they don't — well, there's always something one can do: the dockyard or the victualling yard or something.'

'No, no,' Lucy cried, struggling up. 'You mustn't think of it! Oh Weston, I am glad that you are pleased! I was so afraid that you would look angry or disappointed, and then I don't know how I should have borne it. But you must not think of refusing your commission. That was the very reason I didn't tell you sooner. I shall be all right. I shan't be alone: I shall have Docwra with me, and she saw me through the others with no trouble. And then, when you come back ...' Her voice faltered, but she went on quickly to forestall him. 'Don't you see, it would make me feel quite dreadful if you were to give up your ship. It would make me feel as though I had ... deprived you.'

Weston laughed. 'Lucy, my dear, sweet simpleton, how can you talk such nonsense? My darling, you are to have my child! *We* are to have a child, and do you think that I would go and leave you now, of all times? No, my love, I shall go and see the earl the first thing and talk it over with him. There must be a divorce — it won't be pleasant, but there's no help for it — and then you and I can be together as man and wife ...' His voice trailed away as he saw her expression.

'No, Weston, you don't understand. Chetwyn doesn't want to divorce me. He said he will look after me, but he won't acknowledge the child. He said it must be sent away.'

All the time he had been talking, the layer upon layer of complication, difficulty, and unpleasantness that the situation entailed had been revealing themselves to Weston's imagination in horribly vivid detail; and his initial joy at the thought of their love bearing fruit was sinking under the realisation of what it would really mean to both of them. But his love for Lucy was absolute, and he knew, despite her usual appearance of brisk practicality, how childlike and vulnerable she was. She was putting on a brave show for him, but her eyes were anxious.

'Don't worry, my darling. Everything is going to be all right,' he said firmly. 'I shall go and see him, and make him change his mind. Trust me, Lucy. I'll make everything all right with your Chetwyn.'

Chapter Three

White's and Brooks's, London's leading clubs, faced each other across St James's Street. White's was known as the Tory club, and Brooks's as the Whig, but most gentlemen belonged to both, and used either as the whim of the moment or the excellence of the dinners dictated. Captain Weston, in search of the Earl of Aylesbury and not finding him at his lodgings, enquired for him in both establishments, and discovered him at Brooks's, on the point of dining.

'I'm sorry to interrupt you at such a moment,' Weston said with a formal politeness designed to keep him from trembling, 'but I believe it is important. Might I have an interview with you in private?'

The earl looked at him coldly. 'I see no reason for it. You and I can have nothing to say to each other.'

Weston looked exasperated. 'Sir, I understand how you must feel about me, and I assure you that I like the idea of this interview as little as you do, but you cannot in all reason expect me simply to go away. There are things that must be said: arrangements to be made.'

The earl looked at him for a moment, tight-lipped, and then said, 'Very well. We had better go to a private room. I don't suppose your seeking me out in this public way can give rise to more gossip than is already current.'

Weston thought the earl looked really ill, and was ashamed to have made his life more difficult in this manner. 'I'm sorry, sir. I suppose I should have sent a note first, requesting an interview, but the matter is one of such urgency that —'

'You mistake, Captain. There is no urgency in the case. But I concede that you might well think so. If you please,' — he silenced Weston with a gesture — 'no more talk until we are alone.'

Having asked a club servant to ensure they were not disturbed, he led the way into a private parlour, closed the door and, taking a seat himself, signed the younger man to sit down. Weston obeyed, but almost instantly got to his feet again, hardly aware that he had done so, his agitation too great to let him be still. The two men had been many times in company together since the beginning of Weston's association with Lucy, but they had never been alone together, and nothing in the nature of a confrontation had ever taken place. Aylesbury had been at pains that it should not, and was angry that Weston should have precipitated one now.

'Well, Captain Weston,' he said at last, when the other had paced up and down the room a few times, 'if you have something to say to me, you had better say it, and let us be done with this.'

Weston turned to face him. 'If this interview is painful to you, sir, I assure you it is even more so to me.'

'No, sir. That is not possible,' Aylesbury said, quite gently. 'Proceed.'

Weston flushed. 'Sir, Lucy tells me that you came to see her this morning, at her request; that she had something to tell you.'

'She told me that she is with child,' the earl answered brutally, 'and since the whole world knows that the child cannot be mine, it is to be supposed that you are responsible for its existence.'

Weston bit his lip. 'Yes, it's true. It would be absurd of me to apologise to you —'

'More than absurd. It would be an intolerable impertinence,' the earl said in a hard voice.

'Sir, I am sorry that you, or anyone else, should be hurt in any way by my actions,' Weston persevered. 'I wish with all my heart that things could have been different, but I do beg you to believe that I have not acted lightly, and that I should never have wronged you if it weren't for my great love for her.'

'These protestations are tedious and distasteful to me. Please understand that I have no interest whatever in your state of mind, and come to the point, if indeed you have one.'

'The point is that your wife is with child by me,' Weston said, stung by the contempt in the earl's voice, 'and that I have no wish of concealment in the matter. I have come to ask you to divorce her, so that I may take responsibility for her and the child.'

48

'Divorce is out of the question. I have already told my wife so. She might have saved you the trouble of this application.'

'She did tell me that, but I must beg you to —'

'Captain Weston,' Aylesbury lifted an imperative hand, 'let us understand each other and have done with all this. I have said that divorce is out of the question, and I shall not change my mind. I have no intention of going through all the unpleasantness, scandal and disgrace merely for your convenience. Lucy is my wife, and she will remain my wife, and I shall do my best to retrieve what little reputation is left to her. You, I believe, will soon be going to sea, which will be the best thing for all of us. When you are ashore, you may continue to see her as you do now. I could prevent that, but I have no wish to exert myself; or, as it happens, to make her so unhappy. And that is all I have to say to you.'

'I'm sorry, sir, but I can't leave it there,' said Weston. 'Lucy says that you have told her the child must be placed with foster parents. If you don't mean to acknowledge it, if you feel such aversion to it, why prevent me from accepting my responsibility? I want to look after her — and the child. I know I can't marry her legally, but if you would only divorce her, I would be a husband to her in every other way. I can change my commission for a shore appointment. When the war is over, if you like we could go abroad. You need never see or hear of us —'

Aylesbury sighed. 'I can see I shall have to be plainer still. I married Lucy in the first place in order to get an heir for my title and estate. This was a duty I owed to my family. It happened also to suit the Morland family very well, but that's beside the point. I have always let her do pretty much as she pleased, provided the primary purpose of our marriage was fulfilled. The scandal she has caused by her liaison with you is a fleeting and unimportant thing, but this child — which everyone would know is not mine — and a divorce could cause great damage to my family, and I do not propose to allow it. As to your taking care of her, forgive me if I continue to believe that I can do that better than you.'

'And her wishes in the matter are not important?' Weston asked hotly. 'You would separate her from her own child?'

'Lucy has everything she wants. She has wealth, position,

the protection of my name, and she is free to consort with you as and when she pleases. As to the children, I have never noticed that she is particularly fond of the three she has already — not even the last one you fathered on her, Captain Weston.'

Weston was dumbfounded. 'What do you mean?' he asked at last in a faint voice.

Aylesbury's smile was one of pure malice. 'She didn't tell you, then? We were both quite grateful to you, you know. Our first two endeavours had only produced girls, and I think Lucy found the business as distasteful as I did. The arrival of your boy provided me with the heir I needed, so that we need never go through it again.'

'You mean the baby — Roland — is my son?' He stared, trying to make sense of it.

'No, Captain, not any more. He is *my* son, my heir: Roland Chetwyn, Viscount Calder, who will be seventh Earl of Aylesbury after my death.'

Weston looked stunned, like a man who had been struck a very hard blow. 'I never knew ... I never even suspected ...'

'We were at pains you should not,' Aylesbury said evenly.

'But then — why tell me now?'

'So that you may understand the situation fully. I have my heir, and I'm grateful enough to you and Lucy to allow you the pleasure of each other's company, even though it inconveniences me a little from time to time. But I will not cast any shadow on his inheritance by divorce, or by allowing this new child to come publicly into the world.'

Weston's hands clenched in fury. 'This is intolerable! I tell you I won't stand aside and do nothing, while you —'

Aylesbury's expression hardened. 'Oh yes, you will, Captain. I have been lenient with you so far, for Lucy's sake, but you had better not try my patience. Good God, sir, you talk as if you had some rights in this matter! I will tell you now exactly what will happen. Lucy will go to the country to have the baby privately; the baby will be sent away to foster parents; and you will accept your new commission, which I was at such pains to get for you.'

'You?' Weston said in astonishment.

'Oh yes. I am not without influence, you know. There was

some question of a staff appointment at the Admiralty, but that would not have suited my purposes. It is necessary that you should be out of the country for the next few months. If you return, you may see Lucy again, and I hope you will both try to be a little more careful in future.'

'And if I refuse to co-operate with your plans?'

'You would be wise not to resist them. I can break you, Captain. You see by the way I have already influenced your career that this is no idle threat. You may also like to consider that, for all your protests about love, you are no more than a common adulterer. I could bring a suit against you for Criminal Conversation, which there is no doubt in the world I would win. Considering my rank, the damages which would be awarded against you would be of such an order that you would be faced with the choice of debtor's prison or flight abroad. You should ask yourself, perhaps, how Lucy would like that.'

The earl stood up, and Weston saw the heaviness of his movements and the terrible weariness in his face. 'Now I'm afraid I must ask you to leave,' he said politely. 'It is past my usual hour of dining. You will forgive me, Captain, if I hope that we never meet again.'

Lucy wept, and Weston, who had never seen her tears before, did everything he could think of to console her, but in vain.

'I wish I hadn't told you,' she sobbed. 'It was better as it was. I can't bear to think of you both unhappy! Oh, poor Chetwyn!'

'Lucy, my darling —'

'He has always been good to me. What other husband would let us alone like this?'

'Yes, I know, I know,' Weston said grimly. 'But now he means to make up for it. Oh, Lucy, why didn't you tell me about Roland? I just don't understand.'

'Don't you?' she said, lifting her tear-smudged face from her hands for a moment. 'But — that was why we married, to get an heir. It would have meant it was all for nothing, and he was my husband after all. I owed him that much. But now with this child, we've been apart too long.'

'You mean,' Weston asked slowly, 'that you wouldn't have told me if you and he —?'

Lucy searched in vain for a dry portion of her handkerchief on which to blow her nose, and Weston pulled his out automatically and pushed it at her.

'Of course not, only everybody knows he and I never see each other, so nobody would have believed it was his.' She blew her nose forcefully, and then, seeing Weston's expression, her eyes filled irresistibly with tears again. 'Oh, Weston, don't mind it! I'm not romantic like you — you've always known that. And I ought to behave properly by Chetwyn. But I do — I do care for you!' The tears welled over again, and she buried her face in his handkerchief. 'I'm sorry,' she sobbed unevenly. 'I don't know why I'm like this. It must be my con-condition!'

Weston took her in his arms and let her cry on his shoulder until his coat was wet and warm. He was worn out with emotion, sick with frustration and helplessness. He felt as though he were in a trap; and twist and turn as he might, he could see no way out but to do what Aylesbury told him, which injured his pride as well as going against his wishes.

He remembered so clearly the moment he had first seen Lucy, coming into the Keppel's Head, her face pale from her long journey, her hair raggedly cropped, masquerading as a boy in her burning desire to be a doctor. He had been intrigued by her insane courage, her ferocious determination, her straightforward, childlike frankness; but when he had met her again later as Lady Aylesbury and seen those same qualities struggling for expression through the muffling folds of womanhood, he had loved her as naturally as a bird flies to its nest.

He understood why people talked of *falling* in love: it was as sudden, and as irrevocable. It was as if his heart had left him to live in her. His life, his breath, his blood, were in her, and if he went away from her and never saw her again, those things would not return to him: he could not part from her and live. She was his companion, as close to him as his thoughts, and though it would have been so much easier if they had never met, there was nothing to be done about that now.

Oh, but the child, the child! Not just the one she now nurtured in her belly, but the one she had borne him before without his knowledge. To him, a child of their bodies was something miraculous and precious, the product, the proof, which would live on after they were dust, that once, somewhere in time, he and she had loved. But she did not see it like that. It was a hard thing to acknowledge, that though she loved him, it was not as he loved. 'I'm not romantic like you,' she would say, dear Lucy, hay-haired, freckle-nosed Lucy, who would brave the entire world for him, and yet could not say 'I love you'.

She had stopped crying, and he thought she might have fallen asleep, but after a while she sat up, wiped the smears from her face, and contemplated him thoughtfully. Her fears and anxieties in the preceding days had stemmed from uncertainty; but now that the uncertainties were resolved, she was her old practical self again. Now she knew what had to be coped with, she could accept it and get on with it: there was no point in repining. Weston saw all that in her expression. She was not one to fling everything away in a romantic gesture; but she had said to him that she would not want him any different, and God forbid that he should be less generous in his love.

'I'm all right now,' she said. 'I won't do that again. Now, Weston, we must be practical. There are your trunks to be got ready, the cabin stores to buy, and we have to decide where I'm to spend the summer. That's difficult, until we know where you are bound. But if you are for the Channel Fleet, it had better be Portsmouth or Plymouth, so that I can see you if you come ashore. I don't want to waste a moment we can be together. When will you get your orders?'

'Oh Lucy!' he said with an unwilling laugh. Her eyes were still pink, and her eyelashes wet and spiky, but she looked ready for anything. Tenderness welled up in him. There were so many painful things that would have to be faced, but he could not think about them yet; not just yet. 'I don't think we need to start packing this instant. Perhaps you'd better take off your gown, so that it doesn't get crumpled.'

'My gown?' she said in surprise, and then a slow smile curved her lips, and she stood up. 'Yes, of course,' she said, stepping into his arms and leaning her whole body against him. 'At least now it can't possibly do any harm, can it?'

At the end of the first week of May, Edward made one of his rare visits to London, taking the opportunity of travelling up with his childhood friend John Anstey. They called first at Ryder Street, where they found Lord Aylesbury, in a very splendid Chinese dressing-gown of scarlet silk and a Turkish cap with a tassel, taking a late breakfast of coffee and rolls.

'What London hours you keep, Chetwyn!' Edward cried by way of greeting. 'Still breakfasting at eleven? John and I were up at five this morning, to get on the road!'

The earl started up and crossed the room in two strides to fold him in a fierce embrace which rather took Ned's breath away. When he was released, he was surprised to see that there were tears in his friend's eyes. 'You look as though you've been ill. Is everything all right?' he enquired anxiously.

'I'm well enough, well enough,' Chetwyn said, turning to shake John Anstey's hand cordially. 'Anstey, my good fellow, it's a pleasure to see you. Will you take something? A nuncheon? Your breakfast must be a distant memory by now. Benton! Bring fresh covers, and that sirloin, and fruit! Ned, can you drink coffee? Ale for Mr Morland, Benton! Draw up a chair, Anstey. What brings you both to London?'

'The war, of course, what else?' John Anstey said, bringing a chair to the round walnut table in the window where the earl took such meals as he ate at home. It was laid with a lace cloth, and there was a silver vase of white roses in the centre, whose scent expanded on the sun-warmed air. 'Glorious roses,' he commented. 'Early, too. Ours at home have taken such a knock this year with all the gales.'

'I get them from Chelmsford House,' Chetwyn answered with a smile. 'The garden's so sheltered, they always bloom early. My new man, Benton, used to be a footman there, and he's remained on friendly terms with the Chelmsford butler.'

'What, old Hawkins? Is he still going strong?' Edward put in.

'Strong as ever. I think he feels living in lodgings is rather beneath me, but he's told Benton to help himself to flowers from the garden for me at any time. I'm looking forward to August, if I can persuade Benton to a liberal interpretation of the word 'flowers'. The Chelmsford House cherries are famous!'

Benton came back with a laden tray and set places for the visitors, and when he had gone, Edward began carving thin slices from the handsome sirloin in front of him, and said, 'What's the latest news, then, Chet? Is this war ever to come about?'

'Word was yesterday that Whitworth is still in Paris,' said Chetwyn.

'But surely the seven-day ultimatum is past?' Anstey said. 'Why hasn't he withdrawn?'

'It seems that just as he was about to leave, Buonaparte took care to put about a rumour that he was willing to deal, and Whitworth's orders are such that he dare not take it upon himself to be the aggressor. As long as there's a chance of negotiating over Malta and the Low Countries, Addington's anxious to avoid declaring war. Boney's got to be put in the wrong if the anti-war party are to be persuaded to swallow the pill.'

'He'll be forced to in the end,' Anstey said angrily. 'Damn it, all this shilly-shallying is simply playing into French hands, giving them time to complete their plans.'

'You know that, and I know that, and I'm sure Buonaparte knows that,' Chetwyn said with a wry smile. 'It's just getting it across to Addington that's the problem. But the situation can't last much longer.'

'It had better not, or some of us are going to start making serious demands,' Anstey said sternly.

'It's an uneasy time,' Chetwyn said. 'The financiers don't like it, and 'Change is damned nervous. There've been huge dealings in the Funds, and Lloyds are in a twitter about their premiums. Allowing for the time it takes to communicate, I'd say another week or ten days is all it can last. If you have any relatives amongst the pleasure-seekers in France, Anstey, you had better get them out. I don't like to think what's going to happen to them when war is finally declared. Boney's quite capable of arresting them all.'

Edward had been eating his way steadily through the beef

while the others talked, and Chetwyn now turned his attention to him. 'Is everything well at Morland Place?'

'Oh, we go on much as usual,' Edward said. 'You are coming up for race-week, aren't you, Chet? I've a couple of very promising young 'uns for you to put your purse on.'

'I wouldn't miss it,' Chetwyn answered. 'But how can they spare you, old fellow? You haven't yet told me why you're here.'

Edward told him of his idea for a contract for supplying corn to the navy. 'I suppose the Commissioner of Portsmouth would be the most direct man to approach, but I'm all for trying interest first. That's why I've come up with John. Addington needs every vote in the House he can get, and John proposes to offer to support him, if he will speak to the Comptroller on my behalf. It's of no use his asking St Vincent — he doesn't hold with jobbery, except where dashing young sea-officers are concerned. But in any case, from what I hear, the Comptroller's got more influence than the Naval Lord and the First Lord put together.'

'But I seem to have missed a step somewhere,' Chetwyn said solemnly. 'What does Anstey gain from this?'

Edward grinned. 'Oh, you spotted that, did you? That's partly why we're here, Chet — we want to use the Aylesbury influence on John's behalf.'

'My eldest boy, you see,' John Anstey explained, 'is mad for the navy, wants to make it his career. Well, I don't mind it — I've other sons to follow me in business, and Louisa is all for it. It runs in her blood, you know — father, grandfather and brother.'

'Surely even your eldest lad must be rather young to be going to sea?' Chetwyn frowned. 'I don't recall dates very well, but I remember your wedding, and I can't believe it was more than nine or ten years ago.'

'He's eight this year,' Anstey told him, 'and *I* think it's too young, but Louisa insists he can't begin too early. She says now is the best time to get patronage, before the rush starts. She says that as soon as war is declared, the great naval clans like the Parkers and the Cochranes will start manoeuvring, and all the places will be taken.'

'She may very well be right, but I don't quite see what I

can do for you,' Chetwyn said. 'My influence is limited to
Carlton House, and the Prince of Wales, you know, is not at
all interested in the navy.'

'Well, when I said the Aylesbury influence, I suppose I was
really thinking of Lucy,' Anstey said. 'She's such a favourite
of Admiral Collingwood, and it would be easy enough for him
to find little John a place.'

Chetwyn's face was immobile. 'I'm afraid you are out of
luck. She's not in Town.'

'Oh, what a pity — I wanted to see her,' Anstey said. 'Has
she gone down to Wolvercote?'

'No, to Portsmouth, I believe,' Chetwyn said. Out of the
corner of his eye he saw Edward frown, then open his mouth
to ask an awkward question, and he went on hastily, 'but with
Ned beside you, you can have no scruples about using the
name, if you think you need it.'

He turned to Edward and firmly changed the subject. 'Are
you making any sort of stay, now you're here? Because if you
are, you must come with me to my tailor and let him make
you a coat. I've seen you in that brown thing any time these
five years, and it was always hideous, you know And I've a
new barber, too, who dresses hair to perfection. He could
make a new man of you, Ned, my dear.'

'I'm content with the old one, even if you aren't,' Edward
said with a smile, 'but I admit I could do with a new coat.'

Chetwyn eyed him up and down. 'You had much better
wait until you have it, before you go jobbing. Where are you
staying?'

'Grillons, I suppose,' Ned answered doubtfully. 'Of course,
we both thought we'd be staying in Upper Grosvenor Street,
but —'

'No reason why you shouldn't. The staff are always there
in readiness. I'll write a note for Hicks, and Thorn shall take
it round this morning. No, don't mention it, Anstey. They
might as well be working for their pay. And now, if you'll
excuse me for half an hour while I get dressed, I'll bear you
company across the park.'

Lucy's arrival in the courtyard of the Golden Lion in

Portsmouth, driving herself and Weston in her curricle, caused the sort of mild sensation that she had come rather to enjoy since she became a countess. Two grooms ran up to the horses' heads, two manservants came out from the inn to help her down, and before her feet had touched the cobbles, the landlord himself appeared with his lady bobbing behind him, smoothing her apron with one hand and tweaking at his with the other.

'Welcome, welcome, your ladyship! Welcome, sir. We've a suite of rooms all ready for you, your ladyship, and a cold collation prepared, should you be in need of sustenance. And may I say, your ladyship, what an honour and a pleasure it is to see your ladyship here again?'

'Thank you, Tully,' Lucy said. 'Have my maid and the captain's man arrived?'

'Oh yes, your ladyship, this morning by the mail. They've everything arranged as you like it, and your sheets aired and on the beds.'

'Good. My groom will be arriving later with my horses. He's bringing them on from Kingston, where we made the first change. You'll see they're accommodated, won't you? And have this team taken back to the Green Dragon at Havant.'

'Certainly, your ladyship. At what hour will you be requiring dinner, your ladyship?'

Lucy and Weston exchanged a swift glance, and Weston answered for both. 'We're going straight down to the dockyard, and we'll dine when we return. It won't be before four o'clock.'

'We'll take a nuncheon before we go,' Lucy said. 'Oh, and Tully — send word round to Captain Haworth's lodgings that we are arrived, will you?'

Lucy was no less eager to see Weston's new ship than he was himself, and they paused only for Weston to change into his uniform, to eat some cake and fruit, and to attempt to placate Jeffrey, who was sulking horribly after his long confinement in a basket, before leaving for the dockyard.

A hackney swept them through the great gates, between the tall gateposts surmounted by their golden balls, and the gatekeeper saluted the uniform, and then, peering closer, called out to the driver where they would find the *Nemesis*. As they rattled on over the cobbles, Lucy pressed Weston's hand and said, 'Isn't it wonderful: he not only recognised you, he knew what your new command is, too. Your reputation must be much higher than you thought.'

'I rather think it was you he recognised, my love,' Weston said, laughing, but he was pleased all the same, as he craned out of the window for the first glimpse of his ship. 'There she is!' he cried at last. 'Isn't she a beauty?'

'She has got lovely lines,' Lucy agreed. 'She looks fast, too.'

'Well, everyone knows the French are good ship-designers. Of course, our ships are built very sturdily, to withstand long service and foul weather, but there's no doubt French frigates are more graceful to look at.'

'I didn't know she was French built,' Lucy said.

'She was a prize of the Revolutionary War. She was taken in '98 off the coast of Sardinia. Come on, I can't wait to get aboard!'

When they got back to the Golden Lion for a late dinner, Weston's servant Bates told them that the messenger had come back from Haworth's lodgings to say that the captain was at sea, but that the two young ladies were there in the charge of their nurse, Mrs Farleigh, who would do herself the honour of calling on her ladyship the following day.

'*Both* girls?' Lucy said to Weston when they were alone. 'I thought he meant to take Africa to sea with him.'

'I dare say he thought it too dangerous, since the purpose of the trials is to see whether his ship will stay afloat,' Weston said, helping himself from a dish of peas with mushrooms.

'I suppose he wants to keep them both in Portsmouth until he is given his proper orders, in case he has time to come ashore,' Lucy said. 'It's lucky for him old Farleigh was willing to stay with them. This duckling is very good, Weston. What a pity you can't keep ducks in a ship.'

'If I'm sent on the Brest blockade, I'll be lucky to be able to keep chickens. They don't take kindly to storms and rough seas.'

The moment he said it, he wished he hadn't, for there was no sense in reminding Lucy before time of the dangers of the Brest blockade. They were as well known to her as to anyone.

59

The northern part of the Bay of Biscay was notorious for foul weather and thick fogs; there were hidden rocks everywhere, some far out from land; the currents and tidal streams were strong, and all set towards the rocks of Ushant; and the prevailing south-westerly winds made Brest, with all its hazards, a lee-shore.

A ship of the line might lie off a little and preserve some sea-room, but the frigates, to fulfil their purpose of watching the enemy closely, had to creep in amongst the shoals and the spiked teeth of hidden rocks, with the knowledge that retreating from danger meant clawing their way out against the wind. Only during a settled westerly gale, when the French could not possibly get to sea, could the blockade relax and, if necessary, run for shelter to a home port.

He sought to distract her by saying, 'I wouldn't take it for granted, however, that Farleigh's willing to stay on. What do you think she wants to see you about tomorrow? I'll give you odds she's going to say how wonderful it is that you've come, so that she can leave the children with you. She'll probably arrive with all their bags packed, drop them on your hearth and disappear!'

'Oh nonsense!' Lucy said robustly, 'Though I quite long to see Africa again. I wonder how she has liked living ashore?'

'You'd have loved to have had her chances when you were her age, wouldn't you.' Weston said.

'Well, I would. Will you carve me some of that lamb, please? Of course, there'll come a point when he'll have to send her ashore. It's all right while she's so little, but she can't live amongst sailors for ever, and then I suppose he'll send her down to Wolvercote to join the rest of the brood.'

Weston thought suddenly and painfully of Roland, and his hand faltered in the dissection of the roast leg of lamb, and he looked so utterly stricken that Lucy had no doubt as to what he was thinking.

'Oh Weston, don't!' she said in distress.

'How can I help it?' he said. 'My son — my only son, perhaps — and I can never be a father to him. He is to grow up with another man's name, and not know me.'

'But he isn't any different now from what he was before you knew, and you never cared about him before.'

'Oh Lucy, how can you say that?' he said despairingly,
'You should be proud that he will be an earl one day, and a very rich one at that. What does it matter what name he bears?'

He only shook his head, knowing that he could not make her see it as he saw it. 'And now there's this new child,' he said in a low voice. 'I can't bear to think that it will be lost to both of us — discarded like something useless. Our child, Lucy! It mustn't be!'

Lucy bit her lip. 'I must say I don't care for the idea very much myself,' she said. 'It is such a trouble carrying them and bearing them, and it seems hard to be obliged to do it all for nothing.' He could almost have laughed at the inadequacy of her language. 'But there is nothing to be done about it,' she went on. 'Chetwyn won't change his mind.'

'We could defy him,' Weston said.

Lucy put down her fork and looked at him sadly. 'Oh Weston, you don't begin to understand. I'm his wife, I am completely in his power. He would break you, and ruin you. And he could lock me up and keep me as a prisoner, if he wanted.'

'I would come and rescue you,' he said stubbornly.

'And what use would that be, if you were a proscribed man, a debtor, a beggar?'

'We could go abroad. He couldn't touch us there.'

'Where abroad? We'll be at war any day now.'

'The war won't last for ever. Or we could go to America.'

She shook her head. 'And live on what? I don't want to be a beggar in a foreign country. How could we be happy, always wondering where our next meal was to come from? No, we are better off as we are. He has not said we must not see each other.'

'And how long will that last?' Weston said bitterly. 'We live by the whim of his charity.'

Lucy stared at him helplessly. 'It's the best we can do,' she said at last, gently for her. 'Please, Weston, try not to mind it so much.'

He made an effort, for her sake, and after a moment resumed carving the lamb. 'Where will you go to have the baby? Have you decided yet?'

'I shall stay here for now,' she said. 'There's no need to hide myself until my condition starts to show. Later ... I don't know.'

'I wish you could go back to Yorkshire. I should like to think of you being with friends while I'm at sea.'

'If I stay at Morland Place, everyone in Yorkshire will know I'm increasing,' she said with a faint smile. He laid the slices of lamb on her plate, and she lifted her glass to him and said, 'Let's be happy while we can. We have a few days yet.'

'A week, at least. I have to man her and complete the stores and set up the rigging. I'll be busy every day, but we can dine together and sleep together until I get my orders.'

'I'll find plenty to amuse me during the daytime, I promise you,' Lucy said.

'Including Farleigh tomorrow morning,' Weston reminded her with a teasing smile. 'If she does leave the children with you, you'll have your time well occupied.'

Weston wronged the elderly lady's maid, however. She brought the little girls to visit Lucy the next day, but though she looked thin and drawn and tired, she said at once that she would stay with her charges until Captain Haworth finally sailed and Hippolyta was safely at Wolvercote.

'And I shall not cease to try to persuade him to let me take *both* girls there,' she said firmly.

The sisters were as different as they could be. Hippolyta was almost nine, a dainty child, pretty as a porcelain figurine, with delicate features, and alabaster skin, wide blue eyes, and smooth dark ringlets. Though not in the least shy, she was grave and self-possessed in a way that had always seemed unnatural to Lucy in a child. She sat exactly where she had been placed, with her hands in her lap, and replied to questions with well-schooled politeness.

Africa resembled her sister very little. Where Hippolyta was very like her mother in looks, Africa favoured her father, having his rounder face and irregular features. Her skin was sun-browned and her cheeks were red, her hair an unruly mass of curls, and only dark brown where Hippolyta's was almost black. She did not sit quietly where she was placed, but fidgeted and walked around the room looking at things and peering out of the windows. Her expression was alert, her eyes sharp, and when addressed, she answered in a much bolder way than her sister — not impolite, but freer than was usually considered proper in a small child.

Lucy could see that Farleigh was in agonies about her, fearing that Africa's strangeness would reflect on her. Africa did not remember her aunt, but Lucy engaged her in a conversation about ships which quickly won her the little girl's respect. When it emerged that Lucy had once served as a King's officer Africa's eyes grew wide with admiration, and she demanded the whole story from beginning to end, with details.

'I can't tell it now; it would take too long,' Lucy laughed, 'but I promise you shall hear it all one day. But you will soon have much more to tell me than I can tell you. You can't think how much I envy you.'

Farleigh coughed warningly at this unnecessary encouragement, but Africa nodded in approval. 'I'm to sail with Papa when my ship is ready. She's my ship because I was named after her,' she added in a burst of confidentiality, 'but Papa's the captain. I always lived there until we came ashore. I don't like living ashore. It doesn't smell nice.'

The French continued their game of diplomacy, and Lord Whitworth did not leave Paris until 12 May. Weston had received his orders a few days before that, and had sailed to join two other frigates off Brest, to keep an eye on the invasion fleet which was being constructed there as in other French ports. War on France was at last declared on the 18th, and on the same day five ships of the line under Admiral Cornwallis sailed for Brest to join the frigates and begin the blockade.

Lucy remained at the Golden Lion; while Weston was only just across the Channel, there was always the chance that she might see him, if only for a few hours. She had Jeffrey for company, for Weston would not condemn him to the damp chill of the Brest station, even in summer.

She was badly in need of distraction, and was happy to take an interest in Haworth's girls, or more strictly in Africa, who missed her father and was bored and restless. Farleigh obviously found her more tiring to care for than Polly, and was grateful when Lucy took her away and amused her. A sort of friendship grew up between aunt and niece, each of whom approved of the other as being far more sensible and having more intelligible interests than the majority of the female sex. Lucy drove Africa out in her curricle, and once or twice, when the sea was calm, she hired a little boat to take them out on the water.

It was not until the beginning of June that Captain Haworth returned to Portsmouth, and called on Lucy with the news that the *Africa* was being taken out of commission.

'She's being towed up to dry-dock this moment, poor thing,' he told her. 'She's making water so fast even the Navy Board can't go on pretending she's fit for active service. I thought at one point they were going to make me go on sailing her round and round until she sank under me.'

Lucy commiserated with him. 'I remember when you first got her, she was a new ship. I came down here with you to look her over.'

'Yes, I remember. It was the new timbers that caused the trouble, of course. Your old ships are often more reliable than new ones. There's hardly a decent ship in the service less than thirty years old, and some of 'em are fifty and more.'

'And what will happen to the *Africa* now? Will she be broken up?'

'I don't know for certain. I've heard a rumour that they'll cut her down, and rebuild her using only the old timbers. They might make a sixty-four of her. At all events, she and I have parted company for good.'

'What a shame! Africa will be very upset. But what of you? Will they give you another ship?'

'Yes, I'm lucky. There's a squadron due in from the West Indies any day, and I'm to take over the *Cetus*. She's a seventy-four, which is all I know about her. And you'll have your brother William's company for a while. The port admiral told me that the *Argus* is among them.'

'Oh, William! He's no company,' Lucy said disparagingly. 'Little Africa's got more conversation.'

Her expectations of pleasure from the arrival of the West India squadron were abruptly increased when Mrs Tully came toiling up to her rooms early one morning to say that the ships had been sighted entering Portsmouth Sound, and that the *Nemesis* was with them. That afternoon at dinner Lucy entertained not only her brother William and his wife, and Captain Haworth, but Captain Weston, too.

'What were you doing with the squadron?' Haworth wanted to know.

'The merest chance,' Weston said. 'I caught up with them just as they were rounding St Catherine's Point. I lost a spar in that last blow we had, so I've been sent home with the despatches. I suppose I'll be going back as soon as the repair's finished. How did your trials go?'

Haworth told him about the *Africa*, and about his new command.

'The *Cetus*?' Weston exclaimed at once. 'I served in her back in '95. I went there from the dear old *Diamond* as third lieutenant, and we had a terrible cruise to the Baltic. God, how I hate northern waters! The cold and the damp were dreadful. I shall never forget them.'

'What a play-actor you are,' Haworth laughed.

'You don't believe me? But when I tell you that both the first and second lieutenants died on that cruise, you'll see how awful it must have been. My promotion to first over their dead bodies is the only good thing I can remember about the *Cetus*, though I dare say she may be as good a ship as any in warmer waters.'

'Where are you bound in her?' William asked Haworth politely. 'Shall we have the pleasure of your company in the islands?'

'No, thank God — though I mean that as no disparagement on you, sir,' Haworth added with a bow. 'But I've no wish whatever to visit the West Indies! No, I'm for Toulon, to help our Admiral Nelson guard the nice, warm, safe Mediterranean!'

'They gave Nelson the *Victory*, did you know that, Haworth?' Lucy put in. 'They made poor Collingwood transfer his flag to old *Dreadnought*, and just when he'd got himself comfortable, too.'

'He wasn't best pleased, I imagine,' Haworth said.

'Well, apart from his personal dispositions,' Lucy said, 'he could hardly have liked having to take *Dreadnought* on the Brest station. Her coppering is all but worn out, and she gripes in the stays.'

William raised an eyebrow, and exchanged a look with his wife, but Haworth caught Weston's eye and laughed.

'Oh Lucy, you do one so much good,' he cried. 'I love to hear you talking technicalities like that.'

The next morning Weston's servant Bates woke his master by putting his head through the bedcurtains and whispering that an Admiralty messenger had come with a sealed letter for him.

'Very well, I'll come,' Weston said. 'Wait for me outside.'

When Bates had gone, Lucy rolled over into Weston's arms, and he held her close and kissed her. She was soft with sleep, and her skin smelled like warm new bread. 'It is your orders?' she murmured.

'Probably,' he said. 'They won't keep a useful frigate in port longer than necessary. I'd better go and see.'

She withdrew herself obediently, and watched him through half-closed eyes as he climbed out through the curtains, put on his dressing-gown, and went out. She inched over into the hollow of delicious warmth where he had been lying and drowsed, curling her hands over her belly. What would life be like, she wondered languidly, with no trouble? If there were no war and no Chetwyn; if she and Weston were married in the ordinary way? For the first time she thought about the coming baby with curiosity, and felt a momentary pang at the thought of losing it. She let herself drift into a half-waking dream of living with Weston, perhaps in the little Essex village where they had spent last summer, they and the child in happy obscurity.

'Lucy?'

She started back to wakefulness, and found him sitting on the edge of the bed, leaning over her. Her heart sank, for in his hand was the opened letter, the heavy paper weighted with the official seal. She struggled up on to one elbow, and looked into his face, waiting for the blow.

'It's my orders, I am to go at once,' he said.

'Back to Brest?' she asked.

'Yes.' He put down the letter and used his hand instead to stroke her cheek. 'My love, there is no point in your staying here any longer. It is unlikely I shall leave station again until we need water, and that won't be for three months.'

'Three months.' The words took on a falling cadence of despair. In three months she would be in retirement, in accordance with her agreement with Chetwyn.

Weston had no words to offer that could be of any comfort. It was very hard that he should have to be apart from her at such a time. Unless a miracle happened, the baby would be born before he returned — born and borne away. And Lucy would have to face it all alone; she might die, and he would know nothing about it. He cupped her cheek, and his hand was trembling. 'I must go,' he said.

'Now, this minute?'

'The wind will just serve, but if it backs another point, I may be delayed for days.'

She loved him too much to suggest he delay, in that hope. She watched in silence as he dressed himself and gathered together the few belongings he had brought from the ship yesterday, and all too soon he returned to the bedside to stoop and kiss her: brow, eyes, nose and lips. 'God bless you,' he whispered, and then he was gone. She heard his voice outside, and Bates's, and then the closing of the outer door. In her imagination she saw them clattering down the stairs into the cold, stale-beer smell of the taproom passage, and out into the street.

And then she flung herself almost wildly from the bed, catching her feet in the covers and staggering, before she rushed to the window and flattened her face against it for a last glimpse of him. He still carried his hat in his hand, and the breeze that would just serve ruffled his hair as he and Bates turned the corner, their footsteps echoing behind them. He did not look back, but she had known he wouldn't.

Chapter Four

It was peaceful in the front parlour of the little house named Plaisir, in the village of Coxwold. Though a fine summer rain was drenching the world outside, there was a comfortable fire in the grate, and the ladies of the household were seated around the table at the window, engaged in normal morning pursuits.

Héloïse had abandoned her solitary work on her History of the Revolution in favour of a little companionable sewing, and was stitching some very pretty lace on a new cap for herself. Under the table her enormous hound Kithra was sleeping, lying on her feet as usual. She was beginning to get pins-and-needles, but she didn't like to move in case she disturbed him.

Her faithful maid Marie, who had escaped with her from France and undergone with her all the hardships of flight, exile and poverty, was working her way steadily through the usual pile of mending, and enduring the fourth in a series of colds which had plagued her since March. Beyond her Madame Chouflon, whose fingers were too stiff in this damp weather to sew, was reading aloud to them from a book of French sermons.

Beside Héloïse her little daughter Sophie-Marie, with three cushions under her to raise her to the level of the table, was making a pomander for her mother's wardrobe by the satisfying process of pressing whole cloves into the skin of an orange. Before she began, her mother had told her the etymology of the English word, and while she worked she crooned '*pomme d'ambre*' over and over like a litany under her breath. Brought up bilingually, she had used English and French almost at random all her life, but now at the age of five she was just beginning to separate the languages, and was finding the process interesting.

Opposite Héloïse, in the favoured seat which commanded a view of the little front garden, the white paling fence, and the road, her ward Mathilde was officially working at her daily task of embroidery. But Héloïse noticed that her fingers had not made a new stitch for at least ten minutes, and that most of Mathilde's efforts were given to staring out of the window, peering at the sky to see if the clouds were going to break, and occasionally drawing a deep involuntary sigh.

One of the maids, Nan, came in to see to the fire. It seemed a welcome interruption. Madame Chouflon broke off reading, Marie put down her work to blow her nose, and Héloïse took the opportunity of moving her feet and wriggling them to restore the circulation.

'Has Stephen come back from the blacksmith?' she asked.

'No, my lady, not yet,' said Nan. 'But the butcher's boy's been, and Mr Barnard says the beefsteak he brought is only fit to be given to the dog.'

'How can you know that?' Héloïse asked, intrigued. Barnard, her cook, was a French provincial who spoke English only in the direst emergency, and both Nan and Alice, the other maid, were Londoners who understood no word of any language but their own.

'Well, I don't exactly know what he said,' Nan admitted, brushing down her skirt as she stood up, 'but it's easy enough to know what he means.'

'Ah,' said Héloïse. 'And did the butcher's boy also understand?'

'I think so, my lady,' Nan grinned. 'Mr Barnard threw it back at him, and then he grabbed his big knife and started sharpening it. I never saw anyone move so fast as that boy! But I think all Mr Barnard meant by it was that if he hadn't got no beefsteak to cook for your dinner, my lady, he'd have to go and kill a duck after all.'

Héloïse chuckled. 'It's never wise to assume Monsieur Barnard does not mean the worst. But I expect you're right in this case.'

'Yes, my lady. Will that be all?'

'Yes, Nan. I'll come by and by and speak to him about dinner.'

'That butcher gets worse and worse,' Marie said when Nan had gone. 'It would be much better to let Kexby bring us meat from Thirsk.'

The suggestion was not entirely ingenuous: Kexby the

carrier was in love with Marie, and took her out on his cart on her days off.

'I suppose it will come to that in the end,' Héloïse said, 'but I had hoped to win approval for us all by patronising the village suppliers ... Sophie, my love, put them closer together. There must not be any space between the cloves, or the orange will go bad.'

'Yes, Maman,' Sophie said patiently. 'Why doesn't Nan understand Monsieur Barnard?'

'Because she doesn't speak French, my pigeon,' Héloïse replied.

'Yes, but why doesn't she learn? It's very easy.'

'To us it is, but not to her and Alice, because they are English.'

Sophie frowned over her work, evidently feeling there was a flaw in the argument. 'Perhaps she doesn't want people to think she is French. Is it a *very* bad thing to be French, Maman?'

'Not a bad thing at all,' Héloïse said indignantly. 'Who put such an idea into your head, child?'

'I heard Mr Bates say so to Mr Antrobus after church on Sunday. He said French people are wicked because they make us have a war.'

Reaction to these words was various. Héloïse and Marie exchanged disturbed looks, Madame Chouflon tutted vigorously, and Mathilde started and blushed, then turned to stare out of the window with a particularly languishing expression.

'It is not the French people who wish for war, *chérie*,' Héloïse answered her daughter, 'but this man Buonaparte and his friends. Ordinary French people are no different from ordinary English people. Not,' she added in fairness, 'that you have very much French blood in you, my Sophie. In fact, you are three-quarters English.'

'Good,' said Sophie with satisfaction. 'I should not like to be wicked, for then Our Lady would not love me.'

Madame Chouflon, perceiving that Héloïse had not succeeded in clarifying matters, engaged Sophie across the table in an earnest dialogue in French. Héloïse took up her needle again and said casually to no-one in particular, 'Of course, there are other things besides wickedness which Our

Lady does not like. There is also folly, and ingratitude. It would be very foolish and ungrateful, for instance, to waste one's time moping and sighing and staring out of the window, when one should be working.'

Mathilde quickly removed her gaze from the window and picked up her needle, a red spot of resentment burning in each cheek. Héloïse looked at her with sympathy. 'You think I don't understand,' she said, divining her ward's thoughts without difficulty. 'You think it is so long since I was fourteen that I cannot possibly remember what it was like.'

Mathilde compressed her lips, but did not look up. She was on the verge of womanhood, and was full of doubts and fears and expectations, and didn't know what to do about any of them; and to make it worse she was in the throes of an unspoken and unrequitable passion for Antrobus, the curate. He was a pompous young man, full of long words and his own importance who, because he was rather handsome and was distantly connected to a great family, had high hopes of marrying the local squire's daughter.

It would be useless, of course, to point out any of those things to Mathilde, whose passion had everything to do with her age and very little to do with its object. 'It is a great pity,' Héloïse said, 'that you do not have more company of your own age. Perhaps I ought to have sent you to school.'

'Oh no, madame,' Mathilde said quickly, shocked at the thought of being torn from the parish and proximity of her idol. 'I don't want to go away anywhere.'

'Nevertheless,' Héloïse went on, 'in a year or two, we will probably have to move to a town. It would be of no use to bring you out here, would it? You would have no-one to dance with but Colonel Spencer's sons.'

Mathilde was successfully diverted. 'Shall I have a coming-out ball, madame, like Lizzie Spencer? And a pink gown and flowers?'

'Not pink,' Madame Chouflon cried out at once, shocked to the depth of her mantuamaker's soul. 'Not with your red hair!'

'I hope you will have a much better ball than Lizzie Spencer's.' Héloïse said. 'If I can arrange it with Madame de Chelmsford, I hope we may be able to have it in the ballroom in Chelmsford House, which you have never seen, of course, but which is an exact model of the Galerie des Glaces at Versailles.'

'I have never seen that, either,' Mathilde said; but she had heard it described often enough and now saw herself, in her imagination, dancing down a set with Mr Antrobus to the admiration and envy of all. Despite old Flon's protests, every mirror reflected her gown of pink silk, the same colour as Miss Spencer's, and the pink roses in her hair.

'One's first ball,' Héloïse sighed. '*On ne l'oublie jamais!* Mine was at Chenonceau, before the war. The ballroom there is built over the water, on arches. At midnight they put out all the lights and had fireworks on the river, and we watched from the windows. *C'était un spectacle merveilleux!*'

Mathilde had heard the story before many times, but never tired of it. 'What was your gown like? Who did you dance with?' she asked, resting her elbows on the table in the way that Flon expressly forbade because it made them rough and ugly. But before she could protest, or Héloïse answer, Stephen came in.

'I'm back, my lady,' he announced. 'Both ponies are shod and fit to go.'

'What about the split in Vega's hoof?' Héloïse enquired.

'The smith said it's nothing serious. He's cut it back, and put the nails in so as to hold it together, but he says I should keep an eye on it, and take him back in a fortnight to have it pared again. Did you want me to walk up the butcher's, my lady? I understand there was some trouble over the steak.'

'I'll come and speak to Monsieur Barnard about it. Has the rain stopped?'

'Yes, my lady, and the cloud's breaking up from the southwest. It looks as though we'll have a fine afternoon. If it stays dry, I can get on with mending the henhouse roof.'

'You do everything so well, Stephen,' Héloïse said admiringly, and he smirked a little, trying to maintain an expression of lordly indifference to compliment. 'Would you harness the ponies, please? Mathilde and Sophie are much in need of some fresh air. We shall go for a little drive before dinner.'

Sophie jumped up and clapped her hands for pleasure, and Mathilde gave her guardian a smile of direct gratitude.

72

'Run upstairs with Marie, children, and put on your bonnets,' Flon instructed.

Héloïse, on her way to the kitchen, added innocently, 'I think Mathilde ought to wear her new one with the yellow ribbon. Then if we should happen to pass anyone interesting in the village, she will know she is looking her best.'

Cygnus and Vega, the cream-coloured arabs whom Héloïse had named after stars because nothing else was as beautiful as they, were very fresh, and only good manners kept them from cantering as they set off, drawing the pretty little park phaeton along the road towards Kilburn. They curved their necks and trotted fast, lifting their knees showily, their muzzles touching, and the gold-and-coral ornaments on their browbands jumped and glittered in the sunshine.

The world was delicious after the rain. There were puddles everywhere, looking like fallen pieces of the flax-blue sky. A warm, earthy, weed-fragrant miasma rose from the damp ditches, a green and dim purple composite of cow-parsley and nettle, mullein, loosestrife, hemlock and bryony. Foxgloves lifted their exotic spotted throats and trembled under the weight of visiting bees, and from the higher, drier edges of the fields came the beckoning fragrance of thyme and chamomile. Every leaf in every hedge was dazzling with fat, silver drops, and beyond them the unharrowed crops were gay with scabious and meadow-rue and avens, fumitory and charlock, scarlet poppies, and the shocking blue of the cranesbill.

Soon they were trotting into Kilburn, where the strong light after days of greyness made every house look freshly painted, and the roofs steamed gently in the heat. Here Héloïse was forced to pull up. In the centre of the village the local squire, with the aid of two substantial farmers mounted selfconsciously on plough-horses, was drilling a platoon of local volunteers. Every housewife, child and idler in the village had gathered to watch, and even the innkeeper of the Cross Keys was standing in his doorway in a dazzling apron, philosophical in the anticipation of good business when the parade was over. The blacksmith had emerged from his private Avernus, but his attention was distracted by the thrillingly white forearms of the two housemaids who were leaning out of the attic windows of the house opposite.

It was a scene Héloïse had witnessed in many a village in the past weeks. The whole country seemed in a ferment over Buonaparte's reported boast that he would 'jump the ditch' and conquer England. Volunteers had flocked to take up arms, and the coastal regions were busy devising ingenious defences. Hatred of the First Consul was high, and no calumny was too vile for him. Handbills pinned up in public places exposed his villainy in violent language and crude cartoons, and rhymes and songs about him proliferated like fleas.

The squire, recognising Héloïse's rig, rode over to her and lifted his hat. 'My dear ma'am, how kind of you to honour our little spectacle with your presence! Not a bad turn-out, though I say it myself. A little rough and ready, but they're learning, they're learning. Let Boney try and invade Yorkshire, and he'll find out what sort of a people he's taken on!'

'Quite right, Sir John,' said Héloïse cheerfully, not thinking it necessary to disabuse the old gentleman. 'I am sure they are all brave as lions.'

'Well, they are, ma'am, they are. And an Englishman in the field's worth ten Frogs any day,' he said eagerly, and then suddenly realising what he had said, he turned a dull red and stammered, 'I mean — dash it, ma'am, no offence meant, I promise you! It's this feller Boney we all want to teach a lesson. You're a victim of his yourself, ma'am — we all know that. Your sort wouldn't support him, never thought it for a moment —'

'It's quite all right, Sir John,' Héloïse smiled, intervening before he got himself into worse difficulties. 'I am not offended in the least. In any case, you know, I am only half French, though I was brought up in Paris. My father was an Englishman.'

'Was in Paris once m'self,' Sir John said gruffly, with a grateful look. 'Back in '72. Not a bad sort of place at all, really.'

'Your men are drilling beautifully,' Héloïse replied in kind.

'Drill's all right, ma'am, but when is the Government going to issue arms, that's what I want to know? Had the damned cheek to offer us pikes, you know. Pikes! Refused 'em, straight off. Told them it was a damned insult to York-shiremen. Pikes! Be wanting us to fight Boney with our bare hands next. Not that we couldn't,' he added hastily. 'Fight and win.'

'I'm sure you would, Sir John,' Héloïse said. 'Ah, your men are making a little space on the road. Perhaps I can get by. My ponies are fresh after all this rain, you know, and won't stand for long.' The ponies were standing quietly at that moment, but Héloïse was worried about the restlessness of her passengers. For the past few minutes Mathilde had been having difficulty suppressing a fit of giggles; it would not be long before they affected Sophie too.

'Of course, of course, ma'am. I'll make a way for you. Handsome animals,' Sir John added, eyeing them keenly, 'John Brown, step aside there, will you? Your servant, ma'am.'

'Good morning, Sir John,' Héloïse said with a grave nod, and gave the office to the ponies, who justified her by tossing their heads and springing forward eagerly with little snorts of excitement.

On their return home they were met at the gate by Stephen, who was looking, most unusually, rather upset and flustered. Stephen had come to Héloïse when she first moved into Plaisir, and had set about making himself indispensable. He could turn his hand to almost anything, and prided himself on being imperturbable; so it must, she concluded with foreboding, be something very serious indeed to have shaken his self-possession.

The only clue was the presence, tied to the ring in the wall, of a visitor's horse. Her heart fluttered for a moment before her commonsense told it sternly that the animal was a job horse, and not one from Morland Place.

'My lady,' Stephen said, holding the ponies' heads while Héloïse climbed down. 'There is a visitor arrived to see you.'

'Yes, so I see. Who is it?'

'It is a gentleman, my lady.'

'I can see that, too,' Héloïse said gently. 'The horse does not wear a side-saddle.' Stephen looked more than ever confused. 'What has upset you? Who is it, Stephen?' She came to his side and looked up at him with concern.

'He — I am not acquainted with the gentleman myself, my lady. He gave me his card,' Stephen said in a desperate voice.

'Then you must know what his name is,' Héloïse said reasonably. There was no reply. 'Come, Stephen, was there no name on the card?'

'There was a name on the card, my lady,' he said wretchedly, 'but the fact is ... the fact is, it is a French name, my lady, and I can't pronounce it. Not if I was to die for it.'

Héloïse just managed not to laugh. She looked at her servant affectionately. 'Oh, Stephen! Where is the card of this unpronounceable gentleman?' He produced it from his waistcoat pocket. 'Well,' she exclaimed as she read it, 'I am not at all surprised. I can hardly pronounce it myself. He is in the parlour?'

'Yes, my lady.'

'I shall go and see him at once. Come, Mathilde, Sophie.' She hurried into the parlour, stripping off her gloves, and there discovered the visitor sitting by the fire talking to Madame Chouflon. 'I am so sorry I was not here to welcome you,' she said, looking at him enquiringly.

The visitor stood up and made a very French bow to her. 'Charles-Auguste de Brouilly, Duc de Veslne-d'Estienne,' he introduced himself, and bowed over the hand she offered. 'Completely at your service.'

'I am happy to see you, Monsieur le Duc,' Héloïse said in French, and he fell gratefully into that language.

'As I was in the neighbourhood, madame, I took the liberty of calling. When one is in exile, one longs for the sight of a fellow-countryman.'

'That was kind of you,' Héloïse said, gesturing him to sit down again. 'But indeed, you need not apologise for calling. We have not met before, but I knew your — well, I suppose it must have been your grandfather,' she said, calculating her visitor's age. 'I danced with him at Chenonceau, the year before the Revolution. By a strange coincidence, I was telling my ward about the occasion only this morning.'

'My great-grandfather, it must have been, madame,' he replied with a charming smile. 'My grandfather was killed at Quebec. Great-grandpapa never tired of telling the tale.'

'And as you are in England, I suppose you are in the same unhappy situation as the rest of us?' Héloïse went on.

'I'm afraid so. My family are all dead, my estates confiscated. I am fortunate to have many friends in England, as well as some relatives on my mother's side. The English are all kindness, but now that war has been declared I hope to do something positive to remedy my situation.'

The Duc was about Héloïse's own age, very handsome, tall and well-built, with chestnut hair and blue eyes, and beautiful teeth which he shewed in a most attractive smile. His manners were open and pleasant, and as they talked, he looked at Héloïse with frank admiration which she found unexpectedly pleasant, and a balm to her sad heart. She found herself hoping he would not too soon go away to join the fighting.

'You are staying nearby?' she asked when the opportunity arose.

'With Colonel Spencer, madame. The friend of a close acquaintance of mine.'

'And do you stay long?' she asked casually.

'Colonel Spencer has asked me to stay for the summer. I had not formed any definite plans, but I must say that my inclination for staying is increasing all the time. It seems a most pleasant neighbourhood.'

Héloïse found herself pleasantly flattered by what was evidently meant as a compliment to her. 'Then you must do me the honour of dining with us one day,' she managed to reply.

A sharply indrawn breath from beside her made her glance towards Mathilde, to discover that she was not the only person to have succumbed to the young duke's charm. Mathilde's face was pinker than usual, and her eyes were very bright, and she was gazing at the visitor in a way which suggested that, had Mr Antrobus entered the parlour at that moment and proposed marriage to her on his knees, she would not even have known he was there.

At the end of July, Roberta, widow of Charles sixth Earl of Chelmsford, arrived at Shawes to prepare for a large party

77

she was expecting for race-week. With her was her son Bobbie, the seventh earl, her father Colonel Taske, her son's tutor Mr Firth, and her friend Lady Aylesbury. Shawes was about half a mile from Morland Place, and the walk to it across its beautifully laid-out park was a pleasant one even for lightly-shod ladies; so a party at Shawes had always meant a good deal of coming and going between the two houses.

James was the first visitor from Morland Place to arrive to pay his respects.

'No Fanny?' Lucy asked him at once. 'I'm surprised she let you come on a visit to Shawes without her.'

'She didn't see me go,' he answered succinctly. 'I might equally well ask you where your children are, my dear sister, but unlike you I'm too polite.'

'Fustian!' Lucy retorted. 'My children are at Wolvercote of course. Nobody wants them here.'

'That's not quite true,' Roberta's gentle voice made itself heard. 'I did say that I thought it would be nice for Bobbie to have his cousins to play with.'

'If you wanted Bobbie to pay with his cousins, you should have left him at Wolvercote, as I suggested,' Lucy said firmly. 'The business of removing six children and all their attendant nurses two hundred and fifty miles is beyond anything.'

'Six children?' James queried.

Lucy made a face. 'Lady Barbara found it convenient to leave her two at Wolvercote for two months while she went to Belvoir with Horatio. The Duke of Rutland's got a large house-party there for the summer. He's raising his own troop of cavalry — the Belvoir Volunteers — and naturally he wants his old friends from the Dragoons as officers. He's made George Brummell a major, of all things! Well, of course, Rutland wants his company, or he'd never have done it, because nothing will ever get Brummell out of bed at dawn for inspection —'

'But what's Horace doing there?' James interrupted. 'He can't hope for a commission — he's already got one.'

'What a foolish question! Rutland is amazingly rich and good-natured, and keeps the most expensive table in England,' Lucy said. 'And with their children living at my expense, Horace and Lady Barbara can close up their house and save any amount of money. You should be thankful they have gone to Belvoir,' she added with a stern look at Roberta. 'Nothing else would have kept them from plaguing us here, after Roberta was so weak as to invite them.'

'I could hardly do anything else, when Lady Barbara hinted so dreadfully. And after all, Horatio is my brother-in-law,' Roberta defended herself.

'But you detest him,' Lucy said. 'You shouldn't let yourself be bound by foolish conventions. I don't.'

James grinned. 'No, you don't, do you, Luce? Well, I'm very glad to see you both, with or without children. Young Bobbie can have Fanny to play with if he wants company — and William's boy Frederick, if you don't mind his illegitimacy, Roberta.'

'And Henry?' Lucy enquired.

'No, Henry's not here. His mother's taken him to Manchester to spend the summer with his grandpapa.'

'Oh yes, they went last year, too, didn't they?' Roberta said. 'It must be pleasant for Mary Ann to be with her father.' Roberta was very fond of her own father, so this arrangement seemed perfectly natural to her.

'Well, yes,' James said, 'she does seem fond of the old boy. But, to tell the truth, I think she's more anxious to get away from William and Mrs Smith. She was less than pleased when they arrived, and when she discovered they were likely to be staying for some time, she sent off word to her papa at once.'

'Mr Hobsbawn will be interested to see his grandson, I'm sure,' Roberta said tactfully. 'Little Henry is his heir, after all.'

'And Mary Ann was anxious to keep her precious Henry from being contaminated by Frederick,' James added. 'Not that the poor child is anything but inoffensive, but she has somewhat Gothic ideas about these things.'

'We'll all be more comfortable without her,' Lucy said briskly, shocking Roberta, 'but you won't be able to entertain without a hostess.'

'We'll manage somehow,' James said dismissively. 'I don't suppose we'll be doing much entertaining if you're having a large party, Roberta. Who have you invited?'

'Well, there are Charles's sisters Amelia and Sophia and

their husbands,' Roberta replied, 'and Lord and Lady Tonbridge: they're just coming for race-week. But before that I'm expecting Maurice Ballincrea and his new wife — I haven't met her yet, but I'm told she's very agreeable — and Lord and Lady Greyshott. And Lord Ballincrea is bringing a widowed cousin of his, Lady Serena Knaresborough, and her son Robert. I don't know much about them — they're only cousins by marriage — but apparently he was made trustee over the boy, Robert, when Sir Henry Knaresborough died, and he feels responsible for them, so of course I told him to bring them.'

James smiled. 'You are so kind-hearted, Roberta. You don't like anyone to be left out in the cold, do you?'

Roberta blushed. 'It's very hard, sometimes, when people are in conflict with each other, to do what's right by everyone,' she said. 'But one must try.'

Neither Lucy nor James asked her what she meant by that. There were conflicts enough in the immediate family not to want to probe too deeply. With his wife away, James's thoughts turned more strongly than ever towards Héloïse; and Lucy wondered what she would do if, as was quite likely, Edward asked her to act as hostess at Morland Place after Chetwyn arrived.

She had hoped, with a large party, including Lord Ballincrea and his sister Lady Greyshott, who were fashionable young people with lively manners, to escape notice, and to be able to spend a few more weeks in comfort and with good company before going off to her enforced retirement. It would not at all suit her to have her relationship with her husband dragged into the light by ingenuous questions from her brother Edward. She thought it would probably be necessary very soon to confide in her hostess, and to throw herself on her mercy.

That evening Parslow, whom Lucy had sent on ahead, arrived with her curricle and horses. The following morning Edward, William, James and Fanny walked over to pay a formal visit on Roberta, and since Fanny marched Bobbie off to inspect his apartments and his toys and to boast about hers, and Edward and William were happily exchanging politenesses with Roberta, James quickly proposed that Lucy take him out in her curricle and show him her new team's paces.

'Oh, that's better,' he exclaimed when they were bowling swiftly along the track that led past Morland Place towards the moors. 'I don't know how it is, Luce, but my appetite for polite nothings grows smaller every year.'

She was too preoccupied with holding her team, whose ardour, thanks to Parslow's care, had not been at all damped by the journey north, to do more than throw him a glance, but it was enough to tell her that her brother was not happy. They had always got on well in childhood, and the similarity of their circumstances gave them a sympathy for each other, though Lucy had often been impatient with him. His way of dealing with things was not hers. She had thought when he left his wife to live with Héloïse that he had made a brave choice, and had felt nothing but impatience with him when he came back again, believing it to be an act of indecision. Older and wiser herself now, she was prepared to believe that he had been subjected to irresistible pressures.

'Do you ever see her?' she asked. He shook his head. 'Or hear news of her?' Another shake. 'Roberta writes to her, you know. I expect she could tell you how she goes on. I did wonder . . .'

'Yes?'

'I wondered, with such a big party, and with Mary Ann away, whether Roberta might not invite her to join us.'

James turned to look at her, and his eyes seemed large in his face. 'I want to see her so much; but I don't know if it would be more pleasure or more pain.'

'Well, if it were me . . .' Lucy said robustly, thinking that here was one of the ways she and her brother were different. If she had the chance of seeing Weston only for one moment, she would take it, no matter how it hurt afterwards to be parted from him.

'How are things between you and Chetwyn?' James asked by a natural process of association.

'As bad as they can be,' she answered. She glanced sideways at her brother to see if she had his attention. 'I'm with child again,' she said abruptly.

'Oh?' said James, and then, as the implications occurred to him, 'Oh!'

'Well, Chetwyn isn't the father, of course,' Lucy said impatiently, 'and he says that this time he won't acknowledge it. I tell you this in confidence, Jamie.'

'Of course. But what will you do?'

'Chetwyn says I must go somewhere where no-one knows me, and that when the baby is born, it must be sent away to foster parents.'

'Oh Lucy, I'm sorry,' James said in quick sympathy.

'Well, I must say it seems rather hard,' she said, 'but I can see why Chetwyn says it must be that way. Only I'm not looking forward to it at all, and I can't think where to go to have the baby. If it's somewhere I'm not known, it must be a very dull place indeed, and I shall have to be all alone, without friends.'

'You should stay somewhere in Yorkshire,' James said, 'then I could come and visit you from time to time, to cheer you up.'

'Oh, Jamie, would you?'

'Of course. Why don't you go to Scarborough? That's a jolly place, and the sea air would be very good for you.'

'Don't be silly! Everyone knows me in Scarborough,' Lucy said. 'Besides —'

But James's face had lit up. Envisaging the route to Scarborough, he had come across the perfect solution. 'Why didn't I think of it before? Of course, you must go and stay with Héloïse! She is the kindest creature in the world, and sensible, and as good as a sister to you; and that little village is as far from civilisation as you need. You can be quite private there. No-one need know who you are. You can live in retirement, and yet have the company of someone I know you're fond of.'

Lucy thought it over. 'Yes, I believe you're right. If she'll have me, I think it would answer very well.'

'Of course she'll have you. The wonder is that Roberta hasn't suggested it already.'

'I haven't told Roberta yet,' Lucy said. 'I'll have to, of course, and I was hoping she might have some idea of where I could go. I'll tell her tonight, and if she agrees, she can write to Héloïse for me, and I can go to her when Roberta goes back to London.'

'Is it safe to leave it so long?' James asked.

'Of course it is,' Lucy said indignantly. 'I don't need to go away as long as there's nothing to be seen; and no-one could tell from looking at me, could they?'

James eyed her doubtfully. 'Well — no, I suppose not.'

'What do you mean by that?' Lucy asked dangerously.

'Nothing,' James said hastily. 'I say, Luce, your chestnuts really are a prime team! Let me take 'em for a bit.'

Chetwyn arrived the following day, having spent a few weeks in Brighton where the Prince of Wales and Mrs Fitzherbert had been entertaining a large party. He was in time to witness a minor quarrel between the brothers, which had arisen over the question of a hostess for Morland Place. Edward wanted to have a small dinner-party, and had proposed that Mrs Smith should act as hostess.

Mrs Smith had been William's mistress for many years. He had rescued her from the cruelty of her husband, a wealthy sugar planter from Martinique, and she had lived with him on board his various commands, and borne him a son, Frederick. She was a creole, about ten years his senior, a short and swarthy woman of no beauty or distinction, but William was devoted to her. He would have married her in the beginning had he been able to, and because of that, he had never been ashamed of her or of his relationship with her.

But in the February of that year, while they were in Jamaica, news had reached them that her husband had finally succeeded in drinking himself to death on rum, and William had at once married her in the garrison chapel in Kingston. Now she was his legal wife, he couldn't see why anyone should object to her, or to her son. Edward, who had always liked her, agreed; but though James was loath to associate with his wife's ideas in any way, he felt that Mrs Smith — it was what William called her, which made it difficult for anyone to call her anything else — was not fit to be his mother's successor.

He didn't voice his objection to William — who was twice his size and weight, and had a short fuse where his wife was concerned — but privately to Edward; and it was on this argument that the Earl of Aylesbury walked in.

'Come on, Chetwyn, you loved my mother, too,' James

entreated him. 'Mrs Smith may be a decent enough soul, but as lady of the house, even temporarily —'

'She's William's wife,' Edward said stubbornly. 'She's Mrs William Morland.'

'You've been saying the same thing over and over again like a parrot,' James retorted, 'but you won't answer the point.'

'That *is* the point. She's William's wife, and that makes her good enough for anyone. Chetwyn, surely you must agree with that? He's given her the protection of his name, so it doesn't matter what she was before. She's my brother's wife, and if my brother's wife can't be hostess in my house —'

'It's Fanny's house, actually,' said James.

Chetwyn looked at him with amusement. 'If you've been reduced to that sort of retort, you must feel you've lost the argument.'

'Not at all,' he said with dignity. 'It doesn't matter to me that she was William's mistress: God knows, I am not in a position to preach morality to anyone. But she is, and always has been, a common, ignorant woman, and to put her in my mother's place is an insult to her memory.'

'Damn it, Jamie —'

'What it comes down to is this: does it matter what a person is, or only what their status is? Because if it's only status that matters, then it doesn't signify what anyone does — good or evil.'

If it was a home thrust, Chetwyn gave no sign of it. 'It's no use appealing to me. I always side with Ned,' he said, putting his arm across Edward's shoulders. 'He's my dearest friend in the world.'

'Oh well, if you're going to argue on those lines, I've nothing more to say,' James said with a shrug, and took himself off, leaving the friends alone together.

'It's good to see you,' Edward said at last, scanning Chetwyn's face carefully. 'Lucy's at Shawes, you know.'

'Yes, I know.'

'I suppose she won't come and stay here while you're here?'

'I don't think it would be a comfortable arrangement,' Chetwyn said in a voice that left no room for persuasion. He pressed Edward's shoulder. 'Come, Ned. We'll have a good time together, won't we, just you and I — just as we used to?'

Edward looked doubtful. 'I don't know. I hope so. Things do change, you know, Chet, and you can't put the clock back.'

'We can wind it up again,' Chetwyn said, and seeing no response to his little joke, he turned to face Edward and held him by the shoulders. 'Things do change, of course they do, but we have one thing to hold on to, my dear. We have each other. Don't let that change, Ned, or there'll be nothing left.'

Edward looked at him, troubled. 'I wish Mother were still alive,' he said. 'She kept things right.' But his hands came up to cover Chetwyn's, and he smiled.

Chetwyn made his formal call on Roberta, and having received him, she soon made an excuse to leave him alone with Lucy.

'You are well?' he asked.

'Yes, thank you. I feel perfectly fit. You look tired,' Lucy added cautiously, trying to gauge the present degree of his hostility.

'Too many late nights at Brighton; and the heat of the Pavilion doesn't suit me,' he said. There was a short silence. 'How long are you intending to stay here?'

'Until the end of August. I'm sure it will be all right. No-one will know, if I wear extra petticoats —'

'It's all right, Lucy, I'm not criticising you,' Chetwyn said quickly. 'I just wanted to know if you had made your plans.'

'Yes — that is, I haven't arranged anything yet, but I thought, if you were agreeable, that I would ask Héloïse if I could stay with her until the baby is born. The village where she lives is small and remote. If I went under an assumed name ...'

'It sounds an excellent idea,' Chetwyn said politely. 'Perhaps you might be able to find some sensible family in the district to take the child, too.'

Lucy looked surprised. 'But I thought you would want to arrange that part of it, so that I wouldn't know where the child was.'

He raised his eyebrows, and then smiled painfully. 'Whatever made you think that? Am I such an ogre? No, Lucy, you mistake me. I don't mean to punish you. All I want from you is discretion. The child's identity must be kept secret, that's all.'

'Oh,' said Lucy, and raised her eyes for the first time to meet her husband's. They regarded each other for a moment with a faint regeneration of warmth. He thought ruefully that she had changed very little from the tousle-haired, hoydenish child he had married.

'You do understand why it has to be this way, don't you, Lucy?' he asked her.

'Yes, I understand. I really never meant to hurt you, you know,' she added with an effort.

'I know,' he said. 'Nor I you. You were always my little sister. I wish to God that need never have changed.' She said nothing. 'You're such a strange little thing,' he went on thoughtfully. 'James and Héloïse — they did wrong, they knew it was wrong, and they regretted it. Weston knows what he does is wrong, and wishes it were otherwise. But you — you're like a wild animal that does what has to be done, without any sense of sin. It isn't that you defy the moral code, only that you don't recognise it as applying to you. You don't understand what I'm talking about, do you?' he added with a wry smile.

'No,' she said frankly.

'The wonder of it is, that you could have grown up like that, your mother's daughter.'

'Mother didn't have much to do with my growing up,' Lucy said. 'She was always too busy. Morgan Proom taught me everything I know — well, nearly everything. I read a lot of books, too.'

Now he laughed aloud. 'Oh Lucy!' She smiled politely, not knowing what the joke was. 'Now there's something I want to ask of you,' he said, controlling himself. 'The Earl of Carlisle is having a dinner and ball at Castle Howard in a fortnight's time, and he has sent me an invitation. Will you accompany me, and behave as my loving wife? Everyone of importance will be there, and if we are seen together in a friendly way, it will do a great deal to repair the damage of this last year.'

'Yes, of course I will. I don't know what Roberta will have

arranged for that date, but I'm sure she'll understand.'

'I'd be very surprised if she were not invited too,' Chetwyn said. 'Does she know, by the way, about your condition?'

'Yes. I'll need her help in asking Héloïse if she will have me to stay. But she's perfectly safe, you know. She wouldn't tell anyone.'

'Yes, I know. Well, I'm glad we've had this talk, Lucy. It makes things more comfortable between us.'

But for how long, Lucy wondered, though she didn't say so aloud. As long as Weston was at sea, perhaps. When he came back, all the old hostilities would revive. Here in Yorkshire, with Edward, Chetwyn could regard her as his little sister, but in London he would feel different about everything, although the situation would be the same. She might say she understood, but it was with her intellect only. At a deeper level, he was as unintelligible to her as most other people were.

Chapter Five

Invitations to the ball at Castle Howard arrived the following day for the whole party at Shawes, and made a welcome subject for discussion when they gathered after breakfast in the drawing-room. It was a handsome room, painted in pale grey with a great deal of gilding on the carved, acanthus frieze, and the long French windows commanded a view over the south terrace and down towards the lake, which for the moment was hidden behind drifts of fine, drenching rain. It was too wet even for the gentlemen to go out, and as Lord Greyshott, lounging morosely by the windows, had already several times remarked, Shawes had no billiard-room.

'Can't think what they were about, not to put in a billiard-room,' he complained. 'Vanbrugh built it, didn't he? Always thought Vanbrugh was a good architect! You really ought to have one put in, Lady C,' he turned towards Roberta, who was sitting nearby to get the light on her work. 'You can't think what a comfort it is.'

Roberta murmured a polite reply. Lord Ballincrea, stretching out his legs and admiring the effect of his crossed ankles, said, 'Never mind, Ceddie. They're sure to have a billiard-room at Castle Howard.'

'Tell me about the present earl,' Roberta said, taking another stitch. 'I don't think I ever met him when Charles was alive.'

'Oh, he's a very pleasant fellow,' Ballincrea said. 'He and Papa were great friends in their green days. The earl spent a lot of time at Castle Howard.'

'Gamester, and a friend of Fox's,' Greyshott explained. 'Backed Fox's bills and got himself so far up the River Tick he had to live in the country to economise.'

'So to amuse himself he was always having house-parties,' Ballincrea resumed. 'He used to write plays and get his guests to act them. Do you remember Papa describing them, Helena?'

His sister Lady Greyshott paused in her restless walking

about the room. 'Oh yes! Papa used to act as badly as he could to try to get out of them, but Carlisle didn't notice, and gave him the second lead every time!'

'He was Lord Lieutenant of Ireland, wasn't he?' said Colonel Taske.

'Yes, he had quite a career in politics. Went on a diplomatic mission during the American war,' Ballincrea said.

'That was when he got friendly with my father,' Lucy said. '*He* was a special envoy, too.'

'I know him slightly,' Colonel Taske said. 'Met him once or twice at York House. Intelligent sort of fellow. His son's in the military way — Morpeth, I mean, the eldest.'

'Carlisle and I are related, of course,' came the faint, languid tones of Lady Serena, who was reclining on a sopha in a cloud of muslin scarves and lavender-water.

From the first, Lucy had been fascinated by her, having never before met anyone who spent so much time horizontal. Born Lady Serena Sale, daughter of the Marquis of Penrith, she had been cosseted and protected all her childhood by adoring parents and an army of servants. She had never been allowed to do anything the least energetic, for fear of damaging her tender beauty, and had grown up believing herself to be as fragile as she was precious.

Shortly after succeeding to the title, her brother — who had married Nicoletta, sister of the previous Viscount Ballincrea — arranged a marriage between Lady Serena and Sir Henry Knaresborough, a kindly man twenty years her senior. She bore him one child, Robert, and found the experience so disagreeable that she was obliged to tell her husband her constitution would not allow her to repeat it. On his death some years later, she retired to the sopha for good, to enjoy all the attention her unspecified ailments secured for her, and to ward off anything in the least disagreeable with the threat of their exacerbation.

Lucy was brought up to think of illness as a nuisance, and regarded Lady Serena with astonishment. Her interest in medical matters led her on one memorable occasion to inquire of Lady Serena what her illness was. Lady Serena, her cheeks pink with the delicate bloom of health, described her symptoms with relish.

'But what does the doctor say is wrong with you? What's the name of your disease?' Lucy asked when she paused for breath.

'My dear, he has never come across a case like mine,' Lady Serena said with pride. 'He says it is a wonder I am alive. "My dear Lady Serena," he says —'

'But you look perfectly healthy to me,' Lucy said in frank bewilderment, which caused Lady Serena to fall back on her pillows with a shriek.

'Perfectly healthy? Oh, monstrous! No-one knows what I suffer!' she cried in a faint voice. 'I have puzzled every eminent doctor in the land.'

'Well, I only said ...' Lucy began, and was interrupted by another shriek. 'I think you would feel better for some fresh air and exercise,' she went on, at which point Lady Serena went off into strong hysterics. These soon brought her lady companion, her maid, her son, and Roberta hurrying to her side, and enabled her to be carried up to her room with the most gratifying ceremony.

Roberta, when she was able to quit the scented bower of pain, sought out Lucy and begged her not to upset Lady Serena again.

'But it's all humbug,' Lucy said indignantly. 'There's nothing wrong with her.'

'Perhaps not, dearest, but she gives everyone such a lot of trouble if she's crossed. Maids running about with hot-water bottles and extra pillows, and the kitchen turned upside-down to cook her special meals, and physicians sent for, and drugget laid down outside her room. Please try not to annoy her in future — for my sake.'

Lucy shrugged. 'Well, as you ask me,' she said. 'It's her son I feel sorry for. You can see how she makes him do just what she likes by threatening to die if he crosses her. If I were him, I'd do it,' she added fiercely. 'If she did die, he could go and live with the Ballincreas, which would be a great deal more fun.'

'Oh Lucy!' said Roberta.

But since that time she had kept a severe rein on her tongue, and confined herself to observing Lady Serena with the minute and horrified interest of an explorer encountering a tribe of cannibals. Lady Serena had been extremely wary of Lucy ever since, and called for her vinaigrette if she came too near the sopha.

Everyone else treated her illness with the respect it deserved, and so her languid comment on the Earl of Carlisle commanded instant attention.

'Related, ma'am?' Colonel Taske supplied the correct encouragement.

'Oh yes, on his mother's side. The Sales, of course, are related to all your great families. It's a distant connection, but blood is thicker than water.'

Ballincrea, seeing quite clearly in Lucy's eye what she was thinking, said hastily, 'The connection is enough, at any rate, ma'am, to secure an invitation to dinner as well as the ball. That is a great honour.'

'Oh, Carlisle does not forget what is due to family,' Lady Serena said complacently. 'Remember that, Robert, when we are at Castle Howard,' she added in a sharper voice, 'and try not to be so insipid.'

'Yes, Mama,' said Robert colourlessly.

Lucy did not like to see bullying, of whatever sort, and said, 'I'm sure the rain is less than it was. I think I'll go down to the stables and see how my horses are. Would anyone like to come?' And she looked at Robert Knaresborough, who blushed in confusion.

'You'll be soaked, Lucy,' Roberta said reprovingly.

'Nonsense. What are umbrellas for?'

'I'll come,' Helena said readily. 'I'm tired of sitting.'

'You haven't sat down since breakfast,' Ballincrea smiled. 'But don't let that stop you. Off you go, Nel — and you, Robert. Leave us old folk to the consolation of cards.'

Lady Serena bristled both at being classed with the old folk, and at having her son torn from her side in such a peremptory way, but while she was hesitating over which to challenge first, Ballincrea went about getting up a table of whist, and Roberta asked her what she planned to wear for the ball, and the other three took their chance and escaped.

In the drawing-room at Morland Place the company, being

91

less elegant, had less difficulty in finding something to do. Edward was discussing with James his plans for growing more corn, while Chetwyn lounged in an armchair, not reading a novel. William had managed to get hold of a copy of Sir Home Popham's *Telegraphic Signals or Marine Vocabulary*, which was beginning to be issued to the captains of ships of the line. He was thoroughly absorbed with it, and commented aloud to anyone who would listen.

'Extraordinary! I wonder no-one thought of it before. This is a vast improvement on Howe's signals, I promise you.' He looked hopefully towards Chetwyn, who was nearest him.

'Really?' was Chetwyn's polite response. Edward and James, at the table, did not raise their heads.

'Not a doubt of it,' William went on, sufficiently encouraged. 'Why, with this system, you can say anything you want. You could have a complete conversation with another captain a mile away, almost as quickly and easily as if he were standing by your side! Nothing like it has ever been done before. It's — it's *unparalleled*!'

'How fascinating,' Chetwyn said, hoping that William would not bestir himself to bring over the book to shew him.

'You see, as well as assigning a number to all the commonly-used signals and a large vocabulary of useful words,' William went on, undaunted, 'the letters of the alphabet are numbered, too, so that any other word can be spelt out. Of course, that would take a fair number of flags, but I can see how it could be well worth while, in certain situations.'

'So a message would be a series of numbers?' Chetwyn said, since some comment was wanting.

'Of course. And to understand the message, you simply refer —'

'But what happens if you want to use a number *as* a number? Seventeen ships or forty marines?'

'You precede the hoist with the numeral flag, which tells you the next group is a number, not a code,' William said triumphantly. 'Simple, isn't it? The sooner we have this book issued to the whole fleet, the better. When I think of the number of times I've had to send boats, sometimes in heavy seas, just to deliver a short message ...'

'Oh, quite,' Chetwyn said, stifling a yawn. 'I wonder if it ever means to leave off raining?'

'Bored?' James looked up with a smile. 'You could always walk across to Shawes.'

'I dislike to get wet,' said Chetwyn.

'Order the carriage, then,' James said with inexorable logic.

'It's too bad of you to let your wife go off to Manchester,' Chetwyn returned with interest. 'If she were here, we could have had a house-party of our own.'

'Never mind, you've got the Castle Howard ball to look forward to,' he replied. 'What a pity you aren't acquainted with Carlisle, William.'

'I've half a mind not to go,' Edward said. 'It's too bad of the earl to leave out William and his wife. He invited you, Jamie.'

'Ah, but I know his son. Morpeth and I served in the same regiment together, years ago.'

William was unperturbed. 'I don't particularly want to go. I'm not fond of dancing, and Carlisle's got no influence with Their Lordships. I must show this signal book to Mrs Smith,' he added, getting up. 'She'll be most interested. I suppose she's still upstairs with Fanny and Frederick.'

'I must say I admire her fortitude,' said Chetwyn. 'She manages to spend longer in Fanny's company without strangling her than ever I could.'

When William had left the room, Edward put down his pen with a cross look. 'I wish you wouldn't be so unkind about Mrs Smith.'

'Unkind? Who?' Chetwyn said, raising an eyebrow.

'Both of you. Jamie reminding William about the ball, and you talking about house-parties.'

'It's you that's unkind,' James retorted, 'trying to push the poor woman into a position in which she wouldn't be comfortable. *She* knows she can't be hostess in this house, even if you don't. She spoke to me about it only this morning when I was in the nursery, asking me who it was you wanted to invite, and wondering if it was a good idea.'

'She's never said anything like that to me,' Edward said.

'Because she knows you won't listen. You can't invite people of fashion to dinner and have her at the foot of the table, Ned, however much you like her.'

'John and Louisa Anstey wouldn't mind a bit. They're practically family.'

'Yes, but Sir Philip and Lady Goodman aren't. And do you really want to expose her to Arthur Fussell's wit?'

'He's right, you know,' Chetwyn entered the argument reluctantly. 'There are certain people who would regard it as an insult.'

Edward turned on him. 'It's all your fault,' he said hotly. 'If you'd only behave properly by Lucy, and live with her as a husband should, she would be here now and there'd be no problem.'

James winced at the turn the argument had taken. 'Now, Ned —'

'My fault, is it?' Chetwyn said, his face pale. 'Why is it that you always take her part? You never ask yourself what I've had to put up with.'

'I know she's wild,' Edward said, 'but she always was. You knew what she was like when you married her, but she would never have gone so far if you hadn't neglected her.'

James moved rapidly towards the door. 'I think I'll go and see how Fanny is,' he said. No man likes to be present during an argument between husband and wife, and arguments between Ned and Chetwyn tended to run a similar sort of course.

The Aylesburys, Ballincreas and Knaresboroughs, being the only members of the two households invited to dinner as well as the ball, travelled together, taking Chetwyn's chariot and Roberta's barouche. Roberta, both to save Robert Knaresborough from his mother and Lucy from a tête-à-tête with her husband, observed that it was too far for Robert to travel comfortably upon the barouche-box, and suggested that as he was so slender, he might fit in the chariot without trouble.

Chetwyn had no objection, and for the first part of the journey amused himself with listening to Lucy's attempts to coax conversation out of the boy. He was just eighteen, and since his father died when he was but eight years old, he had had no male influence upon his life to balance his mother's. She kept him in subjection, the more complete because it was

94

not apparent. He really believed her to be frail, and himself to be her only comfort.

He was naturally shy, and Lucy evidently terrified him, and though her attempts to draw him out were meant as a kindness, he was in an agony of blushes until Lucy tired of such a thankless task and dropped him in favour of staring out of the window. For a time there was silence, while Robert wondered how much more of the same was ahead of him at Castle Howard, and Chetwyn brooded over his quarrel with Edward.

In itself it was unimportant; it was the fact that it had happened that was so upsetting. They had not used to quarrel. In the beginning, Edward had gazed at him with adoration, and would never have thought of setting up his opinion against him. All their lives *he* had led, and Edward, unquestioningly loyal, had followed, assuming that Chetwyn, being older and more experienced in the ways of the world, was bound to be right. But now in taking Lucy's part against him, Edward had shut him out, and he was lonely, and a little afraid.

To escape his thoughts, Chetwyn turned his attention to the boy who sat rigid with apprehension beside him. 'Don't worry,' he said kindly. 'It won't be as bad as your first day at Eton,' Robert smiled nervously. 'You were at Eton, I suppose?'

'Yes, sir.'

'Colleger?'

'No, sir. I was at Dame Shepherd's.'

'No, you don't have the look of having endured four years in College. When I remember how the tugs lived in my time, it's a wonder to me any of 'em survived to tell the tale.'

'It's still pretty bad, sir.' Robert ventured, pleased with the attention.

'Not that we oppidans lived in luxury,' Chetwyn smiled. 'I remember being cold and hungry most of the time. Until I became House Captain, that is.'

He lapsed into a musing silence. It was when he was House Captain that he had first met Edward. They both lodged at Dame Weston's, where Edward was fag to an ingenious tyrant called Stevens, from whose cruelties Chetwyn had

95

rescued him. They had been happy days, then and afterwards, until family pressures had forced him to marry. And now — his thoughts circled again, like a donkey harnessed to a mill.

Robert was not offended by his silence. He was happy to have been noticed so kindly by the noble earl, and not to be obliged to speak to the terrifying countess.

They were forty at dinner at Castle Howard, and Chetwyn was placed between the Marchioness of Stafford and Lady Julia Howard, Carlisle's daughter. Further down the table, he saw Lucy engaged in conversation with Lord Morpeth, the eldest son, and from her bright eyes and her gestures he would have wagered Lombard Street to an orange she was talking about horses.

Yet further down the table, he saw young Robert silent between two older women, each talking to her other neighbour. As he looked, Robert's eyes met his, and at once the boy's cheeks coloured, and he dropped his gaze to his plate. Lady Serena, Chetwyn was glad to note, was on the opposite side of the table from him, and therefore prevented by etiquette from speaking to him, which Chetwyn thought would have finished the poor child altogether.

After dinner, in the period before the rest of the guests arrived for the ball, the ladies were escorted upstairs, and the gentlemen assembled in an anteroom. Chetwyn wandered from group to group, listening to the conversation. It was all about the war: he heard the words 'Boney' and 'invasion' on every side, together with bitter complaints about the Government's inefficiency. So great had been the rush to volunteer that it had recently been forced to forbid any further enrolment, as there was no officers or arms for the new recruits. All was confusion and mismanagement.

Noticing Robert watching him from across the room, Chetwyn walked over to join him. It was rather agreeable, he thought, to see the boy's eyes raised so admiringly to him. They were wide, shy, hazel eyes, he noticed, with a delicate pencilling of dark eyelashes.

'I was thinking, over dinner, of the last time I dined here,' said Chetwyn, almost at random. 'A long time ago it was, too. Christmas '75, if I remember rightly.'

'Yes, sir?' Robert said encouragingly.

'I wasn't much older than you are now,' Chetwyn said. 'At dinner I sat next to the most beautiful woman I have ever known: Jemima, Lady Morland. She wasn't an acknowledged beauty ... it was something in her, something more than mere looks.'

'Yes, sir,' Robert said again, longing for the eloquence to tell the earl that he understood just what he meant. But the earl looked at him kindly, and smiled as if he had heard his thoughts.

'Yes. Well, it was a happy occasion, as I remember. I'd just won a good deal of money on a horse — a colt called Persis, you may have heard of it — and, to tell you the sort of man I was then, I'd spent my winnings on a new suit of clothes.' He chuckled at the memory. 'Beautiful clothes we used to wear, too, in those days, not like these dull, plain things. Silver roses and silver lace, it had, and loops of silk ribbons, and true-lovers' knots at the waist and knee. Oh, it was a splendid suit!'

'You must have looked very fine in it, sir,' Robert said. Chetwyn looked at him enquiringly, and the boy blushed, but did not lower his eyes.

'I expect you'd laugh until you were sick if you saw me in it now, but that was how we dressed in those days. And so, you have finished with Eton, and are going — where? If we weren't at war, I suppose you'd be off on your Grand Tour?'

'I'm going up to Oxford in the autumn, sir.'

'Are you indeed! Which college?'

'Christ Church, sir.'

'Oh yes. The Morlands go to The House. I was a Balliol man myself — not that I took the degree, but that was never what one went to Oxford for.'

'That's what Lord Ballincrea says,' Robert volunteered. 'My mother didn't want me to go to Oxford, but cousin Maurice said that if I didn't go I wouldn't get to know the right people.'

'Quite right,' Chetwyn said. The ladies were beginning to come back, now, and the first of the ball-guests was arriving. 'My house is very close to Oxford, at Wolvercote. I shall be

97

there in the autumn, for the shooting. You must come and visit me.'

The boy's face lit with pleasure. 'D-do you really mean it, sir?' he stammered.

Chetwyn had spoken casually, but was obliged now to be serious about it. 'Of course. Come and stay with me, and we'll take a gun out together ... Ah, Ballincrea, good dinner, didn't you think?'

'Excellent, as usual,' Ballncrea said, joining them that moment. 'Hello, Robert. How are you enjoying your first great occasion?'

'V-very much, cousin Maurice,' Robert turned to him eagerly. 'Lord Aylesbury's just said I can go and visit him at Wolvercote for the shooting.'

'With your permission, of course, Ballincrea,' Chetwyn said with a lazy smile.

'My dear Aylesbury, I'm the child's trustee, not his father,' Ballincrea protested. 'I'm sure you can be trusted not to lead him astray. Ah, here are James and Edward. Good God, Edward's powdered! What a difference it makes!'

'Yes, it does,' said Chetwyn. 'He looks ten years younger.'

The women of their party rejoined them soon afterwards, and they stood watching the arrivals and listening to James's account of how he had persuaded Edward to powder his hair. He was interrupted every few moments by gentlemen coming up to ask a dance of Lucy.

'You're very popular, my dear,' Lady Serena remarked with a faint edge of disapproval. 'I'm sure by now you must be engaged right up until supper.'

'The men like to dance with me because I talk to them,' Lucy said. 'There must be nothing worse than having to spend half an hour in the company of a beautiful ninny-hammer with no conversation.'

Lady Serena looked as though she were glad she had never spoken so plainly in polite company, and even Chetwyn was forced to bite his lip so as not to laugh. Just then, Carlisle's major-domo announced with a loud beginning and a marked diminuendo, 'The Countess of Strathord, and His Grace the Duke of Mumble-Cough.'

Everyone looked towards the door.

'*What* name did he say?' Lucy began, and then realised that the diminutive figure beside the unknown duke was Héloïse, and that she was looking straight at James, as if there were no-one else in sight.

'I can't believe you're here,' James said for the third time. 'I can't believe I'm really dancing with you. Tell me you're not a dream.'

'Is this not real?' she asked, placing her hand in his at the demand of the dance and smiling up at him as she turned under his arm.

'Damn gloves,' he replied. 'I want to touch you, not white kid. You look so pretty, Marmoset! No, not pretty, that isn't grand enough.'

'I am not pretty at all, my James; I never have been. But I think I look well, *n'est-ce pas*? Flon has not lost her skill. She was so pleased to have something important to work on again.'

The gown was of almost transparent white gauze over a pale-pink satin slip, with a long train and triple sleeves shaped like flower-petals. She wore a tiara of diamonds, which glittered like frozen fire in her dark hair, and around her throat was the diamond collar which King Charles II had given to her great-great-grandmother Annunciata.

'You are crowned with stars,' James said. 'Dark and starry, like the Queen of the Night.'

'But she was a — *sorcière*?'

'Sorceress.'

'*Eh bien*, the same. And I am a good Catholic, my James, so do not speak nonsense, please. Oh!' she lifted her hands in an involuntary gesture of happiness. 'I am so glad to see you!'

'And who, pray, was that young man who brought you here?'

She gave him a wicked look. 'Monsieur le Duc? He is very handsome, is he not? My papa was acquainted with his family in France, but they are all dead, and he is in exile now, *le pauvre*. He stays with a family who live near me. His is much liked, and goes everywhere, and so I am invited too, which is very pleasant.'

'So I imagine. And what does the neighbourhood think about it?' James growled.

'But naturally, they all think we will marry, because we are the same age, and both French,' she said lightly. 'But we are not very well matched.'

'How so?'

'Because he is very beautiful, and I am very plain,' she laughed, tilting her face up to him. 'But he is such a nice boy, he pretends not to notice, and makes everyone think he admires me very much!'

They reached the top of the dance, and he took both her hands to whirl her down between the rows of blurred faces and glittering jewels to the bottom of the set. 'But you won't marry him, will you? Will you?'

'James, don't hold so tightly, you are hurting me. No, *mon cher*, I don't suppose I will. I am too old for him, though we are the same age. Besides, he will soon be gone to the war. But I enjoy a man's company, after so long alone.'

'Yes. I'm sorry, Marmoset,' James said, releasing her. 'I had no right to ask.' They were silent a while, moving automatically to the music but hearing only their thoughts. James was astonished that he seemed to have nothing to ask or tell her. Just to be near her while he could seemed so important, it left room for nothing else. He was glad when the dance ended, so that he could take her hand upon his arm and feel the warmth of her body close to him.

They rejoined their group to find Roberta deep in conversation with the Duc. She turned to Héloïse as they came up.

'We have had such a good notion, the Duc and I! It is that you should both come to stay at Shawes. I have a large party, as you know, and we all stay until the end of the month. Then I shall be going back to London, and I will be able to offer the Duc a seat in my carriage on the first leg of his journey. Please say you will come!'

James threw Roberta a look of burning gratitude. 'What a splendid idea! Do come, Marmoset,' he said. 'You could go straight back with Roberta from here, and send a message home to tell them where you are.'

'It is most kind,' Héloïse said, looking pleased and bewildered and doubtful. She knew James's wife was from home, but was it quite proper to take advantage of her absence in such a way?

Lucy, always straightforward, answered the unasked question. 'With such a large party, no-one will think anything of it. James does not stay at Shawes, you know. Besides, we are all cousins, and Roberta's acquaintance with you is long established. Why shouldn't she invite anyone she wants to her own house?'

Héloïse hesitated, looking from face to face. The temptation was overwhelming, to be in company again, to be with cousins and friends, to be at Shawes, to be near Morland Place. Surely no harm could come of it? There could be nothing improper, surely, in such a very numerous gathering? And if she was careful never to be alone with him, could it be wrong, just for a little while, to be near James?

The voice of her conscience spoke up boldly, but she crushed it down. I want this, she told it, and I will have it, and do my penance later. 'Thank you,' she said simply to Roberta. 'I will come.'

The days fled by quickly, each one marked with its scheme of pleasure, and the parties from Shawes and Morland Place were meeting every day. Edward and Chetwyn soon made up their quarrel, though there remained a little reserve between them which they could not quite manage to overcome, and made them glad to join with the others rather than go off on their own.

James was at Shawes every day from breakfast until the company retired to bed, and seeing that Héloïse didn't mean to be alone with him, Lucy did her best for her brother by keeping the Duc amused and preventing him from noticing their preoccupation with each other.

All too soon August was over, and the party was breaking up. Lucy and Héloïse were the first to leave, their departure hastened by a letter from Mary Ann announcing her return to Morland Place. Héloïse had agreed readily to have Lucy to stay.

'It makes it a little easier to part from you,' she said to James on the morning of their departure. 'Lucy has something of the look of you; and she will be such good company for me.'

'Let me escort you — part of the way, at least,' he added as she immediately shook her head. 'Then, may I visit you? To see how Lucy goes on, if you need an excuse.'

'No,' Héloïse said, meeting his eyes steadily. 'For us to meet here in a large company is one thing, but for you to come alone to my home is quite different. It would be very wrong.'

He gripped her hand so tightly she winced. 'I have never even seen the child.'

'It is better you should not. We have had this little time together, more than we expected, but nothing has changed, my James. We must go on as best we can.'

He sighed as if it hurt to breathe. 'No reprieve, then?' She said nothing. 'And may I not even kiss you goodbye? Hold you, just once?'

For answer she withdrew her hand from his painful grip. 'God bless you, my dearest love,' she said.

Chetwyn handed Lucy up into the carriage with grave courtesy. 'I shall stay at Wolvercote until I hear from you. You will write to me, if you need anything?'

'Yes. But I shan't need anything,' she said easily. Looking down at him, she thought suddenly how sad and lost he looked. 'I shall be all right, Chetwyn. You don't need to worry about me,' she said, and he pressed her hand briefly before releasing it.

A few days later Chetwyn took his departure from Morland Place. Maurice Ballincrea and Roberta between them had persuaded Lady Serena to allow her son to take advantage of the offer of a seat in Chetwyn's chariot to Oxford. There would be room for her, they said, to travel north in the Ballincreas' carriage, which would save her the expense of a post-chaise for Robert; and since she disliked spending money on anything other than her own comfort, she yielded with a fair grace.

Robert took his breakfast at Morland Place on the morning of departure so that they could make an early start, and between his shyness and his gratitude, he was as little able to eat as to speak.

Edward, James, and William all appeared at the breakfast table.

'We shall soon be after you,' William said to Chetwyn. 'No use waiting around here and hoping for a ship. Not that we haven't enjoyed the rest,' he nodded to Edward, 'but if I don't go and make a nuisance of myself at the Admiralty, they'll forget who I am.'

'It's going to be so dull when you've all gone,' James said feelingly. 'That's the trouble with company — they make you discontented when they go. Just you and me from now on, Ned old fellow. What shall we do?'

'Mary Ann will be home later today,' Edward pointed out. 'And the boy. You could start taking a little notice of him.'

James's expression became veiled. 'I wouldn't dream of poaching Father Aislaby's preserves.'

Edward and Chetwyn walked out into the yard together, a little ahead of the others. 'Young Knaresborough says you've invited him to Wolvercote for the shooting,' Edward said curiously.

'Oh, I said it quite casually in conversation, as one does, and he seemed so pleased I couldn't disappoint him,' Chetwyn said. 'Charming boy, isn't he? He'll be quite enchanting when he's grown out of his spots.'

Edward smiled at that. They reached the carriage and turned to look at each other. 'I've half a mind to come myself,' he said hesitantly.

'Do,' said Chetwyn steadily. 'You know you are always welcome.'

Edward seemed satisfied. 'But you know I can't get away in October. I've far too much to do, even with James's valuable help.' He held out his hand. 'Take care of yourself, Chet. I wish you didn't look so tired.'

'Goodbye, Ned. Keep an eye on Lucy for me.'

It was an apology on both sides.

Chapter Six

It was a long time since Lucy had lived in a small house, and her heart misgave when she saw the size of Plaisir. When she entered the house and discovered how many people were already living there, everything else gave way before astonishment that Héloïse should have asked her to stay, and the conviction that only the warmth of her cousin's heart could have supposed the thing possible.

'But there simply cannot be room,' she expostulated in the crowded parlour, fielding Kithra's passionate advances with strong and expert hands. 'I'm sure you have not enough bedrooms, to begin with.'

'Oh, but I have been thinking about that,' Héloïse said, her arms full of Sophie. 'It is quite easy. Sophie can have a cot in my room, and Mathilde can share with Flon, and you can have the children's room. And I'm sure your maid will not mind to share with Marie.'

Docwra nodded. The two women had already discovered enough about each other in the course of one careful look and handshake to form the basis of a mutual approval.

'*Bien sûr, madame, mais quant à Monsieur Parsleau* ...' Marie said, her English deserting her in the urgency of the moment. There were only the two attic bedrooms left, in one of which slept Nan and Alice. It had been a matter of delicacy to persuade Barnard to share the other with Stephen, and Marie doubted if the volatile cook could be asked to share with a groom as well, without endangering all of their lives.

Docwra spoke quietly to her mistress. 'Parslow had better go back to Wolvercote, my lady. There won't be anything for him to do here.'

'But I can't do without him,' Lucy said at once, more with surprise than determination. She had always taken him and Docwra everywhere with her, and the idea of not having him near to hand startled her, as if she had been told to manage without her right arm.

'You won't be riding for the next few months, my lady,' Docwra told her firmly, 'and as to driving your curricle — well, it won't do, my lady, not if you want to be incognito. If you draw attention to yourself, people are going to start wondering who you are.'

'Come, Docwra, I must have some means of getting about,' Lucy said reasonably.

'You may drive Cygnus and Vega whenever you wish,' Héloïse said, and Lucy brightened. It was she who had been largely responsible for their training.

'Oh yes, I had forgotten them. Well, I suppose I could manage without my horses for a while,' she said grudgingly, 'but I can't have Parslow as far off as Wolvercote. Suppose I needed him? It would take forever to send for him. Perhaps he could put up at the inn?'

'He'd be bored to distraction, my lady, with nothing to do,' Docwra pointed out.

'I have it!' Lucy's brow cleared. 'He can take my horses to Morland Place, and stay there. Ned will be glad of his help, and then I can send for him if I need him.'

So it was decided, and the rest of the day was spent in rearranging the house and settling in. Parslow and Stephen did the heavy moving, while Docwra and Marie looked out linen and discussed her ladyship's approaching confinement with professional interest. Héloïse took Lucy to the kitchen to see Monsieur Barnard, who greeted her with respectful rapture and promised her a dinner equal to anything she had eaten in London.

'You have no competition from my cook,' Lucy assured him. 'Good as he is, he has never approached your genius. Do you remember my wedding feast? The cake you made was so big, we all thought the trestle would collapse under it.'

Héloïse, noting the emulative gleam that arose in Barnard's eye, hastily intervened and drew Lucy away to look round the garden.

'I have been thinking,' she said as they strolled amongst the scented shrubs, 'about your incognito. I shall speak to the servants before dinner, and tell them that you are to be known as Mrs Freeman, and that if anyone should ask, you are a friend of mine from London whose husband is gone away to the war. That will make no surprise, and much sympathy.'

'Your servants are to be trusted?'

'I think so. Besides, now that the Duc has gone away, we shall have very little company, so there will not be the opportunity for them to gossip.'

'Servants always gossip. But it can't be helped.'

'What is to happen, cousin, afterwards,' Héloïse enquired delicately, 'when the baby is born?' Lucy explained about having to find a foster-home. 'We had better leave that to Stephen,' Héloïse said. 'He knows everyone, and he is wonderfully clever at arranging things. He will find exactly the right place for you.'

Lucy shrugged. 'It all seems so far off at the moment. I can't think about it.'

'The time will pass soon enough,' Héloïse said.

It was a wonderfully sunny, golden autumn, and under soft blue skies the preparations against invasion went on apace. A fifty-thousand-strong Army of Reserve had been balloted to repel the French if they should manage to land; while, to make sure they didn't, the navy patrolled the Channel with a force in which volunteers outnumbered pressed men twelve to one. All along the south coast Martello towers were built for defence, and a series of beacons was set up across the entire country so that news of a landing could be transmitted to London within minutes.

With the invasion army camped ready and waiting at Boulogne, needing only for the French navy to gain command of the Channel for a day or two to slip across, it was vital that the Channel ports were never left unguarded. Admiral Cornwallis commissioned victualling ships and water-hoys to take food and water out to the ships on the Brest blockade, so that they need never leave station. It was an unprecedented move, and emphasised, if emphasis were needed, the gravity of the situation. The hoys also carried letters to and from the fleet, so Lucy and Weston at least had news of each other.

She had little to tell him. After a week of feeling cramped by the confines of the small house, she had settled in at Plaisir

106

tolerably well. The fine weather helped, for she could be out of doors a great deal. She drove the phaeton and ponies every day, exploring the area, and taking Héloïse and the children for airings. Mathilde had greatly taken to her, and as she had relieved Farleigh of the burden of Africa, so she often gave Héloïse a morning's peace by driving Mathilde to look at Rievaulx or Helmsley Castle, or to Sutton Bank to pick bilberries.

For the rest of the time she walked in the garden, helped with the apple-picking and jam-making, played spillikins with the children, and spent what was left of the evenings sewing baby clothes and talking to Héloïse . The latter was a new and unexpected pleasure. She had never had a close female friend before; indeed, she had never had any confidant apart from Weston. She was little used to talking about her inner feelings, but as their intimacy increased, she not only welcomed Héloïse's confidences but began to offer her own in return.

One evening they talked about Lucy's mother. 'She was a truly great lady,' Héloïse said.

'Was she?' Lucy said in surprise. 'I didn't really know her. She never had time for anyone but my father and the estate.'

'She meant so much to me, more than just a mother. She was home to me, and a star to guide me, and a place where all good things met. She was holy, in a way.'

'Holy?'

Héloïse smiled. 'It is hard to explain. But she was at the centre of the house, and everything poured out from her. She was holy a little — as Our Lady is holy, not as being God, but as a channel for God to flow through. Do you understand?'

'No,' said Lucy frankly, 'but I should like to.' A few weeks ago she would not have added those words, but the thing that had most struck her about life at Plaisir was its spiritual dimension. Like other ladies of fashion, she was accustomed to go to church on Sundays, usually to the Chapel Royal, where she sat through the sermon with scant attention and departed feeling her duty done. For the rest of the week, religion rarely entered her head.

The household at Plaisir had its Sunday celebration, too, but that was only an outward expression of what was there at all times, every day. It was not that they talked about it deliberately: it was as though it were impossible to leave it out, as if it were a natural quality of everything that happened. Nor did their faith make them solemn: it ran just below the surface of things in a stream of quiet joy that so easily bubbled over into laughter. It enhanced their pleasure and comforted their sadness, and her own life, which had always appeared to her full and rich, seemed curiously monochrome in comparison with theirs. Lucy thought that if she could take a little of that away with her, she would have gained something important from her stay.

At the beginning of November a breath of the outside world reached Lucy in the form of a very welcome letter from Mr Brummell. It had been addressed to her at Shawes, and sent on.

'My dear Lady Aylesbury,' it began, 'I am informed by Lady Chelmsford that you are rusticating — and just when the Little Season is about to begin. It is too bad of you! I am just returned from Cheveley, where the Rutlands held court for the Newmarket races, and your cousin Colonel Horatio Morland was still much in evidence. Does he *never* mean to go to the war?

'London is full of news, and all of it bad. I fear our friend Captain Macnamara has been to Chalk Farm again, despite his narrow escape there in April. He met Captain Manby, favourite of the poor Princess of Wales. Fortunately there were two misfires, and honour was satisfied — if honour was what was at stake — without loss of life. Why will people go out, I wonder? Death and injury can be so inconvenient, especially with the Season just beginning.

'But where, my dear ma'am, is Monsieur Frog? We are all quite disgusted with him, and everyone except the Prince begins to say that the talk of invasion was all a hum. His Majesty, I am told, conducted an enormous review in Hyde Park while I was away, and during the demonstration volleys, a ball passed dangerously close to the Royal Wig. It was a foggy day, so there is no knowing who was responsible, but His Highness came perceptibly closer to the throne that day, and so perhaps he can be excused for wanting to believe the war is really happening.

'I think it very clever of me to be able to tell you that your brother Captain William Morland has got his ship at last — the *York*, a seventy-four. I got it from Admiral Scorton, who was in the pew behind me in the Chapel Royal with the Duke of Clarence yesterday, and who tapped me on the shoulder on purpose to tell me. He is to sail to Sweden — why I cannot say. I meant to ask, but Lady Hester, who was beside me, at that very moment pointed out a woman wearing the most *curious* toilette, which quite drove it from my head.

'I am now on the point of departing for Wolvercote, where I am summoned to slaughter birds in the company of Pierrepoint, the Bagots, the Granvilles, and any number of Russells. The terrible Mrs Fauncett positively pursued me to my box at the Opera on Thursday to tell me that she would be there with her hideous daughter. I was in a quake, until I understood that it is not me she is after, but Lord Aylesbury's new young friend, Knaresborough, who will be quite horribly rich when he comes of age, and is, as yet, as innocent as a lamb. One can only hope Lord A. will take good care of him.

'I wish you may return to civilisation before the hunting season. Hoby has made me some very pretty new boots with white tops — my own thought entirely — which I expect everyone will soon be copying, but which I fear will not stay clean beyond the first covert if there is the least dirt. I quite long for you to see them.

'Until then, adieu!

'Your devoted friend, George Brummell.'

Weston woke and lay staring into the dark for a few moments before he heard the sharp ting-ting of the ship's bell. That would be two bells in the morning watch, five o'clock, he thought drowsily. Two bells in the middle watch had sounded as he went back to bed after being roused because the wind was freshening. It was bitterly cold, and as he moved slightly he felt the clamminess of the bedclothes beyond the small area he had warmed with his body. The hot-water-bottle Bates had filled for him when he went back to bed was long cold; but there was still Jeffrey, curled against the small of his back like a lump of hot lead. The only thing more astonishing than the heat of a sleeping cat, he thought, was its weight.

He must have drifted off again, for the next thing he knew was that Bates was hanging over him saying. 'Three bells, sir, and Mr Osborne wants to shorten sail again, sir.'

'I'll come,' Weston said, feeling for himself, now he was fully awake, how the movement of the ship had changed. Jeffrey groaned and declined to move when he hauled himself out of his cot. Bates was ready with his trousers, sidling about the confined space like a crab to help him into the rest of his clothes, and tucking the ends of his scarf into his coat like a nurse.

'You'll need your gloves, sir. It's mortal cold on deck, sir.'

When Weston emerged, the blackness of night was just beginning to give way to the greyness of dawn, and the air was like knives. The rigging on the weather side of the ship was rimed with ice, and the ratlines were hung fantastically with icicles, but the deck was kept clear with silver sand. The wind had blown steadily out of the east for weeks, relieving the Brest blockade of the hazards of a lee shore, but exchanging it for the very real fear that even the unseamanlike French might manage to get out of harbour. The *Nemesis*, along with the other frigates of the inshore squadron, had clung to their station in the teeth of the wind only by unremitting labour.

But in the last thirty-six hours the wind had backed, and with every point westerly it had freshened. As he reached the quarterdeck, Weston's eye travelled round and took in the situation. The *Nemesis* was close-hauled under topsails and topgallants, heeling over at a fantastic angle so that the black sea broke in masses over her bowsprit whenever she put her head down into the trough of a wave. On the lee bow he saw flashes of white which marked the Black Stones and the Parquette, the rocks which guarded the mouth of the Brest approach, and told him he was on station. To windward were the other two frigates; out of sight beyond the horizon, the rest of the fleet kept their searoom.

Osborne, the first lieutenant, touched his hat as Weston reached him. 'Wind's freshening, sir. I'd like to shorten sail.'

'Very well, Mr Osborne. Get the t'gallants off her. And take a reef in the tops'ls.'

A westerly wind, Weston thought, would also delay the victualling ships from England, along with any letters they might bring. It was 30 December, and Lucy's child ought to have been born by now, but the last letter he had had was written at the end of November. He looked round him as the seamen poured up on deck and ran to their stations, and sniffed the wind, and felt the growing anger in it. Westerly gales were coming, and it might be six weeks, two months before he heard anything.

The blockading ships had been continuously on station for seven months now, an extraordinary feat in response to an extraordinary threat. The French were making ready their ships of war, but very slowly, for the presence of the blockade not only prevented their exit, but considerably impeded the entrance of coastal trade, and it was the coastal vessels which brought the supplies needed to make the ships seaworthy.

At Christmas there had been a new fear, that an invasion of Ireland was planned. Troop movements had been observed along the coast, and several warships had been converted into troop carriers, and with the favourable easterly winds, they had actually started coming down the Brest channel. *Nemesis* and her sister ships had cleared for action, and the crews had been as excited as children at the prospect of a battle to relieve the monotony of blockade duty. But after an exchange of long-range shots, during which the leading French ships, two convoying frigates, had sustained some damage, they had retreated again into the harbour.

With the reef taken in, *Nemesis* stopped lying over so extravagantly, and the ship-noises became more comfortable. The men poured back down from aloft, and Bates appeared at Weston's elbow.

'Breakfast, sir.'

In his cabin, Weston sat at the table while Bates served him a mess of fried, minced salt beef, and a hot drink made from burnt breadcrumbs, which resembled coffee only in its colour. To follow there was an ordinary ship's biscuit, smeared with treacle: the last of the butter ration had gone rancid two weeks ago. It was poor stuff, and Weston eyed it with disfavour.

When he had put to sea, he had assumed, as had everyone,

that he would be putting in at regular intervals to revictual, and he had expected to renew his cabin stores at those times. For weeks now, he and Jeffrey had been obliged to live upon ship's rations, unrelieved even by so much as a dab of mustard. Bates was a skilled cook, and could do wonders, considering the difficulties he laboured under in the captain's galley, but even he could not cook without ingredients.

'When the victualling ship comes out, Bates, you must be sure to get some onions from them, at least,' Weston said sadly. 'I can endure burnt-crumb coffee, but life without onions is intolerable.'

'Aye, aye, sir,' Bates agreed gloomily. The trouble was that as Weston was the most junior of the three captains of the inshore squadron, *Nemesis* was revictualled last, and anything good to eat over and above the basic ration was snapped up by his ruthless seniors.

Through the short winter day, the wind backed and freshened, while *Nemesis* and her sister ships battled their way northward on one tack, and southward on the other, beating up and down like marching sentries outside Brest. Weston remained on deck, listening to the groaning of the timbers and the shrieking of the rigging as wind and sea together tried to break the fragile little ship in half. The *Nemesis* was behaving well, but their safety was precarious. A moment's inattention, or a sudden squall, might carry away a spar, and then they would be driven helplessly down on to the hidden, treacherous rocks.

The light was fading, and the grey sea and sky began to merge into one another in a colourless, formless mass. Close-hauled on the port tack, *Nemesis* presented her port bow to the huge rollers, as fast as galloping horses, whose impetus had built up unchecked over the three thousand miles of open Atlantic between North America and France. Her frail timbers were the first resistance they met, and she lifted, rolled, and pitched as each one passed under her. Weston could feel the planking press upwards against his feet as she rose almost vertically, rolling only a little to starboard until the tremendous force of the wind on her topsails checked her, and rolling back as her head plunged into the trough.

Dusk gave way imperceptibly to darkness, and the invisible

112

wind rose shrieking to gale force. It became imperative to gain some searoom, and Weston, clinging to the taffrail, bellowed the order which brought the hands scurrying up from their below-decks frowst, and up the shrouds to the insanely wheeling yards. The little ship clawed her way out to sea, and with a safe distance between her and the rocky Brittany shore, Weston was able to give the order to heave to under a storm staysail. Yielding to the wind instead of fighting it, *Nemesis* behaved more moderately, and there was less danger of anything carrying away. But still the gale increased, and at the beginning of the middle watch, the *Lively* relayed a signal from the Admiral that the fleet was to run for shelter in Torbay.

Weston ordered the fore-topsail goosewinged, and set about the tricky business of putting the *Nemesis* before the wind. Torbay offered scant shelter, but it would mean they could drop anchor, revictual and take on water. If the sea within the bay was not too rough, there would be shore boats, too, and a chance to renew cabin stores: onions and root vegetables, oranges and store apples, dried raisins and figs, cloves and cinnamon and pepper and mustard. Fresh food, too, he thought longingly of real coffee, and eggs, and crusty bread just baked, and fresh Devonshire butter.

Above all there would be letters. At the representation of Cornwallis, a new road had been cut across the moors between Plymouth and Torbay to serve the needs of the Channel fleet, and that meant that he might receive news from Yorkshire that was only three days old.

The baby was born on 20 December with very little trouble, creeping almost apologetically into the world under the supervision of Docwra and Marie.

'A boy, my lady,' Docwra said with great satisfaction. 'No, no, don't sit up. You shall see him by and by.'

The baby gave a gasp and a whimper by way of greeting to the world, and Marie took him from Docwra and wrapped him in a cloth.

'Why doesn't it cry?' Lucy asked anxiously. 'Is it all right?'

'Perfect, milady,' Marie said, coming round the bed to

113

shew her. 'Look at his dear little hands. He is so beautiful!'

Lucy looked, and was disappointed. Foolishly she had expected this baby to be different, to be special — the child of Weston's that Weston knew about. But, she thought, it was just like all the others: small, very red, and very wrinkled, and entirely lacking the charm of, say, a newborn foal or lamb. 'It's very small,' she said, since Marie seemed to be waiting for some comment. 'I had forgotten how small they are.'

'He'll grow soon enough,' Docwra said briskly, and nodded to Marie to take the baby away and wash it, while she attended to Lucy.

Half an hour later, Héloïse requested and was granted admittance. She came to the bed and pressed Lucy's hand.

'How do you feel?'

'Well enough. Rather sleepy now.'

'Then I shan't disturb you long. The baby is beautiful. May I shew him to the children?'

'If you want.'

'I've made ready the crib which Stephen made when Sophie was born,' Héloïse said. Her soft voice was soothing, and Lucy's eyelids began to droop. 'He's so pleased the new baby will be using it. And Monsieur Barnard is making a special dish for your supper, so you must sleep now and get up an appetite. I will come again later.'

Outside she took the baby from Marie, and looked down tenderly into his sleeping face. It was a long time since her own was small enough to cradle in her arms.

'Poor litle soul,' she said aloud, 'to be sent away, like a criminal.'

Downstairs in the parlour, the new baby was exclaimed over by everyone in turn. Sophie in particular was fascinated, and begged very hard to be allowed to hold him.

'No, my darling, he's not a plaything, you know. And though he's so small, you would find him too heavy. Later, perhaps when you're older.'

'There won't be any later,' Mathilde commented tactlessly. 'Or at least, he won't be here then.'

'Mama, why does the baby have to go away?' Sophie asked plaintively.

'I've already explained it to you, Sophie, my love. He

'doesn't properly belong to cousin Lucy.'

'But who does he belong to?' Sophie persisted. She had touched the new baby's hand, and his tiny fingers had locked around one of hers in a way that made her feel quite proprietorial towards him.

'Well, no-one, really,' Héloïse said absently.

'Then why can't *we* have him?' Sophie asked excitedly. 'If no-one else wants him, he can sleep in my cradle, and I'll look after him, as soon as I'm big enough.'

'Oh darling, it isn't that easy.' The complications of the matter were too much for her to explain to her daughter, and she said instead, 'There isn't room, for one thing.'

'He's very little,' Sophie observed with justice.

Héloïse looked up, and found Flon looking at her. 'Now, Flon, don't!' she warned.

'Oh, *ma chère*! It does seem hard to have to part with him, the poor, dear little waif!'

Héloïse ran a harassed hand through her hair. 'The decision does not rest with me. His lordship might very well not agree. Lucy herself might not like it. He could never enjoy so much obscurity in a household like this, as with respectable poor people.'

'I don't think either of them would care a bit,' Flon said stoutly. 'They just want the poor little mite out of the way.'

'And what would we do when he grew out of the cradle?'

'You always intended to build on to the house, my dear. A new wing with new bedrooms would make us all very comfortable. And you don't really want to part with him, do you?'

Without realising it, Héloïse had been cradling the baby close, as though it were her own. 'It is quite ridiculous,' she said firmly, 'to go on in this way, collecting people as though they were — were *seashells*!'

'And think of poor Captain Weston,' Flon said cunningly. 'How glad he would be if *you* were to take care of his child, instead of a stranger.'

Lucy slept until evening, and woke refreshed and ravenous. A tray was prepared for her, with a number of dishes of special

115

delicacy devised for her and wept into by the tender-hearted Barnard.

As she ate, Lucy could hear the baby crying somewhere in the house. The birth had been so quick and easy, she felt quite remarkably well, and her first disappointment in seeing the baby had dissolved while she slept.

'Her ladyship to see you, my lady,' said Docwra.

'Cousin Lucy, you look very well,' Héloïse said. 'The sleep has done you so much good.'

'And you look guilty,' Lucy said shrewdly. 'What have you been up to?'

'Up to? Oh, nothing at all,' Héloïse said hastily. 'Everyone is charmed with your new baby. They are so adorable when they are very small. I remember how I could not keep from gazing and gazing at Sophie.'

'I've hardly even seen it,' Lucy said, resolutely addressing herself to a piece of white fish with shrimp sauce. 'I suppose I ought to write a note to these people Stephen has found, so that he can take it away. The poor little thing will want to be fed, soon.'

Héloïse clasped her hands together. 'Cousin Lucy, what would you say — how would you think?' — Lucy looked up — 'Would you let me keep the baby?'

Lucy stared. 'Are you serious?'

Héloïse launched into an explanation to which Lucy listened in silence, her face expressionless. At the end of it, she said, 'Are you asking me this because you think it is what I want? Is it for my sake?'

'I do not want to make your life more difficult,' Héloïse said. 'If you would be happier sending the child away, I have no more to say. But I would like to keep him, for my own sake, and for his.' Lucy gave no reaction, and she added, 'I always wanted lots of children. If I can't have my own, at least I may have other people's.'

Lucy looked away, staring out through the window at the top of the apple tree, rocked by the wind. 'I have made a promise to Chetwyn,' she said quietly, 'and the decision must lie with him. But if he has no objection, I would prefer the child to be brought up by you — of course I would.' She turned back to Héloïse, and her eyes were bright. 'It is the

116

best thing I could hope for — for any child, to be brought up by you.'

Héloïse took her hand and pressed it gratefully.

'Well, then,' Lucy said brightly, after a moment, 'it seems I have letters to write.'

'And I suppose I must ask Stephen to try to find a wetnurse, for the baby will have to be fed.'

Lucy made a start on the cheesecakes Barnard had made specially for her. 'I wouldn't put him to that trouble. I can feed the baby myself, for a few weeks. I fed Flaminia, after all, and it didn't kill me.'

Lucy delayed writing to Weston about the baby until she had heard from Chetwyn, and so when the *Nemesis* put into Torbay, on New Year's Eve, there was no news for him. The fleet remained at anchor only one day, before returning to station, but further westerly gales followed, and at the end of January the fleet was forced again to run for shelter to Torbay. This time, the long-anticipated letter was waiting for him. It was typically brisk.

'Cotwold. January 1st 1804.

'Dear Weston, I am happy to tell you I was delivered of a son on the 20th December. You will wonder it was so long ago, but I waited to know the child's fate before I wrote to you. My cousin Héloïse begged me not to send it away, but to let her bring it up herself at Plaisir, because she had taken such a fancy to it. Naturally I preferred that solution, and believed you would too, so I wrote to Chetwyn to ask his permission for the change of plan, which he sent, provided all discretion was used and the child's identity concealed.

'So it is all settled, and I know you will be happy with the result. The boy could not want a better home, and I shall have no fears in leaving him behind when I go back to London at the end of February.

'Everyone seems to be settling in for a long war. Addington is not popular here — people want the war fought more aggressively now they have got over the immediate fear of being invaded. I hope I may be mistaken in thinking the

117

blockade will not be over soon, for I want more than anything to see you again.'

That was all there was by way of tenderness, and Weston smiled ruefully at the firm handwriting which filled the page, but left him hungry. There remained only the signature at the bottom, and two crossed lines. He turned the page sideways and read the hasty post-script.

'We christened the child Thomas. He is perfectly healthy and begins to look more agreeable. I fed him myself at first, and grow quite fond of him.'

Lucy did not go back to London at the end of February. When she had written the letter to Weston, she had been feeling restless, and had named the earliest date for departure she thought Docwra would countenance. But hard weather set in in mid-January, and Lucy caught a cold which, though not severe, left her feeling languid, and content, for the time being, to remain at Plaisir, being looked after and amused and having all decisions made for her.

She was not obliged to bestir herself over the baby. With eight females in the house besides herself, there was never any likelihood that young Thomas's cries would go unheeded, and he was picked up and changed and winded and cuddled and fed by whoever managed to get to him first. Even Stephen revealed a partiality for taking him out into the garden on fine days, and Monsieur Barnard, most mysteriously, proved to have in his capacious memory a receipt for a breast-milk substitute on to which Thomas was weaned without difficulty when Lucy tired of feeding him.

So the first weeks of February, when she would normally have been hunting, found her still at Plaisir. To repay a little of Héloïse's generosity, she took over the instruction of Mathilde, who had remained her most fervent admirer. Though Héloïse had been well taught at the convent, the range of her education was much narrower than Lucy's, who was able to initiate Mathilde into the delights of a number of new studies. Mathilde learned willingly, and the effort involved was just sufficient to stop Lucy growing bored. She was content to spend the rest of the time reclining on the

118

sopha with a book, sprawling on the floor playing games with Sophie, or sitting by the fire talking to Héloïse.

'We are so different, you and I,' she said one evening, when they had been silent a while, staring into the flames. 'If I had been you, when James came to live here, I would never have let him go back. It is all I want in life — to be with Weston.'

'Even for you, that is not *all* you want,' Héloïse said. 'You do not do yourself justice.'

'And you do me too much,' Lucy said with a grimace. 'I am completely selfish.'

'No, cousin Lucy,' Héloïse smiled. 'For, tell me, why are you here, if it is not because you wish to do the right thing?'

'Well, never mind that now,' Lucy said hastily. 'But tell me, why *did* James go back to Morland Place? Why did you let him?'

Héloïse looked at her doubtfully, as though wondering how much Lucy would be able to understand. 'Because it was wrong.'

'But that isn't it,' Lucy said restlessly, 'You love James, and you were happy when you were with him, and unhappy when he left. You've told me so. I don't believe you would give that up, just because — because some priest told you to.'

'The priest did not have to tell me. I knew already.'

'But *why*? I want to understand, truly I do. Why be unhappy all your life? Surely you can't believe that's what God wants for you?'

Héloïse sighed and put down her work. 'I will try to explain,' she said, 'but it is hard, because it is a thing I know in here,' she tapped her chest, 'without words.' She thought a moment, and Lucy waited, almost holding her breath, for what she hoped would be the great illumination.

'So,' Héloïse said at last, 'I have a garden; and Stephen and I work in it, to make the flowers grow, and the trees bear fruit, and it is very beautiful. But sometimes we have to pull up the weeds, or cut back a branch, or kill a nest of ants, for the good of the garden. And how much do you think the weeds, or the branch, or the ants, will understand of our purposes? But so it is in the world, I think, which is God's garden. And though I am not able to understand why things happen as they do, I believe that He knows best. If I go

119

against His will, I shall never know what He had planned for me; but if I obey Him, it will all become clear one day.'

Lucy waited for more, and when it was plain that Héloïse had finished, her disappointment was so transparent that Héloïse laughed.

'Oh Lucy, did you think I would make everything suddenly clear for you, like a great light from the sky?'

'Of course not,' Lucy said with dignity. 'Do you take me for a simpleton?'

'Nothing that is worthwhile is understood without effort,' Héloïse said. 'When you were a child, did you not struggle with Latin and Greek?'

'That was easy, compared with this,' Lucy sighed. 'I think I had better stick to what I know. Like horses.'

'Horses are very holy, I think,' Héloïse said comfortably, taking up her sewing again. 'They do what is in them to do, which is a good way of praising God.'

Now Lucy laughed. 'You bring God into everything.'

'But how can you leave Him out?' Héloïse replied.

A milder wind blew, and the snow dissolved, and there was brown earth to be seen, and patches of green grass, and snowdrops, and fat green spikes that would be daffodils. Suddenly the air was almost tangible with smells, and the robin's solitary song was augmented by the great tit, the chaffinch and the wren. Not spring yet, they said, but soon.

The empty roads beckoned to Lucy too strongly to be resisted. She had almost a hunger for her horses and for freedom. The little house, which had been a haven for six months, was now a prison, intolerably full of women and too far from London.

'I shall miss you,' Héloïse said as Stephen carried Lucy's bags out to the waiting post-chaise. A small crowd of village children had collected, drawn by the irresistible sight of four horses, and two post-boys in drab coats and black caps. Parslow had gone ahead with the curricle and her chestnuts, to meet her at St Albans, so that she could have the pleasure of driving herself into London.

'I shall miss you, too,' Lucy said, discovering it to be true.

'I have so much to thank you for, Héloïse.'

'I will take care of Thomas for you. Be sure to write to me as often as you can.'

Lucy went along the line with a hug for everyone, even for Barnard, who had emerged — as he very rarely did — from his kitchen on purpose to say goodbye, and to hand up into the chaise a large basket of food to guard against the horrors of post-house cooking. Despite her delight at the thought of getting away, Lucy was forced to bite her lip as she parted from the last pair of loving arms, and climbed into the chaise to drive away from what had become her family over these last months. She abandoned dignity to lean out of the window and wave, and Kithra ran alongside as far as the bend in the road, and stood there waving his tail until she was out of sight.

Chapter Seven

When Lucy halted her curricle outside the house in Upper Grosvenor Street, Hicks beat Ollett to the door and flung it wide, and beamed at his mistress all the way up the steps.

'Welcome home, my lady!' he cried feelingly. 'It's such a pleasure to have you back, my lady, if you will forgive me.'

Lucy blinked. 'Thank you, Hicks. I suppose it's still very quiet?'

'A number of the great families are still in the country, my lady,' Hicks said, receiving Lucy's gloves, 'but there is a tolerable degree of company. Quite a dozen invitations have arrived since it was heard that you were coming to Town, and a number of people have left their card: Lady Tewkesbury, Mrs Fauncett —'

'Oh yes, they would! Longing to know where I've been, of course.'

'As you say, my lady. And Lady Chelmsford and Lady Barbara Morland; and Major Wiske called this morning, but hadn't a card about him. He wished me to say he is entirely at your service, and will call tomorrow if he does not hear from you sooner.'

'Very well,' said Lucy. She cocked an eye at her butler, whose expression was that of a cat accidentally shut into a dairy. 'And what else have you to tell me, Hicks?'

Hicks actually smiled. 'His lordship is here, my lady. He has been staying in his old room since Tuesday. He is out at the moment, my lady, but will be back before dinner, and means to dine here, if you have no objection.'

'None at all,' Lucy said, bemused. Chetwyn, staying here and not in his lodgings? What could his reason be? It was clear that Hicks was in ecstasy, believing his master and mistress were to be reconciled, but whether he had more to go on than Chetwyn's simple presence, she had no way of knowing. 'Pray tell Jacques we shall be two, then; and send up hot water at once. Docwra, bring my cloak-bag please.'

Lucy had washed away the dust of the journey, changed into a dress of pale yellow embroidered muslin, and was sitting in the breakfast-parlour going through the pile of invitations, cards and letters, when Chetwyn walked in.

'Lucy, welcome home,' he said cheerfully, crossing the room to kiss her cheek in greeting. 'You're looking very well,' he went on, stepping back to regard her.

'So are you,' Lucy said, with little effort to hide her surprise. The last time she had seen him, he had looked drawn and tired, and though his cordiality to her had been greater than for some time, there had still been a gravity and reserve in his manner. But now he looked much more like his old self, healthy, rested, and above all, cheerful. 'What has happened?' she asked bluntly.

'Happened? Why, what do you mean? Are you surprised that I'm looking well? It must be the effect of a long spell in the country,' he said with a smile. 'Fresh air and healthy exercise. I have been out twice a week since January, you know.'

'Hunting? You?'

'Yes, me! I have a new horse, called Ranger; bought him from Mildmay, for next to nothing. You wouldn't think much of him, I know, but he suits me perfectly. He has a sweet temper, and looks after me very well.'

Lucy regarded him doubtfully. Chetwyn had never been particularly fond of hunting, preferring always to lie about in an armchair than to exert himself, but there was no doubt that something had brought a healthy colour to his face and a light to his eyes. 'I'm very pleased for you,' she managed to say. 'I've sorely missed hunting this year. Has someone been taking my two out?'

'Oh yes, they've been exercised regularly, just as you ordered.'

'Good. I was especially worried about Minstrel, since I had Parslow with me. Anyone could ride Mimosa, but Minstrel's so strong. Who did you find who could hold him? Not your man Thorn, I hope — his hands are like sides of beef.'

'No, no, Thorn had nothing to do with either of them, I promise you. Your instructions were heeded to the letter. You'll find their mouths just as you left them.' He gestured at the cards in Lucy's lap. 'Have you made any plans for this evening?'

'Not yet. Docwra says I haven't anything fit to wear, and that I ought to stay home until she has had time to get me some new gowns.'

'Then we'll have a chance to tell all our news,' he said, sitting down opposite her and laying his hands on his knees. 'First of all, though, I'm afraid I have a rather disagreeable task to perform. I was at the club this morning. I just stepped in to read the newspapers, and I met Tonbridge, who'd been talking to Admiral Scorton.'

Lucy's hands had clenched themselves in her lap, crushing an invitation to Mrs Fairfax's rout. Her face, even her lips had paled. 'Bad news?' she managed to say.

'It's about your brother William,' Chetwyn said, wishing he might not notice her quickly drawn breath of relief at the name. 'As you know, he and his family sailed from London Dock in the *York* in December; and it seems that she did not arrive at her destination. You'll remember that there was a terrible storm which swept up from the south-west on Christmas Day?'

'Yes, it was quite a hurricane,' Lucy answered automatically.

'Some fishing boats out of Yarmouth which were caught in the storm and trying to ride it out, reported sighting the *York* at dusk on the 26th, but so far enquiries have not been able to discover any further trace of her. It's to be feared that she may have foundered.'

'But there is no report of a wreck? No evidence of a mishap?'

'Nothing. She seems simply to have disappeared, and all her crew with her. Of course, there is still hope that she may be found. It's early days yet.'

'If they were driven off course and ran aground on some remote island, it might take them many months to get back home,' Lucy said.

'Indeed. There's always hope. But I thought I had better prepare you.'

'Thank you.' Lucy considered the possibility — probability even — that William and his wife and child were dead, but found it hard to feel anything other than the sort of remote shock that would be aroused by any reported disaster. William came from the other end of the family, was fifteen years her senior, and had been almost continuously at sea since before she was born, and it was hard to feel more deeply for him than for a stranger.

Besides, anything remotely connected with naval matters was difficult for her and Chetwyn to discuss comfortably. After a brief, awkward pause, Lucy resolutely changed the subject. 'Hicks said you meant to dine here?'

'If you have no objection.' Chetwyn eyed her curiously, and suddenly smiled. 'Dear Lucy, you are longing to know why I am here, but are just too polite to ask. Five years ago you would not have hesitated. Are you growing up at last?'

'You are in a whimsical mood,' she observed with a frown. 'Well, what are you doing here? It's early for you, for London.'

'Great things are afoot. Haven't you heard? We are certain to have a new government before long. You know that the King is ill?'

'They were saying at the inns that he has gone mad, like before,' she said.

'He caught a chill while reviewing troops in the rain — he's been indefatigable in taking the salute, you know, ever since last summer — and that cause an inflammation, which brought on his old symptoms. And then what should Addington do, but call in the Willises!'

'What, those men who practically imprisoned and tortured him the last time? But I thought he said he would have nothing to do with them ever again?'

'So he did, and made the Royal Family promise they would not be allowed near him. Fortunately, Cumberland and Kent were on hand, and barred the door to them, so Addington sent them away, and called in another doctor, from the insane asylum. His methods don't seem to be much different. He soon had His Majesty in a strait-jacket, and the Prince has had just as much difficulty as ever in finding out what his father's condition really is.'

'Addington's the man for making himself unpopular, it seems,' said Lucy.

125

'And without the King's support, he has hardly a friend in the world. At any rate, there have been flockings to Carlton House, and reconciliations all around, and the Prince is planning to recall Pitt and make up a government with him and Fox and Grenville — a strong team, if it comes about, to take the war into the enemy's camp.'

'The King will never accept Fox,' Lucy said. 'I suppose the Prince is hoping for a Regency. So what are you doing here, Chetwyn?'

'Have I not just given you reason enough?'

'Yes, but I mean what are you doing *here*? Why here and not Ryder Street?'

'Because I'm hoping very soon to have some guests to stay. You won't have any objection to company, I hope? I know you enjoy playing hostess, and you do it very well.'

'Guests to stay here? Who? It's such a small house, I hope there won't be many.'

'Just one to begin with — Robert Knaresborough. Later I expect his mother will want to join him.'

Lucy stared, aghast. 'Oh no, Chetwyn, how could you? Not that dreadful woman! She'll drive me mad. You can't be so cruel as to foist her on to me.'

'Do you feel so strongly about it? Very well, I'll tell her we haven't enough room here to make her comfortable. When she wants to come to London, I'll get Roberta to invite her.'

'How callous you are! Poor Roberta.'

'Oh, she won't mind. But you've no objection, at any rate, to having Robert here?'

'Lord, no!' Lucy said, too grateful to be spared Lady Serena to object to anything. 'Let him come for as long as he likes, so long as he doesn't bring his mother.'

Chetwyn gave a small, closed smile, and stood up. 'Thank you, Lucy. Well, I had better go and dress for dinner. If you would like to go to the theatre, or the opera afterwards, I shall have no objection to escorting you in that gown. It looks very well to me.'

Lucy could only stare in astonishment as he walked with a light step towards the door. As he reached it, she found her voice.

'Chetwyn!' He turned enquiringly. 'Who was it, who took

my horses out at Wolvercote? You didn't say.'

'Didn't I? Oh, it was Robert, of course. You needn't worry; he rides beautifully, and he has such hands as even you would not object to.'

Lucy found Robert much improved: still very shy, but not overwhelmed nor awkwardly embarrassed; and when he had gained a little confidence in her company, she found him occasionally worth talking to. He evidently admired her husband enormously, and Chetwyn treated him with an amused and fatherly affection which Lucy thought quite pretty to see.

After the first few days, she was not much troubled by either of them. When Chetwyn was engaged on business, she sometimes took Robert riding with her in the Park, and was able to observe for herself that he rode quite nicely and was not heavy-handed, though she did not think his horsemanship anything out of the way. Sometimes all three of them went to the Opera or a ball or a rout, and once Chetwyn made up a party to go to Vauxhall, to eat the ham-shavings and listen to the orchestra. Robert had never been there, and Chetwyn's design seemed to be to shew him all the sights, but usually he did not bother Lucy with them.

She had her own circle and her own amusements, and Major Wiske to escort her, but it was evident that Society as a whole was looking more kindly on her that season because she and her husband were apparently reconciled. She and Chetwyn gave several dinners and evening parties, he inviting his friends and she hers, and they planned to give a ball later in the season. He was pleasantly polite to her when they met, now, and their relationship was almost what it had been when they first married. He never once, however, mentioned the baby, and following his lead, she did not bring the subject up.

April brought showery weather, the first of the spring greens, and Addington's resignation. The Prince of Wales courted Pitt, who, however, did not trust the Prince's professed friendship, and disapproved of his publicly expressed contempt for his father. May brought warm sunshine, and a partial recovery to the King, who sent for Pitt to form a Government, but refused to have anything to do with Fox. Since Grenville and his supporters had previously agreed not to serve unless Fox did, the old lines of battle were drawn, with Pitt and the King on one side, and the Prince and Fox in opposition on the other.

In the clear and sparkling days of early summer, the news came from France that Buonaparte had declared himself Emperor, and, in his usual way, had proceeded to have the *fait accompli* confirmed by plebiscite.

'Napoleon the first!' Edward snorted in contempt. He and James were waiting for Mary Ann to join them to go in to dinner. She had just returned from a three-week visit to Scarborough with little Henry.

'I suppose it was the obvious next step, after making his office hereditary,' James said.

'I can't understand why the French — particularly the ministers — would accept the hereditary principle,' Edward said. 'They were eager enough to get rid of their king.'

'Well, that's the point, isn't it? The one thing they don't want is a return of the Bourbons. They believe a new dynasty will keep the old one out. And, of course, more to the point, a new emperor will need a new aristocracy!'

Mary Ann entered at that moment, wearing a gown of dusky pink, which admirably suited her colouring, and pink roses tucked into her bodice, and in her hair.

'So that's what you were doing out in the gardens earlier on,' Edward exclaimed. 'What a pretty notion! How well you look.'

Mary Ann glanced inevitably towards James, who gave her a faint smile and said, 'Indeed, ma'am, it was worth waiting for.'

'Am I late?' she asked.

'Not the slightest,' Edward said quickly. 'We were just talking about this business of Boney's. There was a very amusing cartoon in the newspaper — did you see it? — of a frog in a crown and ermine, puffing itself up to the size of an ox.'

'Yes, it's a pity he is such a small man,' Mary Ann commented. 'We saw him when we went to Paris — do you remember, James? Quite a handsome young man, but very

128

small. Somehow one expects a king to be tall.'

'And an emperor even more so,' James said, amused. 'He should be six feet at least to wear the imperial crown.'

'I wonder he has chosen to be called emperor rather than king,' Edward said, with an annoyed glance at his brother. Why must he always tease Mary Ann, and make things uncomfortable?

'Because of his love of all things Roman, of course,' James answered. 'He sees himself as successor to the Caesars, conqueror of the world. Why, he even calls his battalions legions, and gives them Roman eagles as standards; and when he reviewed the troops at Boulogne, he dressed up in a toga and laurel crown. He really is a ridiculous little man.'

'He proved himself a very able general, at any rate,' Mary Ann said quietly. 'I should not like to think of him marching through England as he marched through Italy.'

'He'll never get as far as Dover,' Edward said, 'not while our ships patrol the Channel. Ah, here's Ottershaw. Shall we go in?' He offered his arm to his sister-in-law, and she laid a gloved hand lightly upon it. 'I must say, it is very good to have you back, ma'am. Dinner has become something to look forward to again.'

Mary Ann only smiled at him, because she could not in honesty say it was good to be back. She had enjoyed her sojourn at Scarborough, the new sights and the freedom, and the admiring glances other women with small children had cast towards Henry's golden curls and blue eyes. She had little pleasure at Morland Place, Edward's kindness nothwith-standing.

When they were seated at the table, James roused himself to say, 'Had you an agreeable time at Scarborough? Did the sea air answer?'

'It did us both a great deal of good, I'm sure,' she said calmly.

'It's a pleasant place,' he said, and met his wife's eyes for an instant, amused at the hostility she could not quite conceal. It was inevitable that she should have heard frag-ments of gossip over the years about James's former visits to Scarborough for disreputable purposes. Only her dedication to the cause of Henry's health could have persuaded her to visit a place with such associations.

It was also inevitable that she should have learned, through her maid, Dakers, of Héloïse's visit to Shawes last year. Sometimes she wished that Dakers was less devoted to her welfare, for she reported faithfully to her mistress many an uncomfortable fact that Mary Ann would sooner not know. On this ocasion, since the secret of Lucy's pregnancy had been well kept, Dakers had not understood the underlying reason for Héloïse's visit, and had assumed it was arranged for James's benefit. It made Mary Ann sad to have to think ill of Roberta; but it also made her determined that she would not be at Morland Place this summer.

'Papa so enjoyed my visit last year, that I mean to make a longer stay this year,' she said abruptly. 'If you should have no objection, I mean to take Henry to Manchester at the end of the week.' She addressed the remark impartially to the air between the two brothers.

Edward looked disconcerted. 'But you will be back for race-week, I hope?'

'No, I'm afraid not,' she said calmly. 'I mean to stay until September. August is Papa's only period of leisure, and he does so like to entertain, and to enjoy Henry's company.'

'But we shall have no hostess,' Edward said. 'Not even ...' He broke off, remembering last year. It was hard to think he would never see Mrs Smith or William again. He was the only one in the family who had really mourned William, for he had been brought up with him, and his faithful heart retained the affection he had had for the fair-haired boy he remembered; and there now seemed little hope that any good news would be learned of the *York*.

'We mustn't stand in Mary Ann's way,' James said to his brother. 'Of course, we'll miss her, but it's only right that little Henry should visit his grandpapa. And if we don't entertain, we won't need a hostess.' He looked at Mary Ann and smiled genially. 'I hope your father will forgive me for not coming with you, but there is so much to do here in the summer, I can hardly get away.'

'Papa does not expect it,' she said shortly.

'Neatly put,' James said with a grin. 'How your heart would sink if I proposed to accompany you!'

'Jamie!' Edward said, shocked.

'Come, Ned, no hypocrisy. You know it's true. Mary Ann and I understand each other pretty well.' He eyed her thoughtfully. 'Neither of us would stand in the way of the other's innocent pleasure — would we, ma'am?'

Mary Ann declined to answer.

'Now hold still, miss, do,' said Dipton as Africa wriggled with excitement, 'else I'll never get this bow tied.' He threaded a narrow length of blue ribbon through her brown curls with fingers that had become increasingly skilled in the refinements of a little girl's toilette. He had always done little sewing jobs for his master, such as darning a shirt or hemming a cuff, but over the last year on blockade duty he had steadily extended the range of his skills, and the muslin frock that Africa was wearing for her birthday party was entirely the product of his needle and scissors.

'There now, miss,' he said, giving her sash a final tweak. 'What do you think of yourself?' And he took down the captain's shaving-glass from the bulkhead and held it for her.

Africa eyed herself cautiously. She had few opportunities of exercising personal vanity, and was not sure how to go about it; but then Dipton, misunderstanding her silence, said in disappointed tones, 'Don't you like it?' and she knew what to do about that.

She flung her arms around his waist and cried, 'Yes, it's lovely. Thank you, dear Dipton!'

His thick fingers touched her curly head tenderly. 'Off you go then, miss. Your pa'll be waiting.' Miss Africa might not be a beauty like her mother, he thought, but she had something of Mrs Haworth about her, all the same.

In the great stern cabin of the *Cetus* the table was already laid for dinner, and Captain George Haworth was waiting to receive his daughter and her guests. It was natural that his thoughts should turn towards his wife, who had died six years ago in Aboukir Bay. He held in his hands the miniature of her which her brother James had executed, for the captain to take to sea with him when they were first married. It was a skilful piece of work, and the ivory miniature was a suitable medium for Mary's delicate, porcelain beauty.

She smiled up at him, tiny and far away. Their marriage had been all too short, but supremely happy, and she had left him, in departing, his two lovely daughters. Polly would be as beautiful as her mother one day, and it was right that she should learn the ways of polished society in Lucy's household, because one day she would make an excellent marriage and become a great lady of society, as her mother would have been if she had not thrown herself away on a penniless sailor.

Polly was Mary reborn — ah, but Africa was for him, for his daily comfort, pleasure, amusement, and love! She had too much of him in her to be a real beauty, but it would have taken a brave man to suggest as much to any of the six hundred souls on board the *Cetus*; for just as she had won the hearts of the crew of the *Africa*, so she reigned supreme aboard her new ship.

Today was her sixth birthday, and he cast his mind back over the past year on the Toulon blockade, and thought how much harder it would have been to bear without her. Through the stormy autumn and winter, and the calm and lovely spring and summer, they had remained at sea, patrolling the Gulf of Lions with no friendly port closer than Malta, five hundred miles away.

There were eight French battleships and several frigates under the command of Admiral Latouche-Treville inside Toulon, while the blockading force's number varied between nine and twelve. When *Cetus* had first joined them, Nelson had explained his strategy to Haworth, as was his custom, over dinner.

'Naturally, in the Channel, the fleet's business is to see that the enemy never gets out,' the Admiral said, 'but my system here is the very opposite. My numbers simply are not sufficient to do all that needs to be done in the Mediterranean. There's the *Armée d'Italie*, for instance, all ready to overrun the Two Sicilies. There's Malta to protect, and Alexandria. Now, if the French remain in harbour at Toulon, my ships have to remain here too, to guard them.'

'*Quis custodiet ipsos custodes*,' Haworth murmured.

'Precisely, Captain,' Nelson said with a quick smile. 'So my business is to tempt 'em out, so that we can destroy the whole

132

fleet, and release our ships for other duties. I keep a couple of frigates close in, while the rest of us remain out of sight over the horizon. The system had the added advantage that the enemy cannot know when we are off station renewing our supplies.'

'I understood, my lord, that we were to be supplied from Malta and Gibraltar?' Haworth said.

'Only with ration stores, Captain,' Nelson said. 'You know that we are already short of men, and there is precious little chance of replacing any we lose. It is vitally important, therefore, that we keep our men healthy — easier to keep 'em healthy, than to cure 'em when they get sick.'

'Indeed, my lord.'

'So we get fresh food whenever possible. Onions, green vegetables, fruit, beef and mutton when we can. Fresh food, I've discovered, can make all the difference to a crew's health. And we have no water-hoys in the Mediterranean. We have to refill our water casks wherever we can, usually at streams along the uninhabited coasts of Corsica and Sardinia.'

'I understand, my lord. But is there not a chance that the French may slip out while the fleet is off station, and that we might lose them, as we did in '98?'

'Ah, but we found 'em again, didn't we, Haworth?' Nelson smiled. 'Found 'em and thrashed 'em. And so we will again, if Monsieur Latouche will only put his nose out of port! No, no, the chance of destroying the enemy far outweighs the risk of losing him.'

So they had spent the past year, cruising out of sight of Toulon in the hope of tempting the French into battle. The strategy had so far met with little success. Once or twice a couple of French ships had appeared in the roads, like mice peeping out of their holes, only to scuttle back in as soon as the English bore down. Only once, six weeks back, had Latouche come forth in fighting order. A couple of French scouting frigates were threatened by five of Nelson's ships off the Hyères islands, and eight French ships had issued forth to the rescue. The English ships drew off into the open water and hove to, offering battle, but the French declined, content with rescuing their frigates, and went back into Toulon harbour.

133

The sequel to the episode caused Haworth some amusement. All around the coast of France there were spies ready to provide the English with news of events within France, and a copy of Latouche's report to his superiors soon reached Nelson's hands. In it he said that the English had turned tail and fled, and that he had pursued them until nightfall. This piece of gallantry had been rewarded with promotion to the *Légion d'Honneur*, the highest award the new Emperor could give.

Nelson had been incensed, called Latouche a poltroon and a liar. 'I'll give him *la touche!*' he said. 'If I catch him, I'll give him the Nelson touch! I've got a copy of his letter by me, and by God, if I take him, he shall *eat* it!'

The opening of the door recalled Haworth from his thoughts to the present, and he turned and smiled a welcome as Africa came in, walking rather stiffly in her unaccustomed finery, white muslin frock, blue sash, and blue satin slippers on her normally bare feet. She paused just inside the door and looked at him hesitantly for approval, and his heart gave a painful tug.

'You look beautiful, my darling,' he said, holding out his arms, and Africa's face broke into a smile, and she ran to him to be hugged. 'Now,' he said, taking her hand and going to the door, 'shall we pass the word for your guests?'

Three of the officers aboard the *Cetus* had been with Haworth at the Battle of the Nile, and they were the principal guests at the birthday dinner. They were First Lieutenant Angevin, a dour man whom Africa's mother had secretly dubbed The Anchovy, Third Lieutenant Webb, and Mr Midshipman Morpurgo, now aged fourteen, the youngest son of a noble but impoverished family who hoped he would provide for himself by making a successful career in the navy. Haworth had taken him to sea when he was eight and, apart from the period of the Peace of Amiens, the boy had been with him ever since, and had known Africa all her life.

Because it was Africa's party, the other guests were chosen from the youngest members of the ship's company, the 'young gentlemen' who had come aboard rated as captain's servants, or, as they were now officially called, Volunteers of the First Class. They were not, of course, servants, but officers in embryo, who would be rated midshipman as soon as they were old enough. They lived in the Gunroom under the paternal eye of the Gunner, and were between nine and thirteen years old.

On normal days they were Africa's playmates, but today, in their best clothes and on their best behaviour, dining in the captain's cabin, they were like stiff and formal strangers. Only after dinner, when the table had been cleared, the two lieutenants had taken their leave, and Haworth had initiated some games, did they relax a little and become more like their usual selves. After a strangely polite game of Barley Break, Hoodman Blind degenerated rather rapidly, and Mr Morpurgo had just tentatively suggested a game of French and English, when, to Haworth's relief, Angevin interrupted them.

'I beg your pardon, sir, but there's a deputation here from the crew asking to speak to you.'

Haworth stepped outside onto the quarterdeck, where four seamen stood politely bareheaded, rather pink in the cheek and infinitely embarrassed.

'What's all this?' he asked sternly.

Evidently Bullen, Captain of the Foretop, had previously been nominated their spokesman, for after a little shuffling and nudging, he spoke up, turning the end of his pigtail nervously between his fingers as he endured the grave eyes of his captain and the disapproving glare of his first officer.

'Well, sir, it's like this, sir. Me and the lads — well, all of us, sir, what was with you in the old *Africa* — being as how it's Miss's birthday, and, like, the same day as the battle of the Nile, sir, what was so glorious a victory — well, sir, we took the liberty, an' hopin' you'll forgive the same, sir, of making some presents for Miss, an' we've got together a bit of an entertainment, like, and hoped as how you might let us present it to Miss in the second dogwatch, sir, if that'd be in order, sir?'

Four pairs of eyes gazed at him with anxious humility, and Haworth was well aware that many more were watching covertly from other parts of the ship. It might have been a silly attempt to win favour, but their bearing told him it was not. They were anxious that their gifts should be acceptable, not because they wished to impress Haworth, but because they loved 'Miss'.

'Very well, Bullen. I think I can allow that. What have you in mind?'

'Thankee, sir. Thankee, sir,' said Bullen in enormous relief, while the other three grinned foolishly. 'If you'd be so good, sir, and Miss, to be at the taffrail when the second dogwatch is called, me and the other lads'll be on the weatherdeck, sir, an' — an' all will be revealed, sir.'

Haworth laughed at this evidently rehearsed last phrase, and the men shuffled away, pleased. Haworth was about to return to the birthday party when the lookout hailed from the mizzentop.

'Deck there! Sail on the starboard quarter.'

Angevin trained his glass on the horizon. 'Looks like a new ship joining the squadron, sir. She's flying the private signal, but I can't read her number.'

A few minutes later Haworth could just make her out with his naked eye, a tiny scrap of sail, pressed between the sea and the sky.

'She's coming up fast, sir,' Angevin said. 'God, what wouldn't I have for a run like that! She must be doing ten knots.'

The lookout hailed again. 'Captain, sir! I see her now. It's a frigate. I can't see her number, but she's the *Nemesis*, sir, sure as a gun. I reckernise her.'

'*Nemesis*, 36, Captain Weston, sir,' the signals officer translated, and Haworth smiled to himself with satisfaction.

'Yes, I know,' he said. She'd be bringing news from Brest, news from home, letters, too perhaps.

'She's the fastest frigate in the service,' Angevin said, not without a touch of envy. 'I wonder if she's joining us permanently?'

It would be very pleasant to have Weston with them, thought Haworth; but even if he were not to stay, there was every chance that Nelson would at least take the opportunity to have all the captains to dine with him to hear the news first-hand . The admiral knew very well the benefits of social intercourse to blockading officers.

'Flagship's signalling, sir,' said the signals officer. 'All ships — send boat.'

'See to it, if you please, Mr Angevin,' Haworth said, and returned to his cabin to bring the birthday party to a decorous close, and send the boys about their business.

The boat sent to the flagship returned with *Cetus*'s mailbag, and two letters to the captain from the admiral. The first, written by a secretary, contained the information that the *Nemesis* had arrived with despatches, and would be returning the following day to Brest; and that she had brought out fresh food from Gibraltar for the squadron, and would deliver *Cetus*'s share the following morning, and would collect any letters for England at the same time.

The second was written in Nelson's own hand. 'My dear Captain Haworth,' it said. 'Once again the anniversary of the Battle of the Nile has arrived, and all of us who took part in that glorious victory must remember it with pride, and with humble gratitude to our Maker who guided our endeavours that day. But I do not forget that you have another cause for celebration, and I therefore beg to offer my sincere felicitations to your daughter on her birthday, and enclose a small memento of the occasion which I hope will be acceptable.'

It was a medal, enamel on gold, depicting an English battle ship in full sail on a blue sea, with the letters round the rim 'Battle of the Nile August 1st 1798' on the obverse; while on the plain gold reverse were engraved the words, 'presented by Lord Nelson of Brontë and the Nile'. There was a ring at the top of the medal so that it could be hung on a chain and worn as an ornament. It was typical of Nelson's painstaking kindness, he thought, that he should remember that it was Africa's birthday, and that he should go to the trouble of writing, and sending a gift; and it was typical of him in another way, that the gift should commemorate himself as much as her.

The presentation by the crew duly took place at the beginning of the second dogwatch. Haworth had a shrewd idea as to what was behind it. Most of Africa's toys had been made for her by the crew of her first ship, and amongst them she counted as her greatest treasure a large wooden camel on wheels, which she had been used to tow about at the end of a length of cord all day, and even, unless prevented, take to bed with her at night. The crew of the *Cetus* was extremely jealous of the crew of the *Africa*, even though there were many old *Africa*s amongst them. Haworth was sure they had determined Africa should have birthday gifts that would entirely eclipse the camel in her regard.

They proved well designed for the purpose. Under a host of eager eyes, the deputation headed by Bullen presented Africa firstly with a large, soft toy lamb which some member of the crew, skilled with needle, had cut out from a piece of brown velvet and stuffed with old rags. It had embroidered blue eyes, and a long tail and ears, and was exactly suited to cuddling in bed.

The second gift was a Noah's Ark made of wood. It was about three feet long, the hull being beautifully polished, the superstructure brightly painted in red, white and blue. One glance told Haworth that it would sail perfectly; and that the builder had drawn heavily on his experience of warships for its design. It had bluff bows and a long bowsprit, a raised poop, and a considerable tumble-home to its sides, and gave the impression that it had only just escaped having gunports, too.

'The roof comes off, you see, miss,' Bullen explained and, with a glance at Haworth for permission, he knelt down on the deck and shewed her how the bright-red roof was cunningly rebated to lift off completely. Inside, to Africa's patent and flattering delight, was the entire Noah family, carved from wood and painted, and a menagerie of animals.

'Nearly everybody had a hand in it, miss, sir,' Bullen explained, unable to prevent himself from grinning with his pleasure as Africa began lifting out the animals and examining them with cries of excitement. 'All different people made the creeturs, and others did a bit of painting and so on.'

Some of the animals were carved out of wood, others of bone, whale- or shark-tooth, even shell and stone, yet others cut out of cork or pinched from clay. Africa's immediate favourites were a cedar-wood lion with a handsome curly mane and a little bone unicorn whose features had been delicately carved by some scrimshaw expert amongst the crew.

It was the sort of plaything that even a rich child on shore would be delighted to have, and was made even more valuable to Africa by having been made especially for her, by her friends.

Now Bullen asked permission to present the entertainment.

'It's by way of a concert, sir, what we'd got up, begging' your pardon, sir. If you and Miss was to seat yourselves, sir, just here —'

Canvas chairs were brought, and the other off-duty officers gathered along the taffrail, while the concert was presented down below. The sun was setting over a calm sea, and the warm, still air carried up the sounds to them along with all the other ship noises they had long grown accustomed to, the creaking of the timbers, the singing of the rigging, and the chuckle of the water under the pintles.

Music was provided by old Hudson on the fiddle, MacAfee on the tin-whistle, and Oldroyd on the fife, while O'Neill, Captain of the Fo'c'sl, joined in with his bagpipes to accompany the dancing. Hornpipes and reels were performed with the accomplished agility of ballet dancers, and Price, the brawny holder, did a sword dance, his bare, horny feet patting the deck boards between the shining blades with astonishing delicacy.

All the old favourite songs were sung. Many were melancholy and hideously continental: 'The Mother's Lament', 'Farewell to Jenny', and 'Now a Sheer Hulk lies poor Tom Bowling' were hooned by swaying groups in intricate close harmony; and the lugubrious 'Poor Billy's a-hanging' and 'Bury Me in the Briny Deep' was squeezed out of himself with evident pain by Davis, the Welsh gun-layer, in a nasal tenor. There were love songs, too, some of them made suitable for young ears only by severe editing. But Africa had heard them all, and more, many times before while sitting with her tarry nurses on the fo'c'sl on fine evenings, and Haworth knew the men would die rather than offend her innocence.

The sun sank splendidly into sea, and the soft dusk crept up over the ship. Some of the officers lit cigars, and their scent hung on the warm air. One of the concert party begged for a song from Miss Africa, and she obliged with 'I have a Garden Gay', and then 'I long to See Kitty's Blue Eyes' which had the whole of the afterguard sniffing and swallowing, and reduced the quarterdeck starboard carronade crew openly to tears.

In the silence that followed, the ship's bell struck three bells with crystal clarity. The midshipman of the watch lit the binnacle lamp, and at once everything around grew suddenly darker. The eastern sky was black velvet, and in the west one white planet shone steadily against the last streaks of transparent blue. Haworth rose from his chair, took Africa's hand, and looked down into the waist, searching for the right, the eloquent words with which to close the proceedings, which would both express his gratitude and love, and restore them to their usual steady frame of mind. There could hardly have been a man on board at that moment who was not thinking of home, or of someone left behind.

'Thank you, lads,' he said at last.

Shortly after dawn the following day, the *Nemesis* hove to within hailing distance, and boats transferred a bullock, two lambs, casks of butter, whole cheeses, and nets of vegetables to the *Cetus*. Haworth was not at all surprised that Weston took the opportunity to come aboard on the first boat, to shake his hand warmly and give him the news first-hand.

'I was hoping to have the chance to dine with you,' Haworth said, 'but I suppose the Admiral has urgent messages, and wants you on your way at once.'

'I'm afraid so,' said Weston. 'Boney's on the move again. He arrived suddenly in Boulogne two weeks ago, and held a grand review of the troops there, and inspected the embarkation craft, which all looks very much as though he's planning an attempt at invasion for this autumn. He has 120,000 men and 3000 craft, according to our spies, at Boulogne alone.'

'Happily, having them at Boulogne is not the same as having them at Dover,' Haworth said.

Weston grinned. 'True — and Boney, for all his skill as a general, simply hasn't the first idea about the sea. He can't understand about weather conditions and contrary winds, and thinks his sea-officers are cowards or traitors when they tell him such-and-such a thing can't be done. The day after arriving at Boulogne, he ordered all his ships out to sea to perform a sort of review for him. The admiral in charge refused, because the sea was rough and a gale was rising, and it seems that Boney threatened to beat him with his riding-crop unless he obeyed.'

'Good God! He offered to strike a gentleman?'

'Hard to believe, isn't it? The admiral walked out, but Boney got his way in the end. The fleet put to sea under the second in command, and the storm duly broke over them. They lost a dozen craft and two hundred men before they could get back to anchorage.'

Haworth shook his head. 'I feel sorry for the French sea-officers. Many of them are perfectly decent fellows. They deserve better.'

'True. Well, the disaster doesn't seem to have deterred him at any rate. The talk is now that he has ordered Latouche and Ganteaume to break out of Toulon and Brest and join together to command the Channel while the crossing is made, so we must all be on our guard. With any luck, they'll be fool enough to try it, and we'll have one good battle and be able to go home. I can't tell you how I long to see Lucy again. You're a lucky man to have your daughter with you.'

'Have you had any news from home? Is everyone well?'

'I must assume that they are, since I haven't been told otherwise. But you know Lucy — her letters tell one nothing,' Weston said with a rueful smile. 'Ah, it looks as though my men have finished. I'm afraid I must be off. Have you your letters ready?'

'Yes, there's a bag going down now.'

'Then I must bid you goodbye, sir,' Weston said with a return to formality. He touched his hat, and then grasped the hand that Haworth held out to him.

'A good journey, Weston. I pray God we'll meet again soon, preferably on shore.'

'And have time for dinner next time, sir,' Weston said. 'If the French come out, we could all be home for Christmas.'

By the end of the month it was learnt that Napoleon had left Boulogne as precipitately as he had arrived, and that Latouche had died suddenly on board his flagship, the *Bucentaure*, anchored in Toulon roads, on 20 August. Nelson said he must have died of a heart attack brought on by mounting so often to the outlook post to stare through the telescope at the English fleet.

Nelson, too, had been unwell, suffering from recurrent bouts of fever, and his remaining good eye had become inflamed to the point where he feared he would lose the sight of it. He wrote to Lord Melville, the First Lord, asking permission to go home. His health, he said, would not permit him to endure another winter like the last at sea, but a few months of leave on shore would set him up, and enable him to return to active service in the spring.

Their Lordships' reply would be many weeks in arriving, but it looked to Haworth and the other captains of the Toulon blockade as though there would be no decisive action that year after all, and that 1805 was likely to find them in exactly the same situation as 1804.

BOOK TWO

The Seahorse

Mourn and rejoice! Horatio's spirit
Well pleased, beholds a friend inherit
The honours paid to valour's merit
   He smiles on gallant COLLINGWOOD.
Mourn for your martyrs on the wave,
Mourn for your NELSON in the grave,
Rejoice and cheer the living brave,
   With modest, gallant COLLINGWOOD.

Anon
(Published in *The Times* of 7 November 1805)

Chapter Eight

Mary Ann's first task on arriving at Hobsbawn House was always to initiate a grand cleaning programme, to rectify the neglect of the months since she had last been there. There were such washings and beatings and scourings and polishings as gave the impression that a giant hand had stirred up the household like a stick in an ants' nest; but at the end of a week the whirlwind departed, leaving the house spotless, shining, comfortable, and smelling of beeswax and fresh flowers.

'By God, love, it's like having your mother back again,' Mr Hobsbawn remarked, between admiration and apprehension, as he picked his way through unrecognisable, dust-sheeted rooms, and consumed pic-nic meals from trays in unexpected corners. 'But it's worth it,' he would say when it was all over, and the sense of cheerfulness and order that belonged to a well-run house pervaded the rooms. 'It's as if the sun shines more often when you're here,' he added simply.

'I like to be here,' she said. 'And so does Henry.'

Mr Hobsbawn and Henry shared a deep and largely word-less affection for each other, expressed in smiles and chuckles and a predilection for each other's company. Henry liked to ride on Grampa's shoulder, to sit on his knee and examine the innards of his watch, to explore his pockets for sweetmeats, to be carried up to bed by him. For Mr Hobsbawn, the prospect of shewing off his grandson was one of the few things that would tempt him away from his mills, and he liked to ride in the park in an open carriage with Henry on his knee, and stop every few yards to exchange compliments with his neigh-bours.

He took him to the mills, too, nominally to 'let him see what would be his one day', but in reality to listen to the effusions of his managers and overseers on the boy's beauty and intelligence. No praise was too fulsome for him. He truly believed that no such remarkable child had ever lived.

It was all very pleasant to Mary Ann. She revelled in the warmth which surrounded her, and the consequence she enjoyed in the society in which she had grown up. Morning visits were very different in Manchester from those she endured in Yorkshire. Here she was sought out, admired, flattered; an invitation from her was something to be prized, and an acceptance of one by her a source of self-congratulation. She liked to see her father and Henry so fond of each other, and to see how the child was already beginning to carve a place for himself in the kingdom that would one day be his.

The longer she remained, the easier it was to forget Morland Place and James. Here, her consequence derived from being her father's daughter, and at times she was even momentarily surprised to hear herself addressed as Mrs Morland instead of Miss Hobsbawn.

One day at the end of August 1804 she accepted an invitation to drink tea with Mrs Pendlebury, the widow of the master builder who had been largely responsible for the construction of Hobsbawn House. Pendlebury and Hobsbawn had been friends since the earliest days of their enterprise, and had risen side by side to wealth and social eminence, a consequence Mrs Pendlebury still enjoyed in her widowhood. She lived with her son and three daughters in an imposing stone villa of her husband's designing.

Mary Ann accepted her invitation with some curiosity, for Mrs Pendlebury prided herself on being a leader of society, and always had the most talked-about people of the moment at her gatherings, which sometimes meant that one met some very queer folk indeed in her drawing-room. But the widow's self-consequence was so great that she had no apprehension that an acquaintance with unsuitable people might affect her own standing or reputation. She considered herself far above any possibility of taint.

'Ah, there you are, my dear,' she cried as Mary Ann was announced. 'Now, I think you know everyone here, except the two gentlemen.' Mary Ann had taken in at a glance the familiar faces, and in some cases the even more familiar hats, of the leading matrons of Manchester's society; but the two people on their feet were a grizzled man with a lined, tired face, who looked vaguely familiar to her, and a younger man, very tall and dark, with a beak of a nose and high cheekbones, which gave him a foreign look.

'Allow me to present John Ferriar, the physician, you know, at the Infirmary,' Mrs Pendlebury was saying. 'Mrs James Morland, daughter of our Mr Hobsbawn of Hobsbawn Mills.' The older man looked at her with sharp interest, but merely shook her hand without comment.

'And this is Father Thomas Rathbone of the St Anthony Mission.'

The younger man took her proferred hand. He was so tall she had to turn her face up to look at him. Her eyes met his dark, intelligent gaze, and she felt a warmth and embarrassment rushing through her. It was a long time since any man had looked at her so intently.

'I'm honoured to meet you, ma'am,' he said. 'I beg your pardon, but I think we have an acquaintance in common, by the name of Aislaby?'

'He is my chaplain at home — in Yorkshire,' Mary Ann said in surprise.

'I thought so. We were at seminary together. Might I trouble you to give him my regards when you see him?'

'There, didn't I say so?' said Mrs Pendlebury, with her usual magnificent disregard of tact. 'All you Catholics always know each other. Mr Ferriar here has been fascinating us with the details of the survey he is taking for the Board of Health, of the mill-workers' homes. He is quite chilling our blood with threats of all the plagues of Egypt.'

'Prophecy is rather more in Rathbone's line, ma'am,' said Ferriar drily. 'My task is simply to report on what I find.'

'I suppose you must often go amongst the mill-workers, Father?' Mary Ann said politely to Rathbone, as she had been seated next to him. 'I believe many of them are Irish.'

'Ferriar and I stumble across each other daily,' Rathbone replied. 'Our work overlaps to a great extent, and we have often been able to help each other — though not, I'm afraid, the unfortunate objects of our concern.'

'Father Rathbone has been telling us about the Peel Act that was passed through Parliament two years ago,' said Mrs Spicer, the attorney's wife. 'How has it affected your father, dear Mrs Morland? Do tell us.'

Mary Ann turned her mild gaze on the sharp-faced little woman, well aware that the question was designed to discompose her. Mrs Spicer had a jealous nature, and a smaller dress-allowance than Mary Ann. 'I have never heard of it, ma'am,' she said.

'It's a law for the protection of pauper apprentices,' Rathbone supplied. 'It lays down conditions and hours of work and so on. Unfortunately, making a law, and implementing it, are two very different matters.'

'I suppose your father must have had to make many changes because of it,' said Mrs Spicer.

'My father does not discuss his business with me,' Mary Ann said calmly. 'I have never seen his mills, or his apprentices.'

'Of course she hasn't, Emily,' Mrs Pendlebury interposed. 'You don't think Joseph Hobsbawn would encourage his daughter to visit that part of town, do you? Ah, here is tea at last! Mr Ferriar, do go on about the cellars. I am quite fascinated by the cellars.'

As the servants handed cups and plates, the physician said, 'I am quite serious, ma'am, when I say that the cellars present a grave problem. Many have no windows, nor any form of ventilation. Most are so damp that they are unfit for habitation. I have seen those in which there is actually a sheet of water across the floor, so that beds have to be raised up on rafts or platforms to keep them dry. Of course, it is not so bad at this time of year, but in the winter many useful, industrious families are carried off in consequence of living in such damp conditions.'

'That is a sad waste,' Mrs Pendlebury said, directing a maid by a sharp glance to offer Mrs Morland the macaroons.

'At this time of year,' Rathbone interposed, 'it is the privies and dunghills which present the gravest problem.' A sharply indrawn breath of affront from the company made him look around defiantly. 'They are left open to the air, outside the very windows of the workers' houses. The effluvia, the noxious vapours, cannot be described. And the consequence is the most virulent fevers, which pass rapidly from one person to another in those crowded tenements, and carry them off like flies.'

'The lower orders are always suffering from something,' said Mrs Ardwick plaintively. 'I'm sure I am always dosing my servants for one thing or another. They do it on purpose to annoy, the tiresome things. It's getting to be quite impossible to find decent servants in Manchester these days,' she added to a murmur of sympathetic agreement from the other ladies. 'And the price of things is more than I can understand. Why only the other day —'

'I tell you, we shall have an epidemic of fever very soon if nothing is done about these conditions,' Rathbone said desperately, as the conversation threatened to slip away from him. 'A plague of such proportions that you will all have to take notice.'

But it was no use. Mrs Pendlebury had begun a private interrogation of Mr Ferriar, which left the rest of the gathering to go on to the much more interesting subject of the iniquities of servants and the terrible rise in prices since the war began.

Mary Ann eyed the young priest with sympathy. 'They will not listen,' she murmured. 'You cannot expect them to be interested in what they have no knowledge of.'

'But if they listened, I would give them knowledge,' he said burningly. 'I expect everyone to be interested in what is vital.'

'Vital to them?' Mary Ann said. He turned to look at her. His dark, hawklike face was more full of life and feeling than anyone's she had ever seen. She compared him briefly with her cynical husband, laughing at everyone and everything, caring for nothing but his own comfort. I could admire a man like this, she thought.

'Vital to everyone,' he said.

'Tell me,' she said. 'Tell me what it is I must know.'

He looked at her for a long time, as if gauging her mettle, and she returned his look steadily, hardly knowing why she wanted him to trust her, knowing only that she wanted him to understand that she was not like the others.

'You said that you knew nothing of the mill-workers and the conditions they live in — no more than them.' He gestured towards the other women in the room, but his eyes never left her face. 'How can you be interested?'

149

'I'm different,' she said. And so began the strangest conversation of her life.

On 2 December 1804, Napoleon's coronation took place in the cathedral of Notre Dame in Paris. It was reported to be a ceremony of the utmost pomp and splendour. Although Pope Pius VII was present, his role was restricted to that of on-looker, since the new Emperor, magnificent in ermine and velvet, chose to crown himself with the crown of Charlemagne, to signify that no-one else was high enough to do it.

On 12 December, Spain delcared war on England, in consequence of a naval action in the Atlantic, when a small squadron under the command of Captain Gordon Moore, the general's brother, captured a Spanish treasure flotilla bound for Cadiz, and confiscated a vast quantity of silver coin. Though Spain had been officially neutral until that time, it was perfectly well known that she was supplying Napoleon with money, and the huge consignment of treasure would have been so valuable to the Emperor that it was decided Spain would be less dangerous as an open enemy to England than as a secret ally to France.

Pitt meanwhile, though on the brink of a treaty with Russia and Sweden, and with the hope of stiffening Austrian resistance, was finding his fellow countrymen harder to handle. With a strong opposition of Foxites and the Grenville 'cousinhood', he was forced to a confusing reconciliation with Addington, and throughout December, the clubs were filled with shrill dispute and the clamour of pension- and place-seekers.

Chetwyn was saved the unpleasantness of being driven out of his own club by quarrelling factions, for he was down at Wolvercote. He had spent most of the year there, ever since it had become clear in May that the King was recovering and there would be no regency, and in December he wrote to Lucy asking particularly that she spend Christmas at Wolvercote, where he intended to assemble a large party.

'I can't imagine what he has found to do down there,' Lucy remarked to Wiske and Brummell as they rode in the Park. 'He was always such a Town bird. And why isn't he going to

150

Morland Place? He always spends Christmas at Morland Place. Edward will be most put out.'

'Perhaps he has invited your brother to Wolvercote, too,' Wiske said.

'Why not? After all, he seems to have asked everyone else,' Brummell said. 'My invitation was most pressing. He absolutely *swears* that I shan't feel cold for an instant, but I can't think how. My memories of Wolvercote,' he added with a bow to Lucy, 'are that it is just like every other family seat — too large, too dark, and too draughty.'

'Oh, you needn't look apologetic,' Lucy said cheerfully. 'I freely admit it. Wolvercote is the most dreadful old pile. I did something to modernise the kitchens and offices when I was staying there a few years ago — after all, if the servants haven't proper facilities, they can't make one comfortable — but I never bothered much with the apartments.'

'It would hardly have been worth your while,' Brummell said. 'I dare say you weren't indoors often enough to notice.'

'But you are coming, aren't you?' Lucy asked. 'Both of you? Because Lady Barbara called this morning to say she's been invited, too, and I must have someone to leaven the lump.'

Wolvercote, like many a nobleman's seat, was a heterogeny of styles, as Aylesbury after Aylesbury, all down the ages, had added this and adapted that with a magnificent disregard for architectural harmony. The result was that it was a shapeless edifice of rambling corridors and icy draughts. Some of the rooms were inconveniently large, some gloomy and dark, others low-ceilinged and cramped, and the decorations were shabby from long neglect.

Lucy arrived a few days before Christmas to be received by Charlcott, the new butler.

'Welcome to Wolvercote, my lady,' he intoned. He was a thin man with a pinched face and an air of impenetrable gloom. Lucy wished she could have brought Hicks down, as she had used to in the old days, but since Chetwyn had been spending so much time at Wolvercote, he obviously needed a butler to be there permanently.

'His lordship and Mr Knaresborough are in the Octagon Room,' Charlcott offered, receiving Lucy's gloves and driving coat with the air of one accustomed to better things.

Lucy wrinkled her nose. 'What on earth are they doing there?' The Octagon Room was a large, cold chamber on the ground floor at the junction of the west and south wings, which had never been used in Lucy's memory, except for passing through on the way to somewhere else.

'Waiting for you, my lady,' Charlcott said patiently.

'Yes, but why there?' Lucy insisted.

Charlcott's gloom deepened. 'I could not undertake to say, my lady.'

Lucy snorted with impatience, and hurried across the echoing staircase hall and through the door at the end, to find herself in a room transformed.

'Lucy! I thought I heard a carriage,' Chetwyn said, getting up from his chair by the fire and coming to meet her. 'Come and get warm.'

Lucy spared a nod for Robert, who had risen from the sopha on the opposite side of the fire, but otherwise was occupied in revolving on the spot to look around her. The room had been redecorated in the Chinese style, the ceiling made lower by a canopy of silk drawn up, tent-like, to a central point, the cold stone floor carpeted with thick Chinese rugs. A fireplace had been put in one of the walls, and a huge fire roared there, while Chinese lacquer screens cleverly placed ensured there were no draughts. The room, she discovered, was actually warm, quite apart from being bright and welcoming.

'I'm astonished,' she said at last, turning to the two men. 'I thought for a moment I had stepped into the Pavilion at Brighton.'

'Do you like it?' Chetwyn asked, with a pleased glance at Robert, who met it with a shy smile. 'One can't receive guests in that damned draughty old hall, and there ought to be somewhere nearer than the drawing-room. All this was Robert's idea,' he added with a wave of the hand at the lacquer cabinets, the side-tables supported by goggle-eyed dragons, the silk hangings and intricately-patterned wallpaper. 'He just looked at the room, and imagined the whole thing.'

Lucy eyed the blushing youth as though she couldn't

believe that exterior concealed an imagination so unfettered. 'It's certainly much cosier,' she said with monumental tact.

'And this is just the beginning. Wait until you see what we've done to the rest of the house,' said Chetwyn, handing his wife to a chair and pouring her a glass of wine. 'I've left the east wing alone: it really ought to be pulled down — there's nothing you can do with those old Tudor rooms. But we've made vast improvements to the west and south wings. New fireplaces, new windows; some rooms made smaller; everything redecorated; lots of new furnishings. And the ball-room's been completely refurbished, and the floor mended. We shall have some proper entertaining, for the first time in years. Do you know, there hasn't been a ball at Wolvercote since before my mother died?'

'So this is why you promised George Brummell he'd be comfortable,' Lucy managed to say. 'You have been busy. I wonder Robert has found time to do his studies.'

Robert blushed more deeply. 'Well,' he said, 'to be honest, I ... I haven't been in Oxford very much this term.'

Lucy raised an eyebrow. 'I wish you may not be sent down,' she said. 'Your mother wouldn't be pleased.'

'Oh, Mama wouldn't care about it,' he said, faintly defiant. 'She didn't want me to go in the first place, and I'm sure I learn much more here than ever I did at the House.'

He cast an appealing look at Chetwyn, who grinned and said. 'No need to attack poor Rob, Lucy. He's been working his way through my library — I've seen to that — and besides, he's meeting more people through me than he would at Oxford, and that's all his mother will care for.'

'Oh, it's nothing to me what you do,' Lucy said easily, standing up. 'I think I'll go to my room now, and change.' She hesitated. 'I suppose I have got a room? You haven't demolished it to make a boxing booth, or something?'

Chetwyn grinned. 'No, you have your old apartments, as before, but we've altered them quite a lot. We'd better come with you and shew you, or you might not recognise them.'

'You alarm me,' said Lucy, preceding them from the room. The family's apartments were all in the west wing.

'I've put in a false wall in your bedroom and made you a proper closet beyond,' Chetwyn told her as they walked up the stairs, 'and by knocking the old closet and the linen-room together into one, I've given you a decent-sized dressing-room on the other side. It gives the bedroom much better proportions, too, and the new window makes it lighter.'

It was also completely redecorated and refurnished in shades of blue and brown, and the effect was light, comfortable, and pleasing. She looked around her, more puzzled as to why Chetwyn had done it, than pleased at the result. He had never cared any more about his surroundings than she had.

'Do you like it?' he asked.

'Yes,' she said with an effort. 'Very much.'

'I thought you would. Now come and see your sitting-room.'

It, too, was transformed. It had always been a handsome room, dating from the best period of the previous century, but its beauty had been obscured by heavy colours and ugly furniture, and it had never been warm enough in the winter. Now Chetwyn had installed a second fireplace at the opposite end to match the first, and an enormous new chandelier, which he promised would make the room 'as bright as day'.

The terracotta walls had been repainted in pale grey, the ceiling in pale pink, and the elaborate plasterwork of the frieze and cornice picked out in gold. The curtains were of velvet, and their old-rose colour matched the upholstery of the new, modern furniture. A rose-and-white Chinese rug covered most of the floor, and various pieces of pink-and-white Sèvres porcelain — bowls and vases and urns — decorated the side-tables and chimney-pieces.

'What do you think of it? The porcelain used to be in my mother's sitting-room, and the clock. I hope you like the colours.'

Lucy had never had any particular views about colours, but she could see that the grey and pink combination was subtle and elegant, and the whole room looked far more like the setting for a countess than the shabby, damp, dark room she had used to use, when bad weather or advanced pregnancy forced her to be indoors.

'It's very pretty,' she said.

'Robert chose it,' Chetwyn said, placing a proud hand on the young man's shoulder. 'It is all his taste. I rather doubted you would care for anything so ... so feminine, but he said it was what the room demanded. I let him have a free hand, once I'd seen what he did with the Octagon Room. He has a real talent for these things: I had nothing to do but sign the bills. We've had such fun all this year, planning and choosing. I never realised before what a pleasure it could be.'

'I suppose it was never worth doing before,' Lucy suggested tentatively, 'since you've lived mostly in London.'

'True,' Chetwyn said. 'But that's all changed now. I mean to spend much more time here in the future. The estate needs personal attention if it is to run properly, and I owe it to Roland to keep everything in order. It wouldn't do to leave him a run-down house and estate to inherit.'

'Oh, quite,' Lucy said, and regarded him thoughtfully. He never normally mentioned Roland to her unless she enquired directly of him, and he had certainly never spoken of the child with so much warmth. Evidently more things had altered at Wolvercote than the decorations of the house. Chetwyn had changed drastically in the last sixteen months, and though the changes seemed all to the good, Lucy would have liked to understand what had caused them.

'Well, I'm sure you must want to wash and change,' Chetwyn went on. 'We'll leave you alone now, and meet again at dinner.'

Docwra was waiting for her in the bedchamber. 'Well, my lady,' she enthused, 'this is much more like it, I must say. You'd never know it was the same room! And so warm, and not a bit damp, the way you could walk about in one o' them scraps o' muslin and never catch a cold! There's hot water waiting for you, my lady, through in the next room there.'

Lucy allowed herself to be undressed, and went through into the closet where there was a handsome porcelain bath filled with hot water, and towels hanging to warm before the fire. Docwra had grown accustomed at last to the Morland habit of frequent bathing, and she no longer kept up a monologue, while washing her mistress, on the perils of getting wet all over.

Instead she said, 'What a wonderful thing it is, my lady, the change that's come over his lordship. I'd swear he's even lookin' younger! A blessed thing it is, to see a gentleman

155

taking proper care of his house and his lands. And Parslow says that Mr Thorn says there's to be a grand ball on St Stephen's day, my lady, for the whole county. Ah, sure, God, what a grand sight that'll be, you and his lordship, side by side, receivin' together at the top of the stairs!'

Lucy grunted. 'I just don't understand why he's done it all.'

'For you, my lady, to be sure,' Docwra said.

'Very romantic,' said Lucy. 'You've been reading novels again. That will do, Docwra. I want to get out now.'

When Lucy was dressed, as there was still plenty of time before dinner, she thought she had better go and see Miss Trotton, and warn her, in case no-one else had thought to do so, that Bobbie Chelmsford and Lady Barbara's children would be arriving the following day.

The nurseries occupied the whole top floor of the west wing, consisting of a large day-nursery, two smaller night-nurseries, and a number of rooms for governesses, tutors and servants, so that, apart from the provision of food, the childrens' quarters were self-contained. Miss Trotton reigned there supreme, with a large staff under her, and her own private sitting-room as well as a bedroom.

Lucy found them all in the day-nursery. It was a long room, shabby but comfortable, with windows looking west over the gardens, giving it all the afternoon light, and a good fire at either end. Here the children played, did their lessons, and ate their meals.

When she entered they were divided into two groups around the two fireplaces. By the nearer fire were Polly Haworth and Lucy's elder daughter Flaminia, usually called Minnie, who, judging by the pair of globes to hand, were taking a geography lesson of Miss Trotton. Lucy's glance noted that Polly, who was ten now, seemed to have grown still more beautiful since she had last seen her, while Minnie, very like her father with her reddish curls and green eyes, had grown chubbier.

At the far end of the room was her younger daughter, Rosamund, tall for her seven years, plain, freckled and sandy-haired; and her son Roland, aged five and just out of petti-coats, looking so like Lucy herself that it gave her an odd feeling, as if the reflection in a mirror had taken on a life of its own. They were listening to a story; what was odd was that it was being read to them by Robert Knaresborough. Roland was sitting on his lap, and Rosamund on the floor, leaning on his knees, and there was about them such an air of ease and accustomedness that Lucy knew without asking that it was a scene which that room had often witnessed.

Miss Trotton and the elder girls had risen, and as Robert looked up from the book, Lucy waved a hand at him not to disturb himself.

'I heard you had arrived, your ladyship,' Miss Trotton said. 'Girls!'

'Aunt Lucy,' Polly said, curtseying gracefully, and Minnie, looking to her cousin for a lead, bobbed, and moved her lips in a soundless greeting. Minnie was not clever, and was rather shy, but since babyhood she had adored Hippolyta, obeyed and copied her in everything, and as Hippolyta was both clever and sensible, Minnie got by very well.

'I came to tell you, Trotton, that you are to expect some additions to your charges tomorrow.'

'Yes, your ladyship, it was mentioned Lord Cholmsford is coming, and Master and Miss Morland, I believe.'

'Quite right. Colonel Morland's regiment is gone abroad at last, and Lady Barbara naturally doesn't want to spend Christmas alone.'

Her cynical eye suggested that the real reason was that Lady Barbara didn't want to spend Christmas at her own expense.

'Naturally, your ladyship,' said Miss Trotton with complete understanding.

'And how is everything? Are the children well? Do they behave themselves?'

'Yes, your ladyship. We have had a very healthy year, after all the colds at Easter, and everyone is coming along very well at their lessons. We have learned some new pieces to perform for you, if you should have the time to indulge us.'

'Yes, later perhaps,' Lucy said vaguely, her eyes going irresistibly to the group at the far end. 'Trotton, isn't it time Roland had a tutor, now that he's been breeched?'

'I have mentioned it to his lordship, but he has not yet told me what he has decided. Of course, Mr Knaresborough has spent a lot of time with Lord Calder recently. He has been teaching him to ride, too.'

Trotton met Lucy's eyes, and a number of questions and answers flitted rapidly between them.

'That is kind of him,' Lucy said. 'But not satisfactory. Lord Calder must have a proper tutor. I'll speak to his lordship.'

'Yes, your ladyship,' Miss Trotton said. Lucy nodded to her to continue with her lesson, and walked down the room to the other group.

The warmth of the fire and the soothing process of being read to had evidently lulled Roland almost to the point of sleep. His eyelids were drooping, he was sucking his thumb, and his head was lolling against Robert's shoulder in the most comfortable and accustomed manner. Rosamund, her face rosy from the heat of the fire, was kneeling facing him, with her arms on his knees and the point of her chin resting on her arms, evidently deeply absorbed in the story. She looked up crossly when Robert stopped reading.

'What is it you're reading?' Lucy asked. 'It seems to be having a very different effect on your two listeners.'

Robert looked faintly alarmed. 'It's from a book of history stories, ma'am. Quite educational, you know.'

'It's about King Charles the Martyr,' Rosamund supplied, glaring up at her, 'and we were just getting to the execution.'

Lucy ignored this. 'It's very kind of you to take an interest in the children, Robert. I had no idea how much at home you were here.'

'Oh — well ...' He evidently didn't know if he were being thanked or criticised. 'It's a great pleasure to me, ma'am. I never had any brothers or sisters, or really anyone to play with, when I was young. I usually come up here at this time of day, and read to them, or play a game. I hope — I hope you don't disapprove?'

Lucy wasn't quite sure what she did feel about it. Surprise, yes; amusement; a slight touch of jealousy, perhaps, that her children evidently liked him so much? She felt she didn't want Robert Knaresborough teaching her son to ride, but on the other hand the idea of living here at Wolvercote in order to do it herself bored her. There could be no harm in it, surely, she argued with herself. He was a well-behaved boy, with pleasant manners, and she had guessed enough about his oppressed upbringing to feel sorry for him. If he had found a more congenial home here at Wolvercote, why should she deprive him of it?

'No, I don't disapprove,' she said. 'Please go on with your story. I just came up to speak to Trotton. I don't wish to disturb you.'

She turned away and left them, and before she had reached the other end of the room Robert had resumed his reading, and they had all, she was sure, entirely forgotten her.

The man who replaced Admiral Latouche at Toulon was Pierre Villeneuve, a young officer who had joined the navy during the American war and had been the only French captain to get his ship away unscathed from the Battle of the Nile. His appointment was a factor in the decision of Admiral Nelson not to go home on leave, despite the arrival in December of Their Lordships' permission.

On 19 January 1805 the Toulon squadron was off station, anchored under the lee of Maddalena Island, which lay between Sardinia and Corsica, renewing their water supply at her streams. The wind had been freshening all day, and the sky to the northwest was darkening with an approaching storm, and no-one was in a hurry to leave the shelter of a comparatively safe anchorage. Six bells in the afternoon watch had just struck, when two frigates appeared on the horizon, running down to them fast before the wind.

Lookouts on every ship identified them almost simultaneously as their own *Active* and *Seahorse*, which had been left behind to keep watch on Toulon, and as soon as the signal flags could be distinguished against the background of black clouds, the reason for their presence was understood. The message flying from *Active*'s masthead was: 'Enemy fleet has put to sea'.

By the time the commanders of the frigates were on board the *Victory*, the rest of the squadron's captains had been summoned, so that all could hear the news and receive their orders together. The *Active*'s captain reported that Villeneuve's fleet, eleven of the line and seven frigates, had left Toulon two days ago on the evening tide, heading south. The frigates had remained with them until that morning, and then had left them to make their report to the Admiral.

After the long, wearisome blockade, the news that the French were out at last was like champagne to the spirits. Within two hours the orders had been given and the squadron had raised anchor and was under way, passing through the narrow channel between Maddalena and the north-east tip of Sardinia and out into the open sea. The French fleet, Nelson determined, was heading either for Naples, Sicily, or Alexandria.

But as soon as they were clear of the island, the full force of the wind came hurtling down on them. By nightfall, a gale was raging, which forced them to remain hove-to for three days, and it was almost a week before any enquiries could be made about the French fleet. The information was all negative: they had not been seen in Sardinia, and they had not landed in Sicily. 'Unless they have gone to the bottom, they are in Egypt,' said Nelson, and the squadron set sail for Alexandria.

'It's like '98 all over again,' Haworth heard The Anchovy remark to Mr Webb when they arrived off Alexandria on 7 February and found no sign of the French. They set sail again, this time for Malta, and arriving twelve days later learnt that, as in '98, the fault had been in overestimating the French. While the English squadron had ridden out the storm in safety, the French fleet had been thrown into disarray, had lost some spars, and had run for shelter back to Toulon, where they had been ever since.

Lucy was exercising her chestnuts in the Park early one bright, cold morning in April, with Parslow up beside her, when she was hailed from the footpath by Admiral Scorton who, like her, had never broken himself of the habit of taking his exercise early.

'Ha! There you are!' he called. 'Made sure I'd find you here, m'dear. Something in particular to say to you.'

Lucy pulled up, and Parslow stepped down to take the leaders' heads.

'Well, Admiral?' she said cordially.

Scorton eyed the horses cautiously. 'Don't think your beasts'll stand long enough for what I've got to tell you. More than a five-minute chat.'

'Jump up, then, and we'll take a circuit or two,' Lucy offered. 'Parslow won't mind waiting.'

'Sooner you walked with me, while he takes the drive,' the admiral said frankly. 'Never get seasick, except in sportin' carriages.'

Lucy laughed, wound the reins, and held out a hand to him. 'Whatever you say, Admiral. Jump me down, and I'll take your arm with pleasure. Keep them moving, Parslow, and pick me up at the gate, if you don't pass me first'.

The horses went off at a fine pace, and Lucy tucked her hand under the admiral's arm and matched her step to his as they walked after them.

'Ha,' he said, 'that's good! You've a fine way, m'dear, of pacin' along, that makes all very comfortable. My dear wife was just the same, but some young women take such mimsy little steps, there's no walkin' with them, unless it's round and round a sopha! They teeter along like a rat on a wet cable. It quite makes one nervous to be alongside 'em.'

'Quite right, Admiral. But what was it you wanted to tell me?'

'Oh, ah, yes! News, m'dear, of a vast upheaval at the Admiralty. It will be all over Town in two shakes, but I thought you'd like to be first with it. Melville's resigned.'

'Melville? The First Lord?'

'This morning. Nothing else to be done. Royal Commission, you see, goin' over the Naval Treasury books, uncovered what they call "irregularities" while he was Treasurer.'

'But that was years ago,' said Lucy.

'Oh, quite; and there was nothin' dishonest about it. Merely an unauthorised speculation. But Melville, you see, wouldn't trouble himself to be civil to the Commissioners when they interviewed him. Cursed 'em for wastin' his time, so of course they went after him like Spanish luggers. Bound to turn up somethin' if they only looked long enough. There never was a public servant yet who was beyond reproach, you know.'

'Except Pitt, perhaps,' Lucy said drily. 'The incorruptible.'

'Ah well, that's where it is, you see,' said Scorton. 'It's Pitt they're attackin' really. Friend of Melville's. Daring Pitt to defend him, and so on. It's all politics, m'dear, all politics. I thank God I'm a simple sailor.'

'I wonder who Pitt will find to replace him,' Lucy said thoughtfully.

Scorton pressed her arm in triumph. 'I think I can tell you. It won't be generally known yet, but when you think of it, it's the only sensible choice. Senior admiral; and after all, he's been Melville's confidential advisor, and Pitt's, these two years.'

Lucy wrinkled her brow. 'You're talking of yourself?'

Scorton chuckled. 'You flatter me, m'dear! Oh, I've been called in once or twice, it's true, when I've had somethin' particular to say, but Middleton's kept his finger on the pulse all along, and there can't be a better man in the present crisis.'

'Sir Charles Middleton? But surely he retired years ago? I didn't even know he was still alive. He must be — oh, any age!'

'Seventy-eight, but as hale and hearty as an oak tree. Well, I know he hasn't been to sea in an age, but that's not the be-all and end-all! Officers on the spot don't like havin' their decisions made for 'em anyway. Middleton understands the workings of the navy better than any man alive. He got the navy back on its feet when he was Comptroller durin' the American war, and with three-quarters of our ships in need of overhaul, and others rotting at their moorings when we desperately need 'em at sea, he's the man for the job all right. You'll see.'

'Well, I suppose you know best,' Lucy said doubtfully, 'but I'd have thought you were a much more likely candidate.'

'Haven't got the brains, m'dear,' Scorton said cheerfully. 'I can sail a ship — none better, though I say it m'self. But I haven't enough wits to bless myself — never did have. What do you think of this business of Villynoove, by the by? Escapes from Toulon, appears outside Cadiz harbour with nineteen of the line, calls out the Spaniards, and disappears again.'

'I think it's a pity Admiral Nelson ever let him get out of

Toulon. What on earth is a blockade for, if not to keep the ships in harbour?'

'Mediterranean's a big sea,' Scorton said apologetically, 'and Toulon's a bad station to watch. Point is, where's this Villy feller gone with his combined fleet? Twenty-five enemy ships — nasty thing to lose, you know.'

'I can't imagine,' Lucy said obediently. 'What's your opinion, Admiral?'

'It's my belief they've gone to the West Indies. Where else should they have gone? And that other Frenchy's there ... what's his name? Out of Rochefort?'

'Missiessy,' Lucy supplied.

'That's right. Damn' silly name. Taken Dominica and St Lucia already, from what we hear. I think this Villynoove's gone to join him. Take a few of our island possessions, and if it tempts our ships away from the Brest blockade, all the better.'

'But would we be so silly as to leave the Channel undefended?'

'No, but it's just the kind of damn' fool notion Boney would think up. Grand, military sort of scheme. Diversionary tactics. Not a sailor, you see,' he explained simply. 'After all, he's had all those troops waitin' in the Channel ports for months. He's got to make a push to invade us soon, or he's goin' to look a fool with his own people. He's up to somethin' all right, and we'll need every ship and every man out there to fox him.' He glanced down at Lucy, and seeing her troubled expression said, 'Talking too much. Don't you worry, m'dear. Things never turn out to be as bad as anyone thinks they will. Take an old man's word for it.'

'Which old man is that, Admiral?' Lucy asked innocently, and Scorton laughed.

'That's my naughty puss! Heard from young Captain Whatsisname recently? Cornwallis's last report spoke handsomely of him. No easy job, inshore squadron at Brest.'

On 27 April, Chetwyn and Robert drove to Upper Grosvenor Street for a long visit. The hunting was over, and Robert was eager for more social pursuits than Wolvercote could offer, and had persuaded his patron and mentor that it would be a great pity to miss the best of the Season.

They arrived to find the house in an ordered confusion, and leaving Robert in the breakfast parlour, Chetwyn ran upstairs to Lucy's chamber, where she and Docwra were packing her trunks.

'Lucy! What's going on? Hicks says you're going away somewhere. Going away at the height of the Season? It must be something serious.'

Lucy turned from sorting through her glove-box and frowned at him. 'Of course it's serious. What are you doing here, if you don't think it's serious?'

'We've come up for the plays and balls,' Chetwyn said mildly. 'Do put that box away and talk to me properly.'

'You mean you don't know about the Toulon fleet? You haven't come to safeguard your investments? 'Change is in a turmoil, Consols have plummeted, the Government has been on the brink of resigning five times, and you've come to Town for the theatres?'

'We've been very busy at Wolvercote,' Chetwyn said with dignity, sitting on the edge of her bed. 'Polly, Minnie and Rosamund have had three fearful colds in the head, and we've had to look after Roland all day to keep him from catching them. We took him out hunting last week — only to the first draw, but he was so proud, and behaved like a little gentleman. He's going to be a fine horseman. What's the trouble, then?'

'A letter has come from one of our spies in Paris,' Lucy said. 'It seems Villeneuve's almost certainly gone to the West Indies to join up with Missiessy, and Ganteaume's squadron is making preparations for departure, with eighteen thousand men on board.'

Chetwyn shrugged. 'It doesn't seem to me to be cause for immediate concern. The situation is no different from before.'

'The difference is that there's a combined fleet of thirty ships loose in the Atlantic, and no-one knows for certain where it is. Cochrane's been sent in pursuit with six of the line, but every other ship is already being used on blockade service, and can hardly be spared. And nobody knows where

Nelson and his squadron are. They haven't been seen for three weeks, and there are letters in the papers about the navy letting the country down.'

Chetwyn picked at the fringe of the counterpane. 'Harsh words.'

'As dear old Admiral Scorton says, it's all politics. He warned me about this weeks ago, the clever old creature, guessed the Combined had gone to the West Indies. But he thinks it's all a prelude to a concerted attempt at invasion.'

'Well, that would be serious, I agree. But where exactly are you going? You can't be fleeing London for fear of Boney's imminent arrival. I'd back you to man the barricades with the best of them.'

Lucy smiled for the first time. 'Thank you for your good opinion. No, of course I'm not fleeing.' She hesitated. He was sitting and talking with her so companionably she didn't want to spoil his mood by introducing the forbidden subject.

'So, where are you going?' he prompted.

'To Plymouth,' she said. She eyed him apologetically. 'I have to be nearer than London. I can't bear just to sit here when something is going to happen at any moment. I want to be on hand, as close as I can be, in case ... in case there is news.'

To her astonishment, he grinned. 'Just like any poor officer's wife, eh, Luce? You're going to tuck yourself into some lodging-house run by a fisherman's widow, and walk down to the harbour every day to look for sails on the horizon?'

'I suppose so, except that it will be the largest suite in the most comfortable inn I can find,' she replied. 'I'm sorry, Chetwyn.'

'Don't be. I expect I'd do the same if I were you,' he said, standing up. 'Are you leaving at once, or will you be here for dinner? Because if you won't be, I think I'll take Rob to dine at Brooks's. He wants me to put him up for membership, and it would be as well to introduce him to some of the more influential members.'

'No, I shan't be here,' Lucy said vaguely, astonished at the change in his attitude. He didn't mind about her wanting to be near Weston; he didn't much care, it was evident, about the threat of invasion; he wasn't in the least worried about the turmoil in the City. He was simply looking forward to dining at his club with a friend.

'I'll leave you to pack,' he said, heading for the door. 'Come and say goodbye before you leave, won't you?'

The door closed behind him, and Lucy turned to meet Docwra's almost equally perplexed gaze.

'Sure God, I think I liked him better the other way,' said Docwra.

Chapter Nine

At the beginning of April, Nelson's squadron was in the Gulf of Palmas, off the southern tip of Sardinia, where they had arranged to rendezvous with the storeships from Malta. On 3 April the frigate *Phoebe* arrived from Toulon to report that Villeneuve's fleet, eleven of the line and six frigates, had cleared the roads at sunset on 30 March, heading south, as if to pass down the eastern side of the Balearic islands.

On this course, Nelson reminded his assembled captains in the stern cabin on the *Victory*, it was probable that the eastern Mediterranean was Villeneuve's objective. 'Naples, Sicily, Malta, or Egypt, gentlemen? They are all vulnerable: the question is, which?'

No-one spoke, but each man consulted the map of the Mediterranean which by now was engraved on his mind. Many, like Haworth, had served here in the last war too, and all had patrolled every mile of it for far too long.

'I'm not going further east than Sicily, or further west than Sardinia, until I know something more certain,' Nelson concluded. 'The narrowest part of the route to the east is the channel between Tunisia and the south-western tip of Sicily. The capital ships will patrol that area, while the frigates cover the channel between Tunis and Sardinia. That way, there's no possibility they can elude us.'

Day after day aboard the *Cetus*, Captain Haworth subdued his doubts as he cruised up and down the Sicilian channel without sight or sign of the French. The pattern was becoming horribly familiar.

'It's just like last time, Papa,' Africa said unhelpfully. 'Do you think the French have gone back into harbour again?'

'There's been no storm this time, my love,' he replied steadily. 'You must remember the French sail more slowly than we do, because they aren't used to being at sea. I expect they'll appear any day now.'

'It's been nearly four weeks since they left Toulon,' Africa

167

pointed out. 'I don't think they're coming at all. Papa, may I take my sewing up on the fo'c'sl, and sit with Blind Billy? He promised to tell me a story about a mermaid.'

It was not until 16 April that another sail was sighted. It was a single merchantman, whose captain reported to the admiral that some French ships had been seen leaving Cartagena on the 6th, heading south-west. Signals rushed up the halliards, and the squadron was ordered to set sail north-westward, first to make sure the French fleet had not returned to Toulon, and then to check on the Spanish coast.

They were no sooner under way than the wind turned dead foul, and for three days they could only struggle to hold their position, making no headway. On the 19th they were met by a brig sent out of Gibraltar to find them, to tell them that Villeneuve's fleet had passed westwards through the straits on the 9th, ten days earlier, and had been joined by the Spanish admiral Gravina's five ships out of Cadiz.

Once again the captains were called on board the *Victory* to hear the news and receive their orders.

'We are heading west, gentlemen. Evidently the enemy is making for the Atlantic, but thereafter, his objective might be one of many.'

'Ireland, my lord?' suggested Keats of the *Superb*. 'They might be planning a landing. We know they have troops on board.' And Ireland, always in a state of barely controlled ferment, was a useful back door into England.

'It may be Ireland; but then again they may be intending to join Ganteaume at Brest. We must cover both eventualities. I am sending the *Amazon* to Lisbon to try to obtain more information. Meanwhile the eleven ships of the line will head for Cape St Vincent, join up with the *Amazon* there, and unless we have further news, we'll take up position to the west of the Scillies, where we can intercept the French whether they head for Ireland or Brest.'

'And the frigates, sir?' asked one of the commanders.

'They are to remain here, patrolling the channel between Tunis and Sardinia, to intercept any expedition the French may send against Egypt.'

Haworth and Pellew of the *Conqueror* exchanged a glance

at that. Still hankering after Egypt! was the thought in both their minds.

The captains returned to their own ships, and there was a flurry of activity as boats were sent off to the *Amazon* with all the letters for home. The wind had backed just sufficiently for them to get under way, and the *Amazon* was soon hull-down of them, moving several knots faster than the best of the ships, and three times as fast as the poor old *Superb*, which was heavily fouled and in dire need of a refit.

But before they had gone twenty miles, the fluky wind veered dead foul again. It was one thing to plan a strategy, and quite another to put it into effect, and while London was seething with panic, and demanding to know where Nelson was, the Toulon squadron was struggling slowly towards Gibraltar, unable to reach the Rock until 7 May. Here the news greeted them that Villeneuve was on course for the Caribbean.

With home waters protected by Cornwallis's and Keith's forty ships, and the West Indian possessions only by the small force Cochrane had taken in pursuit of Villeneuve, there was at last a clear choice for Nelson. The ships renewed their stores, and the Admiral interviewed his captains.

'Though we are late, yet chance may give them a bad passage, and us a good one. The wind is favourable, and we must hope for the best. In any case, even if we don't find the combined fleet, we can be back in home waters by the end of June, before the enemy finds out where we are.'

They had been at sea for almost two years continuously, and most of the ships needed a refit; but the crews were in good health and spirits, with the most experienced officers in the world to command them. They set sail at seven in the evening of 11 May to pursue Villeneuve across the Atlantic. There was a fine following wind, and with studding sails set, even the old *Superb* logged six knots.

During the voyage, the Admiral issued to the captains his fighting instructions, in case they should manage to bring the combined fleet to battle. As at the battle of the Nile, the English numbers would be smaller than the enemy's, and the instructions were essentially the same: to break the enemy line, concentrate the attack on one part of it, and overwhelm

169

it before dealing with the remainder.

The crews were excited at the prospect of action, and skylarked about their daily routines. It was exhilarating to run free at last, with every sail set, leaping over a blue sea under blue skies. Africa spent most of each day on the fo'c'sl, watching the white water as it broke dazzlingly against the forefoot; gazing out at the horizon, where the frigates scouted ahead, like flecks of foam against the rim of the world; exclaiming with excitement at her first sight of a school of dolphins; and in the dogwatches, learning to dance the hornpipe, barefoot on the warm deck boards, and singing songs about the great sea-battles of the past as they sailed steadily towards the setting sun.

The month of May was a nervous one in England, for with two enemy squadrons and one English one missing, and signs daily at Brest that Admiral Ganteaume was preparing to come out, it was hard for anyone to know what to do. It seemed that the man with the most responsibility in the case — the First Lord, now elevated to the peerage as Lord Barham — was the least agitated, as he gave his orders, adapting them daily to the new circumstances as news and rumours dribbled in.

It was the same sort of nervousness which had driven Lucy down to Plymouth, where she had installed herself at the George. Docwra had been prepared to see her mistress fretting herself into an illness, but fortunately she had the company of Admiral Collingwod for part of the time, as he prepared a squadron for sea, and was delayed first by storms and then by conflicting orders.

In the middle of the month, John Anstey drove down from London with his eldest son, aged nine, whom Collingwood had now agreed to take into his ship. When he had delivered the boy on board, he called on Lucy, and was invited most pressingly to stay to dinner.

'Stirring times to be going to sea,' Lucy commented, when Anstey told her about little John. 'I can't tell you how I envy him.'

'What is going on, Lucy?' John Anstey asked. 'Have you any better information than I could get in London? I have to tell you that Nelson's reputation is very low. Everyone seems to think he has been fooled by the French and gone to Egypt. Lady Bessborough said to me yesterday that he must think the French grow there.'

Lucy laughed. 'I hope you warned little John not to repeat such things in Collingwood's ship! The admiral won't hear a word against his friend. He thinks Nelson must be hard on Villeneuve's heels.'

'You think Villeneuve has definitely gone to the West Indies?'

'Collingwood does. He also believes that the French went to the West Indies purely to draw off our ships from the Channel, so we had better hope that Nelson finds Villeneuve and defeats him, or we shall surely have a battle closer to home.'

'What do you mean?'

'Collingwood thinks that Villeneuve and Missiessy will bring their ships straight back to attack the Brest blockade so that Ganteaume can get out; and there's no-one in the world guesses better what the French are about than Collingwood.'

'I hope little John will be safe,' Anstey said, 'Have you any idea where he will be going?'

'It was to have been the West Indies, but I think it's more likely now to be Cadiz. The Dons are fitting out ships as hard as they can go. Blockade duty — dull, perhaps, but good training. But tell me the London news. Have you seen anything of Chetwyn?'

Anstey eyed her curiously. 'One can hardly get away from him — he seems to go everywhere! I never knew him so sociable. There's a great change come over him in the last year or so, hasn't there?'

'All to the good,' Lucy said shortly. 'He was growing very strange and dour, but since Weston went back to sea, he seems to have become cheerful again.'

'Is that what it is?' said Anstey neutrally, and helped himself to some of the excellent West Country mutton before asking, 'What do you think of this young friend of his?'

'Robert? Oh, he's well enough, I suppose. A pleasantly-behaved boy. He seems to be very fond of my children, for some reason.'

'I met his mother in Town last week. She seems to be in ecstasies over his friendship with Aylesbury. Introducing him into the best circles and so on, she said.'

'Thank God I left Town before she arrived,' Lucy said fervently. 'I loathe the woman. I suppose she's installed herself in my house?'

'Yes.' He reached for the caper sauce, and placed a spoonful with great deliberation on the edge of his plate. 'It's fortunate, really, that she has, since you've left. Otherwise they'd be there on their own.'

Lucy frowned. 'Why shouldn't they be? You don't think they'd break the furniture, or burn the place down, do you?'

'No, of course not,' Anstey said hastily, and changed the subject. 'How long are you meaning to stay in Plymouth? Shall you be coming to Yorkshire in the summer? You'll hardly believe it, but your brother tells me the new stables at Twelvetrees are going to be finished in time for race-week.'

'You're right,' Lucy laughed. 'I don't believe it.'

When Collingwood and Anstey had both left, Plymouth became a lonely place, filled, as Chetwyn had said, with the wives of sea officers, waiting like Lucy, for news of their men; yet not like her, for they had each other for company, and their children around them. Most of them knew who she was, but they held aloof from her, and she from them. Ship's captains and their wives came mostly from the middle orders. They made devoted couples, and, from the uncertainty of their lives, tended to adhere to a strict moral code by way of compensation. They did not approve of Lucy; she hardly knew they existed.

Her patience was rewarded at the end of May. On the morning of the 22nd, while she was eating her breakfast and looking over the newspaper which the innkeeper of the George acquired for her daily, Docwra came into the room in a state of great excitement.

'Oh my lady, quick, quick, let me get your hat and pelisse. He's coming, my lady!'

'What! How do you know?' Lucy was on her feet instantly. There could be only one 'he' in their conversation.

'Parslow was exercising the horses along that straight bit of road by the harbour, when a ship was signalled coming in, and a shoreboatman there who knows him, told him it was the *Nemesis*.'

'Oh, thank God! Is he quite sure?'

'Yes, my lady. It seems everyone knows the *Nemesis*, her bein' famous as the fastest ship in the service. Anyway, Parslow came straight back here, and he's below now with the horses turned round, so you can be there before she drops anchor. Oh, pray God he can stay a while!'

In moments Lucy was running down the stairs, throwing orders over her shoulder to Docwra who panted along behind her. 'He may not have much time. Have fresh coffee ready, and bread and meat, and have them make up the fire in the coffee room, in case his clothes need drying.'

Parslow was in the curricle at the door, and the chestnuts were plunging against his restraining hand, sensing the urgency in the air. No single moment had been wasted, and Lucy was waiting at the steps when Weston came ashore. He was looking tired and drawn, his face very brown, his hair too long, straggling out of the ribbon with which he had tied it back. For one instant he seemed unfamiliar, and she felt absurdly shy; but then his face creased into a grin of astonished delight and she was in his arms.

'Lucy! Oh, my dearest, dearest girl! If you only knew how often I've dreamed about this!'

Her arms were round him under his boat cloak, her face against his shoulder. His clothes smelled of sour dampness, his skin of salt air, and he was so thin, so thin! But he was her Weston, and she closed her eyes against the painful rush of joy at being close to him again.

'But what are you doing in Plymouth?' he asked, kissing the top of her head, pressing his cheek against it, while she simply clung, uncharacteristically silent. 'How did you know I was coming?'

'I didn't. I just hoped you might.'

'You've been waiting here at Plymouth just in case I put in?' he asked, looking down at her, laughing. 'That must mean you've been missing me after all! Oh, but I have no moment to waste,' he cried, putting her away from him as he

173

remembered his duty. 'I must report at once to the port-captain. I've urgent news, which I don't doubt he'll tell me I must take post-haste to London.'

'Yes, I understand,' Lucy said, gesturing towards the curricle as she hurried along beside him. 'See, I have horses waiting. I'm putting up at the George — it's the posting inn. We'll drive there straight away.'

'Bless you,' he said, grateful for her rapid intelligence, that wasted no time in exclamation or question. She was ready in the driving-seat when he emerged from the office, a bag of despatches under his arm, clapping his hat to his head as he climbed up beside her. She nodded to Parslow to let go the chestnuts' heads, and he leapt to his seat behind as the rig passed him.

'I have food waiting for you at the inn,' Lucy said, frowning with concentration as she sprang her horses along the harbour road. 'I thought you might be in a hurry.'

Weston, holding the side of the curricle with one hand and his hat with the other, as they rattled and swayed over the uneven surface, said, 'It was a kind thought, but I dare not stay for anything. I have news for Their Lordships which must be taken to them at once.'

'Yes, yes, I understand, but you will take a mouthful of something while Parslow hires the chaise and sees the horses put-to. No time will be wasted, I promise you. Oh Weston, I am so glad to see you!'

In minutes they were at the George, and Lucy hurried Weston into the coffee-room.

'My God,' he said, 'I'd forgotten how you drive! Oh, what a glorious fire! And is that coffee I smell! Lucy, my darling, you are the most wonderful woman in the world. I've dreamed of real coffee almost as often as I've dreamt of you.'

Lucy was already pouring a cup for him. 'Here's bread and meat, too,' she said.

'Fresh bread! Oh, the heaven of it, after ship's biscuit! But I haven't time, I haven't time!' He gulped coffee, scalding his mouth in his haste.

'Come, Weston, there's no need to injure yourself. We'll take the tray in the chaise with us, if you really cannot spare even a few minutes to eat.'

'Did you say *we?*' He opened his eyes wide over the rim of his cup.

'You don't think I'd just watch you drive off in a chaise without me, do you? We can be together all the way up to London — and back, I suppose, if they send you back straight away.'

'I think they will,' he said. 'You see —'

'Ready sir!' Parslow said, poking his head round the door at that instant. 'I've picked you the best horses they had.'

'I'm going too, Parslow,' Lucy said, as Weston bolted for the door. 'Bring that tray along, will you?'

'Yes, my lady. You won't think of travelling back on your own, will you, my lady?'

'No, I'll come back with the captain. Don't worry.'

Docwra was in the yard, where the post-boys were already mounted, and handed Lucy a cloak-bag. 'Just a few things. Parslow said you'd be going. Take care, my lady.'

'I'll be back in a few days. Pass up the tray, will you?'

The door was clapped to, the boy sounded his horn, and they were off, with no greater mishap than a sad spillage of coffee as the chaise swung violently out of the innyard.

'Well, that was neatly contrived,' said Weston when they regained the upright. 'Now I can enjoy my breakfast in peace. Lord, I'm hungry for it, too!'

'You are very thin,' Lucy commented as he tore into a piece of bread with more appreciation than elegance. 'I hope Bates looks after you properly.'

'He tries to, but I make his life difficult for him, I'm afraid. There are so often more important things to do than eat. You haven't asked what the news is, yet.'

'I assumed you'd tell me. It must be important, to warrant all this haste.'

'It is. Missiessy's back in Rochefort! He slipped in with his five ships two days ago, while everybody thought he was still in the West Indies. I was with Calder's squadron when we spotted them off Finisterre, and he sent me to trail them and then report to the Admiralty.'

'Then it looks as though Collingwood was right,' Lucy said. 'He believed that the expedition to the West Indies was a ruse to draw us off, and that Missiessy and Villeneuve would be back as soon as possible.'

'He's a smart man, our Colly,' said Weston through a mouthful of cold beef. 'If that's the case, it would account for all the activity that's been going on in Brest. We've been expecting a sortie every day for months, but Ganteaume keeps getting as far as Bertheaume Bay, at the mouth of the road, and then putting back again.' He grinned. 'Some fishermen we've got friendly with along the coast have a nice little song they sing about him.

> There was an Admiral Ganteaume,
> Who when the wind was in the east
> Sailed out from Brest to Bertheaume;
> And when the wind was in the west,
> Turned round and sailed back home to Brest.'

'What were you doing with Calder's squadron?' Lucy asked.

'Reporting on Ganteaume's movements, of course. That's the joy of commanding a fast frigate — you get released from blockade every now and then. I must say, I didn't expect to be seeing you while I was here, though. I thought I might be able to find time to scribble you a letter and have it sent round to Upper Grosvenor Street, but no more than that. How long have you been in Plymouth?'

'A month.'

'There's dedication for you! And how are things with you?'

'Very well, on the whole,' she said, and told him about Chetwyn's improved state of mind.

'And the child?' he asked eagerly. 'How is he? Has he grown?'

'Héloïse sends me letters from time to time, about teeth and colics and so on. I think she said in the last one that he was walking well and talking a little — or was it the other way round?'

Weston looked at her, perplexed. 'You haven't been to see him?'

'No,' she said, and gave him a helpless look. 'Weston, I can't help it. He's just a baby. I don't find babies very interesting. He's being well looked after, you know.'

He turned his face away from her and stared out of the

window unseeingly, and she watched him, gripping her hands together in her lap against a new and unfamiliar hurt. In a moment he spoke, his head still turned away.

'I think about him so often. I imagine holding him, playing with him. I think what it would be like to be able to watch him grow up, with you beside me. I'm sorry.' He looked at her now, and she hated the sadness in his face, because it made her feel so useless. 'I shouldn't say things like that. You can't help your nature, any more than I can help mine. And I've always loved you as you are.'

'You don't understand,' she said with difficulty. 'I've thought, too, about —' She frowned, seeking words for things she was not used to expressing. 'Do you remember the summer we spent at Great Wakering? I've imagined what it would be like to live there with you, like ordinary people. We were happy there. But we aren't ordinary people.'

He took her hand and stroked it warmly. 'No, I suppose not.'

They travelled in silence for a while, and when she looked at him again, she saw he had fallen asleep from sheer exhaustion, his head tilted back against the dusty squab. He was worn out, she thought, by months of unending tension. He was pale under his tan, and there were deep grooves beside his mouth which had not been there before, and his cheekbones were too prominent. His eyelashes trembled as he slept uneasily, and she had a sudden, foolish urge to kiss his eyelids, and his sleeping mouth, and to cradle his head against her breast, as if he were a child.

The sensation surprised her. She had never felt protective towards him before, nor towards anyone; but now she wanted to be everything to him, not just lover and friend, but mother, and wife. She had a brief mental picture of her and Weston walking along the overgrown path beside the creek at Great Wakering, with a small child between them, each of them holding a hand as its uncertain feet stumbled on the uneven turf. Did such things ever happen, even to other people? Would they be pleasurable? Far back in her mind, behind the picture, she had a dimly perceived apprehension that pleasure of that sort was only bought at the price of an equal pain.

His eyes flickered open, and he looked at her unrecognis-

177

ingly for an instant, blank from the deadness of sleep. She felt a surge of fear that made her clutch his hand, waking him properly, so that he shrugged himself upright, and apologised.

'I didn't mean to go to sleep. I'm sorry. Lucy, what is it? You look quite pale.'

She shook her head, still holding his hand tightly, unable to tell him that she had seen the image of a world without him, and it had terrified her. 'I missed you when you were away,' she said at last.

From her, he knew, it was a great deal.

While he was in the Admiralty she went with the chaise to the nearest post-house and changed the horses, and was waiting for him when he came out. He noted the change of team, and nodded to her as he climbed up beside her.

'Yes, I have to go straight back. They never have enough frigates, and can't spare mine even for a day.'

Lucy gave the order to the post-boys, and sat back. 'We'll take our dinner at Kingston. Even sea-officers have to eat.'

'One good piece of news,' he said. 'I'm to join Collingwood's squadron, off Cadiz. Barham thinks that if Villeneuve does come back from the Caribbean, he'll probably head for Cadiz, to try to pick up more Spanish ships. The old boy didn't say anything, but I think he's desperately worried. One of the secretaries said that the shortage of men and ships was so bad that Barham's afraid we might have to give up the blockade by the end of the year.'

The journey back to Plymouth was accomplished almost as fast as the journey to London. They slept on the road, as before, stopping only for meals, and arrived at the George very weary in the late afternoon.

Parslow came out to meet them in the yard, with the latest information about wind and tide. 'I thought you'd need to know, sir, so I made sure I kept myself apprised of the situation. And the harbour master says that the *Nemesis* was revictualled and watered in accordance with your instructions, and she's all ready to sail at an hour's notice.'

'You're a remarkable man, Parslow.'

'Thank you, sir. I took the liberty, sir, of making some purchases of cabin stores on your behalf, and having them sent aboard. And there's a fire in your chamber, my lady, and I can have a bite of food brought up within the hour.'

Lucy looked enquiringly at Weston, and he nodded towards the stairs. 'I can spare an hour. If high tide's not until seven, provided I'm back on board by six, we can sail on the ebb.'

In the privacy of her chamber, Lucy turned towards Weston, and he took her in his arms with a weary sigh.

'When this crisis is over, my Lucy, I am going to give up the sea, and find myself some occupation on shore, and dedicate all my waking hours to you. This piecemeal business is very bad for love.'

She leaned against him, trying to make herself feel to the full the joy of being with him, but all she could think was that he was going away again in such a very short time. Behind him she could hear the crackling of the fire, and the relentless ticking of the clock eating away at their only, precious hour.

'Weston,' she said urgently, tilting her head back.

His eyes had been shut again, but he opened them and smiled down at her with a sleepy, 'Hmm?'

'I don't want to waste any of the time we've got left,' she said.

His smile became a grin. 'Quite right. Whatever was I thinking of? Shall we lock the door, or have you warned the servants not to disturb us?'

Her cheeks grew a little pink. 'I wasn't thinking of that,' she said.

He cupped his hands over her breasts and bent his head to kiss her on the lips. 'Ah, but you are now.'

Despite everyone's doubts, James's new stables at Twelvetrees were finished at the end of July, in good time for a grand opening ceremony to coincide with the beginning of race-week. Roberta was coming up to Shawes, and had offered James the ballroom and her services as hostess for a cele-bration ball in honour of the occasion.

'So it won't matter if Mary Ann doesn't come back in

time,' he said to Edward.

'I'm sure she will,' Edward said. 'She knows how important the stables are to you.'

'I'm sure she won't. Not even for a fountain that really works, and music, and fireworks after dark. It really doesn't matter. She evidently enjoys her visits to Manchester, and I've no wish to deprive her of that pleasure.'

'Chetwyn's coming, at any rate,' Edward said with deep pleasure. 'I don't know how it is, but I don't seem to have seen him for an age.'

'We've been busy,' James said. 'The time goes by so fast. But I'm glad he's coming — and Lucy, too. She'll love the stables.'

'If only poor William could be here.'

'Now don't start that, old fellow, or we'll have to go through the whole list! I must say, I was pleasantly surprised that Chetwyn decided to bring the children. Fanny's going to be so excited when I tell her how many cousins she'll have to play with.'

Fanny's initial reaction was cautious. 'Are any of them older than me, Papa?' she wanted to know.

'Well, your cousin Polly is. You remember her, don't you?'

'No,' said Fanny firmly.

'She lived here for a little while. Aunt Lucy says she's getting to be very beautiful, like her mother.'

Fanny frowned. 'I don't like her.'

'But you just said you didn't remember her.'

'I don't care. I don't like her. I don't want her to stay here.'

'Well, that's all right, chicken. I expect Aunt Lucy will want them to stay at Shawes with Bobbie Chelmsford. But they can come over and play with you. The younger ones, Minnie and Rosamund, will want to see your baby house, I know, and all the new furniture I've made for you. They haven't got anything half so fine.'

Fanny brightened. 'And my rocking horse?'

'I expect Rosamund will love that. She's nutty on horses.'

'Is she pretty?'

'No, she's the plain one of the family, poor little thing. Freckles and mousy hair.'

Fanny smiled. 'Perhaps I'll teach her to ride,' she said

generously. 'I could let her sit on Tempest while I hold the reins. I don't expect she'd be able to manage him on her own.'

Lucy travelled post, and stopping to change at Grantham, discovered amongst the vehicles in the innyard her husband's chariot, with the Aylesbury arms on the panels, and his mother's elderly berlin. As they were horseless and pushed to one side, she assumed they must be resting or taking a meal within, and told her post-boys she would stop for half an hour.

On entering the inn and enquiring for his lordship, she was taken to a private parlour, where a large meal was laid out on a long table, around which sat not only her husband, but the four children and Trotton. Three nursery maids were attending to the girls' needs, and Chetwyn's man, Benton, was seen at that instant by the astonished Lucy, indisputably to be tucking a napkin into young Lord Calder's neck.

'So it's you that's responsible for blocking up the innyard!' Lucy exclaimed. 'I took it to be a travelling circus at the very least. Good afternoon, Trotton. Benton, I hope your new master is as considerate as your old one!'

Chetwyn started up with a smile and came to greet her. 'Well, here's a famous coincidence! I wondered if you might pass us on the road. Will you stay and eat with us? There's plenty.'

'So I see. Really, Chetwyn,' she added quietly, 'this is the outside of enough, to be eating at the same table as the children. What will the inn servants think? You ought to think more about your dignity as an earl.'

'In the first place,' he returned easily, 'they are very busy here, and this was the only private room they had free. And in the second place, the best thing about being an earl is that you can do anything you like, and no-one can criticise you. You, of all people, ought to appreciate that.'

She allowed a servant to place a chair for her and fetch her clean covers. 'There are things, and things,' she said darkly.

'Let me help you to some of this beefsteak pie — it's excellent,' said Chetwyn by way of reply.

'That was your mother's berlin I saw outside, wasn't it?'

Chetwyn grinned. 'Enormous, isn't it? The girls and Trotton travel in that, and Benton and Roland and I squeeze into the chariot. There are two other hired carriages, too, for the maids and the luggage.'

'Benton said he would rather travel with the luggage,' Roland offered suddenly, his wide eyes fixed admiringly on his mother's hat. 'That was after I was sick — not the first time, but the second.'

'I don't blame him at all,' Lucy said mildly. 'Why were you sick?'

'Papa said it was the *infernal* road, but Benton said it was the game pie I had for breakfast.'

'You seem to be having an exciting time,' Lucy said to Chetwyn. 'Why on earth are you travelling with them?'

'My dear Lucy, because I want to! I actually rather like my children, I've discovered. There's something so delightfully honest about them.'

Lucy wrinkled her nose. 'You have a strange taste.' She thought how Weston had said he wanted to play with his child, too. 'Men are so sentimental,' she concluded. 'Where's Robert?'

'Gone to Bath, at the urgent summons of his mother. She thinks she's dying, and wants him to be with her for a few weeks while they still have time.'

'If she stays in Bath in August she will die,' Lucy asserted. 'And not before time, either. Does Robert really think she's ill?'

'How cruel you are! Well, he did at first, but I persuaded him not to worry until he'd seen her, and he wrote quite a comfortable letter once he arrived, to say that she's more upset than ill, but that he's staying with her at least until September. And so here I am. I can't wait to see the stables. Ned's promised pageants and fireworks and I don't know what besides.'

'Fireworks are very unwise when there are horses round.'

'Dear Lucy,' he said with a smile. 'I don't suppose he's going to let them off actually in the stable! And there's to be a ball at Shawes, for which I hope to have the honour of your hand for the first dance, and a picnic ride to Plompton Rocks, besides the races themselves. I'm glad you've come,' he added genially.

'I'm glad you have,' she returned with faint surprise.

182

'Have some of the smoked duck, and some peas to go with it. Benton, will you carve for her ladyship? And how is the wide world in general, and the King's navy in particular? The last thing I heard was that everyone is raging at Admiral Calder for letting the combined fleet get away from him somewhere out in the middle of the sea —'

'Off Cape Finisterre. He engaged them in fog and a heavy swell, and the action was inconclusive.'

'It seems most unfair to me to vilify him, considering that no-one seems to be blaming Nelson for having been in the West Indies with them for two weeks without sighting them once.'

'What does it matter what ignorant people think?' Lucy said shortly. 'Bobbie Calder's a fine seaman with an unblemished record, and no-one who wasn't there can say that he ought to have done better.'

'Public opinion is so fickle,' Chetwyn said with a mocking smile. 'No-one had a good word to say about Nelson until it turned out that he had chased Villeneuve to the West Indies after all, and then he was everyone's darling again. Travelling twice across the Atlantic seems to be a splendid thing to do, even if it doesn't achieve anything.'

'I wish you wouldn't talk so foolishly. You don't seem to understand how serious the situation is.'

'My dear, I have implicit faith in our sailor heroes. Yours, I must say, seems strangely shaky.'

'Oh, that reminds me,' Lucy said, ignoring the barb, 'I have a letter for you, Polly, from your father. It's in my luggage. You may come to me for it, when we reach Yorkshire.'

'Thank you, aunt.'

'Mama,' Rosamund said, now that Lucy's attention was on her side of the table, 'shall we be allowed to go on the picnic ride?'

'I shouldn't think so. What would you ride? Your uncles breed carriage horses and gentlemen's hunters, not ponies.' She had answered automatically, her mind turning instantly elsewhere, but in that moment she caught Rosamund's eye, and saw her deep disappointment, and suddenly remembered herself as a child, being denied some treat to do with horses.

183

An unexpected sympathy touched her, and just for an instant she felt connected to the stranger who was her daughter. She is made of my blood and my flesh, she thought in surprise. Is this what Weston means, and Chetwyn?

'I expect we might be able to hire ponies from somewhere,' she said. 'There must be plenty of them in Yorkshire.'

'Have some wine,' Chetwyn said with an approving smile. 'Age is making you kind, my dear Lady Aylesbury.'

The letter for Polly from Captain Haworth had been sent off with all the other letters and despatches from Nelson's squadron, from Antigua by the brig *Curieux*, which came into Plymouth on 7 July.

The letter was dated 13 June, and told the story of the run across the Atlantic, and of the ten days the squadron had spent sailing from island to island searching for the French. It had been a fruitless task, for at every step they had been given false information about the whereabouts of their quarry, which had sent them the wrong way.

'We have missed them at every turn, and the admiral now believes that they are gone back to Europe,' Haworth wrote, 'so I conclude this in haste, my dearest Polly, as we are to weigh anchor and set off after them. The admiral is sure they are gone to Egypt, so we are for Gibraltar, to take on stores, and then into the Mediterranean. I will write to you again and send it off from Gibraltar, and hope that I may have the opportunity to see you soon, for my poor old *Cetus* is long overdue for docking, and I fear this sojourn in warm waters has only increased her fouling.'

On her journey home, the brig *Curieux* had had the good fortune to sight Villeneuve's fleet on far too northerly a heading to be making for the Straits; so her commander, on his arrival in London, had been able to give Their Lordships the information that enabled them to send out Calder's squadron to intercept Villeneuve off Cape Finisterre.

But Nelson's ships had no such reassurance. The journey back to Europe wearied Haworth. Everyone was feeling the strain of being so long at sea without respite, and a double crossing of the Atlantic meant short commons for all; but the

Cetus had received the minimum of attention before he took her over, and she was now as heavily fouled as the *Superb*, and in need of several new spars and timbers, and sailing her was relentless and exhausting work.

In addition, the journey to the West Indies had been undertaken in hope of action after long tedium, and action had been denied them. Haworth had no faith that the journey back would bring them any closer to the French, especially since the Admiral still clung to the belief that Egypt was their object. They had been wrong at every turn, had spent the whole of this year sailing around in futile pursuit of an enemy who was always somewhere else. He did not expect to receive any news of Villeneuve when they reached the Rock; all his hopes were pinned on the chance of being sent home for refitting.

They crossed the Atlantic in just over a month, anchoring in Gibraltar Bay on 19 July, to find no trace of the French. While they were revictualling, a letter came for Nelson from Admiral Collingwood off Cadiz, giving his view that the combined fleet would head for Ferrol, release the ships there and at Rochefort, and then sail on to Ushant, Nelson had time to consider these ideas while they were replenishing their stores, and as a result, on 23 July, he ordered his squadron into the Atlantic to make for Brest.

They made slow progress northward against contrary winds, saw nothing of the combined fleet, and could gain no news of it until they joined Cornwallis off Ushant on 15 August. Here they learnt of Calder's inconclusive action on 22 July, and that the combined fleet had been sighted in Ferrol on 9 August, but had disappeared again.

There was no further call for decision on Nelson's part, however, for Cornwallis had a copy of orders which had missed him at Gibraltar, ordering him home on leave. There were orders, too, for Captains Keats and Haworth to bring in the *Superb* and the *Cetus* to Spithead for repair. Haworth received them with inward relief, as the first good tidings he had had that whole year.

Chapter Ten

Mary Ann had had a lifetime's experience of schooling not only her behaviour, but her feelings, too, and if she went on her annual visit to her father in 1805 with any desire of seeing Father Rathbone again, it could only have been because she had a letter to deliver to him from Aislaby. Even that was no urgent reason — 'It's nothing important,' Aislaby had assured her. 'Just if you happen to see him ...'

The first two weeks were fully occupied with settling in, and with paying and receiving formal visits. It was not until the third week that Mrs Pendlebury, in the course of a longer visit, brought up the subject.

'Have you happened to see the report to the Board of Health that John Ferriar was working on last year?'

'The report on the mill-workers' houses, you mean?'

'Yes, my dear. He has had it published, and sent copies to several of the leading people of Manchester. I have had mine a sennight, and simply can't put it down! It is such thrilling reading, quite like one of dear Mrs Radcliffe's stories. Something horrid on every page! I must ask him to send you one, dear Mrs Morland.'

'Thank you, ma'am,' Mary Ann said, and added diffidently, 'And what of the other gentleman, whom I had the pleasure of meeting on the same occasion? Have you seen anything of him?'

Mrs Pendlebury's brow furrowed under her much-plumed hat.

'Other gentleman? Who can you mean? Not Mr Adubon, the mesmerist? My dear, he does such thrilling things! Quite, quite horrid! Poor Mrs Ardwick went off into strong hysterics when he performed a demonstration at Mrs Withington's card-party, and had to be revived with burnt feathers.'

'No, no, ma'am. I was referring to Father Rathbone.'

'Oh, I understand you. No, my dear, I believe he is in Ireland. The mission sends him here and there, you know.

But you look disappointed?'

'I have a letter for him,' Mary Ann said hastily, 'and I am wondering how to deliver it.'

'The mission would doubtless know where to send it,' said Mrs Pendlebury, 'but if it is not urgent, it may be less troublesome to wait until he returns. He is sure to be here again before you leave. He often goes to Ireland, but he never stays very long.'

Mary Ann smiled. 'It's of no consequence at all, ma'am, I assure you. I shall keep the letter by me, and if he should happen to return, I will give it to him. And now, ma'am, I very much want to consult you about the subscription concert at the Exchange, but may I ring for some refreshments for you first?'

John Ferriar duly sent a copy of his report to Hobsbawn House, but Mary Ann, with no desire for the sort of *frissons* which had made Mrs Radcliffe's books so popular amongst ladies of quality, received it simply as a mark of attention and put it aside unread. A spell of very wet weather, however, confined her indoors, and without the usual means of occupying her time, she was driven to take it up.

She found it absorbing and very disturbing reading. She had little imagination, and no taste for novels, but John Ferriar's dry, unemotional account of the living conditions of the mill-workers not two miles away gave her a clearer picture than she was really comfortable with. She was reading it for the third time when her father returned from his day's labours at the mill, and came at once to greet and kiss her.

'What is it you're reading, love?' he asked, noting her preoccupation. 'A pamphlet, is it?'

Mary Ann told him. 'Some of the things he has discovered, Papa, are quite dreadful. Listen: 'At number four, Blakeley Street, the range of cellars consists of four rooms, communicating with each other, of which the two centre rooms are completely dark. Each contains four or five beds, and they are very dirty.' And this: "The houses at the corner of Cross Street have been built with windows not intended to open. The ceilings are so low that a man standing outside may touch the sill of the upstairs windows at a stretch of his arm."'

187

'Nay, love, what sort o' reading is that?' Mr Hobsbawn protested.

'No, but listen, Papa: 'The ground floor rooms have no floor-boards, but are of bare earth. As they are at the foot of a slope, there is much seepage into them of effluvia from higher up the street.' Effluvia, Papa! You know what that means.'

'Aye, I know,' Mr Hobsbawn said, growing rather red in the face, 'but I never thought I'd hear such a word on my daughter's lips! Who is it that's given you this trash to read, hey?'

'It isn't trash, Papa. It's the truth. Look, it's a report made to the Manchester Board of Health — you can't say that's trash, can you?'

'I can say it, and I will say it. If the Board of Health wants to trouble themselves with that sort o' thing, that's their business, but it's not the thing for a lady to be reading. You leave it to them whose concern it properly is.'

'It may soon be the concern of all of us,' Mary Ann said, undeterred. 'He says that there are many houses where dangerous fevers subsist permanently, and new lodgers fresh from the country lay themselves down in beds full of infection, from which the corpse of a fever victim has been removed only hours before. If these fevers should spread further —'

Hobsbawn reached down and snatched the paper from her fingers. 'That's enough! I'm taking this away and burning it, right now. If your mother were alive, to hear you talk so ungenteel about fevers and corpses and efflowers, and after the good sisters brought you up so carefully to be a lady!'

'The good sisters also taught me that we ought to care about our fellow man, and help those in affliction,' Mary Ann said.

Hobsbawn ruffled his hair in consternation. 'Aye, love, very proper, I'm sure, but our fellow man doesn't mean these sort of folk. These are none of our concern.'

'What about the pauper children who work in your mills, Papa?'

'Aye, and what about 'em? They don't live in these houses. They live in the 'prentice house, and I feed and clothe 'em at my own expense. Do you know how much it costs to keep one of 'em for a week? Three and sixpence! That's more than most mill-owners pay in wages. And then the ungrateful little devils up and run away, or die on me, out of sheer contrariness. Aye, it's no wonder Kennedy and the others are going over to free labour! Keeping 'prentices is more trouble than it's worth, and no thanks you get for it, besides the overseers complaining about having to beat the little ones to keep them working. Now if it was free labour, their parents'd do the beating, and all would be well.'

'Except for the children, perhaps,' Mary Ann said quietly.

'Nay love, you don't understand,' Hobsbawn said affectionately, patting her shoulder. 'Hard work never hurt anyone. Look at me — when have you known me lie abed after six in the morning? I'm down at the mill before any of my men, and stay longer. If you was to come there — not that I'd want you to, but if you did — and you was to see the rows of pauper children, working away, all industry and innocence, saved from destruction and vice, and turned into useful members of society — why, I tell you your eyes would be overflowing.' Mary Ann said nothing. 'Now let's have no more of this sort of talk, hey? I come home to be peaceful and happy, and to enjoy your company, and my little grandoon's. How is the little lad?'

Obedience, she had been taught, was one of the first duties of a child to its father. Mary Ann dropped the subject, and since Ferriar's report was never seen again in the house, she put it from her mind, and applied herself instead to the usual pleasures of her visit. Her brother-in-law Edward had asked her most urgently to return to Morland Place for the opening of the new stables and race-week, and though she anticipated little pleasure from the proceedings, her sense of duty suggested to her that she ought to cut short her stay. In the last week of July, however, she returned from a morning's drive to find Father Rathbone's card, and the message that he would call upon her formally the following day.

The visit was duly paid, and it was the purest coincidence that Mary Ann had just had delivered a new and very becoming morning-gown, which, in justice to the mantuamaker, demanded an early call by the hairdresser. Rathbone entered, so tall he seemed to darken the doorway, his sallow, hawkish face drawing her eyes like a moth to a candle-flame. He bowed over her hand, and she wished she might control the most improper colour in her cheeks.

'I hope I find you well, ma'am?' he said. His dark eyes surveyed her face for a moment and then he smiled, his teeth very white and rather savage-looking. If Mary Ann had been a novel-reader, the words 'corsair' or 'pirate' might have sprung to her mind. 'But I do not need to ask,' he added, taking the seat she offered. 'I can see you are in excellent health, as blooming as a rose.'

It was not the sort of comment she expected from a gentleman of slight acquaintance, but she supposed that he presumed upon his cloth, which, of course, made him not really count as a man at all. 'I understood you have been in Ireland?' she managed to say.

'I have indeed, and a terrible state things are in over there. Not that it's so quiet this side of the water! I've never seen so many musters and drills going on, on every village green I pass. So the French are really coming at last, are they?'

Mary Ann looked puzzled. 'I don't know,' she said. 'I do not read the newspapers very often.'

'Of course, you have other things on your mind,' he said, grinning at her. 'And more proper concerns for a lady, too, I'm sure, like hats and French gloves' — his eye flickered over her much too knowingly — 'and a very becoming gown, whose colour complements the eyes to perfection. And with those very finely stroked gathers on the sleeve, I can say with confidence that you have had the good taste to call upon the services of Madame Renée.'

Mary Ann hardly knew where to look. 'Oh, how can you be so —'

'So strange? But I am a priest, my dear Mrs Morland, and must not be judged by common standards. Besides, Madame Renée and I are old, old friends, she being from the same part of Dublin as myself.'

'I thought she was French,' Mary Ann said foolishly.

'Everybody in Dublin is half French at least,' he answered with a smile. 'French is our second language, which of course is what makes the English so suspicious of us, and rightly so! We're a treacherous people, not to be trusted.'

'Oh, but you, I'm sure, can be trusted!' Mary Ann cried,

190

and then wished she hadn't, for the opening it gave him.

But Rathbone only gave her a small, satisfied smile, and said, 'Well, if it isn't your pretty gown you have been thinking of, pray tell me what has been occupying you to the exclusion of Boney's Grand Design?'

Seeking for a subject that would interest him, Mary Ann said, 'I have received from Mr Ferriar a copy of his report on the mill-workers' houses.'

Rathbone's face at once became grim. 'So, you've read that, have you? I have wronged you, Mrs Morland, and I apologise.'

'My father would not think it an insult for you to consider me entirely frivolous,' Mary Ann said. 'I'm afraid he took the report away from me and destroyed it. He did not think it a proper concern of mine.'

'I tell you, it will be everyone's concern when we have another outbreak of fever,' said Rathbone harshly. 'You remember how they panicked when it happened in '96?'

'I wasn't here then,' she said. 'Do you really think it is likely?'

'I do. I've seen the same sort of thing in India and Turkey and North Africa, and for the same reasons — overcrowding, open sewers, poor ventilation, and no washing water. Where these conditions subsist, the evil humours collect, and breed fever. Mrs Morland' — he sat forward, clasping his hands between his knees and fixing her with his burning eyes — 'may I ask for your help in bringing this state of affairs to the notice of those who can do something to remedy it? A woman of your standing could do much to influence thought.'

Mary Ann felt a little faint under such a penetrating gaze. 'You may count on me for anything of which I am capable, but —'

'But your father would not approve.'

'I am a married woman. I am not in my father's governance.'

'Spoken like a woman of spirit,' he smiled. 'And now, I see I have exceeded the polite quarter-hour of convention, and had better take my leave lest I offend propriety.'

You have been doing that all along, Mary Ann thought, but rose and rang the bell without comment. She held out her hand automatically, and Rathbone, towering over her, took it and held it, looking down at her in a way that would have struck Mr Adubon with deepest envy.

'Goodbye, Mrs Morland,' he said. She heard the servant open the door behind him, but still he held her hand.

'Goodbye,' she said faintly, and then, remembering, 'Oh, but I have a letter for you from Father Aislaby. It quite slipped my mind.'

'Keep it for me,' he said. 'It will give me an excuse to call again.'

She wanted to say, you need no excuse, but aware of the listening servant, she drew back her hand firmly, and said formally, 'It was kind of you to call, Father.' And as if he perfectly understood all she had been thinking, he only smiled and left her.

Edward and Chetwyn strolled arm in arm along the Long Walk, kept under observation by two of the swans drifting on the moat with the utmost casualness, as if they just happened to be going the same way. A magnificent full moon rode high in a clear sky, pouring down such intense light that one almost expected it to burn, like sunlight. The moat, where it turned the corner of the house, was a sheet of beaten silver, but close to, the water was striped black and silver like birchbark, broken into ripples by the strong movements of the swans' black webs.

Around this side of the house all was peace, with no indication of the revels that were going on within, the silence broken only by the small noises of night. Chetwyn was smoking a cigar, and its fragrance mingled with the warm night smell of damp earth and grass, and the flat, weedy dankness of the moat.

'How many times have we done this, do you think? Escaped from a ball to walk and talk on our own?' Chetwyn said at last.

'We haven't been doing much talking,' Edward observed.

'I was just enjoying the quiet after all that noise in the saloon. What strange things people enjoy — being crushed together in a hot, noisy room, when they might have all this.'

The glowing end of the cigar made a red circle in the air as he gestered towards the gardens.

'If they were all out here, it wouldn't be peaceful,' Edward pointed out. 'Just be thankful not everyone likes the same things.'

'You should be fully occupied with being thankful that Lucy's staying here, so that you can have all your entertainments here instead of at Shawes.'

Edward smiled. 'I do seem to enjoy them so much, don't I? Wouldn't miss a moment of them.'

Chetwyn laughed and pressed his arm. 'I had to drag you away.'

'It is going well, though, isn't it?'

'And you have such a lot to celebrate: the stables finished, and a good harvest of corn safely on its way to the Navy yard! You were right to try for that contract, old fellow. In a year or two, you will be wealthier than me.'

'I don't think so,' Edward said ruefully. 'Any profit I manage to make from the corn, Jamie will find a use for in his building schemes. But at least I have the satisfaction of knowing that I'm helping to keep the navy afloat.'

'You were moved, I'm sure, solely by patriotic motives when you ploughed up your pastures,' Chetwyn agreed solemnly. 'I am almost persuaded to do the same. If only my patriotism were stronger than my sloth.'

Edward laughed. 'I am so glad you're here, Chet! It seems so long since we had any time together.'

'Demands of your growing wealth and my growing family,' Chetwyn said.

Edward looked away towards the moat, where the pen had paused by the bank to smatter the weed with her bill after some fragment of food. 'Is that really all it was?' he asked casually. 'Just being too busy?'

Chetwyn stopped and turned, holding Ned's arms just above the elbow to look into his face. Chetwyn's face was partly shadowed by the moon behind his back, but his voice, to Edward, sounded warm and amused. 'Of course it was, my dear. What else? Out with it, Ned, what have you been worrying about?'

'Nothing. Nothing at all,' he said feebly. Chetwyn waited

insistently. 'I only wondered if, perhaps — if everything was all right between us?' he finished hesitantly.

Chetwyn laughed, and turned to resume their stroll, drawing Edward's arm through his again. 'What could possibly change?' he said. 'We have been friends almost all our lives, haven't we?'

'Yes,' Edward said. 'It's silly of me to think —'

'It is,' Chetwyn said firmly.

'Only you have seemed different recently. I mean, for instance, you never used to care about your children like this —'

'They weren't very interesting before. Now they're growing up. You don't see them as rivals for my affection, do you? That would be very silly indeed. They're your own nephew and nieces. I want to share them with you. Roland, for instance — don't you think it's time we taught him some of the refinements of horsemanship?'

'What, you and I?' Edward asked, pleased. 'Won't Lucy mind?'

'Just us,' Chetwyn smiled. 'Lucy's far too worried about international affairs to have time for such purely domestic matters. The trouble is, what could we teach him on? His legs are too short for any of the horses. I suppose we might borrow Fanny's pony, though.'

Edward laughed. 'That is the silliest thing either of us has said tonight.'

Very early on the morning after the ball, when the servants might properly have supposed that their masters and mistresses would remain decently abed until noon, Parslow and James's groom Durban were standing in the courtyard, enjoying the air and chatting. Durban had got his pipe drawing nicely, and Parslow, whose hands never liked to be idle, was weaving a hay wisp for strapping his horses. Hens were croodling and fluffing in the sunshine, sparrows perched in fat rows along the guttering, and the yard dog had just rolled over on to his back and was scratching an itch on his haunches deliciously against the ground, tongue lolling and legs waving in the most foolish manner.

'My father had a dog once ...' Parslow began, when

Durban, who was looking towards the house over his shoulder, nudged him, and Parslow turned his head to see Lucy coming out through the buttery door, the great door being still closed and bolted. 'Well, dang me,' he said mildly.

'Dancing until all hours, too,' Durban answered the spirit of the comment. 'What's to do, Mr Parslow?'

'Dressed for riding,' Parslow murmured without moving his lips. She looked very pale, and rather grim about the mouth, but that might be the effect of a late night. 'You best scarper.'

But Lucy, her long skirt folded over her arm, walked briskly, and her eye encompassed both men as she said, 'Good morning.'

'Morning, my lady,' Parslow said, and Durban ducked his head in greeting.

'I wish to go riding, Parslow, and you are to accompany me. What is there here for me to ride?'

Parslow and Durban exchanged a perplexed glance. 'Well, my lady, the good horses are all out, or up at Twelvetrees,' said Parslow.

'We could fetch you one down in an hour or so, my lady,' Durban offered. 'Have it groomed and tacked up for after breakfast.'

'No, I must go now,' Lucy said firmly. 'Surely you have some horse that will carry a sidesaddle?'

'There's Missy, the dun mare, my lady, that Mrs Morland rides sometimes.' Durban said doubtfully. 'She's always kept up, because she doesn't do well at grass. Her paces aren't so very good, but —'

'Her ladyship, ride a horse with hocks like that?' Parslow protested, shocked.

'Never mind that now,' Lucy said impatiently. 'Saddle her up at once will you, and something for yourself, Parslow.'

Parslow exchanged a speaking glance with Durban, and the two men went into the stables, while Lucy waited, biting her lip and slapping her crop restlessly against her leg. In a few minutes the horses came clopping and blinking out into the yard. Parslow threw his mistress up and helped her drape her skirt, and then he mounted the bay Durban was holding for him and they were off. All this time Lucy did not speak, not even to tell Parslow their destination, but when they came up to the Thirsk road just past Overton, she did not seem surprised when he pointed out to her the best way to go across country.

They stopped when they reached Huby to breathe the horses, and to let them drink at the little stream that ran beside the village street. Parslow jumped down and went to the mare's head, and holding both horses, glanced up covertly at Lucy's face. It was pale and set. He saw that she had made up her mind to do something she did not much want to do, but he could not yet guess what it was.

At last she sighed and, catching his eye, said, 'You know where we're going, I suppose?'

'Yes, my lady.'

'You always know everything. I've thought and thought about it. It never occurred to me to go back, and yet the Captain was surprised that I hadn't. Do you think I should have gone before?'

Parslow knew her too well to say 'It isn't for me to say, my lady' — the standard servant's answer to the unanswerable question. 'There was no need to go, my lady,' was what he said. 'The arrangements were all made.'

She twisted the mare's mane between her fingers. 'I don't want to go now. I wonder why? I would sooner run away. But I need to find out something.' She gave him a crooked smile. 'Idle curiosity, you see.' She gathered up the reins with a restless movement. 'Let's get on.'

The little house looked even smaller than she had remembered; the front garden behind the white paling fence was full of the tarnished flowers of August. The bedroom windows were open to air the rooms, and the curtains within hung motionless in the still, warm air.

Parslow came to jump her down. 'I'll tie them up in the shade, over there, my lady, where there's a little bit of grass. I dare say they'll give me a bucket of water for them in the kitchen.'

Lucy knew he was talking to comfort her. I must look nervous, she thought. She stood undecided as he walked the horses away to the big chestnut tree at the end of the garden wall, and then walked up to the door of the house, and knocked on it with the head of her riding crop.

The door was opened by Stephen, whose self-control was so magnificent that he blinked only once to betray his surprise before stepping back to invite her in, saying, 'I'm afraid the mistress is not at home, my lady. She and Miss have gone for a ride in the carriage. She ought to be back before very long, though.' He took her crop and gloves. 'Would you care to wait, my lady? Can I get you something?'

'Nothing, thank you. Only some water for my horses.'

'I'll see to it, my lady. And a glass of lemonade for you?'

She licked her dry lips. 'Yes, lemonade. Thank you. Where is everyone else?'

'Madame Chouflon is in her room, my lady. It's one of her bad days, and she hasn't been down yet. I could tell her you're here —'

'No, don't disturb her. And the others?'

'Marie has gone to visit a friend, and the children are in the garden, my lady.'

'I'll go out, then, and wait for your mistress there,' Lucy said. Stephen bowed and escorted her to the back door, and she stepped out into the heat and fragrance of the walled garden.

The children were sitting on the warm, flaking red brick of the path, between the lavender bushes, oblivious of the full sunshine. Sophie was in a white muslin frock and a wide straw hat, which looked comfortable and cool, and her thick, dark hair had been braided into a long plait at the back to keep it out of her way. She was playing fivestones with great concentration, explaining every movement in great detail to her companion.

Lucy stood still just outside the door. The baby was not quite two, a chubby child, made stouter in appearance by the bundling of baby clothes under his faded blue frock. He had a white linen sun-hat over his silky brown hair, and he was sucking the forefinger of one hand while using the other to interfere with Sophie's game by picking up the stones out of turn. Sophie retrieved them with enormous patience, as absorbed in teaching the baby as in playing herself.

She looked up as she felt Lucy's eyes on her, and jumped up to make an automatic curtsey, but she was clearly puzzled by the visitor.

'Don't you remember me, Sophie? Come, it's not so very

197

long ago that I was here.'

Sophie's face cleared, and she smiled. 'Oh yes, of course, madame, I remember. Have you come to see Maman? She isn't here.' A look of consternation crossed her face. 'You haven't come to take Thomas away?'

The baby, hearing his name, looked up, and Lucy found herself regarded by a pair of solemn brown eyes underneath fine, delicate eyebrows whose exact shape and texture she knew with such intimacy that it made her feel faint. Oh, I was right not to come before, she thought, staring and staring to seek out what exactly it was that was Weston in that face. It was a likeness so vivid, so haunting, that she felt it must reside in some particular feature, and yet when she tried to pin it down, it became elusive. It was as if Weston himself were there, looking at her through a veil that both obscured and revealed him.

'No,' she managed to say at last. 'No, I haven't come to take him away.' She dragged her eyes from Thomas to look at Sophie. 'Would you mind so much if I had?'

'Well, I would,' Sophie said politely but firmly. 'Because you didn't really want him, did you, and I look after him now, and Maman said that he wouldn't have to go away until he was quite grown up. Except,' she added with scrupulous fairness, 'perhaps to visit.'

Lucy had nothing to say to this. She wished they would not look at her so with their bright eyes. 'Shew me what you're playing,' she said, and Sophie obliged. Lucy sat nearby and watched, and soon both children had forgotten her presence. Stephen brought out her lemonade, and she sipped it, and felt guilty that she had not brought anything, presents for the children, something for the boy — a dress or a pair of shoes or something — a gift for Héloïse.

She felt very strange. It was too hot here in the garden. The air was too heavy with fragrance, and the boy's likeness to Weston was confusing, making her feel as though she were in the grip of a dream. She stood up, swaying a little, and said, 'I have to go,' and her voice sounded strange too in the enclosed space. And then there were sounds from behind her, and Héloïse came running from the house with exclamations of surprise and pleasure.

'Lucy! How lovely to see you! But why didn't you let me know you were coming, then I should not have gone out.'

'I came on impulse — I can't stay,' Lucy said.

Héloïse looked concerned. 'But how pale you are! You have been sitting in the sun, it is too hot for you. Come at once into the house, cousin Lucy. Here, take my arm.'

Héloïse helped her inside. The darkness after the bright sunlight made her dizzy, and for a while she could not see properly. Everything was red and black, and faces came and went indistinctly. A tall girl with red hair pinned up and a grown-up gown — could that really be Mathilde? A cold, wet nose pressed helpfully into the palm of her hand was Kithra, instantly banished, with the children, out into the garden again. Héloïse hung over her affectionately, bathed her temples with lavender water, and made her sip more lemonade, and her vision cleared to find that they were alone together in the peace of the parlour, dim and cool with the sun on the other side of the house.

'Sorry,' Lucy said when she could speak. 'Foolish of me. I'm not usually so missish.'

'It is hardly any wonder,' Héloïse said cheerfully, 'for Parslow tells me you had little sleep, and no breakfast at all. And then since you go into a hot garden after a long ride and sit in the sun, it must mean you really wanted to faint away. But now you have done it, will you let me have some food brought for you?'

'I don't want to eat anything.'

'Ah, I understand, you wish to faint again,' Héloïse said kindly.

Lucy couldn't help smiling. 'I feel sick,' she explained.

'That is because you have got too hungry. *Attendez un instant,* I will fetch you something that you will like.' She was back in a few moments with a plate on which rested some freshly-baked madeleines, pale golden and fragrant, and a sprig of grapes with the bloom still on them. 'There, such little things you may eat without fear. The grapes are from my own vine, a great wonder to me, for I never thought one could grow such fruit so far north, or in England at all.'

Lucy nibbled tentatively, and soon had cleared the plate, and felt better for it. Héloïse watched her, her enormous dark

199

eyes filled with sympathy. 'So, cousin Lucy, have I cared for him well?'

Lucy put down the plate. 'You must think me careless — heartless — not to have come before, or to have written more often. I'm not ungrateful, truly I'm not.'

'I know it,' said Héloïse easily. 'Don't worry. I understand very well what you must feel.'

Lucy sighed. 'Yes, I think perhaps of all people you may.'

'Then, why suddenly today?' Héloïse asked.

Lucy frowned, and tried to piece it together. 'I saw Weston a few months ago, just for a little while, and he asked about the boy. I could see that for him, he was real and important, even though he had never seen him. I felt — I felt that there was something I ought to be feeling, but wasn't. I want to share everything of his, Héloïse. I want to understand.'

Héloïse looked down at the plate, decorated with grape pips, and reached out with a finger to push three of them apart from the others in a triangle. 'Three is the number of the Trinity. A very special number, complete, eternal. Father, Son and Holy Ghost. Man, woman and child. It is everything, and enough.'

'I never thought of it before,' Lucy said, 'but just recently I have begun to wonder if it might not be enough, even for me. The baby looks so like him, Héloïse! How can that be? I can't see why he does, but he does.' Héloïse smiled encouragingly. 'Only,' Lucy went on, a little pleadingly, 'if one had all that, there would be so much to lose. I keep thinking about you and James, and Sophie. I'm not strong like you. I don't think I could bear it. It's safer without anything to love very much.'

There was silence between them for a while, and then Héloïse said, 'One can only do one's best. It is no use to try to bend yourself out of your nature.'

Lucy looked up with a faint smile. 'Nature can change,' she said. 'Perhaps it ought to.' Héloïse said nothing. 'I had better go. No-one knows where I am.'

'Won't you stay to dinner?'

'No, I had better get back. I have intruded on you long enough.'

Héloïse smiled. 'Ah, you cannot imagine how my heart began to beat when I saw horses tied up outside my house.'

'Oh, I'm sorry. I didn't think . . .' Lucy was contrite.

'No, I am teasing. I was very glad to see you. I only wish you might stay longer.'

'Come and see me in London,' Lucy said impulsively, holding out her hand. 'Next year, in the Season. I'm sure you would like a little Town gaiety for a change.'

Héloïse took the hand. 'I should like it very much.'

'Good, then it's settled. And now I really must go. Where is Parslow?'

'In the kitchen with Barnard,' Héloïse said with an impish grin. 'He has a great deal more sense than you, cousin: he has eaten salmon in egg-sauce, half a cold chicken, and most of a plum pie, while you were refusing all but grapes.'

Lucy rode back to Morland Place as silently as she had made the journey out, but Parslow could see by her face that her mood was very different. In fact she was trying, as she rode, to compose in her head a letter to Weston, telling him about her visit to Coxwold, and how Thomas had looked, and what she had felt. It seemed suddenly very important that she should tell him, though she hardly knew how to go about it.

At various moments during the next few days, whenever she was at leisure and alone, she tried to write the letter; but though she stared and stared at the paper, and chewed the end of the pen until her mouth was full of damp shreds of feather, it would not come out as anything other than a factual account of having ridden over to Coxwold, seen the boy, and remarked that he was stout and well. The underlying thoughts remained elusive, dislimned as soon as the ink touched the paper, leaving her feeling restless and unhappy.

She was very glad when, a few days later, something happened which gave her an excuse for running away from a situation grown too complicated. An express came from Captain Haworth announcing his arrival in Portsmouth, and requesting that Hippolyta might join him and Africa for the few weeks that he would be on shore. Lucy was prompt in offering to take her niece in her chaise, and thus save every-

201

one the trouble of arranging for her to be sent with a servant by the mail or stage.

'And will you come back afterwards?' Edward wanted to know.

Lucy caught her husband's eye, but he merely lifted an eyebrow and gave her an amused and almost sympathetic look.

'No, I don't think so,' she said.

On the 20 August, while Lucy was travelling back to Portsmouth, Weston was walking the quarterdeck of the *Nemesis*, cruising up and down outside Cadiz with the rest of Collingwood's small squadron, keeping watch on the nine or ten Spanish battleships within. Cadiz was an unhappy town, short of supplies of all sorts, riddled with fever, and frustrated by the endless blockade. The blockaders were only a little better off. They had all been at sea for an inordinate length of time, and this was a comfortless station, with no fresh food to be had, except the grapes the neutral Portuguese sometimes brought out to them; but at least they were in good health, and the weather was fine, and the seas moderate, which made for easy sailing.

The *Nemesis* was not the only frigate on the station now: she had been joined by the *Euryalus*, Captain Henry Blackwood, and the two of them kept the inshore station together. As Weston turned at the end of his walk, his eyes automatically made the sweep of the horizon, marking the position of the ships in sight. There was *Dreadnought*, the flagship, heavily fouled and overdue for docking, but sailing like a machine with her highly-trained crew, and beyond her the elegant lines of Captain King's *Achille*, French prize of the American war. The other seventy-four was farther out, almost hull-down from Weston's viewpoint, while to leeward wallowed the bomb-vessel, unweatherly and unhandy with her stumpy mainmast stepped far back to make room for the mortars amidships.

Jeffrey came picking his way delicately along the deckboards, weaving sideways to brush Weston's leg as he passed, making for his favourite position inside a coil of rope by the mizzenmast, warm from the sun. The cool summer seemed to be giving way to a pleasantly sunny autumn. Weston reached the taffrail and paused, noted the hand reaching out for the rope on the ship's bell to ring six bells, and turned again, thinking about his dinner. Bates had bought a couple of lobsters from a friendly Portuguese fishing-boat they had encountered yesterday, which would make a pleasant change from ration-pork.

It was at that moment when, almost simultaneously, flags began racing up *Achille*'s halliards, and the lookout at the foretopmast yelled 'Sail ho! Deck, there, sails on the port bow.' A pause, and then, frantically, 'Dozens of 'em! Cap'n, sir, it's the Combined!'

Achille's signal confirmed it: thirty-six French and Spanish ships, led by Villeneuve's *Bucentaure*, came bearing down on the English squadron of three of the line, two frigates, and a bomb. Collingwood's response was swift. This was not a time for false heroics. He ordered his ships to tack towards Gibraltar, out of the combined fleet's path.

It was a nerveracking moment, prolonged when it became evident that Villeneuve had ordered sixteen of his ships of the line to pursue and, presumably, destroy them. It would have been easy enough for Collingwood's squadron simply to flee through the Straits to safety, but this was the combined fleet which had been loose on the high seas for over six months, and to lose sight of it now would be a serious error. The Admiral kept just out of gunshot, tacking whenever the enemy tacked, drawing them all the time nearer to Gibraltar where there would be reinforcements; and when, finally, the enemy tired of the game and turned for Cadiz, the English squadron followed them, and watched them in.

The combined fleet filled the harbour, their topmasts, when the sails were furled, thick as winter trees in a forest. Collingwood sent for the two frigate captains on board the *Dreadnought*, and they were conducted into his day-cabin, where he sat at his desk writing. Bounce was lying at his feet under the desk, and the little dog jumped up and came politely to meet Blackwood and Weston as they entered.

Collingwood wasted no time. 'Well, gentlemen, we may have a rattling day of it soon! I've always said that superiority of numbers dulls the spirit, but I'd as lief have some help to keep the Combined in its place, so I'm sending you two gentlemen off with the news. Blackwood, you are to go straight to England with all possible speed. Do not stop for anything. Your orders will be ready in a few moments, as soon as my secretary has finished copying them.'

'Aye aye, sir,' said Blackwood, unable to repress a grin of excitement.

Collingwood turned to Weston. 'And you, Captain, are to take despatches, first to Admiral Calder at the Ferrol, who I hope will send me some ships, and then to Ushant, to Admiral Cornwallis. I shall ask you to wait for the squadron's letters, too, and if Sir William has no other plans for you, you may take them to England before returning to me.'

'I understand, sir,' said Weston.

'I should like to take the opportunity of penning a few lines to my wife,' Collingwood went on. 'Will you both excuse me? I shall not detain you long. Smith, a glass of madeira for these gentlemen while they wait.'

Weston and Blackwood withdrew to the other side of the great cabin, and Collingwood's servant brought the decanter and glasses. 'What price glory, eh?' Blackwood murmured. 'I give you a toast, Weston — to the crushing of the Combined — but not until after we've got back!'

'How will the old man keep 'em in until reinforcements arrive?' Weston pondered.

'The usual trick, I suppose,' said Blackwood. 'Signalling to an imaginary fleet over the horizon. It may do to keep the timid French in harbour for a few days.'

'They will need to refit, anyway, after so long at sea,' Weston said, 'and there being no supplies will delay them.'

Blackwood nodded. 'All the same, those Spanish captains are as proud as Lucifer. They'll want to fight, and if Ville-neuve don't overrule 'em, Old Cuddy may have to thrash 'em single-handed.'

Weston glanced across at his admiral's white head, bent over the letter he was scribbling to his wife and daughters unimaginably far away amongst the ancient swards and trees of his estate in green-and-grey Northumberland.

'Well, he's the man to do it,' he said affectionately.

Chapter Eleven

Lucy and Captain Haworth were strolling along the ramparts at Portsmouth on the afternoon of 2 September, while Polly and Africa ran on ahead, the light sea-breeze tugging at the ribbons of their bonnets. The girls, after an initial period of reserve, had become as friendly as their very different natures would allow, and in lieu of any better pursuit they were quite willing to talk and play with each other.

Lucy had remained in Portsmouth to enjoy Haworth's company, rather than return to Plymouth to fret in solitude. She found her brother-in-law a very soothing companion, sensible, easy to talk to, understanding. She had always liked him, from the first time Hannibal Harvey had introduced him to Mary and her in Bath, and over the past ten days she had come to feel very comfortable with him.

A woman in a bonnet and shawl coming towards them smiled at the children, and then gave a sympathetic nod to Lucy and Haworth as they strolled by arm-in-arm.

'She thinks we're all one family,' Lucy said when she had passed. 'I wonder how many other people see us together and think you and I are wed?'

'You've been all the mother Polly has ever had,' Haworth observed, 'and done wonderfully well with her, too. I'm grateful to you. She is very much a lady, even at so young an age.'

Lucy shrugged. 'There's nothing to thank me for. Trotton looks after her manners and her education. In any case, she doesn't need much teaching. She was always like that, even as a baby. Chetwyn used to call her the Infant Alderman, because she was always so solemn and proper.' She sighed. 'I don't think I should make a very good mother if I had to bring up my children myself.'

Haworth eyed her shrewdly. 'Should you like the opportunity?'

For a moment Lucy was tempted to tell him everything that was in her mind, but it was all too complicated, and she evaded the intimacy. 'I should not, indeed!' she said quickly, with a light laugh. 'I've always said sheep and horses had much more interesting young.'

They paused and turned towards the sea, calm in the warm afternoon sunshine. 'I shall be sorry when you have to go back to sea,' she said after a moment.

'So shall I,' Haworth said. 'I could quite happily spend the rest of my life like this, walking in the sunshine with you on my arm, watching my girls running about, healthy and happy.'

'But don't you long to be back in the thick of it?'

'No, not any more. Two years of blockade service have quite taken away my appetite: I've no relish for another winter off Ushant. But one must go where duty calls. As long as the threat to England remains, none of us sailors can rest easy.'

Lucy looked at him affectionately. There was nothing heroic or dashing in his appearance, and he spoke so quietly and matter-of-factly about duty, and yet it was on him, and others like him, that the safety of the country depended. They were the real — and the unsung — heroes.

'Will you have supper with me tonight at the Golden Lion, Captain Haworth?' she asked abruptly. 'I have a fancy to broach a bottle of champagne, and one cannot drink champagne alone.'

He smiled at her quizzically. 'Is there something to celebrate?'

She tucked her hand under his arm and turned him to walk on after the children. 'Nothing I could tell you about.'

It was while they were lingering over the remains of the elegant supper Lucy had ordered in his honour, that a commotion was heard downstairs, and not longer afterwards there was a knocking on the door. Dipton opened it to reveal the landlord, Tully, his wife, one of the tapsters, and some assorted maids, all jostling one another in a state of great excitement.

'News, m'lady, Captain!' Tully cried out. 'Wonderful news! We just heard it from a post-boy what knows one of our lads, m'lady, and I came straight up to tell you, knowing you'd want to be the first to know. The Combined is found! They're in Cadiz, all right and tight, and our Admiral Collingwood sitting on 'em like a cork in a bottle to stop 'em coming out again.'

'Cadiz?' cried Lucy, and Haworth caught her eye sympathetically.

'Praise be to God!' Mrs Tully said fervently. 'Now we can sleep safe in our beds again!' Everyone began talking at once, and Lucy had to raise her voice to be heard.

'Who brought the news from Cadiz? What ship was it?'

'The *Euryalus*, m'lady, and Cap'n Blackwood's posted off to London as fast as he can go to tell Their Lordships. Now they'll have to send Nelson, won't they, m'lady, and he'll trounce 'em, like what that Calder should have done before, the villain.'

'Hanging's too good for that one,' Mrs Tully opined.

'It's excellent news, Tully,' Haworth said, seeing that Lucy could not speak. 'It calls for celebration. Here's a drink for yourself and your good wife. Confusion to the French!'

'Amen to that, sir!' said Tully, pocketing the coin dextrously.

When they were alone again, Lucy said, 'What does it mean, Haworth? Will this be an end to it?'

Haworth frowned. 'It's hard to say. Of course, it is wonderful news that the combined fleet has been found at last, and no doubt Barham will order ships there at once to reinforce the blockade. But whether they will come out and fight is another matter. They've never shewn themselves particularly courageous before, and in this case, they may well just stay put and try to outlast us. The blockade costs us dear, and another winter of it may stretch our resources too thin.'

'That's how it seemed to me,' Lucy said. 'I suppose this means you will be ordered back to sea very soon?'

'As soon as *Cetus* is out of dock, I imagine. Well, at least I shall have the advantage this time of knowing where I'm likely to be sent.'

'I can't think why Collingwood didn't send *Nemesis* with the news,' she complained. 'She's the faster frigate.'

'I expect he had other urgent despatches,' Haworth said comfortingly. 'Cheer up, Lucy! Let's drink a toast to the good news, at any rate, and hope that the French are fools enough to come out again and give us battle.'

The thoughts of battle, however, seemed to bring Lucy little comfort.

The *Nemesis* made Portsmouth only a week after *Euryalus*, by which time the First Lord, making use of the new system of telegraphs along the south coast, had ordered the port admirals of both Portsmouth and Plymouth to make ready all the ships they could to send to Cadiz. Weston was told to renew his ship's stores, and to hold himself in readiness to sail whenever his orders should arrive.

He had expected to have to send word to Plymouth for Lucy, but an idler met him outside the port admiral's office to tell him that her la'ship was waiting for him at the dockyard gates. Weston patted his pockets for a shilling.

'Go back to her ladyship and give her my compliments. Say that I must attend first to my ship, but that I hope to dine with her. Have you got that?'

'Aye aye, Cap'n,' the man grinned, pocketing the shilling, where it nestled against the half-crown Lucy had given him to take her message and bring back the captain or a reply. 'Her la'ship's staying at the Golden Lion, Cap'n,' he offered, feeling a certain obligation to give value for money.

Dinner was not uppermost in Weston's mind when at last he took Lucy in his arms in the familiar parlour at the Golden Lion.

'How did you know I was coming?' he asked as soon as he could speak.

'Blackwood told me,' Lucy said breathlessly. Her arms were round his neck, and her fingers were hooked over his coat-collar as if to ensure he was not snatched away from her again. 'When he came back from London, he called on me to tell me that you would be bringing the letters in from the fleet.'

'Obliging of him. And how did you come to be here and not in Plymouth?'

Lucy told him about Haworth and the girls.

'So I've a rival now, have I?' he said, kissing her eyes and nose and revelling in the sweet smell of her which owed nothing to salt or tar.

'Don't be silly,' Lucy said. 'How long can you stay?'

'How I wish that need not always be the first question! A few days, at least, while we revictual. I have to hold myself ready to sail, but I don't know when my orders will arrive. It's possible they may keep me here until the new squadron is ready to sail, or they may send me on ahead.'

'A few days,' Lucy said happily. 'That's more than I expected, after last time.'

'There's not so much urgency about it, now that we know where the Combined is.'

'But might they not come out? They say there's plague in Cadiz.'

'Calder and his fleet will be there by now — I passed them heading south when I was on my way to report — and Cornwallis will have sent more ships. I don't think there is any likelihood that Villeneuve will be so foolish as to come out and risk battle against those odds.'

'Then, it's the blockade again?'

Weston sighed, and pulled her against him for comfort. 'I'm afraid so. Another winter like the last, and when will it end? Poor Colingwood is worn out with it. His man Smith told my man Bates that he means to haul down his flag and go ashore for good next spring, and if any man deserves it, he does. Cornwallis and Nelson have both had spells of shore leave to brace them up, but Collingwood hasn't set foot ashore since the war began.'

He was silent a while, resting the point of his chin on the top of Lucy's head. Then he said, more cheerfully, 'But at least we can be glad that the threat of invasion is finally over. The Boulogne camp is broken, the troops are being marched away, and Boney himself has trotted off to sniff at another rabbit-hole.'

'And we are to have dinner together,' Lucy said, returning to her own particular source of pleasure, 'and I have spent most of the day thinking of all the things you would like best to eat. And I have invited Haworth to eat his mutton with us —'

'Lucy, you haven't!' Weston cried, his face a mask of comic dismay.

'— tomorrow!' she concluded, laughing. All the confusion of the past weeks seemed no more than a dream. He was here, he was real, flesh, blood and bone, and to be near him, to talk and eat and sleep with him, was the only thing that mattered.

He slept late the next morning, after a broken night, for he could not at once get used to the leaden stillness of the bed after the airy swooping of his cot on board the *Nemesis*. The silence troubled him too, as it always did for a night or two, and he had dozed and woken every half hour, listening subconsciously for the ship's bell, or the swift rush of feet as the watch was changed.

But waking was a delight: waking to a warm bed, clean, dry sheets, and Lucy beside him, fragrant and sleep-hot like baking bread. He touched her, and, still half asleep, she curled with instant response into his arms, her shape fitting down into the contours of his body as though she had been moulded in them. She made a little langorous sound of content, and nudged her face into his neck so that her tousled hay-coloured curls tickled his cheek, and he folded his arms around her, filled with such a huge upsurge of love that he could only lie still and endure it.

'What is it?' she said at last, and he opened his eyes to see that she was looking up at him, still half drugged with sleep, from under her furry eyelashes.

For answer, he kissed her, and she unfolded like a flower in sunlight, and they made love with such a mixture of new passion and old accustomedness, that when it came to the end he felt as if his soul were being dragged out of him by the soft, inexorable pull of love.

Afterwards they lay still for a while, listening to each other's breathing, without any need to talk. Then he said, 'I've been thinking, my darling, that perhaps the time has come for me to leave the service.'

'Hmm?'

'Perhaps in the spring, like the admiral. Haul down my pennant. What do you think?'

She was a long time answering, and her voice came at last hesitantly. 'What would you do then?'

210

'Be with you, of course,' he said.

She made no reply, and he pushed himself up on to his elbow to look down at her. She met his gaze warily, and he smiled at her, traced the contour of her lips with one finger. 'What is it, my Lucy? Doesn't the idea please you? Do you want to keep me as a once-a-year lover?'

Her eyes were suddenly bright, and she pulled away from him to rub them with a knuckle, defensively, like a child. 'What has made you suddenly change your mind?' she asked from behind her hand.

'Oh, it isn't sudden. I've been thinking about it all this year, but while there seemed to be a crisis looming, it was hard to see beyond it. But now the invasion threat is over, and it seems that there will be nothing more to come in the future than endless blockade duty, I begin to feel my presence is not so essential on the high seas. I might do as much while staying ashore.'

'Then it's not just for me?'

He looked at her curiously. 'I can't tell from your voice whether you want me to say it is or it isn't.' He took her masking hand and planted a kiss on it, and put it down out of the way. 'The truth is, that I can't separate the motives which concern you from those that don't, because you are woven into every aspect of my life. I can only say that I have had enough, that I want to come home and be with you, if you'll have me.'

She was a long time answering, but he could see it was not from reluctance, but because she was thinking out something difficult. At last she said, 'I went to see him while I was in Yorkshire. The baby, I mean.' Her eyes came to meet his. 'You were angry that I hadn't been before.'

'No, not angry,' he said, stroking her cheek. 'You were right not to go, given the circumstances. I shouldn't have said anything.'

'You didn't,' she said in fairness. 'I went of my own accord.'

'And?' he prompted, but she seemed to have run out of words, only looked at him as a cat looks at a door, willing it to open. 'Shall I leave the service, Mr Proom?'

'That must be for you to decide,' she said gruffly, but he saw from her eyes that it was the right door.

'It's settled then,' he said. 'I shall see out this one last winter, and then come ashore for good, and if your husband won't let us be, we'll go somewhere where we'll be out of reach, and be poor and happy together. Or rich and happy — I'm not particular which.'

'Rich would be better,' said Lucy, the practical. 'Then we could keep some horses.'

He laughed and took her in his arms again. 'Rich, then,' he said, 'Whatever you say.'

They had four days. On the evening of the 11th Haworth came to visit, and gave them the dockyard gossip, which the lovers had been too absorbed in each other to gather.

'They're sending Nelson,' he said. 'The whole town's talking about it. I never knew so much excitement! The people seem to think he's a saint or a saviour or something of the sort: they believe that he's only to appear outside Cadiz and the enemy's as good as defeated. Even Barham's gone completely over. He sent for him and gave him carte blanche — forty ships, and choose his own officers. Nelson told him to choose for himself. Said every officer in the profession was moved by the same spirit, and he couldn't choose wrong.'

'It's true,' Lucy said. 'I like him the better for saying that.'

'*Victory*'s up at Spithead,' Weston mused. 'I suppose they'll give him her?'

'Yes, and he's to take *Royal Sovereign* — she's just had her coppering renewed — and *Agamemnon* and *Defiance* if the dockyard can get 'em ready in time. They were in Calder's squadron, you know. I wonder if he'll be pleased to see 'em back?'

'Poor Calder,' said Lucy. 'The papers have said dreadful things about him.'

'And what of you, Haworth?' asked Weston.

'*Cetus* was warped out today,' he said, betraying a grin. 'I'm promised my orders by tomorrow noon — I'm to sail with Nelson!'

'You sound as though you were looking forward to it,' Lucy frowned. 'I thought you didn't care about going back to sea?'

'All this excitement is infectious,' Haworth admitted. 'I half believe our little admiral will be able to get the French to

212

come out and fight us after all. But I have to ask you, Lucy, if you'll take charge of Polly for me, and arrange for her to be taken back to Wolvercote?'

'She can take her herself,' Weston said, and turned to meet Lucy's eye. 'I won't be here much longer. If they don't send me ahead, they'll send me with Nelson for sure. There'll be no point in your hanging on here any longer, my love.'

'You may come ashore again,' she said stubbornly.

Haworth tactfully examined a picture on the wall, while Weston took Lucy's hand and said, 'I would be happier if you went back to London. I should prefer to know you were sitting out this autumn and winter in comfort, with friends about you. It would be poor sport for you here, alone.'

'But supposing —'

'No. Whatever Haworth hopes, I don't believe there will be a battle. Sending Nelson may cheer up our men, but it won't tempt the French out of port — rather the opposite! Ville-neuve's no fool — he knows he only has to sit tight to wear us down, and sooner or later we'll be driven off station. One more winter of blockade, Lucy, and then we'll be together, I promise you.'

She held his eyes for a moment, and then nodded. 'Very well. I'll take Polly back to Wolvercote, and then go on to London. You'll send for me there, if you should come into port?'

'Of course.' He kissed her hand reassuringly, and then released it. 'Now, Haworth, a glass of wine with you? I'd like your opinion of this claret — I've bought three dozen to send on board to keep me going for the next few months. Port, of course, we can get on the spot, but I warn you there's nothing else to be had off Cadiz, so you'd better order in your cabin stores with a lavish hand before you sail!'

Weston's orders came the next morning, while they were breakfasting. Bates brought them in, and exchanging a pointed look with his master, went through into the bed-chamber to begin packing. Jeffrey, who had been sitting on Weston's lap under the table-cloth, hit the floor with a thump and disappeared under the sofa with his tail in bloom.

213

Lucy put down her knife and watched in silence as Weston broke the seal and unfolded the stiff paper. He read, his face expressionless, and then put the paper aside and took a sip of coffee to moisten his mouth before looking at Lucy.'

'I am to sail at once,' he said, and saw the breath leave her in a rush. 'I have to take the despatch bag to the Brest squadron, and then rejoin the fleet off Cadiz under Nelson's orders.'

Lucy took a piece of toast and buttered it carefully. 'When will you leave?'

He got up and went to the window, flung it up to lean out and test the air. It was raining steadily, but the sky was ragged, and there was a fair amount of wind. Still studying her toast, Lucy heard the sharp clatter of the rain as the gusts blew it sideways to glance off the window pane, and smelled the damp coolness of the air he had let in. There was a rattle and thump as the window was closed again, and Weston came back to sit down opposite her and drain his coffee cup.

'I must leave at once,' he said. 'I shall have to go to the ship and make the final preparations, and we'll sail with the tide. It turns about one o'clock today.'

She nodded, calmly eating toast, her eyes on her plate, making no demands on him, knowing she must not get in his way. He looked at her with enormous love. 'You're the perfect naval wife,' he said. He got up. 'I'd better go and gather my belongings. Don't disturb yourself. Finish your breakfast.'

'I'll drive with you to the dockyard,' she said, and stood up too, and reached for the bell-pull by the chimney, and he caught her halfway and kissed her thoroughly, before hastening into the bedchamber.

The rain was not heavy, but persistent, and they drove to the dockyard in a closed carriage. Everything was glistening and wet, cobbles and slate roofs shining blue with it, trees dripping, gutters gurgling, the horses' ears and loins darkening slowly from gold to auburn as their coats soaked through.

'Don't get out,' Weston said when they pulled up. 'We'll say goodbye in here.'

She lifted warm lips, her hands cupping his face briefly.

'Goodbye, Weston,' she said evenly.

'Goodbye, my darling. Only a few more months.' A swift

hug, and then he jumped out, clapping on his hat and tugging his cloak round him against the rain. Bates followed him with the luggage and Jeffrey's basket, and still Lucy's calm held. Then as they turned to walk away, she was suddenly out of the carriage and calling him in a panic.

'Weston!'

He turned back in time to receive her full against his chest, and her face, turned up into the rain, flinching as the cold drops touched her eyes, was pale with urgency.

'Darling!' he said, half enquiry, half protest.

Her lips worked as she fought with the unfamiliar words. 'I love you,' she whispered.

He grinned triumphantly. She had said it at last, the one thing she had never been able to say — such a small, enormous, important thing. But there was no time for discussion. He kissed her once, hard, on the lips, and then pushed her determinedly back into the coach, and walked away, turning at the gate to wave a hand before they disappeared.

Lucy stayed there long after they had gone, staring at the empty gateway, her mouth still tingling with the imprint of his lips. The front curls of her hair dripped water, soaked even in that brief exposure. It had suddenly seemed vitally important that he should not go away without her telling him; and now that she had told him, everything would be all right. The familiar spreading feeling of emptiness, of not knowing what to do to fill the day, seeped into her; but beneath it, like solid ground under mist, was the knowledge that this would be their last parting, and that when he came back next time, it would be for good.

On the calm, sunny afternoon of 28 September, Nelson's small squadron joined the Cadiz fleet. *Nemesis* was with him, having caught him up just off Lisbon, and Weston was able to witness at first hand how the ordinary sailors loved and believed in the one-armed admiral, for every ship they passed was lined with cheering, waving jacks, who were certain that they could now expect an end to their long vigil on the seas.

There was much to-ing and fro-ing amongst the fleet over the next few days. Collingwood, tired out, and weighted with responsibility, had not encouraged visiting between ships, but Nelson, rested after his shore leave and cheered by the faith the First Lord had shewn in him, was eager to meet and dine with all his officers, to get to know those who had not served with him before, and to discuss tactics. Signals officers were busy all day long, and boats bobbed across the sparkling water between the ships, carrying messages, gossip, gifts, and officers bent on social intercourse.

Going up the side of some of the ships was a hazardous business, for they were hung with cradles and sticky with paint, as eager hands redecorated the hulls to match those which had been serving with Nelson in the Mediterranean fleet: black, with broad yellow bands along the sides at the level of the gunports, but with the port-covers themselves black, so that when they were closed, the ships had a chequerboard appearance. If there were to be a battle, it would be easier in the thick of it to pick out friend from foe if they were all painted alike.

Not all the business of those early days was so genial, for part of Nelson's orders from Barham had been to require Admiral Calder to return to England to face a court-martial for his failure to defeat the combined fleet off Cape Finisterre in July. Haworth and Weston discussed it when they met about the *Victory*, where both had been bidden to dine, while they waited for the arrival of the more senior captains.

'Nelson didn't like above half having to tell Calder,' Weston said. 'He maintains the criticism is all a lot of nonsense.'

'Well, so it is,' Haworth replied, leaning on the taffrail on the weather side of the quarterdeck and watching the approach of another captain's barge. 'How can the laymen of the newspapers know whether he did everything he could or not?'

'Harvey of the *Agamemnon* and Durham of the *Defiance* evidently think he didn't,' Weston observed. 'They've refused to go back to England with him to give evidence.'

'Yes, but Durham's got a grudge against Calder, for not giving him the credit in his report for being the first to spot the Combined. I can't believe it will come to anything.'

Weston shook his head. 'Guilty or innocent, I don't

216

suppose Calder's career will ever recover. But Nelson's done his best for him, at any rate. The Admiralty ordered him to send Calder home in *Dreadnought*, so that she could be docked. You know she's badly overdue. But Blackwood told me this morning that Nelson said it would look like a condemnation to part Calder from his own ship, so he's sending him home in the *Prince of Wales* after all.'

'And Collingwood keeps poor old *Dreadnought*?'

Weston grinned. 'I've heard Nelson's going to ask Collingwood to transfer his flag to the *Royal Sovereign*. I wish him joy of it! Coll won't want to give up his crew, after he's spent years training 'em to the peak of perfection, even for the fastest of the three-deckers.'

'The joys of command, eh, Weston?' Haworth laughed. 'Who'd be an admiral?'

'Not me, at all events. Oh, look, you see who's over there? It's Digby of the *Africa*! You'll be able to ask him how she sails, now she's been rebuilt. Aren't you green with jealousy, Haworth, seeing the man who's run off with your girl?'

'Digby's a very good sort of fellow,' Haworth said serenely. 'I'm sure she couldn't be in better hands. And how could I be jealous, since I've got the best seventy-four in the service?'

'Fighting talk from a fighting captain,' Weston remarked. 'Ah, here's Scott with that whipper-in look in his eye. I think we're being summoned. Nelson gives famous dinners, I'm told.'

'He does, and it isn't only the excellence of his cook, either. You wait and see.'

'Gentlemen,' said Nelson, and waited for the talk to die down. The candlelight glowed on the snowy linen, the shining silver and sparkling crystal, the tawny-gold and blood-red of port and brandy, the brown faces and bleached hair of the officers around the long table. Glasses were set down, hands came to rest, and all eyes turned attentively to the small, shock-headed, green-patch-eyed admiral at the head of the table.

'Gentlemen, the enemy are still in port. I had hoped that famine or plague or even courage might make them come forth, but there they sit, forty sail of them, and we can't get at

217

them.' A growl went round the table in response to the words. 'Something must be done immediately to provoke or lure them into a battle, before the winter gales set in. Once they are out, gentlemen, I think we all know what we have to do.'

He looked around the table, gathering the nods from these firm-faced, responsible men. Here was the difference, Haworth thought, between the English fleet and the French: every captain here could be, and was, trusted to act on his own initiative. But the Corsican general expected his orders, impossible or not, to be obeyed to the letter, and woe betide even the admiral who adapted them to circumstance.

'It is not merely a splendid victory our country wants — honourable to the parties concerned but otherwise useless,' Nelson went on. 'It is the complete annihilation of the enemy fleet, so that Bonaparte can never again threaten our shores.'

A murmur of agreement and some tapping of knives against glasses.

'I am able to tell you all that intelligence has reached me, from our informants in Paris, that Boney has sent new orders to our friend Villeneuve. Since the invasion of England has had to be cancelled for the moment' — laughter rippled round the table — 'it seems he has ordered the combined fleet to sail for the Mediterranean and land reinforcements at Naples. I propose therefore to withdraw the fleet to a distance of fifty miles to the west from Cadiz, out of sight of the enemy, leaving only the frigates inshore to report on the enemy's movements.'

The one eye roved round the table, gathered in Weston and passed on to Blackwood. 'Captain Weston, Captain Blackwood, I am confident you will not let these gentry slip through our fingers. You are the eyes of the fleet. I would to God I had more frigates! I have written to Their Lordships on the subject — I should like to have at least eight. But a man may survive with only *two* eyes ' — a comical look from the Admiral, and more laughter '— and so for the moment must the fleet. I will give you your individual orders later.'

'Aye aye, my lord,' said Blackwood for both.

'If this combination of Boney's orders and our apparent absence can tempt the enemy out of port, I shall intercept them between here and the Straits, and bring them to battle.

218

Now, as you know, they are around forty, and we are thirty-three, and no day is long enough to arrange two fleets of that size and fight a decisive battle according to the old system, in two parallel lines broadside to broadside. This, therefore, is what I propose.'

There was to be no formal manoeuvring for position, for the days were too short and the October weather too uncertain to be wasting time. They were to attack from whatever course brought them most swiftly into gunshot of the enemy's centre. The attack was to be made in two divisions, one under Collingwood's command breaking the enemy's line about twelve ships from the rear and overwhelming and rearguard, while the other under Nelson attacked the centre of the column. Thus the Admiral hoped they would have defeated two-thirds of the enemy fleet before its van could turn and get into position to help the rear.

'There can be no hard-and-fast rules for the detailed conduct of the battle, since we cannot know under what conditions it will be fought. Something must be left to chance — nothing is certain in a sea-fight. Each division must look for instructions to its own commander; but in case signals can neither be seen or perfectly understood, no captain can do very wrong if he places his ship alongside that of an enemy. And finally, gentlemen, need I say that the battle cannot be considered to be over so long as a single enemy ensign remains flying?'

The response to the last question was unanimous, and the captains cheered, applauded and tapped their glasses for fully five minutes before conversation was able to break out again, and each man turned to his neighbours to discuss what he had heard with eager approval.

'This plan of Nelson's it's singular — it's simple!' said Hargood of the *Belleisle* on one side of Haworth. 'By Gad, it must work, if they will only let us get at 'em!'

And Grindall on his other side rubbed his hands and said, 'If I can get my old haystack of a *Prince* up to them before you fellows have polished them all off, I'll shew you how it's done. You're a lucky man, Haworth, coming out from Portsmouth with a newly refitted ship.'

'You forget the two years I had sailing her *before* they

219

scraped her bottom,' Haworth grinned. 'Twice across the Atlantic with rotting spars and a wilderness of barnacles below me!'

'Well, we shall have a pell-mell battle of it, after all this damn' dreary blockading,' said plump-faced, balding Cooke of the *Bellerophon*, from across the table. 'It'll be like the Nile over again, eh, Haworth? Our little admiral can pull a trick or two out of the bag when it comes to it. Remember how we cut the line then? Of course, they were at anchor, but the principle's the same.'

'By Gad, there's a man who inspires confidence!' Hargood burst out with an admiring glance at Nelson. 'He makes you feel like a personal friend. He makes you feel you could do anything he asks. The port's with you, Haworth.'

'But will the French come out?' Haworth said, filling his glass and passing the decanter. 'Our being out of sight won't convince Villeneuve that we've gone. He knows that trick from Toulon, and he's never shewn much of a desire to fight us.'

'But one thing we do know about Villeneuve,' Grindall pointed out, 'is that he obeys orders. You have to, when it's Boney giving 'em. And if he's been told to sail, then he will. The only question is: when?'

'The sooner the better,' Hargood growled. 'I'm damned if I want to spend another winter in the western approaches. I've got a wife at home.'

Murmurs of agreement: they all had wives at home.

'Well, then, gentlemen,' said Grindall, lifting his glass, 'may the Frogs hoist their topsails without delay!'

'Amen to that!' said Cooke feelingly.

On 19 October, Weston was on deck at dawn. He had been unable to sleep, dreaming fitfully of post-chaises and hurried journeys to London, and of frantic searchings in the pockets of the coach for something he had mislaid. The wind had changed last evening, swinging round from the south-east to the north-east, and had remained light but steady all night.

Without calling for Bates he got up, dressed himself, and went on deck. They were close inshore, along with *Euryalus*, the sloop *Weazle* and the tiny schooner *Pickle*. Out on the horizon, just visible as the first light touched her topgallants, was the *Sirius*; and beyond her, out of sight, the *Phoebe* and the *Naiad*. These were the extra frigates the Admiralty had sent in response to Nelson's request. Beyond *Naiad* were the ships *Defence*, *Colossus*, and *Mars*, each visible only to the next in the chain, between them covering the fifty miles of sea between Cadiz and the main fleet. Thus from ship to ship a message could be passed, by means of Popham's wonderful new flag system, from *Nemesis* to *Victory* and back again, without their ever sighting each other.

If a message were ever to become necessary, Weston added inwardly. So far they had had nothing to say to the admiral but 'situation unchanged'. Osborne, the first officer, touched his hat as Weston reached the quarterdeck. Weston returned the compliment, and walked to the port-side taffrail and looked towards the shore. The sun was just coming up. They were so close inshore that Weston could see the quiet waves breaking on the beach, and smell, over the tar and salt and hemp of the ship, the damp morning freshness of the land.

There was the city of Cadiz, built on the spit of land which enclosed the bay. The sun, as yet still unseen, was gilding the tips of her square towers and battlements, while the lovely white walls to seaward were in deep shadow. Beyond the town was the forest of spars which was the Combined, at anchor in the harbour, safe and untouchable, except by plague, shortage, and depression. Weston drew in a deep breath and was about to turn away when a movement called his eye, and he stiffened.

'Osborne, your glass,' he said urgently. He trained the telescope on the enemy fleet. Surely there was movement? Yes, those were men going up the ratlines. 'Masthead!' he yelled. 'What do you make of the enemy?'

The voice came back so quickly that he guessed the man had been on the point of hailing. 'Enemy hoisting their tops'ls, sir!'

'By God, sir —!' Osborne said, and broke off, his excitement too deep for words. Could this be it? Were they about to come out at last?

Five minutes later, Weston could see it for himself. 'Mr

221

Osborne,' he said, his eye still glued to the glass. 'Signal to *Euryalus* — Enemy are hoisting their topsails.'

'Aye aye, sir.'

Blackwood was the senior captain, and in command of the inshore squadron. He would decide what to do with the information.

'*Euryalus* acknowledges, sir.'

'Very good. Send a midshipman aloft with a glass, if you please, to help the lookout. Who has good eyesight?'

'Reid is the best of 'em, sir.'

'Very well. Pass the word for Mr Reid.'

The gangling young Scotsman came hurrying on deck in great excitement, his clothes awry and his cheeks and chin stubbled with gold like a newly-harvested wheatfield. He clattered to a halt before his captain, shrugging his right arm into his pea-jacket and saluting all in the same movement.

'Mr Reid, it looks as though we may have something to report to the admiral at last. I want a sharp pair of eyes at the foretop. I want to know everything the enemy does, every detail, however small. Understood?'

'Aye aye, sir!' said Reid fervently.

'Take a glass then, and up with you.'

Reid dashed away, and before many minutes not only his, but every glass in the ship was trained on the harbour.

The sun came up, dazzling gold in a pale sky, filling the world with light so that the very air seemed luminous. Each wave was a dark, glassy emerald on one side, and slicked with gold on the other, running peacefully towards the shore. Weston watched a seagull, almost close enough to touch, hanging on the invisible air, keeping pace with the *Nemesis* while it tilted its head this way and that, its bright black eye like a bead of polished jet. The sunlight streamed through its spread tail-feathers, dazzling white and gold, as it rocked on a gentle gust of wind, and then, with one effortless beat, it soared away into the lambent sky.

It was difficult to look eastwards into the light, but even so, the observers saw topsail after topsail being hoist and then unfurled. There was no doubt of it: taking advantage of the light but favourable wind, the enemy was moving at last. As long as they weren't frightened off, Weston prayed fervently.

They must be able to see *Nemesis* keeping her insolent watch just outside the harbour, and probably *Euryalus* and *Weazle* as well, but the other frigates ought to be out of sight of the land, and *Pickle* was probably too small for them to pick out from the surrounding dazzle. They must be hoping to get away, as they did from Toulon, and lose themselves in the vastness of the ocean before the inshore vessels could summon help. What they could not know, was that this time the frigates need never leave them to report to the admiral.

Just after six bells the first of the enemy topsails filled and then narrowed as it was braced out to the wind, and Weston signalled to *Euryalus*, the code-group 370: 'Enemy ships are coming out of port.' It was the message everyone had been waiting for these three weeks, and which many of them had not thought ever to see. *Euryalus* acknowledged, and then signalled to *Sirius*, 'Repeat signals to look-out ships west,' followed by the group 370. Weston saw *Sirius*'s pennant dip and rise, and moments later the first flurry of flags went soaring up her halliards. The all-important message was on its way to the fleet.

223

Chapter Twelve

Fifty miles away to the west, Captain Haworth had seen the same sun rise over the same sea, and had gone below to have his breakfast in his cabin, with Africa seated opposite him, presiding over the coffee-pot like a very small version of her mother, and chattering to Dipton as he brought in dishes and handed bread.

Midshipman Morpurgo came down while they were still eating.

'Flagship signalling, sir,' he reported. '"Admiral to captain, will you dine with me?" and then several ships' numbers, sir, and ours is amongst them.'

'Very well, Mr Morpurgo. Signal the assent, if you please. I am coming on deck.'

Africa looked disappointed. 'Aren't you going to finish breakfast, Papa?'

'Perhaps later,' Haworth said, throwing down his napkin, 'but I have to go now and lay in a new course so that we'll be close enough to *Victory* by dinner-time. An admiral's invitation has to be acted on at once, you see.'

When he reached the quarterdeck, the signals rating was hauling the assent flag up, but Webb, the signals lieutenant, was not looking at the *Victory* any more. He was staring in the other direction, towards the east, where the topgallant mastheads of the *Mars* were just visible on the smudged grey-blue line of the horizon.

'Captain, sir,' said Webb, and then hesitated. He was evidently not sure of what he saw.

'Yes, Mr Webb?'

'*Mars* is signalling, sir. I think it's 370.'

There could hardly have been an officer in the fleet who did not know the signal code for that longed-for message. 'Let me look.' Haworth took the glass from him and trained it on the distant speck. The mastheads appeared in the circle, tiny as a wren's foot-prints against the curve of the world's rim, and as the image steadied, Haworth could see the flags strung out, but they were simply dark, indistinguishable shapes. She was too distant for him to be able to make out the colours. His eye ached as he strained to see more than was possible, and he lowered the glass, disappointed.

'She's too far away. I can't read them.'

'I'm sure it is 370, sir,' Webb said eagerly, his gaze fixed imploringly on his captain.

'I'm sure you are, Mr Webb,' Haworth said. 'It's the signal we'd all like to see.'

'But, sir, begging your pardon, sir, I've always had very good eyesight, and I'm sure I've read it correctly. Won't you pass it on to the flagship, sir?' He shifted from foot to foot with the urgency of the matter. 'It would be such an honour, sir, to be the first to report it,' he added persuasively.

'I can't risk passing on a false message, Webb. I'm sorry.'

'If someone else could make out the flags, sir, would you then?' Webb pleaded. Haworth consented, and every glass in the ship was trained on the eastern horizon. Morpurgo even climbed partway up the ratlines and hung there perilously with a telescope, but no-one was confident enough to confirm Webb's sighting.

'She's hauling it down, sir,' Angevin reported. 'Must have realised no-one can read it.'

'Now she'll make the distant signal,' Webb said eagerly. 'You'll see. It'll be 370 all right.'

The distant signal, a combination of ball, pendant and flag hoisted at different mastheads, for use in just such a circumstance as this, went up a few minutes later, and now they could all see that it was indeed 370. Cheers broke out, and several of the younger officers thumped Webb heartily between the shoulder-blades in congratulation.

'Well done, Mr Webb,' Haworth said, conscious of a quickening of his own pulse. 'Signal to the flagship, if you please.'

But before the flags could be hoisted, *Victory* was already signalling acknowledgement of the message to the *Mars*. The flagship's next signal cancelled the invitations to dinner, and then followed the order 'General chase south-east'.

Haworth gave the orders for changing course and resuming their place in the line, and the whole fleet set sail towards the

Straits of Gibraltar and the hoped-for interception point with the enemy fleet.

At half-past seven, *Euryalus* signalled for the *Weazle* and the *Pickle* to come alongside.

'Sending them off with the news, I dare say,' Osborne remarked to no-one in particular. 'Gibraltar, probably.'

Bates came on deck, closely followed by Jeffrey, who picked his way across the deck to a sheltered and sunlit spot under the starboard bulwarks.

'Your breakfast is ready, sir.'

Jeffrey began a meticulous cleaning of his whiskers which suggested he had already had his, and Weston realised that he was enormously hungry; but he could not leave the deck at a time like this.

'Bring me something up here.'

Bates sighed and went away, returning later with a tray of coffee, bread, and fried fat pork. A hand set up a canvas chair, and Weston sat to consume his breakfast and watch as first the *Pickle* and then the *Weazle* hoisted their courses, shook out their reefs, and sprang away over the bright water to the southward.

'Sun's sucking up the wind, sir,' Osborne observed disappointedly. Weston saw that it was true. On a shore like this, at this time of the year, calm days and light, fluky winds were only to be expected; but the enemy fleet shewed a surprising determination to come out. The Spanish ships had been the first to get under way, and when the wind failed them, they hoisted out rowing boats, and began the painfully slow business of towing the great, unwieldy ships towards the harbourmouth.

By noon the wind had died away altogether, and the English frigates lay becalmed in the sunshine, their sails limp, drifting a little on the tide. There was nothing for anyone to do. The watch on duty leaned against the bulwarks and stared at the lovely white city framed with the dark-blue autumn sky, and some of the idlers brought their work on deck and sat like Jeffrey in sunny spots and basked.

The only enemy ships that were moving were those under tow, and Weston could imagine the scene in the boats: the men leaning against the oars in the gruelling heat, sweating and labouring under the curses of their petty officers, their muscles cracking and their hands raw with friction, as they tried to haul the huge, unwilling ships another foot forward.

Ships of the line were never designed for towing, and the men who struggled to drag them out into the open water must have been doubly miserable, knowing that any chance of slipping away unseen was gone, and that if it came to battle, they had little chance of winning.

In the afternoon a light breeze got up again, and the first of the enemy ships began to emerge from the harbour mouth. *Euryalus* and *Nemesis* drew off to about three miles distant, and tacked back and forth just out of gun-range, keeping the enemy under observation and reporting everything along the chain to the fleet. After their rest during the midday calm, the hands now had unceasing labour making and shortening sail and tacking, to keep the frigates on station in the light and variable breezes.

By nightfall twelve of the enemy were out, and heading slowly northward in an untidy group. The beacon light of Cadiz blazed up as darkness fell, and the frigates crept a little closer to the enemy. It was important not to lose them during the hours of darkness.

All day the fleet sailed south-west, painfully slowly in the light breeze. The slow sailers, *Britannia, Dreadnought* and *Prince*, sagged off to leeward, barely making one knot. Nelson signalled to them to take whatever station was convenient, and they soon fell behind. The rest of the fleet sailed in line-ahead, and keeping station and maintaining an exact distance from the ship in front was all that anyone had to do that long, still day.

At dusk Nelson ordered *Cetus* and five other fast sailers to go out ahead, carrying lights. The line of communication with the frigates had been maintained all day, and they knew that twelve of the enemy were out. The weather conditions prevailing at Cadiz meant that there was a sea-breeze by day, and a light breeze off the land all night, which the enemy might use to get out of harbour under cover of darkness. It was worrying, therefore, that no further messages came from the frigates after dark.

When dawn broke, a grey, wet and squally one, *Cetus* was in the mouth of the Straits, six miles ahead of the flagship, and there was no sign of the Combined. The direction of the wind was such that the enemy could not have reached Gibraltar before them, so the Admiral ordered the fleet to wear and retrace their course, hoping to hear soon from the frigates exactly where the Combined was.

Weston had been having a bad time of it during the hours of darkness. Thick weather had come down not long after dark, and he had lost sight of the enemy, and then, more seriously, of the *Euryalus*. With a hostile shore to leeward and twelve enemy ships, all more powerful than the *Nemesis*, at large, the situation was perilous, and he remained on deck all night, huddled in his greatcoat, straining his eyes into the darkness and chivvying the lookouts.

It was an enormous relief, at dawn on the 20th, to discover the twelve enemy ships anchored a few miles to the north of Cadiz, the rest of the Combined still in harbour, and the other frigates still on station. Villeneuve had evidently weighed the shortcomings of his crews and the hazards of a night sortie in the balance, and decided to wait for daylight.

The squally weather, which the fleet had encountered at Gibraltar, reached Cadiz at ten in the morning, while the Combined were still working their way out of harbour. For the next two hours it was difficult to keep them under observation, for the teeming rain reduced visibility dramatically, and the enemy ships, once clear of the harbour mouth, straggled over a wide area. It would be all too easy to stray amongst them during one of the sudden downpours.

In the early afternoon, the weather cleared, and the Combined was visible again, a rough mass of ships, barely under control and in no proper sailing order, heading westwards. This may have meant that they were going into the Atlantic, but Weston thought it more likely that their destination was the Mediterranean, and that they were simply trying to gain enough sea-room to be able to weather Cape

228

Trafalgar on a single long tack. To judge by the confusion that seemed to reign amongst them already, he did not think Villeneuve would want to risk more manoeuvres than was absolutely necessary.

Blackwood was signalling to him. 'I am going to the Admiral, but will return before nightfall'.

Weston acknowledged, and watched *Euryalus* turn to the southwards and shake out her reefs, bending with a lovely, flexible strength to the wind. If Villeneuve were also watching, he thought, it must almost break his heart to see how easily the little frigate manoeuvred, how close she lay to the wind, and how swiftly she dropped out of sight.

Nemesis remained with the enemy fleet, shadowing it effortlessly, unwelcome witness to all its struggles. The squalls which were an annoyance to the frigate were a serious hazard to the French, with their untrained crews. Through his telescope Weston watched as they attempted to reef down against the weather, saw how slow and clumsy they were even with this routine procedure. The most inept of them were driven down to leeward, scattering the fleet still further, and Weston calculated that they would need to stand at least twenty-five miles out to the westward before they could fetch the Straits in one tack.

But then in the middle of the afternoon the wind veered westerly, a favourable wind for the Straits, and it was not hard to guess that the signal the *Bucentaure* quickly hoisted was the order for the enemy fleet to tack. The leading ships did so, but others were slower to comply. Some had been taken aback by the change of wind, and were wallowing in the troughs without steerage way, while others were still far down to leeward, having only just managed to comply with the earlier order to reef. The crew of the *Nemesis* watched with sad shakings of the head the hopeless confusion which ensued. It was dusk before the whole fleet was on its new heading, sailing very slowly towards Gibraltar.

All through the night of the 20th the English fleet shadowed the Combined, remaining far enough out of sight not to frighten them into changing course, while the frigates kept them informed of the enemy's progress. It was a dark night, with occasional squalls, and with the necessity of keeping the Combined's light in view and reporting on them to Nelson, Weston and Blackwood had no chance of rest.

In the early hours of the morning both fleets were in sight, heading on converging courses which would bring them together at dawn, and the frigate captains were able to go below and snatch some sleep, their task now completed.

When the first greyness was beginning to seep into the sky, Haworth went on deck, and found Africa already there, standing by the taffrail staring in fascination at the lights of the enemy fleet sparkling like distant candles in the murk.

'Look, Papa!' she said softly.

He came to stand beside her, resting his hand on her shoulder. Gradually the shapes of the ships began to appear, their spars like bare trees populating the horizon. And there were the *Euryalus* and the *Nemesis*, small and snug and black, sailing serenely between the two rows of lights, 'Like a couple of jarvies trotting down Piccadilly,' Haworth murmured.

The Combined was trapped between the fleet and the shore; there was nothing it could do now to avoid battle. The squalls had cleared away, and a fine dawn was breaking, and the sun was coming up, burnishing the water and gleaming on the white cliffs of Cape Trafalgar beyond the enemy fleet. It was to be today, then, the battle for which they had all been waiting these two-and-a-half long, weary years. Every man in the fleet must be glad that the end of tedium was come; every man must be quite sure that the battle would end in victory for Nelson's fleet; and every man must also wonder whether this would be the last dawn he ever saw.

Africa looked up into her father's face searchingly, and he smiled and touched her dark curls. 'Let's go and have breakfast, my love, before we have to dismantle the whole cabin.'

Everything had been taken care of, every detail that Nelson could think of. He had ordered all the English ships to fly the white ensign, because it was easier to distinguish from the

French flag, even though Collingwood's division ought by rights to have flown his blue ensign. He had noticed that all the English ships had their mast-hoops painted yellow, except for the *Belleisle*, which had them painted black like the French ships. He ordered the *Belleisle* to repaint them, and pointed out to his fleet that this made a useful means of identification, when all but the masts were obscured by smoke.

At ten past six he ordered the ships to take up their pre-arranged stations, although this was only a confirmation of what was already the case, for despite the long night of manoeuvres, the fleet had remained in its correct order, all but the *Africa*. She had, presumably, missed the order to wear ship during the night, for she had stood on alone to northwards, and was now hurrying back with all the sail she could cram on. Haworth heard this story repeated from hand to hand through his ship, and gave a small, private smile at the indignation of many of his men that their old ship might not be in time to join the action.

'Wouldn't have happened if we was still in her!' they grumbled. 'Suppose she misses the whole battle?'

It seemed unlikely that she would, for the winds were so light it was taking a very long time to sail into reach of the enemy. Nelson gave the change of course at a quarter to seven, turning the fleet from one line almost parallel with the enemy, into the two divisions, parallel with each other and heading for the enemy line almost at right-angles to it.

Cetus's position was fifth in line in Collingwood's division, with the flagship, and the *Belleisle*, the *Mars* and the *Tonnant* in front of her, and the *Billy Ruffian* immediately behind. The *Prince*, steering like a haystack, as Grindall had predicted, was already far out of line to port, and at half-past seven Nelson signalled to her, and to *Dreadnought* and *Britannia*, to take whatever station was convenient without regard to the established order of sailing.

Ten minutes later he called the captains of the frigates on board the *Victory* to give them their orders, which were to stay out of gunshot and render such assistance as might be required. Their usefulness would lie in rescuing men from the water, taking crippled ships in tow and receiving surrender from enemy ships already overpowered. Their frail scantlings

231

would not withstand enemy fire: that was not what they were built for.

Weston returned to the *Nemesis*, and as everything necessary had been done, he occupied himself for a while with writing to Lucy, to tell her of the events leading up to this morning.

'A few nights ago, I dreamt all night of taking despatches to London,' he wrote, 'and now I can see why. It was an omen, I believe, that I shall soon be bringing home news of our great victory over the Combined. No other result is possible. No doubt they will fight bravely, but they are no match for us, as they must know as well as we; and that very knowledge will fight for us and against them.'

The morning passed. By ten o'clock the enemy was about six miles away, clearly visible, some flying the French tricolor, others the red-and-yellow ensign of Spain. They had gone about on the other tack, heading northwards, back towards Cadiz, and had found the manoeuvre so difficult in the light wind that it had taken three hours for all the ships to wear. Their line of battle was not straight, but a long crescent with its concave side towards the English fleet, doubled in places where some ships had fallen off further to leeward than others.

Captain Haworth made a round of the ship, not so much to see if everything was in readiness, for clearing for action was a routine drill, but to observe the morale of the men. Most of them had stripped to the waist, and the old hands, who had been in battle before, had advised the gun-crews to tie a handkerchief round their heads over their ears, to deaden the percussion of the guns, otherwise a man might be deaf for days afterwards.

Complicated arrangements had been made amongst them for the inheritance of personal effects should they fall in battle, but otherwise most of them did not seem to be concerned by the prospect of death. They were excited at being able to see the enemy at last, and constantly put their heads out of the gun-ports for another squint at the opposing ships. Haworth stopped here and there for a word with a familiar face, and they grinned cheerfully and expressed themselves eager to get at 'Johnnie Crapaud'. Some of them had chalked a slogan on the bulkhead above their gun, such as 'Victory' or 'Death or Glory'. One crew had written 'Maria' on the gun itself, leaving Haworth to wonder whether it were the work of a Catholic gunlayer or simply their nickname for the gun.

At eleven it was obvious that they were not going to be in action for another hour or more, and so he ordered bread and cheese and beer for the men, so that they should not have to fight on an empty stomach. He himself ate a cold chicken and some Portuguese grapes on the quarterdeck with Africa, for his cabin had been dismantled, and all his cabin furniture hoisted aloft in a net between the main- and the mizzen-masts for safety. The ships moved so slowly through the water that there was hardly a sound from the rigging, or from the water under the ship. Haworth had an extraordinary, dream-like feeling that this would go on for ever, and to shake it off, he ordered Hudson and Oldroyd and McAfee on to the fo'c'sl to play some cheerful tunes to pass the time as they sailed slowly towards the enemy.

At last they were close enough for individual ships to be identified. Near the centre of the line was the unmistakable bulk of the giant *Santisma Trinidad*, with her four red stripes and one broad white one along her hull — the biggest ship in the world, which Haworth had encountered before at the Nile. Four ships further back was the crow-black *Santa Ana*, 112 guns, and Collingwood, well ahead of his division in the fast *Royal Sovereign*, seemed to be steering for her. Because of the curvature of the enemy line, it was clear Collingwood's division would make contact before Nelson's: to them would fall the honour of first blood. It was time for Haworth to send Africa below to safety.

She had been at his elbow all this time, her toy lamb, which she had elected to keep with her when the cabins were cleared, tucked firmly under her arm. Haworth stooped to kiss her, and called young Morpurgo to escort her below to the orlop deck and place her in the care of the carpenter's wife.

'You'll be safe there, my love,' he said, 'but you must stay

233

there until I send for you again. You would be very much in
the way anywhere else. Do you understand?'

'Yes, Papa,' she said, lifting her cheek for his kiss. It felt
like warm velvet under his lips. Her eyes met his anxiously.
'You will send for me as soon as it's over?'

'Of course I will. Off you go, now.'

She went without fuss, walking between the gun crews
who grinned after her and called out 'God bless you, miss!'
and 'We'll thrash 'em, miss, don't you worry!' Haworth
watched her go, with a small smile as he saw her take
Morpurgo's hand, a weakness she would not normally have
permitted.

She glanced back, just once, as she disappeared from view,
and Morpurgo, understanding her very well, bent his head to
whisper, 'Don't worry, the Cap'n'll be all right.'

'Will you stay with him? All the time?' she asked urgently.

Morpurgo nodded. He was message midshipman, and his
battle station was on the quarterdeck. 'Yes,' he said. 'All the
time. I promise.'

Africa smiled, reassured, and followed him down into the
dark and odorous safety of below-decks.

Collingwood's division was no longer in a column, for each
captain was steering the shortest route into battle, which
meant that each was a little to starboard of the ship in front.
Nelson's ships were still in line-ahead, heading for the centre
of the enemy fleet, their numbers increased by the *Prince*,
which had sagged so far out of line it had crossed from
Collingwood's to Nelson's division. To port and astern of
Nelson's line were the frigates, and the schooner *Pickle*,
returned from Tetuan. She had her four tiny guns run out in
readiness, as Lieutenant Webb pointed out to his captain.

'They look about as dangerous as two pairs of sea-boots,
sir,' he added, which raised a laugh and eased the tension a
little.

Haworth was studying the enemy line through his
telescope. Astern of him, Cooke had swung old *Billy Ruffian*
still further to starboard and was heading for the Spanish
seventy-four *Bahama*. The ship in front of her was the French

Furieux, also a seventy-four, and Haworth pointed her out to his officers.

'There she is, gentlemen, our chosen target, all ready and waiting for us. Mr Angevin, starboard a point, if you please.'

It was a quarter to twelve. 'Flagship signalling, sir,' said Webb. 'General signal ...'

Haworth looked towards the *Victory*. It was a long signal, twelve groups, and he waited with slight impatience that they should be receiving more instructions at this late stage, when they all knew very well what to do. At last Webb turned to him with the slate in his hand.

'Message reads, "England expects that every man will do his duty", sir,' he said, sounding faintly puzzled.

Biggs, one of the larboard side carronade crews, was heard to mutter, 'Do my duty? I've always done my duty. Just lay me alongside the Frenchies, and I'll do my duty all right.'

'Thank you, Mr Webb,' Haworth said. 'Mr Angevin, you will read the Admiral's message to the men, if you please.'

Shouted out from the quarterdeck taffrail, it had a more resounding ring to it, and the men at the weatherdeck guns sent up a cheer which Haworth could hear echoed from other ships across the water. The cheering died away to a buzz as the message was repeated from hand to hand, and the musicians on the fo'c'sl struck up with a squeaky but heartfelt rendering of 'Rule Britannia', with which many of the men joined in, in a sort of muted roar.

Moments later the song was drowned by a different kind of roar, as the *Fougeux*, the ship next astern of the *Santa Ana* opened fire on the *Royal Sovereign*. She made no reply, steering steadily to pass close under *Santa Ana*'s stern and swing up her starboard side.

'Look at old Cuddy!' Biggs said cheerfully. 'Brave as a lion! He don't care about a few pebbles rattling round 'is ears!' There was a chatter of approval from all the larboard-side crews, who were watching *Royal Sovereign*'s progress with interest.

At exactly noon she fired her first broadside, and she and her opponent disappeared in a cloud of smoke.

Next astern of the flagship, the *Belleisle* was now under fire from the *Fougeux* without replying. 'Hargood means to cut

235

through the line, whatever it costs him,' Haworth muttered to himself. He turned his glass on to the *Mars*, steering to pass astern of the *Fougeux*, and saw her torn by a terrible raking broadside.

'Tell the men to lie down, Mr Angevin,' Haworth said. It would be some minutes more before any of their guns would bear, and they were about to come within range of the *Furieux*.

'Here it comes,' muttered somebody. 'For what we are about to receive . . .'

The French ship vomited smoke, the roar coming a fraction of a second later, and then the crashes as the shot struck home. There was a terrible shriek from somewhere forrard, and a swirl of disturbance at one of the weatherdeck guns as the surviving crew drew back in instinctive horror from the remains of a colleague, beheaded and flung across the deck by a cannonball.

'Still, there!' the midshipman of the division shrieked at them, his voice slipping several years upwards in his excitement.

'Starboard a little,' Haworth said. 'Steady.'

The next volley struck murderous splinters from a bulwark, and there was a crash and an ominous creaking as the foretop stays parted and it began to sag.

'Foretopmen! Mr Styles, see to that damage!'

'Aye aye, sir!'

There were more wounded now. One man was sobbing with fright as he staggered towards the hatches with a great rent across his chest from a two-foot splinter.

'Steady, men,' Haworth shouted. 'We'll have our turn by and by, and then we'll give 'em as good as we get.'

There was a cheer from the carronade crews, and then all hell seemed to have been let loose. The Spanish *Bahama*, astern of the *Furieux*, had opened fire on the *Cetus*. The quarterdeck disappeared in a dense billow of smoke. Haworth felt the hot wind of something passing close by him, followed by a stunning crash, and half a dozen screams, rising in pitch to an insanity of pain.

'Starboard guns, open fire!' Haworth yelled, coughing as the bitter smoke filled his mouth. Feet were running through the fog behind him, and as it rolled away upwards he saw that one of the shots had struck the starboard carronade nearest him, smashing two of the crew into pulp, and toppling the gun over on top of two others. It was one of these who was shrieking. The other was staring upwards at nothing and panting shallowly, like a dog run down by a carriage.

But *Cetus* was no longer a silent victim. Her starboard-side guns were bellowing out her rage at her enemy, and moments later, as the gilded stern of the *Furieux* came into range, Haworth ordered the larboard guns to open fire.

Now firing was continuous, and it was impossible to see anything of the rest of the battle through the dense pall of bitter smoke. It was as if they were quite alone in a hellish darkness of sound and fury, lit only by the flashes from the gun-muzzles. Occasionally the smoke swirled away so that the masts of their opponents could be seen, but apart from that, their isolation was complete.

But the long months of training were bearing fruit, and despite the chaotic noise, and death all around, the *Cetus* was functioning like a well-oiled machine. Every gun was working, firing and reloading rhythmically. The quartermasters were silent and steady at the wheel, the topmen standing ready at their posts, the powder boys running past with fresh charges. Here was a work party come to remount the toppled carronade. The screaming man was carried away, while two others dragged the dead out of the way and dumped them against the mizzen-mast.

Angevin appeared at Haworth's shoulder for an instant. 'Hot work, sir,' he said. The *Bahama* seemed to have dropped away astern, and the larboard guns fell silent, but the *Furieux* was alongside now, and the two ships were pouring shot into each other. 'Two rounds to their one, as you'd expect, sir,' he added judiciously.

There was a violent jar, and a crash forrard as the *Furieux* ran her bowsprit across *Cetus*'s fo'c'sl.

'Stand by to repel boarders!' Haworth yelled. 'Mr Styles! Mr Bittles!'

'Musketmen in her crosstrees, sir,' Angevin said urgently, as a high-pitched whine was followed by the sharp smack of a rifle-bullet embedding itself in the coaming.

'God damn those bloody Frenchies!' yelled one of the gun captains, and his crew howled in agreement. English sailors felt it to be unsporting to use sharpshooters in a naval battle. The enemy was the opposing ship, not the crew, who were all brother seamen.

'Keep pounding 'em, lads!' Angevin shouted in reply. 'We'll shew 'em! Good work, there, number three —'

The sentence was cut off. Haworth looked round to see Angevin staring at him with a puzzled expression. Then he lifted his hands, gave a curious little sigh and collapsed on to the deck.

'You — Hobbs! Walters! Get Mr Angevin below to the surgeon!' Haworth shouted.

A slight breath of wind rolled back the smoke like a theatre curtain and revealed the ferocious fight going on up forrard where the crew of the *Furieux* were attempting to board, and were being driven back by the maddened jacks under the command of Lieutenant Styles. Haworth saw Midshipman Bittles, with a dirk between his teeth and a cutlass lashed to his wrist, go running along the bulwarks like a monkey along a branch, and then the breath of wind strengthened and there was a rending noise as the *Furieux* began to turn away and her bowsprit parted company with *Cetus*'s fo'c'sl. There was a flurry of frantic activity as those hands locked in the fighting hastened to jump back into their own ships before it was too late, and a group of half a dozen Frenchmen pinned against the base of the foremast saw their escape cut off and flung up their hands in surrender.

'Mr Morpurgo! Run and tell Mr Styles the captain says well done. And then go below to the cockpit and find out how Mr Angevin is.'

'Aye aye, sir!'

The same light breeze continued to push away the smoke, and for the first time other ships in the battle became visible. *Cetus* had not been fighting all alone. On the port quarter there was the *Belleisle*, with her mainmast down and trailing over her port side, locked in combat with the *Fougeux*; the *Mars* seemed to be drifting out of control away to starboard; and up ahead the *Royal Sovereign* had beaten the *Santa Ana* to a mastless hulk.

The *Furieux* was still turning away, so that her stern was coming round into view, and her guns would no longer bear. A moment later Haworth could see why she had placed herself in that vulnerable position: most of her stern including her rudder had been shot away, and she had no means of steering.

'Give her another, lads!' Haworth shouted, and the gun crews nearest him glanced up, black and glistening from a mixture of sweat and powder, and cheered as they poured another broadside into the French ship's helpless stern. Beyond her another ship loomed out of the smoke, her yellow stripes and white ensign revealing her as friendly moments before Haworth recognised her as Moorsom's *Revenge*. Her gunports spoke orange fire as she passed, and a volley of crashes sounded from the *Furieux*. Then, in an awesome moment, the French ship's mizzen-mast began to fall forward, seemed to hang poised for an instant, and then, with a rending sound like a great tree being torn up, it toppled, taking the mainmast with it, and ending in a horrible tangle of wreckage over her port bow.

The *Cetus*'s crew yelled in savage joy, the men capering like mad things beside their guns, waving their arms in the air. Tyler, the second lieutenant, appeared beside Haworth, taking Angevin's place, his teeth white in his grimed face.

'She's striking her colours, sir! She'll be our prize, sir!'

'So she will,' Haworth said.

'Sir!' Here was Morpurgo, trying to attract his attention.

Haworth turned to him. 'Mr Morpurgo, ask Mr Styles to —'

He got no further. A bellowing roar from astern, crashes, screams, splinters hurtling past like flying razors; a great, hot breath and a huge numbing blow in the small of the back flung Haworth forward and sideways, knocking him off his feet across the deck.

Another French ship, the *Neptune*, coming up on their port quarter, had rendered passing honours, smashing a whole section of the poop into matchwood, and sending a piece of it flying to knock Haworth over. It was this which was the saving of him, for the mizzen-mast was shot clean through three feet above the deck, and pivoted by its shrouds, the bottom of it swung forward like a deadly pendulum and crashed into the taffrail, smashing it like eggshells.

The air was full of sawdust. Morpurgo, with a jagged cut across his brow, helped him to his feet.

'Are you all right, sir?'

'Yes, yes — only shaken.' His lower back felt numb, and below the numbness was the knowledge of a horrible pain, though the pain itself was not yet present. He gripped Morpurgo's shoulder to support himself and looked around.

The *Neptune* was passing on down the larboard side, heading to the rescue of the *Algeciras*, which was in combat with the *Tonnant*. The larboard gun-crews were firing into her as fast as they could, but the slow Spanish crews took so long to reload that they only managed to fire one more round into *Cetus* before their guns ceased to bear.

The *Furieux* was still drifting away to starboard, the wreckage hanging over her side acting like a rudder. As to the *Cetus*, she was not mortally hurt, though she had had to cease firing in default of any enemy ship within range. There were dead heaped about her masts, but all the guns were still manned, and the division officers were still at their appointed stations, waiting for orders.

On the quarterdeck the men still unhurt were already struggling to move wreckage and extricate the wounded, but the mizzen-mast was hanging, creaking ominously, from its chains. There were several urgent things to be done: the mizzen-mast must be secured in some way before it fell straight through the decks and sank them; they must get under way again, so as to follow up the damage they had managed to inflict on the *Neptune*; and the *Furieux* must be boarded before some other captain got to her first. She's our prize, Haworth found himself thinking fiercely, and no-one else is going to have her.

He began to bellow orders, for the sails to be got in to take the strain off the mizzen, for the afterguard and the carronade crews to get a rope round the butt of the mizzen-mast to stop it swinging, for Styles to get together a boarding party to go off to the *Furieux* in whatever ship's boat was still intact, and received her surrender, for the boatswain to find some spare yards with which to fish the mizzen-mast to its stump, and the carpenter to look at the damage to the stern.

He discovered he was still holding on to Morpurgo's shoulder — gripping it, in fact, so hard that it must have been hurting the lad, though he had not made a sound of protest. Forcing himself to relax his grip, Haworth at last became aware of the pain in his lower back, which was so bad it made him feel sick. And at the same instant, the ship's bell rang seven bells. It was three and a half hours since they had gone into battle. It seemed to Haworth more like fifteen minutes.

Chapter Thirteen

The battle had seemed much longer to Weston, in the unenviable position of watching it from a safe distance. Not long after the *Royal Sovereign* had opened fire, the *Victory* was being fired upon by three of the enemy ships: the flagship *Bucentaure* and the two ships in front of her, the giant *Santisma Trinidad,* and the *Héros.* It was plain that they were trying out the range, for they were only firing single shots.

'They're aiming high, sir,' said Osborne with interest. 'Trying to cripple her. Just like the Frogs.'

Weston rather doubted it. From what he had seen of the enemy fleet, they were not capable of anything so sophisticated as aiming a gun. It was surely the heavy swell which was sending all their shots upwards.

Some of the ships of the van began firing also, though they were too far ahead of the *Victory* to hope to hit her, and they soon gave it up in favour of firing at the *Africa,* who was passing them as she came down from the northward, alone.

A hole appeared in *Victory*'s main topgallant, and almost at once the French began firing their broadsides.

'She must be getting pounded, sir,' Osborne said anxiously. *Victory* sailed on unflinchingly, aiming for a gap in the line.

'She'll pass astern of the flagship,' Weston said. 'What's that ship behind her? Oh yes, the *Redoutable.* See, she's trying to close the gap. There's one French captain who knows his business, anyway.'

'They're going to collide!' cried Osborne. Moments later, *Victory*'s bows hit those of the *Redoutable* with a crash they could hear quite clearly across the water; and she ground on, forcing the *Redoutable* round to starboard. Then with a roar, *Victory* opened fire at last, smashing the beautiful gilded stern of the *Bucentaure* into splinters with an entire port broadside, and pumping her starboard broadside into the *Redoutable.*

The *Temeraire,* immediately behind *Victory,* broke the line to the rear of the *Redoutable* and lay up on her starboard side, and the *Fougeux* ran up on the *Temeraire*'s other side, so that the four ships were locked together, side by side, their yards touching, pounding each other with their guns. The familiar pall of smoke began to obscure the scene.

The rear of the combined fleet was catching up with the centre, where the action was taking place, but the vanguard was sailing away out of reach. Weston and his officers watched in amazement as the enemy van held to its course, expecting every moment that they would turn to help their colleagues, but apart from firing at the *Africa*, the smallest of the English ships of the line, as she passed, they seemed to want no part of the battle.

Weston's view of the battle was now limited to tantalising glimpses whenever the smoke rolled away. One glimpse revealed the magnificent *Santisma Trinidad* with all three of her masts down, hanging over the side so that her huge bulk rolled helplessly like a gigantic log. The *Belleisle*, too, was completely dismasted, but she had cut her wreckage away and was still firing at anything that came within range. The slower of the English ships were now joining battle with the fresh ships from the enemy's rearguard, so that the struggle in the centre was constantly renewed. But it was plain who was getting the worst of it, and after two hours, ships of the Combined began to strike their colours.

There were men in the water now, and Weston tacked the *Nemesis* nimbly here and there to pick them up. A stray shot whined past and parted a forestay, and the boatswain's party went running forward to reeve a new one. Even on the fringes of the battle, Weston reflected, one was not entirely safe.

'Sir, I think the enemy van's turning,' said Acton, the third lieutenant. Weston trained his glass on the distant ships.

'I think you're right. I wonder how long it will take them? It took them three hours to change course yesterday.'

'Good God!' Osborne said in disgust, 'they're trying to tack, instead of wearing. Haven't they any more sense than that, with the wind so light?'

'They'll be in trouble,' Acton predicted. 'Yes, look, that one's lost her steerage way. She's all aback! Now what'll they do?'

It took an hour for all the ships to turn. Some had to hoist out boats and tow themselves round; two others collided, and one lost a foremast; but at last they were on the opposite tack, and heading southwards on the windward side of the battle. All the ships of Nelson's column were now engaged except the *Spartiate* and the *Minotaur*, which now altered course to stand in the way of the enemy van, shewing their teeth and offering battle. Seeing this, all but the first four of the enemy ships hauled their wind and hovered about out of range; and even those four, after exchanging fire with the two English ships, thought better of it, and continued on their south-westerly course, away to safety.

The *Royal Sovereign*, having lost her masts, signalled for the *Euryalus* to take her in tow. At the southernmost end of the battle, the French *Achille*, which had been fighting with her English namesake and the *Prince*, had set fire to her own rigging by using musketry in the crosstrees, and Weston took the *Nemesis* to offer help. A ship on fire was no longer an enemy ship: her crew must be taken off, if possible.

Before he reached her, however, Weston saw that the *Pickle* was already on the spot, and several other ships had sent boats, and seeing that his immediate presence would only hamper them, he looked around for some other ship that might need his assistance.

Nearby was the *Cetus*, not at present engaged, her stern battered and shapeless, her fore- and main-topmasts gone, and a working-party still labouring to secure the mizzen-mast. Haworth was on the quarterdeck, and Weston hauled his wind and hailed him.

'Is everything all right, sir?'

Haworth grinned. 'Some minor damage, as you see. How many have struck?'

'Fourteen or so, I think. None of ours, of course.'

'I should hope not.' He jerked his thumb over his shoulder at the *Furieux*. 'We have a prize, too, you see.'

'Congratulations, sir. Have you heard what happened to the *Africa*?'

'No. Did she manage to get into action?'

'Oh, yes, sir. But she found the *Santisma Trinidad* already dismasted, so Digby sent a lieutenant on board to receive her surrender. The Spanish admiral told him politely that it was a mistake, that he hadn't struck, and escorted the lieutenant back over the side.'

Haworth grinned. 'Poor old Digby.'

'I haven't had any better luck,' Weston said ruefully. 'No prize for me yet. Do you need any help, sir?'

'No thank you, Weston. I shall need your help later to celebrate, however, when we get back to Spithead.'

'What a story we'll have to tell!' Weston said, grinning. 'There never was a battle like this!'

The *Pickle*'s boats were now heading back for her side, and there was room for another rescuer on the spot, so Weston touched his hat to Haworth, gave the order to come before the wind, and the *Nemesis* turned away from *Cetus*'s side to head for the burning *Achille*.

The mizzen-mast was secured, the immediate danger over, and Haworth was able to turn his attention to other matters.

'Shot hole below the waterline, sir,' said the carpenter. 'We're plugging it, sir, but we're taking in water. Could we have four more men on the pumps, sir?'

'Mr Angevin's dead, sir,' said young Morpurgo, a message he had been trying to deliver to the captain for half an hour at least. 'He was dead when they got him below. Mr Parry says he must have died instantly, sir, shot in the chest.'

'You're wounded yourself,' Haworth remembered, seeing the crust of blood on the boy's forehead, and feeling, now that he had the leisure, the savage, sickening pain in his own lower back.

'I'm all right, sir, but what about you?' Morpurgo said anxiously, seeing Howarth's grimace of pain as he tried to straighten.

Styles was hailing from the quarterdeck of the *Furieux*.

'All secure, sir,' he called. 'Things are pretty bad here, though, sir. I could do with some more men, if you could spare 'em.'

'I'll see what I can do,' Haworth said. 'Do your best for the moment, Mr Styles. You had better send the unwounded French officers here, for safety's sake. Mr Tyler, see to it, will you? And let me know as soon as we are ready to make sail again. I'm going below for a few minutes, to see how things are in the cockpit. Mr Morpurgo, you had better come with me, and have that wound attended to.'

On the lower deck, the smoke had almost cleared, and the light coming in through the gunports gave more illumination than usual. The crews were still standing to their guns in readiness for further action, but Haworth was glad to see that the division officers were releasing them in turn to drink at scuttles. They were all dog-weary, but they straightened up as the captain passed, looking to him trustfully for guidance and praise.

'Well done, my lads,' he called to them. 'We've given the Frogs a trouncing, and taken ourselves a prize, and we may still have the chance to take another, God willing!'

One or two of them managed a cheer, and the others grinned at each other, thinking no doubt of prize-money and Portsmouth whores.

Down again, and the orlop deck was hellish, dark except for the pools of lamplight, stifling hot, the air thick with the smell of sweat and the coppery, butchery reek of blood. From out of the darkness came the tormented moans of mutilated men. There were wounded everywhere, sitting on benches, lying on the deck, propped against the ship's knees; some were crying out with living pain, others silent with shock, or locked in the solitude of approaching death.

But others were still cheerful, making light of their wounds for the sake of their reputations or the spirits of their neighbours, cheering whenever any piece of news was passed down to them of the battle. Here was one man, his face indistinguishable beneath a mask of blood, grinning painfully through broken lips, and knuckling his forehead as Haworth approached.

'Well, Bullen, what's happened to you?' Haworth said, recognising the Captain of the Foretop at the last moment.

'Got hit in the face, sir, by running a cleat, when the foretop went down,' he mumbled. He had some teeth missing, too, by the look of it.

'Bad luck,' said Haworth.

'Twarn't nothing, sir,' Bullen said modestly. 'It were the fall that broke me arm. One thing, sir, I'll be able to whistle a treat through me gap, now.'

In the cockpit itself the surgeon and his assistants were working by candlelight, cutting out splinters, probing wounds, amputating smashed limbs.

'How are things, Parry?' Haworth asked.

The surgeon looked up with a harried expression. 'I need more help, sir,' he said abruptly. 'I've sixty or seventy wounded here.'

'Everyone needs more help,' Haworth grimaced. 'I'll do what I can. For the moment you can have the cook and his mates. They can begin by giving every wounded man a tot of rum to celebrate our victory.' Someone raised a feeble cheer. 'Morpurgo here's got a bit of a knock; and I've taken a blow to my back. Just take a look at it, will you, old fellow, and tell me its nothing but a bruise, so that I can get back on deck.'

Parry wiped his reeking hands perfunctorily and took Haworth aside to examine him. He pressed here and there, making Haworth wince and break out in a sweat. 'Nothing broken, so far as I can tell,' he said at last. 'Just a massive contusion. You'll be as stiff as a board tomorrow, but that can't be helped. You were lucky, sir.'

'Thanks,' said Haworth wryly.

'Hill, take a look at Mr Morpurgo's head, will you. I'd better get back to my man,' Parry said. The man face-down on the table was writhing in a slow, aimless way like a wounded snake, and Haworth could see the purple-black shape of a foot-long splinter under the skin of his back. Splinters, being barbed, could rarely be drawn out by the route they went in, in this case a jagged hole under the armpit. The surgeon usually had to cut down to the point and drag them out through flesh and muscle with forceps. Haworth tucked his shirt back into his trousers, not much wanting to witness the operation, and with a reassuring pat to Morpurgo's shoulder, he went out into the murk of the orlop.

There were women moving about amongst the wounded, bandaging minor wounds, doing what they could for the others. There was Lieutenant Phillips of the Marines, cheese-coloured with approaching death, his white breeches ending in bloody bandages. Haworth stopped to speak to him, and then realised that the woman crouching by him was the carpenter's wife. She looked up apprehensively.

'What are you doing here? Where's my daughter?' he demanded. She was not obliged to answer, for Africa's voice came from further off in the gloom.

'Here I am, Papa.'

Haworth went towards her, staring in horror, for she was squatting on the bloody deck beside a jack with a bandaged stump instead of a right arm, supporting his head with one hand while she fed him sips of water from an iron cup.

'What are you doing? Come away from there!' he said, his voice hardly more than a whisper from the shock of seeing her in such a position. But she only looked at him calmly, and there was no child in her eyes, except in the simplicity with which she saw the situation.

'It's all right, Papa,' she said. 'They're my friends. I must help them.'

'It's not fitting,' Haworth said. 'You shouldn't be here. Mrs Colley had no right to allow you to see this.'

'It's not her fault,' Africa said. 'She tried to stop me, but poor Mr Parry had so much to do.'

Haworth turned back to the carpenter's wife, who had stood up, and was twisting her apron nervously in her fingers.

'Mrs Colley, take my daughter back to your quarters at once, and keep her there.'

'Begging your pardon, sir, but I haven't got no quarters. It's all shot away, sir. Colley's in there now, sir, with his mates, trying to plug the leak.'

So that's where the hole was. Haworth paled as he thought about it. If she had been in there when the shot came through the hull . . .!

Africa stood up and laid her small brown hand on his arm, looking up steadily into his face. 'I'm all right, Papa, really. You can go back on deck,' she said, and he remembered suddenly how her mother had helped with the wounded during the first battle she had ever witnessed, before Africa was born.

He laid his hand over hers, and smiled uneasily. There was so much for him to do, and she knew it, and was trying to help him by taking herself out of his hands.

One of the midshipmen, a boy of twelve, came picking his way, round-eyed with horror, through the wounded towards him.

'Captain, sir, Mr Tyler's compliments, sir, and we're ready to make sail.'

'Thank you, Mr Dixon,' Haworth said automatically. This boy was no younger, inside himself, than Africa, his erstwhile playmate; and indeed, his eyes had strayed from his captain to her, and she was giving him a little, brisk nod for reassurance. He could not protect her from the knowledge to which his decision to bring her to sea had exposed her. 'Tell Mr Tyler I'm on my way,' he said.

'Aye aye, sir.' The boy took one more awed glance around, and hurried off. Haworth laid the tips of his fingers on Africa's head, and exchanged a smile with her, and walked away.

But there was little left to do. It was past five o'clock in the afternoon, and the battle was as good as over. The main mass of the ships clustered around the centre, where the mastless *Royal Sovereign* wallowed helplessly, having lost her tow-line to the *Euryalus* when a random shot from the enemy van severed it as they passed on their flight south. The *Belleisle* and the *Victory* were also dismasted, and many others had lost topmasts or spars. Of the whole fleet of twenty-seven ships, more than half were seriously damaged.

But all around, too, were battered French and Spanish ships, rolling on the swell, and all wearing the white ensign over their colours. Four ships of the enemy van were fast disappearing over the southern horizon, while another group, nine or ten, Haworth thought, were fleeing northwards, hoping to regain the safety of Cadiz; and the French *Achille* was burning briskly in a circle of clear water prudently left around her. It seemed a most complete victory.

The firing had almost ceased; certainly there was none on the vicinity of *Cetus*, for there was no enemy near enough to fire at. It was time, Haworth thought, to report to Collingwood for orders, for since neither *Victory* nor *Royal Sovereign* had a mast from which to fly a signal, it was plain there could be no orders sent that way.

'Mr Tyler, secure the guns if you please,' he said. 'The men had better not stand down until we have orders from the Admiral, but see to it that they have something to eat at their posts.'

'Aye aye, sir.'

'Have we any boats left?'

'No sir, only the one that Mr Styles took to the prize, sir.'

'It's back, sir, the boat,' said Robins, master's mate. 'Here's Mr Bittles, sir, with the French officers.'

More distractions. The prisoners came picking their way across the quarterdeck, escorted by young Bittles, who probably had no idea that he was grinning like a monkey in his excitement and pride. The prisoners looked a sorry group, their faces grimed, their clothing awry, dejected in their defeat, ashamed of having surrendered, of having always known that it would end like this. But they had to be received with courtesy, compliments exchanged, arrangements made for their accomodation under guard.

Only the man at the head of the group had the spirit to look around him with interest at the workings of a foreign ship. He was a very short young man with a plump, puggy face divided across the middle by a bushy black moustache. The group came to a halt before Haworth.

'Dugasse,' said the moustached one, doubling himself with his hat over his stomach in the French manner.

'First lieutenant, sir,' Bittles explained. 'The captain's dead, sir, killed in our first broadside.'

Dugasse drew himself up to his full five-feet-two. 'To whom do I have the honour of rendering myself?' he asked with dignity.

'I am Captain Haworth of His Majesty's ship *Cetus*.'

Dugasse raised his eyebrows. 'Ah, le Capitaine Haworth! Of the ship *Afrique* at the battle of Aboukir?'

Haworth bowed. 'You have heard of me, sir?' he asked in surprise.

'But of course. I also was at Aboukir, sir, in the *Formid-*

able. I am glad to be able to render the *Furieux* to such a distinguished officer.' He bowed, and Haworth bowed again, and the other French officers, who presumably did not speak English and were looking blankly miserable, bowed too.

Haworth turned to Tyler. 'Mr Tyler, would you see to it that these gentlemen are taken below to my cabin, and given some refreshment. Gentlemen,' to the French officers, 'I'm afraid your accommodation will be a little cramped for the moment, but we will do our best to make you comfortable. Mr Bittles,' turning in relief from more bowing as Tyler ushered the prisoners away, 'are there any boats intact on the prize ship?'

Bittles frowned in thought. 'There's a gig, sir, that doesn't look too badly damaged. We could probably repair it.'

'You had better give Mr Styles a hail: my compliments, and ask him to have it patched up and sent for you. I must have our boat go to the flagship.'

'Aye aye, sir.'

Morpurgo was by his side again, his fair hair falling across the bandage round his forehead. 'Mr Morpurgo, can you find me some paper and a pen and bring it to me here?' With the French prisoners in his cabin, there was nowhere else for him to write to the Admiral.

'Aye aye, sir,' said Morpurgo, as if it were the easiest request in the world. Haworth felt a renewed surge of affection for the boy.

A dozen people were waiting to gain his attention, and the dreamlike feeling was returning. He fought against it, aware that it was largely fatigue, forcing himself to concentrate on what they were asking.

'Boat pulling off from the *Victory*, sir,' Webb reported. 'I'm not certain, sir, but I think it's Captain Hardy in the sternsheets, sir.'

'Hardy?' said Haworth vaguely. Where could Hardy be going in a boat? The thought slid effortlessly out of his mind as he tried to concentrate on writing his brief report and request for orders to the Admiral, and sent it off with Webb to the *Royal Sovereign*.

'All firing seems to have ceased, sir,' Tyler said. 'May I tell the men to stand down?'

'Very well, Mr Tyler. And if Mr Parry can spare the cook, as soon as everything is secure, he can start cooking something for the men's dinner.'

As Tyler turned away to implement the orders, the *Achille* blew up. She had burnt almost down to the water amidships, and the fire had reached her magazine at last. The huge gout of flame was followed by the dull, flat-sounding explosion, and a mushroom-shaped cloud of black smoke rose into the pale evening sky, while all around her there was a rain of debris.

Nemesis and *Pickle* were still on the scene, and the *Revenge* also sent a boat to pick up the last survivors. The boat sent by Styles from the *Furieux* to bring Bittles back, diverted at once and picked up two men from the water, one badly burned, and brought them to the *Cetus* to add to Parry's problems. The story was soon running round the ship that the *Pickle*'s boat had picked up a completely naked young woman who had been clinging to a spar, and another boat had picked up a fat black pig.

'Just our luck,' muttered Robins. 'All we get is a couple of Froggie sailors! Can't eat 'em and can't —'

'Boat's coming back from the flagship, sir,' said Morpurgo. His face was white with fatigue under his tan. Webb came up the companion, his eye fixed on Haworth's, and an odd look about his mouth, as if he were a young child trying not to cry. A strange sort of sensation rippled across the men in his wake, as some message was passed instantly from mouth to mouth.

He came to a halt in front of Haworth and saluted, and his mouth worked silently. Haworth saw with amazement that his eyes were full of tears.

'Make your report, Mr Webb,' he said briskly, hoping to brace him.

'Sir —' He swallowed. 'Sir, I gave your letter to the Admiral, sir. He's moved his flag to the *Euryalus*. Cap'n Hardy was there, sir. He came in person to tell the Admiral ...'

Webb's lip was trembling, and he caught it between his teeth, and his adam's apple moved up and down his throat several times. 'Admiral Collingwood, he was crying sir, and

Cap'n Blackwood, quite dreadfully. Admiral Nelson's dead, sir.'

Now the Commander-in-Chief's pendant flew from the *Euryalus*. Collingwood had inherited an unenviable command: a fleet of forty-four ships, of which only a dozen were fit to sail and fight, with insufficient crews, on a dangerous lee shore. The wind was light and westerly, there was a heavy swell running, darkness was coming on, and there was an ominous gathering of coppery clouds on the horizon.

It was no difficult decision to head westwards, towards open sea and away from the menacing shore. Orders went up the *Euryalus's* halliards, for the able ships to take in tow those without masts or rudders. The frigates *Sirius* and *Naiad* took on the *Victory* and *Belleisle*, and *Nemesis* threw a line to Haworth's prize, the *Furieux*. Though physically and spiritually exhausted by the battle, the victorious fleet was to have little rest.

On board the *Cetus*, the shot hole below the waterline had been roughly plugged, the debris cleared from the decks, the dead committed to the deep. The bulkheads had been replaced, and such furniture as had survived brought out and set up. Some of the wounded had been moved into the wardroom and the captain's day cabin was being used to house the French officers, while Dipton took care of Africa in the night cabin. He reported to his captain that he had fed her and tucked her into her cot, and that though she was naturally exhausted, she did not seem unduly distressed by what she had witnessed that day.

'I think she's glad to have been able to help, sir,' Dipton said. 'The only thing that's upsetting her is that we can't find Cleopatra, sir, and she thinks it might have gone overboard when we were clearing for action. You know what jacks are, sir — any excuse to chuck stuff overboard.'

'Cleopatra?' Haworth asked vaguely.

'The camel, sir,' Dipton prompted. 'Not but what she loves her lamb, sir, but Cleopatra's very close to her heart. But Colley's promised to make her another one, if it don't turn up.'

When these things had been done, Haworth saw to it that the men were fed, and normal watches were resumed, which meant that the watch below could sleep. Most of them simply folded up on the deck where they stood, too weary to sling their hammocks, even where their hammocks had survived the shot and splinters of the battle.

But for the officers and the prize crews there was no rest. There was simply too much to do. A third-rate's normal complement of men was five hundred and ninety, but after so long at sea, *Cetus*'s company had numbered only five hundred and fifty before the battle. Of these thirty-seven had been killed, and seventy-three were wounded. Of the six lieutenants, Angevin and Beaton, the fifth, were dead, while Styles was in the prize with midshipman Bittles and thirty hands. This meant that *Cetus* was short of a hundred and eighty men, or a third of her normal complement, at a time when she needed every hand to sail her, what with two of her topmasts gone and a mizzen-mast which was only fished to its stump.

But if Haworth had a hard task ahead in sailing *Cetus* to safety, that of Styles in the *Furieux* was even less enviable. With her main and mizzen masts gone, and no rudder, she was almost helpless; besides that, she was riddled with shot-holes, and the unnumbered French wounded filled the orlop and lower deck. Styles and his small party had managed to rig a jury mizzen-mast, and to perform hasty repairs on the foremast rigging, so that they could carry some sail and help the *Nemesis* which took them in tow. All the same, towing a ship of the line in swell conditions with only a light wind was a hazardous task, and both the prize crew and the crew of the *Nemesis* had an exhausting ordeal before them.

By nine in the evening, the swell had worsened, and the wind was backing south-westerly, which meant it was blowing straight towards Cape Trafalgar with its hidden shoals. Haworth ordered a man into the leads to take soundings, for in the dark it would be hard to see how close they were to the shore.

'Keep it going all the time,' he told Pitcairn, the junior lieutenant, who was taking the watch, 'and see that the leadsman is relieved every two hours.' Taking soundings was gruelling work, and the men were already tired. 'And double the lookouts. They can keep each other awake.'

'Aye aye, sir.'

'Flagship signalling, sir,' said the midshipman of the watch. 'General order: prepare to anchor.'

'Acknowledge.' Collingwood, too, was wary of that hidden lee shore.

'Sir,' Pitcairn's face was white and black like a Greek mask in the light from the binnacle, his mouth bowed downwards for tragedy. 'We can't anchor. That broadside from the *Neptune*, sir, it severed the anchor cables.'

They would not be the only ship in that predicament, Haworth thought. Probably the present signal was Collingwood's means of discovering how many ships were capable of anchoring. 'Signal to the flag, if you please, Mr Pitcairn: have no anchor cables.'

In the next few minutes other ships were seen to be making the same signal, and it was enough to decide the Admiral that there was no point in making the executive signal. The damaged fleet continued to struggle away from the hidden shore, while the wind grew more squally, and backed another point.

Dipton appeared at Haworth's shoulder.

'I've screened off a bit of the night-cabin for you, sir, and rigged a cot, and I've got a bite of supper all ready for you, if you'd like to come now, sir.'

Haworth looked at him in dull amazement, hardly able, through his fatigue, to understood what was being said to him.

'You're worn out, sir, begging your pardon. Everyone else has had a bit of a rest, sir, bar you,' Dipton went on. 'The French gentlemen is sleeping like babies.'

'Nonsense. How can I go to sleep at a time like this?'

'Well, sir, p'raps you could just come below for a minute and take a bite of supper, and change your coat,' said the wily Dipton. 'That one's wet through, besides having a terrible great tear in it. I'd like to get it mended, sir, before we get to Gibraltar, in case you need it for going ashore.'

It was his best dress coat, which he had put on that morning for the battle. Could it really only be that morning?

'Very well,' he said. 'Mr Pitcairn, I am going below for a few minutes. Keep your eye on that mizzen-mast.'

'Aye aye, sir.'

Below in his night-cabin, Haworth put his head through the screen to look at Africa, who was soundly asleep, her head and that of the brown velvet lamb side-by-side on the pillow.

'Here we are, sir,' said Dipton. 'Let me help you out of that coat, sir. That's right. A glass of wine, sir, to warm you up. You must of got chilled in that wet coat. If you'd like to sit down on your cot, sir, I could get those wet stockings off. You'd be more comfortable in your sea-boots, sir, if you're going back on deck.'

The wine heartened him enough to discover he was hungry and he savaged a round of cold roast beef, some bread and a bunch of grapes, while Dipton removed his stockings and chafed his legs and feet with a coarse towel until they grew warm. The comfort of dry clothes and the wine and food soon reversed their effect, and he became very sleepy — intolerably sleepy. He found himself drifting even between one mouthful and the next, jerking awake where he sat as his head lolled forward.

'Perhaps if you was just to lie down for five minutes, sir,' murmured Dipton, like a siren. 'No need to take off your clothes, then you can be back on deck in a jiffy, if you're needed, sir. Let me help you . . .'

Haworth didn't even feel his head touch the pillow, or Dipton draw the blanket over him: he had swum backwards and down into the black sleep of utter exhaustion.

Weston had hardly noticed the time pass since taking the *Furieux* in tow. Everyone admired the French ships as being more elegant and graceful than the English ones, but however graceful a ship of the line was under sail, she was an unutterable bitch to tow. Styles did his best, with his handful of a prize-crew, keeping them at the sheets the whole time to try to mitigate with the best possible use of the sails the deadweight drag to leeward that the ship exerted on the frigate; while Weston stood on the quarterdeck with the speaking-trumpet in his hand, watching the swell, the cable, the two ships, and his own masts and sails, bellowing orders until his voice cracked.

At one minute the *Furieux* would hang back sulkily so that the cable rose from the water and tightened like an iron bar, and the masts of the *Nemesis* would creak ominously under the strain; and at the next the swell would bring her surging forward, big and black and senseless as a boulder, bearing down on the frail frigate like a mad bull bent on destroying her.

The headway they made was pitiful; the lee shore was less than ten miles away, and the wind backing dangerously, and growing squally. Then, despite everyone's vigilance, just before ten o'clock a sudden violent gust of wind together with the running swell brought the *Furieux* surging up to fall on board of the *Nemesis*'s starboard beam.

Her murderous bowsprit tore through the main course like a sword, while her bows stove in the quarterdeck bulwarks and smashed the jolly-boat and its davits. The *Nemesis* lurched horribly, taken aback, and there was a terrible rending sound aloft as the main and mizzen topgallant masts were torn away. A severed halliard whipped through the darkness with a sound like a hornet, and Weston felt a sharp, cold pain in his cheek, and putting up his hand, brought it away bloody.

'All hands, fend off there! Afterguard, cut those hammocks away! Mr Harris, slacken off those sheets! Helm a-lee!'

Five minutes of frantic activity, as the *Furieux* seemed bent on mounting the frigate and cutting her in half, and the hands strained and shoved at her great senseless bulk with their puny spars; but then with a terrible tearing and snapping of yards and running rigging, she suddenly sheered off, and the *Nemesis* righted herself with a lurch.

'Towing cable's parted, sir,' Acton reported. 'She's going down to lee.'

'Give her a hail before she's too far away, Mr Acton. Tell Mr Styles we've got to repair our rigging before we can take her up again.'

'Aye aye, sir.'

'You're wounded, sir,' said Davie Reid in concern.

Weston dabbed at his face again, and then fumbled for a

257

handkerchief. 'It's nothing. Just a cut. I'll have it seen to by and by.'

'Here, have mine, sir,' Reid said proffering a handkerchief.

Weston took it with a murmur of thanks. 'That'll spoil my beauty, won't it, Reid?'

'Depends on your point of view, sir,' Reid said, meeting his captain's eyes with a sudden access of sympathy, and they both grinned.

Haworth woke with a violent start, tried to get up, and couldn't. The bruising to his back had stiffened while he slept, and he couldn't move. He tried hooking his hands round the edge of his cot and dragging himself over, but the pain made him sweat. He had not meant to sleep. Anything might have happened. He bellowed for Dipton.

'How long have I been asleep?'

'Only about an hour, sir,' Dipton said soothingly.

'You should have woken me. Help me to get up, damn it. I can't move.'

'You needed a sleep, begging your pardon, sir. Can't you rest a bit longer, sir?'

'Help me up, damn you,' Haworth said, hating his helplessness. He was like a woodlouse on its back.

Between them, he and Dipton managed to get him to a sitting position, though not without a great deal of pain.

'Shall I send for Mr Parry, sir?' Dipton said anxiously.

'It's only stiffness. It'll loosen up as I move around,' Haworth said, without much inward conviction. But the hour's sleep had refreshed him amazingly: he felt deeply weary, but perfectly alert. 'Help me on with my boots. I daren't bend.'

On deck he felt at once that the wind had freshened, and the next thing that caught his attention was the rhythmical groan and thud as the mizzen-mast moved in its lashings with the slow pitching of the ship on the swell. Webb was on deck, and touched his hat as Haworth appeared.

'We'll have to get some of the strain off that mizzen-mast, Mr Webb.'

'Take in another reef, sir?'

'I think we'll goose-wing it,' Haworth said. That exposed less sail than reefing.

'Aye aye, sir. Hands to shorten sail!'

'We'll have to watch it carefully,' Haworth went on as the topmen came running for the ratlines. He squinted upwards apprehensively into the formless shadows of the rigging. 'If the wind freshens much more, it could give us trouble.'

When dawn came at last, all forty-four ships were still in sight, widely scattered over the heaving sea. Four of them, the *Defence* and three of the prizes, had anchored after Collingwood's preparatory signal, and were riding the swell off Cape Trafalgar. The others, which had had no choice, were struggling to claw away from the land against a rising wind.

The Admiral signalled for the frigates to relinquish the task of towing to some of the sound ships of the line, which would be more equal to the task. All day the weather worsened. The wind continued to rise to gale force, and at noon it began to rain heavily, and the horizon disappeared behind sheets of driving water.

During the afternoon, the prize *Redoutable* hoisted 314, the distress signal. She had been sandwiched between *Victory* and *Temeraire* during the battle, and to avoid firing straight through her and into each other, the two English ships had depressed their gun muzzles and fired downwards into her, with the result that she had numerous holes below the water-line, and was leaking like a sieve.

The *Swiftsure*, which was towing her, sent boats to take off as many of her men as possible. By nightfall she was evidently deeply waterlogged, wallowing heavily, but the sea was now too rough, and the gale too fierce, for boats to be launched in the dark. There must still, Weston knew, be hundreds of wounded below decks, perhaps already drowning as the water crept up inside the *Redoutable*'s ravaged hull, but nothing could be done for them. Just after ten that night, she sank by the stern with her gruesome cargo.

By the morning of the 23rd the gale had risen almost to a hurricane force, blowing from the south, and in the mountainous seas the tow-cables parted again and again. The *Thunderer* had taken over the task of towing the *Furieux*, and just after dawn the prize ship's foremast stays, which had been damaged in the battle and hastily repaired, parted, and the foremast went over the side, shortly followed by the jury mizzen which could not take the strain alone. Without sails or rudder she was going down on to leeward fast, and *Thunderer* signalled urgently for assistance.

Under storm jib and triple-reefed topsails, Weston took *Nemesis* as close as he dared. The *Furieux* was lower in the water now, too, and it was obvious that there was no hope of saving her. *Thunderer* put out a boat to try to reach the crippled ship in the hope of taking off at least the prize-crew, and Weston did the same. The seas were very heavy now, and at times the boats disappeared altogether in the troughs of the black-green waves, but however hard they pulled, the crippled ship went down to leeward faster than they.

The crew of the *Nemesis* watched dry-mouthed and in silence as those on board the *Furieux* managed, in spite of the appalling difficulties, to rig a jury foremast and shew a scrap of sail; but their pathetic struggle was unavailing. Without a rudder, they could not keep her to the wind, and the *Furieux* was driven inexorably down to lee, to be wrecked on the Spanish shore.

Chapter Fourteen

In the *Cetus*, Haworth and Tyler had decided to keep 'watch and watch', four hours on and four hours off, so that one of them should always be on deck. Haworth was on deck when disaster overtook the *Furieux*, and watched with a sick feeling of helplessness as she was driven to her doom, taking Styles, Bittles and the rest of the prize crew with her.

The *Cetus* was not out of danger herself: she was making water through the shot hole below the water-line, and the heavy seas were also coming in through the smashed lower-deck gunports. During the morning the main topsail, which was full of shot-holes, split and was torn to ribbons by the wind before it could be got in, and the sudden loss of it broke away the jury topmast. The topmen worked for hours in the reeling, heaving tops, rigging a main-topgallant-yard in its place. The mizzen-mast, which Haworth worried about constantly, seemed fit to carry nothing more than a scrap of sail, simply to take some of the strain off the men at the wheel.

When Tyler took over from him, Haworth went below and tried to rest, knowing that it was necessary for the safety of the ship, but anxiety made it difficult, and the injury to his back now throbbed all the time, and he could find no position that eased it. Down below, he knew, the injured were suffering horribly in the heaving ship. Those lying on the deck were rolled helplessly back and forth by the motion, and even those lashed in hammocks were bumped agonisingly against each other or the bulkheads, bursting their stitches and making their wounds bleed afresh. Many who had undergone amputation did not survive: being thrown about broke the artery ligatures and they quickly bled to death.

Every time he went on deck, there was some new trouble to be reported. The *Fougeux* suffered the same fate as the *Furieux*, broken adrift from her escort and driven down on to the shore with the loss of all those on board. Two other prizes, the

Bucentaure and the *Algeciras,* also parted company with the ships towing them, and a little later the tricolor was rehoisted in both of them. Evidently the Frenchmen on board had taken the opportunity to overpower the prize crews, or to persuade them to yield in the interests of saving the ship. They managed to get themselves under sail, and headed for Cadiz and were soon lost to sight. No-one could be spared to try to retake them.

During the afternoon the wind moderated a little, and five enemy ships and a handful of frigates, which had escaped intact from the battle, put out from Cadiz, despite the terrible weather, and came down on the fleet to try to retake some of the prizes. Collingwood ordered the able ships to cast off their tows and form line of battle. Haworth brought *Cetus* before the wind and took his place with the others, beating to quarters as they stood towards the enemy. Seeing themselves outnumbered, the French yielded and returned to Cadiz, but the manoeuvre had not been without value to them: their frigates had been able to retake two of the prizes, and were escorting them back towards Cadiz. The prospective prize-money was shrinking before the English captains' eyes, for those who had time and energy to consider the matter.

The respite from the wind was as brief as it was partial. Towards dusk it rose again, higher than ever, shrieking through the rigging and piling up mountainous seas which broke against the ships and sometimes washed over the decks. It seemed Providence had no pity on the victors of a great sea-battle; and for the third night the weary, disheartened fleet prepared to face the same exhausting hazards of wind and weather and lee shore.

Haworth struggled up from blackness into lamplight with the greatest reluctance. He seemed to have been asleep only minutes. Who was this waking him, shaking his shoulder now, since his eyes and lips would not obey his weary brain?

'Sir. Captain, sir.'

It was Morpurgo. Haworth unglued his eyes a fraction. His mouth was sticky with sleep. 'What time is it?'

'Three bells, sir.' He had been asleep an hour and a half.

Oh, not enough! 'Mr Tyler's respects, sir, and the wind's freshening, and would you come on deck, sir?'

'Very well,' Haworth said. His legs felt completely numb, and when he tried to push himself up, the pain of his bruising seized him like lion's teeth. Morpurgo helped him to his feet and into his pea-jacket, and he limped up on deck.

The *Cetus* was close-hauled under storm jib and staysails, leaping in the extravagant sea like a bucking horse. The hurricane drove the sea towards her in glassy walls, and she set her head into them, her bowsprit carving them into foam as the water broke over her bows and washed the fo'c'sle waist-deep. She seemed weighted by the sea, as if she would never rise, but slowly, slowly she lifted, the water fountaining out through the scuppers as her bowsprit pointed now at the invisible sky, corkscrewing as the water passed under her towards her port quarter, lifting her stern and dipping her head to the next wave.

Dip — roll — lift — roll, she performed her monstrous dance, while every timber in the ship groaned with her working, as the tremendous pressure of wind and water bent her this way and that like giant hands. And all the time the wind shrieked in the rigging in twenty different pitches, like the demented voices of demons, and the mizzen-mast groaned and thudded with an irregular, unnatural sound.

'I don't like the feel of her, sir,' Tyler yelled, bringing his mouth close to Haworth's ear so that he could hear him in the din. The wind was hurling hatfuls of icy water over them, breaking it into needle-fine spray against the standing rigging. 'She feels sluggish to me; and there's something else. I don't know what it is, but she doesn't feel right.'

'Have you sounded the well?' Haworth yelled back.

'Yes sir. We're still making water. I've got the pumps going all the time, but one of the larboard ones was knocked to pieces in the battle, and the water's gaining. I wish we could heave to.'

Heaving-to would ease the working of the timbers, and let in less water; but with Cape Trafalgar dead to leeward, they dare not risk it.

'If you want to wish, don't stop halfway: wish we had three good masts,' Haworth shouted.

'Pardon, sir?'

Haworth shook his head, and turned to speak to the quartermaster. There were four men at the wheel now, and it was all they could do to hold it.

'How does she feel to you?' he yelled, but before the man could answer, Tyler grabbed his arm hard.

'There, sir! Did you hear that?'

They listened tensely for the one sound in the storm's cacophany which had struck an unnatural chord. It was a strange sort of creaking, muted, but ugly.

'It came from below decks,' Haworth decided.

'There it is again!' Tyler yelled. 'I don't like it, sir.'

'You'd better investigate, Mr Tyler. Take Morpurgo with you. I'll take over here.'

'Aye aye, sir.'

It seemed a long wait on deck. The darkness lifted a little at one point as the clouds parted for a moment, enough for Haworth to see another sail not far from him up to windward. It was a frigate — he thought it was the *Nemesis* — and the sight comforted him a little before the cloud closed over again. He strained his eyes into the darkness. Now he knew where she was, he thought he could still see a glimmer of her, just a faint greyness in the blackness.

'Captain!'

Here came Tyler and Morpurgo, struggling up the sloping deck towards him. The water streamed down Tyler's face like tears; his face was set and white.

'That noise sir — it's the main mast. It's cracked nearly right through below decks, between the orlop and the lower deck, sir.'

'Good God!'

'It must have happened when the mizzen-mast went, sir. We'll have to heave to, and take the strain off it, sir, or it'll snap. You can see the crack widening every time she rolls.'

'Is it possible to repair it?'

'Well, sir, it's a diagonal crack, so we might whip it, sir, with rope and a couple of yards — sort of splint it, sir. I don't know if it'll hold.'

'It'll have to. Very well, Mr Tyler, we'll heave to while you do that.'

Tyler gave the order, and the boatswains calls began to shrill.

'All hands! All hands to shorten sail!'

But the weary men had not even reached their posts when the wind gusted demoniacally, laying them over, and with a sound like the end of the world, the main mast sagged forward, and the mizzen-mast snapped its moorings and fell too. The *Cetus* was thrown violently aback; the staysails exploded, the jib was whipped away in shreds, the larboard mainstays parted, and she fell off the wind, turning to run with the sea down to leeward, with the mass of wreckage hanging over to port.

'Mr Morpurgo!' Haworth screamed into the wind. 'The *Nemesis* is out there somewhere. Hoist the night signal for 314 at the foretop. Clear away one of the bow-chasers, and keep firing it until she hears us.'

'Aye aye, sir.'

The main mast was sagging forward and to port, and the mizzen-mast was resting against its cross-trees. Now they must face the appallingly difficult task of cutting away the wreckage so that it fell overboard, and hope that the *Nemesis* would be able to get a line to them and take them in tow before the wind and sea drove them after their late prize on to the rocks of the Spanish shore.

There was no time for fear, no time for weariness. Now they were fighting for their lives against their oldest enemy, the sea itself. The men, weary beyond thought, performed feats of strength and endurance that would have killed a landman, their discipline and the long months of training standing them in good stead now, when all their lives depended on their co-ordinated skill.

The axemen were cutting away the wreckage on the deck, the topmen performing the same task aloft, balancing on the footropes up in the corkscrewing tops, where the wind battered at them, trying to snatch them away into the howling darkness. At last the splintered mass of masts, yards and rigging came free and fell away overboard into the black, racing sea, and the *Cetus* righted herself, leaping more extravagantly without the weight, which had acted like a kind of sea-anchor.

Now here were lights, thank God! Here was the *Nemesis* flying down to them like a dancer, and as she passed they could see a man on the quarterdeck with the octopus shape of the grapple and line in his hands, ready to fling it on to the fo'c'sl of the *Cetus*. The boatswain was there with his mates, ready to pass the line down, haul in the cable, and make it fast when the grapple struck.

The first throw missed them, and the second, and *Nemesis* had to beat back to windward for another pass.

'Breakers, sir!' cried Webb suddenly. 'Breakers on the lee bow!'

The coast of Spain; waves leaping to fantastic height against the waiting rocks.

Nemesis again, and the flying starfish of the grapple, and a cheer, instantly whipped away, as it struck.

'Line fast, sir. They're pulling in the cable now.'

With the wreckage gone, *Cetus* had developed a quick and vicious movement, and without her tophamper she rolled, too. It would be a horribly dangerous operation for the *Nemesis* to get her under way. When that colossal drag came on the line, the strain on the frigate's masts would be frightful.

'Breakers on the starboard bow!'

'Breakers dead ahead!'

White as bared teeth in the darkness. No, it was not quite so dark now. Was dawn coming? They longed for dawn more than a thirsty man longs for water.

'*Nemesis* signals: ready to get under way, sir.'

'Acknowledge.' The word was passed rapidly down the ship to the signals rating on the fo'c'sl. 'Stand by, at the wheel.'

The cable rose out of the sea, spouting water as it tightened; the breakers flashed white, distractingly, at the corners of vision. They watched the frigate's sails with horrid fascination. If they were to split under the strain, all would be lost.

'*Nemesis* signals, sir: prepare to go about.'

'Acknowledge.'

'Signal's down, sir!'

'Helm a starboard!'

For a long, frightful moment there seemed no response. To Weston, standing on the raised poop, the better to view the situation, the *Cetus* seemed to hang like a deadweight, sulkily refusing to move, as though the sea held her in a kind of suction, and the loom of the grey shore and the breakers were close, so close that there seemed no escaping them.

Beside him, Davie Reid was cursing the big ship rhythmically under his breath, exhorting her with a string of Scottish oaths to yield. Weston could hear *Nemesis*'s masts groaning with the strain of the drag astern, and out of the corner of his eye he saw Osborne's hands twitching as he watched the taut sails, longing to cast off the tow-line which was endangering his precious ship.

Then the party which had been working frantically on the fo'c's'l of the *Cetus* managed to haul out a new flying jib, and the scrap of sail gave the extra leverage needed for the rudder to bite. She began to come round, turning her head away from the terrible rocks and the white water, and someone, somewhere, raised a feeble cheer.

Weston lifted the speaking-trumpet. 'We'll shake out a reef in the foretops'l,' he shouted. He saw Osborne open his mouth to protest, and then think better of it as he realised, as Weston had, that it would help to counteract the tremendous drag of the *Cetus* astern. The big ship began to move slowly forward, still rolling with the ugly movement of a mastless vessel. Weston could see another party working as fast as they could to fish a spare jib-boom to the stump of the mizzen-mast so that they could rig a sail of some sort. Any canvas they could shew would help.

And then suddenly the wind gusted again, so violently that it actually checked the *Nemesis*'s way for an instant, driving her sideways over the surface of the water as the sea dropped away under her stern and her rudder was exposed; pushing her into the path of the *Cetus*. She was still turning. Weston saw the bowsprit come plunging towards them, forwards and sideways, like a giant unicorn's horn, and without time for thought he flung himself at Reid, bearing him to the deck, as the massive spar, big as a tree, smashed into them, pinning them against the transom.

He heard himself scream, felt a terrible agony of dissolution inside him, knew he was to die, crushed between the two immovable masses of wood. He heard the rending crash as the bows struck, splintering the quarter galleries, and then the pressure on him was gone. Above him there was a rush of air as the bowsprit, lifted by the sea, continued its sideways career of destruction, smashing away the transom rail and dropping clear.

Pain battered him. He fought to retain consciousness, to understand what had happened. It had all taken only an instant. He was sinking into darkness, and he struggled against it, angrily, feeling no pain now, only a bitter fury. Not now, not like this! his mind cried. There were people calling him, come to rescue him now, when it was too late. A sound came from his mouth that he did not recognise, and the darkness overtook him, black and suffocating and absolute.

On the *Cetus* they watched in grim silence, waiting to know their fate. *Nemesis* hung helpless, wallowing in the troughs, pale gashes on her splintered stern where new wood was exposed, but her masts and sails were intact, and they could see the flurry of activity on her decks as they worked to bring her to the wind again.

One man on the quarterdeck was throwing over loops of the towing cable, to give them room to gather steerage way before the drag came on her.

'Signal to *Nemesis*: cast off tow if necessary,' said Haworth.

'Aye aye, sir.'

A figure on the quarterdeck waved in response to their signal. They were all too busy to hoist a reply.

'Someone was injured, sir. Two people. I can see them carrying them below,' said Pitcairn. 'Poor devils.'

Haworth nodded. He had heard that thin, inhuman scream even through the din of the crash, but it was too dark to see who it was.

Nemesis was gathering way again, taking up the strain, hauling *Cetus* away from the hostile shore. The darkness was definitely less, greyness seeping, unwillingly into the sky. *Cetus* managed to hoist a staysail on the jury mizzen as a kind driver, easing the task both of the *Nemesis* and the quartermasters, but still the storm shewed no sign of abating, and their progress was painfully slow. The sun had long risen over the battered fleet before they were close enough for Haworth to signal to the Admiral and report *Cetus*'s condition.

The Admiral did not hesitate. To lose a prize was one thing, but to lose one of their own ships would be intolerable. The flags rushed up *Euryalus*'s halliards: *Nemesis* was to tow *Cetus* to Gibraltar for repair, leaving immediately.

There was sunshine at Gibraltar, and blue skies, fantastic after so many days of howling storm. There was the rock, like a great bony forehead, crowned with a green wig of vegetation; and the town, climbing over the lower slopes; and the battery, with the Union Flag flying bravely, watching over the shipping anchored in the bay.

'There's the *Belleisle*, sir,' said Tyler. The *Naiad*, who had towed her in, had gone straight back to the fleet. They had passed her on her way back the previous day.

'I'll bet she caused a stir,' Pitcairn commented. 'That will have been the first news they had of the battle.'

'Mr Tyler, there will be salutes to be fired. Have the larboard foredeck gun cleared away, and send for Mr Partridge, if you please,' said Haworth.

'Aye aye, sir.'

'And send word to Mr Parry to have the certificate ready for the port officer, and ask him to make his arrangements for sending the wounded ashore to the hospital. Mr Webb, signal to *Nemesis*, if you please: can you spare an anchor cable?'

'Aye aye, sir.'

'Mr Morpurgo, run below and give my compliments to the French officers, and tell them that we have reached Gibraltar, and that I shall be transferring them to the charge of the Governor. And pass the word for my servant to have my dress uniform ready.'

'Aye aye, sir.'

There was so much to be done, including finding time to complete the report he had been writing over the past several days. The warmth, now that they were stationary and in an enclosed bay, was enough to make his hands sweat, and the ink ran and smeared on the damp paper. Africa, holding her toy lamb perilously by the tail, was wildly excited, and begging to be allowed to go ashore with him; and Dipton was mourning over the wreck of his dress-coat, though Haworth's hasty glance could not discern the repair he had had to make to it.

And then, in the midst of all this, Lieutenant Dugasse came to interrupt him with an enquiry about cartels of exchange which Haworth could not possibly answer, and Midshipman Rose, appearing innocently at the door with a message, almost had his head bitten off.

'Mr Tyler's respects, sir, and the boat's come from the *Nemesis*, and could you come, sir?'

'My compliments to Mr Tyler,' Haworth said tautly, wrestling with a sealing-wafer which *would* stick to his fingers, 'and I am confident he can deal with the new anchor-cable without my presence.'

Rose's ears crimsoned. 'Begging your pardon, sir, but there was somebody in the boat, sir, that was asking to see you urgently, sir.'

Haworth cursed inwardly, but only sighed outwardly. Though knowing it would turn out to be some petty problem that there was no need to disturb him for, he was too just to execute the messenger. 'Very well, Mr Rose. Tell Mr Tyler I shall be there directly.'

He managed at last to seal the report, and brushing off Dugasse with a bow and putting Africa gently but firmly aside, he went up on deck, taking the steps slowly, for he was still very stiff, though now the bruising had begun to come out in a spectacular display of colours, it was not quite so painful. The fo'c'sl was a-throng as the boatswain's party hauled the new cable up from the *Nemesis*'s boat, but on the comparative quiet of the quarterdeck the visitor was waiting for him, bareheaded in the sunshine, his hands twisting anxiously before him. It was Bates.

'What are you doing here, Bates?' Haworth asked in astonishment.

'Oh, Captain Haworth, sir, it's my master — it's Captain Weston, sir. He's badly hurt, and asking for you, and please will you come right away, sir?'

'Hurt? How is he hurt? What's happened?'

'It was when you ran on board us, sir, in the storm,' Bates said, lifting his eyes to Haworth's, his face drawn with distress. 'The Cap'n threw himself on Mr Reid, sir, to save him, and the bowsprit hit him and crushed him, sir.'

'Good God!' The horror of it hit Haworth like a blow to the stomach. He remembered the scream he had heard. 'We saw someone had been hurt, but I never dreamed it was the captain. How bad is it?'

'Mortal bad, sir. Mr Oakleigh — the surgeon — says he doesn't think ...' Bates swallowed, unable to complete the sentence. 'Only he's been asking for you, over and over, sir, and now we've anchored, Mr Oakleigh thinks you ought to come at once, sir, if you can, because he doesn't know how long ... how long he'll last.'

Haworth hesitated only an instant. There were so many official things he was obliged to do as soon as he arrived in port, but technically he had not yet anchored, and that would serve as an excuse if excuse were needed. Weston was his friend, almost his brother: he must go.

'Very well, I'll come,' he said, 'Take over, Mr Tylor.'

'Aye aye, sir.'

In the boat, pulling for *Nemesis*'s side, Bates spoke again: 'Mr Osborne took over, of course, sir, and then the Admiral sent us straight off to Gibraltar, so there wasn't time to tell anyone, not that there was anything anyone could have done. Mr Oakleigh says there's internal hem — something.'

'Haemorrhage?'

'That's it, sir. He thinks the Cap'n's liver may have been crushed. He's been trying to keep him still, sir, but it wasn't easy in the storm. Mr Reid's got three broken ribs. The Cap'n saved his life, sir,' Bates added miserably.

'You did right to come for me, Bates,' Haworth said, automatically trying to comfort him. Weston dying? He could not believe it. Weston was too young and strong and full of energy. He had promised to help him celebrate the victory at Spithead. He had to live to keep that promise.

Osborne saluted him as he stepped on board the *Nemesis*, but did not delay him on deck. 'He's in his cabin, sir. The surgeon's with him.'

271

'Thank you, Mr Osborne.'

The sentry at the cabin door came to attention; Haworth entered. Even at such a moment, he noticed the difference from his own cabin. *Nemesis* had not taken direct part in the action, and despite the damage to her stern, the cabin furniture was still intact. He glimpsed mahogany and silver, gained an impression of modest luxury and expensive good taste, before the surgeon came forward to greet him.

'Captain Haworth? Oakleigh, sir. I'm glad you've come. He's been asking for you ever since he regained consciousness.'

'How is he?'

Oakleigh shook his head. 'Frankly, sir, I did not expect him to last this long. There is a spinal injury and extensive internal damage, shock, haemorrhage. It was only his great vitality which brought him back to consciousness at all.'

'But now we are here, we can transfer him to the shore hospital,' said Haworth quickly. 'With their better facilities —'

'Even if he were to survive the transfer to shore by boat, sir, they would not be able to help him, I'm afraid. There's nothing anyone can do.'

'Is he in pain?'

'He feels very little, sir. The injury to the spine has numbed his lower body. He is very restless, and that is typical of his condition, but I am sure it has also to do with his desire to speak to you. I hope you may be able to ease his mind, sir.'

Haworth nodded, and Oakleigh led the way into the sleeping-cabin. The cot had been lowered on to its frame, now that the ship was at anchor, and in it, carefully packed with sheets to prevent movement, lay Weston. Haworth bent over him, his mouth dry with shock, his heart contracting with pity at the sight of him.

Weston's skin was yellow-white, moist and clammy, his hair dark with sweat, his eyes seeming already sunken in his face. Haworth carefully took the hand that was lying on the sheet, and it felt cold and impersonal, unreal, as if it were made of wax.

'Haworth?' Weston's voice was only a whisper.

'Yes, I'm here.'

Weston licked his lips, and his brown eyes moved over

Haworth's face restlessly. He seemed to have forgotten what he wanted to say.

'You sent for me, and I'm here,' Haworth said clearly. 'I'm going to see you're looked after. You've had a bit of a knock, old fellow, but now we've reached Gibraltar, we'll get you to the hospital, and —'

'No,' Weston whispered, and he gripped Haworth's hand weakly. 'Listen.' Haworth waited in silence, watching the younger man gathering his strength, arresting his wandering thoughts. 'Don't ...' A long pause. 'Don't bury me here.' He stopped, and lay panting shallowly, his skin seeming to take on a grey tinge from the effort. 'Take me home.'

Haworth pressed his hand. 'You're not going to die. You're going to be all right. You can't die, Weston.'

The hand gripped tighter. '*Promise!*'

Reluctantly, Haworth nodded. 'I'll take you home. I promise.'

The eyes locked on his, filled with the urgency of his struggle. 'Tell Lucy — I love her.'

'Yes,' said Haworth, his throat aching. 'I'll tell her. I'll look after her, Weston, I promise you.'

Weston nodded, and closed his eyes with relief. Haworth waited. The cold, damp hand in his grew limp again, and the surgeon came up to the bedside and took the other wrist to feel for the pulse. Weston was still for so long, that Haworth began at last to withdraw his hand, upon which the eyes flew open again, searching for his face.

'It's all right — I'm still here,' Haworth said gently.

'Cold,' Weston whispered. His eyes wandered again, and a look of great bitterness seemed to cross his face. 'Thomas,' he said, incomprehensibly to Haworth. He chafed the dying man's hand, not knowing what else to do for him.

The surgeon put down the other hand, caught Haworth's eye and shook his head. 'I don't think it will be long.'

Weston was staring at nothing, locked in the unapproachable solitude of his death, his eyes beginning to glaze. His lips parted once more. 'Tell Lucy,' he whispered, quite clearly. His breathing hitched and stumbled, dragged on again more faintly. His lips moved, but Haworth could not catch what he said, and then the breathing stopped and did not resume.

Haworth laid down his hand he held gently on the sheet, and then stood indecisively, not knowing quite what to do. It did not seem possible that it could end like this. There must be something more to be done.

When at last he went back on deck, he was astonished to find bright day, and the life of the ship and the port still going on all around. It seemed an affront for the sun to continue so unheedingly to shine; it felt as though he had been in that cabin for hours.

With two jury masts and her shot-holes roughly but securely patched, the *Cetus* set sail for England on 1 November. In her hold was the lead-lined coffin Haworth had had made for the body of Captain Weston, and his cabin furniture and private papers and belongings packed in his sea trunk. Haworth's cabin was now gratefully free of French officers, who had been transferred to the Governor's charge, and the orlop of wounded, who had been transferred to the shore hospital.

Nemesis was remaining in Gibraltar, receiving her refit and waiting for a new captain to be promoted into her, but on Haworth's representation to the port admiral, Bates, who was dazed with grief, was coming home in the *Cetus*. Dipton had tactfully let him think that he needed help in looking after Captain Haworth and his daughter.

'Give him something to do, sir,' Dipton murmured to Haworth, with a nod towards Bates, who was polishing knives in a bemused manner. 'Keep his mind off, a bit. I told him Miss Africa was a bit of a handful, begging your pardon, sir, and took up all my time.'

Africa, at least, had something to be glad about, for the stowing of the coffin and the trunk in the hold had resulted in the rediscovery of Cleopatra, who had been thrown there with a miscellaneous collection of odds and ends when the ship was cleared for action. She emerged a little scarred, and minus a wheel, but Africa was delighted to have her back. On sunny days she sat with Bullen on the fo'c'sl while he attempted to repair Cleopatra one-handed, and demonstrated his new and painfully-acquired ability to whistle through the gaps in his teeth.

On inclement days she stayed in her father's cabin, and did her best to comfort Jeffrey, who wandered restlessly about the unfamiliar spaces, yowling in a lost sort of way, or slept determinedly on the lap of anyone who would sit still for him.

The winds were unfavourable, and the journey home was slow. *Cetus* carried sail tenderly on her jury masts, and Haworth hove to when necessary, for there was no hurry. The battle off Cape Trafalgar seemed a hundred years ago, and any joy or pride there might have been in it seemed outweighed by the death of Lord Nelson, and the more personal, sorrowing loss of Weston. There would be glory and congratulation, and prize-money, and perhaps promotion, and the jacks looked forward eagerly to the delights of paying-off in Portsmouth. But Haworth, in his off-duty hours, as he absently nursed Jeffrey on his lap, could only keep thinking of how he was going to tell Lucy.

On 7 November, Lucy was eating her usual hearty breakfast, having come back from her early ride in the Park, when the door opened and to her surprise, Chetwyn came in, wearing his Chinese silk dressing-gown.

'What on earth are you doing up so early?' she enquired mildly. 'Do you want some breakfast? I'll ring the bell —'

'No, no, just some coffee,' Chetwyn said, taking a seat opposite her and yawning. 'How you can eat at this time of day, I don't know.'

'I've worked up an appetite,' she said succinctly. 'What *are* you doing out of bed?'

'Robert will be arriving soon. There's a special sale on at Tattersall's and there's a team of match-greys we don't want to miss.'

'Galbraith's?' Lucy said with interest. 'Yes, I've seen 'em. Good action. Nice mouths, too. Are you after them?'

'I might be. You see, when Robert comes of age next year, he's going to set up his establishment in London, and then he'll need some decent horses.'

'Oh, so it's Robert wants to buy them, is it?'

'I thought they might make a suitable coming-of-age present,' Chetwyn said diffidently. Lucy raised an eyebrow, but refrained from comment. What Chetwyn did with his own money was his affair, and he had never been less than generous towards her.

'They won't go cheaply,' was all she said, and poured him a cup of coffee. 'How long is Robert staying this time?'

Chetwyn gave her an engaging smile. 'I don't know. Does he get in your way? Shall I send him off to an hotel?'

'Of course not. I just wondered why he bothers to keep up the pretence that he's up at Oxford. The nearest he ever gets to his college is Wolvercote Park. Perhaps you ought to pay him a salary as Roland's tutor, and be done with it.'

'How acerbic you are this morning, Lucy,' Chetwyn said mildly, reaching for the newspaper. 'You see, rising early isn't good for your temper. Is this today's? What news is there of the Austrians?'

'Nothing more since yesterday. They always were a lily-livered nation, but that surrender on the Danube is beyond anything. Why couldn't they wait for the Russians? Then they'd have beaten Boney easily.'

'I must say in their defence that if I were facing Boney's crack troop, armed to the teeth and thirsting for blood, I wouldn't be inclined to wait for the Russians.'

'Thank God we don't have to depend on such allies at sea, is all I can say,' said Lucy, dabbing mustard on the last of her mutton cutlet, and Chetwyn looked at her with sympathy.

'There'll be some news soon, don't worry,' he said.

'I'm not worried,' Lucy said, standing up. 'I must go and get dressed. Good luck with the greys.'

'Thanks,' Chetwyn began, and then paused at the sound of excited voices down below. 'What's going on?' he said, getting up and going to the door. Hicks was coming up the stairs, with Parslow close on his heels, while a group of servants lingered in the hall, whispering amongst themselves.

'My lady, my lord, there is news at last! A great sea-battle has been fought off the coast of Spain,' Hicks began, and in spite of her claim not to be worried, her eyes flew to Parslow's, to receive the reassurance of a minute shake of the head. 'Our fleet has met the Combined and defeated them, my lady, defeated them completely. Twenty ships taken, so they are saying. A most complete victory.'

'How do you know this?' Lucy asked sharply. Hicks gestured Parslow forward.

'It was when I was exercising the chestnuts, my lady,' he said. 'I always make a point of coming back round by the Admiralty in case there is any news, and this morning one of the porters, who knows me, came out when he saw me, to say that Lieutenant Laponotière of the schooner *Pickle* arrived from Falmouth in the early hours of this morning, my lady, with despatches from Admiral Collingwood.'

'From Collingwood?'

'Yes, my lady. Admiral Nelson is dead.'

'Nelson, dead?' Chetwyn interposed. 'Are you sure?'

'It is true, my lord. The most tragic loss!' Hicks cried. 'Our victory is dearly bought, indeed, if it costs us the life of the Hero of the Nile.'

'That will do, Hicks,' Lucy said quickly. 'You may go and tell the other servants the news. Parslow, I want more details. Tell me everything you know.'

All day little pieces of news and rumour filtered into the house, and there was a constant coming and going. Chetwyn and Robert went out as soon as the latter arrived, but Lady Aylesbury had more visitors than ever before, for the house in Upper Grosvenor Street seemed the natural one to visit in the circumstances. Everyone wanted to tell, ask, and exclaim about the victory over the French, and the death of Nelson. The two things were, of course, inseparable, and most of the day's visitors seemed far more concerned with the latter than the former.

'A glorious, dearly-bought victory,' proclaimed Lady Tewkesbury, endorsing what seemed to be the popular conclusion.

'What are twenty ships in exchange for Our Hero?' Mrs Fauncett moaned. 'I declare, I fainted dead away when Nesbitt told me this morning. I have not felt well ever since.'

'My maid has been weeping like a baby all day,' said Mrs Edgecumbe.

'I feel almost as much envy as compassion,' said Lady Bessborough. 'He could not have picked out a finer close to such a life. I think I should like to die so.'

Lucy listened without comment. She remembered how

277

these same ladies had reviled Nelson earlier that year, when Villeneuve escaped from Toulon.

Docwra brought her the earliest copy of *The Times* the next morning.

'It's got Admiral Collingwood's despatch printed in it, my lady,' she said, handing it over, her fingers lingering on one edge of the page, 'and a list of the killed and wounded.'

Lucy looked up at her sharply, and then laughed, and said, 'Were you worried, then, Docwra? You are a fool. Frigates don't take part in the battle. Their task is to bring the ships together, and then withdraw out of range.'

'Yes, my lady,' Docwra said, content on this occasion to receive the abuse. She hovered while Lucy read.

'He praises Blackwood's vigilance in watching the enemy,' she said after a moment. 'No mention of — but it is a preliminary report, written in haste. He will give more details later.'

'I'm sure of it, my lady.'

'Good God, here's poor Duff of the *Mars* and Cooke of the *Bellerophon* killed!' she exclaimed a little later. "I have yet heard of none others", says Collingwood.'

'Yes, my lady,' said Docwra, turning away with a small, private smile. Lucy's tone of voice had told her a great deal.

There was nothing to do now but to wait for his letter. Lucy felt like a small stillness at the heart of a whirlwind as the excitement over the Battle of Trafalgar swirled around her and left her untouched. There were illuminations, representations of every sort on every stage of the battle and Nelson's last moments, *tableaux vivants*, musical impromptus; there were handbills and paintings and songs and terrible poems; there were Nelson snuff-boxes and tankards, models of every size and varying accuracy of the *Victory*, and every sort of memorial china the ingenious imagination of commerce could devise.

Honours were announced: Collingwood was awarded a barony, and immediate confirmation as Commander-in-Chief of the Mediterranean Fleet, Nelson's old command. Captain Hardy was to have a baronetcy, and there was to be a special Trafalgar medal for everyone who participated in the battle. Nelson's brother was given an earldom, his sisters and his wife large pensions, and there was to be a state funeral for the Hero himself, as soon as his dead body could be brought home. Of Lady Hamilton and the child there was no mention. No-one wanted to remember at a time like this that his private life had been irregularly conducted.

So the three weeks of November wore away, and December came. Chetwyn grew tired of the noise of London and went down to Wolvercote to ride with Robert; and Lucy remained in Town to wait for news.

Then on the evening of the 3rd, when Lucy was upstairs dressing to go to a ball, and Major Wiske, who was to escort her, was standing by the fire in the drawing-room and admiring the fit of his breeches in the looking-glass opposite, the commotion of arrival was heard below.

Lucy was sitting in front of her own glass, while Docwra adjusted her headdress — a fillet of gold ribbon supporting a long plume, pinned with a diamond clip — when Ollett tapped on the door.

'Captain Haworth has arrived from Portsmouth, my lady, and is waiting below.'

'Haworth? How wonderful! Oh, what luck I had not already left for this tedious ball,' Lucy cried, jumping up. 'Never mind that now, Docwra. I can't wait for gloves at a moment like this!'

She scooped her train over her arm and ran out of the room and down the stairs like a child, to where the murmur of voices and the glow of light came through the open drawing-room door.

'Haworth!' she cried as she entered. 'Haworth, I am so glad you are come!' He stood by the fire, his clothes shabby and crumpled, his face drawn and weather-beaten. 'Where is he? Have you a letter from him?'

She started across the room to him, and then stopped halfway, puzzled by the atmosphere which only now impinged on her. Wiske was looking at her with anxious eyes, Haworth's expression held no gladness or welcome. Behind her she heard Docwra come in and say, 'My lady —'

'What is it?' she asked, tilting her head, frowning at Haworth. 'What's the matter? Why do you look at me like that?'

'Lucy,' he said, a world of reluctance in his voice. He put out a hand to her. 'It's bad news. I don't know quite how to tell you.'

'Is he hurt?' she asked, feeling her heart beating faster, though the apprehension did not seem to belong to her, but to someone else nearby. 'It's all right, you can tell me. How bad is it? Where is he?'

'Lucy, my dear.' He took a step towards her, and she backed instinctively.

'No,' she said.

'It was after the battle. There was a terrible storm. Our ship ran on board his. He saved a young midshipman's life.'

'No,' she said again. She could back no further now. There were people behind her, blocking her escape. Would nothing stop that inexorable voice?

'Lucy, I'm sorry. There was nothing anyone could do. He died when we got to Gibraltar.'

His face, and Wiske's, were before her, horrible with pity. She turned. Docwra was there, and Ollett, and Hicks, clustered by the door, and beyond them, Parslow. Her eyes met his, and he came forward. The others parted to let him through, and he came close and laid his hand on her arm, and as he touched her, she shuddered, and knew it was true. He helped her to a chair by the fire and sat her down, taking up his position beside her as she faced Haworth like a soldier facing execution.

'Tell me,' she said.

BOOK THREE

The Anchor

For who, to dumb Forgetfulness a prey,
This pleasing anxious being e'er resigned,
Left the warm precincts of the cheerful day,
Nor cast one longing ling'ring look behind?
　　　Thomas Grey: *Elegy written in a Country Churchyard*

Chapter Fifteen

The night seemed endless. Lucy sat by the window in her bedchamber, staring unseeingly into the dark street, until all the sounds of to-ing and fro-ing, the carriages, the footsteps, the last late revellers, had ceased, and the night was silent, but for the chiming of the church clocks on the hours and the quarters. Then, in the stillness, there was nothing to distract her thoughts from the endless circle they prescribed.

It seemed an age ago that she had sat in the bright drawing-room, listening while Haworth put an end forever to all joy. The scene had been so calm — no great explosion or outcry, only the small, quiet, deadly words, and then she had got up to go away and try to understand them. Only Parslow had come with her. She had seen out of the corners of her mind the little silent exchange between him and Docwra as she walked out of the drawing-room. He knew she couldn't have borne Docwra near her.

Parslow sat in a chair on the other side of the room, not speaking, not moving except occasionally to get up and tend the candles; and Lucy sat with her hands in her lap, and struggled alone with pain and incomprehension. The dark hours passed, the world turned slowly. Eventually the sun would rise again, and a new day would begin, but Weston would still be dead. Hardest of all hard things to understand was that he would always be dead from now on.

The darkest hour. There was no sound anywhere, and the silence was absolute, black and suffocating.

'Parslow?'

'Yes, my lady?' His voice came gentle out of the darkness to reassure her. He had always been there, before Docwra, before any of them.

'What time is it?'

'A little after four, my lady.'

'Dawn is still a long way off. I don't want dawn to come.' She turned towards the pale glimmer of his face across the

283

room. 'I know what you're thinking — it will come, whether I want it to or not. One has no choice in the important things.'

'No, my lady,' he agreed.

'That's why —' She paused, pursuing a thought. 'Was it a *great* sin, do you think?'

'Only you can tell that,' he said. His voice was unobtrusive, sliding in amongst her thoughts like one of them.

'The Church would say it was. But I can't regret it, you see. Not any of it.' She turned again to the window. She felt as though she were convalescent from a long illness, restless and weary and parched. 'I don't want day to come.' Here in the dark there was a brief respite. At the end of it, she would have to know and accept.

Later she said, 'He was everything to me.'

'He knew that.'

'Yes. We didn't waste anything. I'm glad of that.'

An hour passed. The candle nearest her guttered and sank with a hot smell, and went out, and she saw then that there was a greyness in the sky. Her time was running out.

Across the room, Parslow had fallen asleep, his chin sunk on his chest, his large, leathery hands resting on the frail, carved arms of the little gilt boudoir chair. She looked at him with enormous, weary affection, and then got up, moving quietly so as not to wake him, across the room to her writing desk.

Lying on it was the letter Haworth had brought to her, the letter Weston had begun two days before the battle, when the enemy first began to come out of harbour. She sat at the desk and read it again, slowly, while the faint daylight broadened outside.

Then she opened a drawer and brought out a small, ormolu casket which she unlocked with a key. Inside were all his letters, read and reread until the paper grew soft at the edges. She took out one or two and handled them. She did not need to read them: she knew them by heart. Then she sighed, and folded up the letter Haworth had brought, reached for her pen, dipped it in the standish, and wrote on the outside of it in her even, childish script, 'His last letter.'

She sat and looked at it until the ink was dry. She held it against her cheek for a moment, as if it were his dear hand,

and then she placed it on top of the others in the casket, and closed the lid, and locked it, and put the casket away, with an air of finality, in the drawer.

Outside the windows, the pearl of before-dawn was bleaching out the candles, and the first scattered threads of movement were binding into day. She stood up, stretching her aching limbs, feeling her eyes burning with tiredness, and saw that Parslow was awake and watching her.

'There will be so much to do,' she said.

Chetwyn came back from Wolvercote on receiving Captain Haworth's message, apprehensive as to what he would find. Docwra met him in the hall.

'How is she?' he asked.

'Very calm, my lord. I don't like it.' She shook her head. 'She doesn't cry or carry on, just works away, writing letters and such, as if nothing had happened.'

'Writing letters?'

'She's sorting out the captain's affairs, my lord,' she said with some embarrassment. 'On account of he hadn't any family at all. But I wish she'd cry, my lord. It'd be more natural. And she won't have anyone near her, barring Parslow, my lord.'

Chetwyn found her in the breakfast parlour, neatly dressed in a grey-blue round gown, seated at the table, writing, with Jeffrey curled up on her lap. She didn't look up as he came in, didn't even seem to notice that he was there.

'Hello, Lucy,' he said at last. 'How are you?'

She looked up. She was very pale, but otherwise there was no outward sign that things were not as usual. What had he expected? Widow's weeds? Extravagant grief? And yet there was a difference. There were shadows under her eyes, and two lines of tiredness or pain at her mouth corners; but more even than that, she no longer looked like a child masquerading as an adult. For the first time it was possible to look at her and believe that she was the mother of three — four — children.

'You look tired,' he said. 'You must take care of yourself.'

She did not answer. He cleared his throat awkwardly.

'Lucy, I want you to know I really am sorry.' She looked at him impassively, as if she were simply waiting for him to finish so that she could go on with what she was doing. 'I know what you must be feeling. Truly, I never would have wanted it to end like this.'

She drew a tired sigh. 'Go away, Chetwyn,' she said.

He bit his lip. 'Please don't be bitter,' he said. 'I know we have had our differences, but —'

'I'm not bitter. Now please leave me alone. I'm very busy.' She went back to her writing, and there seemed nothing he could do except leave her.

They met again at dinner. She sat opposite him at the other end of the table, but she ate very little.

'Why don't you go back to Wolvercote?' she said when he had exhausted all his attempts to converse with her. 'I don't need you here.'

'Come back with me,' he said. 'Everyone will be going down to the country soon. London will be empty. Come to Wolvercote and see the children, and we'll go hunting, and have a few friends down for Christmas, and everything will be cosy and pleasant.'

She did not quite smile, but her expression softened just a little. 'You don't need to worry about me,' she said. 'I appreciate your concern, but really, I'm all right. I just want to be left alone. Please, Chetwyn.'

He sighed. 'Whatever you want. Just remember I'm there, when you want me.' He went back to Wolvercote the next morning, without seeing her again.

She arranged for Weston's burial amongst his ancestors in the churchyard at Great Wakering. She could not think what else he could have meant when he made Haworth promise to bring his body home. She had meant to go to the funeral heself, but at the last moment she felt could not bear it, and sent Parslow and Bates instead. She ordered a headstone, and a marble memorial for the wall inside the church, which the rector of the parish was glad to accord a prominent place opposite the south door, in return for a substantial contribution to church funds.

Weston's sea-chest was delivered to the house, and Lucy ordered it to be put away in the loft. She could not yet — perhaps never would be able to — open it, and go through his belongings. Amongst his papers she found a will, dating from that September, written during the quiet period on the Cadiz blockade. In it he left his entire estate in trust for 'my natural son, Thomas Freeman', naming Lucy as trustee, and requesting that the boy might be allowed to take his surname.

Apart from Weston's private fortune, which was small, there was the prize-money from Trafalgar. To compensate the captains a little for the loss in the storm of so many of the prizes, Parliament had voted a special award of £300,000, to be divided amongst everyone who took part in the battle, according to the usual rules of prize-money. Weston's share for that day's work was £3,362. Lucy invested it in the Funds on Thomas's behalf. Out of her own private capital, she purchased an annuity for Bates; Jeffrey she took into her home.

That December was a sombre month, not only because of the death of Nelson, whose body was brought up to Sheerness on the *Victory* on the 21st. Pitt's health was fast failing, and when Parliament went into recess he went down to Bath to drink the waters as a last, desperate remedy. Captain Haworth was recalled to Portsmouth where, in the great cabin of the *Prince of Wales*, Admiral Calder's court martial took place. In time of war it was difficult to assemble sufficient captains in one place, and both Haworth and Hardy had been subpoena'd. The hearing took three days, at the end of which they acquitted Calder of cowardice or disaffection, but found him guilty of 'not doing his utmost' to renew the engagement with the French last July. The penalty imposed on him, which for cowardice might have been death, was only a reprimand, but every officer in the cabin knew that Calder's career was over. He would never be employed again.

Then just before Christmas came the terrible news that the allied army had been utterly crushed by Napoleon at Austerlitz. Austria was suing for a separate peace; Sweden was withdrawing from the alliance for fear of losing her Pomeranian territories; and the two English armies Pitt had sent out were stranded and presumed lost, one in the French dominated Italy, where nothing had been heard of it for months, and the other trapped between Boney and the frozen waters of the Elbe. It seemed certain that Pitt would fall, if he did not die first; and when he fell others would fall with him.

Nelson's body, which had been lying in state in the Painted Hall in Greenwich Hospital since 22 December, was taken by river in a great procession of ceremonial barges up to White-hall Steps on 8 January, to lie in the Captain's Room in the Admiralty in readiness for the state funeral the following day. It was to be a magnificent affair, attended by royalty, nobility, ministers, admirals and generals, and the whole of London society. The crew of *Victory* were to march behind the coffin, and Hardy and Blackwood were to carry the emblems, but few of Nelson's friends would be present. Most of them were sea officers and, like the rest of the Trafalgar captains, they were still at sea. Lady Hamilton was most empathically not invited.

Lucy did not attend the funeral either. On 8 January she received a letter from the masons to tell her that Weston's memorial was in place, and on an impulse she decided to drive with Parslow down to Great Wakering to see it.

The little village was always quiet, standing, as it did, at the end of the world; for beyond it, the earth degenerated by salt degrees through marsh into sea. But that windy January day, grey with blustery showers, its street was empty, and they might have been the only people left alive. They drove to the end of the village where the little church of St Nicholas stood on a shallow rise overlooking the marshes. Parslow held the horses at the gate, while Lucy went in alone.

Inside the church was a haven from the weather; the still air smelled of wood and wax and old incense, dry as sand, silent as dust. The new white marble of the memorial stood out opposite the door as if it were illuminated from within. Lucy approached it shyly, and stood beneath it to read it.

Sacred to the memory of Captain James Rivers Weston, who died on the 26th of October, 1805, in the thirty-second year of his life. Isaiah LX, 20.

She looked for a long time, admiring the smooth, sharp edges of the deep-cut words. It said little, but those who knew

288

would understand. The mason had made a nice job of it, she thought.

She walked over to the lectern by the door where the visitor's book stood open, and turned back the pages until she came to the entry she and Weston had made that day in the summer of 1802. She remembered how lightheartedly he had said, 'One day when we're old, we'll come back and look at this, and remember how happy we were.' Oh Weston! she thought despairingly, you ought to have known that the Fates are always listening, and always jealous. She touched the words with a forefinger, as though the ink might convey something of him back to her. His warm and living hand had held the pen that made these marks. The ache of missing him rose up so strongly that she could only stand with her head bowed, waiting for it to pass.

One more thing to do; one thing to be redressed. She had signed herself, that day, in fun, 'L. Morland, nephew of the above'. There was just room between the two signatures to put the record straight. She dipped the pen, and carefully inserted her public signature: Lucy, Lady Aylesbury.

Then she walked away, out of the church, closing the heavy door quietly behind her, out into the grey afternoon and down the gravelled path to the gate, where Parslow waited with the horses. He watched her coming towards him, and saw how exhausted she was now that there was nothing left to do for which she need bear herself up. He had to step forward quickly to take her arm and help her up into the carriage, for fear she might actually fall.

Fortunately the horses were quiet; they stood patiently in the rain while he tucked a rug around her and then got up beside her. He shook the reins and sent the horses forward, to find the nearest decent inn where they might put up for the night. The short day was already darkening, and the rain was setting in, and his lady could go no further.

Mr Pitt died at his villa in Putney on 23 January. Though the event had been expected, it was still shocking, for he was a man of such stature that the loss of him from the political scene seemed to leave as large a void as that made by the loss of Nelson from the naval.

John Anstey came hurrying to London, and called at Upper Grosvenor Street. Hicks welcomed him, but seemed doubtful as to whether my lady would receive him.

'She has seen no-one, my lord, since her return from Essex; not even Mr Wiske, whom, as you know, I was accustomed to admit almost without ceremony, as if he were family, my lord.'

'Is her ladyship in health?' Anstey asked.

'I cannot say there is any outward appearance of ill-health, my lord. Her ladyship behaves no differently towards the household, but she seems not to want to have anything to do with the rest of the world, if I may put it so, my lord. She scarcely stirs out of the house, except to exercise her horses early in the morning, when the Park is empty.'

'Lord Aylesbury is not in Town, I collect?'

'He is still in the country, my lord, at Wolvercote.'

'Well, then, Hicks, perhaps you will just mention to her ladyship that I am here. As I am such an old friend, she may be willing to see me.'

'Certainly, my lord.' Hicks bowed and withdrew, and there was a long wait, during which Anstey became aware of the unnatural stillness of the house. Then at last the door opened, and Lucy came in. Her little face was pinched and grim, and her clothes hung loosely on her, as if she had lost weight. He saw that she had shut herself away to grieve alone.

She advanced across the floor with her hand stretched out welcomingly; but there was no light in her eyes, and when she spoke, her voice was strangely flat and dead.

'John,' she said. 'What a pleasant surprise. How is Louisa, and the children?'

'They are very well. We are hoping for another addition in June.'

'How delightful,' she said politely, and seating herself on the sopha, looked at him enquiringly. 'What brings you to Town?'

'It cannot have escaped your notice that Mr Pitt is dead?'

'Oh — no,' she said vaguely. 'Of course I knew. And what is to happen now? There is not another man of his stature in the country.'

'You are forgetting Charles Fox,' Anstey said with a wry smile.

'The King will never accept him,' Lucy said. 'But I suppose the Tories are vanquished and we shall have the Whigs in at last?'

'Not precisely,' Anstey replied. 'Grenville is the only man capable of drawing together all the threads of opposition, and commanding the respect of Parliament. He is to see the King today and offer to form a Government, but only on condition that Fox is a part of it.'

'Bold words. And you think the King will agree?'

'I think even the King will see that he has to. It is to be a party combining all the talents, wisdom and ability of the nation, including the new Whigs, the old Whigs, and all the Tories except Pitt's closest adherents.'

'And Fox is to lead it,' Lucy said cynically.

'He is to be Secretary of State for Foreign Affairs,' Anstey admitted.

'And he will doubtless be looking for peace with Napoleon.'

Anstey shrugged. 'It's clear we cannot beat him on the continent. We saw that back in '02.'

'And we saw in '05 what Boney means by peace,' Lucy said with her first kindling of emotion he had seen in her. 'Can't you people understand that he is not to be trusted, that the only way to live in the world with him is to defeat him? If he agrees to peace, it will only be to give himself time to rebuild his fleet, and then Trafalgar will have been fought for nothing.'

'No, never that,' Anstey said quickly. 'Trafalgar gave us the strength of position to treat for peace on our terms.'

'If you believe that, you are a fool,' she said, and then, appearing to feel she had spoken rudely, she made an obvious effort to be social. 'Have you heard from little John?'

'Oh yes, we've had several letters since Trafalgar, telling us all about the battle,' Anstey said. 'Did you know that Admiral Collingwood was wounded, by the way? He took a pretty bad splinter wound in the leg, but made light of it, and wouldn't allow his name to be included in the list of wounded. He is pretty well John's hero now!'

'He could not want a better,' said Lucy. Anstey saw how

her face had gained a little animation in the last few minutes, and hoped to build on it.

'John says he is so pleasant to the young officers,' he went on. 'He was joking with John about his little dog, Bounce, saying that now he has become a right honourable dog, he is grown too proud and above his station. He is afraid that when they go on shore, he'll refuse to talk to ordinary dogs.'

Lucy smiled a little. 'And where are they now?'

'Still blockading Cadiz. I suppose we shan't be seeing him for many a long month yet.'

'Surely he'll come home when Collingwood hauls down his flag? He always meant to retire this spring, and now that there is no danger from the French fleet . . .'

Anstey shook his head. 'The Admiralty won't let him retire. They can't afford to. Barham's going, you know, now that Pitt's gone. Lord Grey is to be the new First Lord —'

'What!'

'Oh yes — who else is there? But with Nelson dead, Calder in disgrace, Cornwallis retiring, and St Vincent going out to take his place, we simply can't spare Collingwood. He'll be persuaded to stay on, at least for a couple of years.'

'Poor Coll!' Lucy said, and the contemplation of his weariness seemed to tire her. The animation drained out of her face, and she looked so worn that Anstey stood up at once.

'I must take my leave. Thank you for seeing me.' She stood too, and he took her offered hand and held it a moment. 'You will remember I am your old friend, if you should need me, won't you, Lucy?'

'I'll remember,' she said. 'I'm all right, John.' But her eyes were turned away from his, looking into the middle distance with that blank look that he had seen in men brought out of the ground after pit accidents.

On an unexpectedly mild morning in February, Roberta, returning home across St James's Square with her maid, Sands, encountered Lord Aylesbury and Mr Knaresborough strolling arm in arm, the latter resplendent in a new pair of pale fawn pantaloons and short, tasselled Hessian boots shined to dazzling-point. The gentlemen stopped, and his lordship embraced her affectionately, while Mr Knaresborough bowed so low as to present her only with the scarlet tips of his ears.

'Roberta, my dear girl, what are you doing in Town?' Chetwyn enquired cheerfully. 'It's early — there's hardly anyone here yet.'

'I'm opening up Chelmsford House,' she replied. 'Héloïse is coming up tomorrow for the Season. We are going to bring out Mathilde together with a grand ball at the end of March.'

'Quite right — always give either the first or the last ball of the Season,' Chetwyn grinned. 'Anything else is mediocre. But the end of March is six weeks away.'

'My dear Aylesbury,' Roberta said severely, 'you surely cannot think that Lady Strathord and Lady Chelmsford would sponsor a young woman without ensuring that she had a proper wardrobe?'

'Of course — foolish of me! That will take quite six weeks, I am sure,' Chetwyn murmured.

'And then,' Roberta went on firmly, 'we shall have to introduce her to the principle hostesses at a series of private parties.'

'Do you think she'll take?' Chetwyn asked with interest.

'I really can't tell,' Roberta said. 'She's a good girl, with pretty manners, but she's rather shy. Come along tomorrow and meet her, and give me your opinion.'

'Of course we shall — we'd be delighted,' Chetwyn said. 'What a charming Season we are going to have! Chelmsford House open again, you bringing out a new young protégée, Robert's coming of age ... He will be twenty-one in May, you know. We're planning the biggest, most splendid celebration ever seen in London! Dinner, grand ball, fireworks, and probably a Venetian breakfast to follow. The only problem is that we can't decide where to hold it. I suppose we couldn't borrow Chelmsford House from you for the occasion?'

'Really, Aylesbury, I don't know what to say —' Roberta began, deeply embarrassed, and Chetwyn laughed.

'It's all right — I was teasing you. But now, tell me, what do you think of the new style?'

He waved a ringmaster's hand at Robert, whose blush escaped the confines of his ears and spread over his face as well. Roberta looked at him with mingled amusement and sympathy. He had grown up in the last three years, filling out from a rather gawky boy into a tall and well-built young man. His spots had disappeared, and his carriage and air were greatly improved. He was really, she thought, exceedingly good-looking, with glossy brown hair cut in the latest crop, regular features, and the high colour of health in his cheeks. His eyes were large and surrounded by distractingly long eyelashes, his teeth were even and white, and if it weren't for something rather soft about his mouth, she would have found him very attractive.

That was no reason, she caught herself up sharply, for staring the poor child out of countenance. 'What new style?' she asked quickly. 'What are you talking about?'

'Why, these pantaloons, of course, and the Hessians, instead of breeches and topboots. Admirable, don't you think? Of course, the problem is that the pantaloons wrinkle so when one has been wearing them for a while. The only way to avoid wrinkles seems to be a certain unnatural stiffness of gait.'

'And do you think that is a fair price to pay for fashion?' Roberta asked, trying not to smile.

'How severe you are! You must let us poor peacocks strut a little. Wrinkles or not, this is going to be the thing, you know, from now on. In a year's time, breeches will be as *passé* as powdering. I'm thinking of making the change myself. I have the calves for it — a better calf even than young Robert, here,' he added, slapping the back of Knaresborough's leg amiably with his walking stick. 'How do you think I would look, dear Lady Chelmsford?'

'Ridiculous,' Roberta said firmly. 'By my advice you will save your money. But where are you off to, now?'

'We were just going to Jermyn Street, to Roberts and Parfitt, to see about a dress-sword for Robert,' Chetwyn said. 'He will need one, you know, for his presentation.'

Roberta nodded. 'My poor Charles always went to Grey and Constable, in Sackville Street.'

'And so do I,' Chetwyn smiled, 'but that would not do for Robert. He has a mind of his own, you see!'

Roberta, glancing at the handsome, silent, blushing young man, thought that that was the last thing she would have supposed he had. 'I hope you find something you like,' she said politely. 'And now I really must go. I haven't interviewed my cook yet, and Héloïse being used to her Monsieur Barnard's cooking, he will have his work cut out. Goodbye — I will see you tomorrow, I hope?'

She left them bowing, and walked on thoughtfully.

They appeared at Chelmsford House the following morning at the polite hour for calling, and were received by the two ladies, together with Mathilde and the young Lord Chelmsford, who was now nine years old. Roberta saw with mixed amusement and exasperation that Chetwyn, too, was now sporting the new pantaloons and filling them, as promised, excellently. Héloïse, having stared at him in astonishment while the greetings were performed, addressed the matter with her usual frankness.

'But what is this, Lord Aylesbury? Is it a joke? You look like a *drôle, enfin!*'

'How very rude you are,' Chetwyn said admiringly. 'But you have been so long in the country, you won't know about the new fashions.'

'Oh, I am *véritable rustique,*' she agreed cheerfully, 'but even I have heard about these things. It is a reaction against the French revolutionaries, who wore the topboots, is it not? And the Hessian boots are German, and therefore very much *comme il faut,* because the royal family are German too. You see how knowledgeable I am?'

'I think they both look *splendid,*' said Bobbie fervently, turning admiring eyes from one to the other. 'Your neckcloth, sir,' he addressed Robert shyly, 'is it the Trône d'Amour tie? I wish I could learn how to do it, but m'tutor is against excessive use of starch.' He sighed. 'I shall never get on if I don't have the chance to learn the important things.'

'If you can learn to be like Mr Firth, you will get on very well,' Héloïse told him comfortingly, but Bobbie looked unconvinced.

'Why did you not come up at Christmas, Aylesbury?' Roberta asked. 'You were missed, you know. Poor Edward was quite lost. He had no-one to walk with, to avoid the dancing.'

'Oh, I'm quite a reformed character now,' Chetwyn said quickly. 'You wait and see. When the Season starts, I shall dance every dance and be the favourite of every hostess. How are the plans progressing for the launching of Miss Nordubois?'

He gave a smile and a bow in the direction of Mathilde, who was sitting as quietly and demurely as any girl 'not out' should. She was rather too thin and too tall, he thought, but those things could be corrected with careful dressing. Though not precisely pretty, she certainly had very lovely white skin and her hair was at least unusual. The worst thing a young woman entering society for the first time could be was insignificant.

'We have not had the opportunity to do anything yet, except look through some of the ladies' journals,' Héloïse said, with a smile at her protégée. 'Of course, we shall have to choose colours very carefully, to make the most of her hair.'

'Just what I was thinking, ma'am,' Chetwyn said. 'The most important thing is to be noticed, and the second most important, to be noticed in the right way.'

Héloïse laughed, and was about to reply when the door opened and Hawkins, taking it very slowly, announced the Duc de Veslne-d'Estienne. Héloïse's face lit up. He came in wearing his coat loose on one shoulder, for his right arm was in a sling. He had been in the fighting at Austerlitz, and was recovering in the safety of London from a broken arm. He had been fortunate to escape, for, as Bobbie explained, round-eyed, to Chetwyn, 'Boney would have had him shot, if he'd caught him.'

He had been the first to call on Héloïse at Chelmsford House when she had arrived yesterday, having learnt of her visit from his servant, who had learnt of it in the usual roundabout but infallible way that servants always knew everything.

Now the greetings were renewed, and everyone had something to say to the pleasant young man, except for Mathilde, whose blushes clashed painfully with her hair, and who could only look at him at all when he was looking elsewhere. However, as the topic of Mathilde's come-out was now resumed, and the Duc joined in with a discussion about the guest-list for the ball with great and bilingual good-humour, she was not often able to lift her eyes from the floor during the following quarter-hour.

When Chetwyn and Robert finally rose to leave, Héloïse tore her attention away from the Duc to say, 'But tell me, how is Lucy? I have not been able to call on her yet, but mean to do it tomorrow.'

Chetwyn shrugged. 'You may call, of course, but she may not see you. She sees no-one now.'

'What, is she ill?'

'Oh, she's well enough, as far as that goes,' Chetwyn said. 'But she doesn't seem to want to talk to anyone. We hardly see her ourselves, though we live in the same house. She takes her meals in her room, and only goes out to ride in the Park with her groom. But Hicks told me she thinks of going down to the country in a few days' time, and I'm sure that will be better for her.'

'Héloïse regarded him thoughtfully. 'Perhaps it may,' she said. 'Well, I shall call tomorrow in any case, and hope she may receive me.'

After talking it over with Roberta, Héloïse went alone to Upper Grosvenor Street the next day, for they both thought it more likely that Lucy would see Héloïse alone, than both of them together. When she arrived, however, she found that Lucy already had a visitor. Hicks shewed Héloïse into the breakfast parlour, where she was entertaining, or rather being entertained by, Mr Brummell, in an even more exquisite version of Robert Knaresborough's outfit.

Heloïse thought at once that Lucy had the harried look of an animal that had been mistreated, and that she was much too thin.

'But Lucy, you are ill,' she cried, crossing the room to take her hands. 'And your husband told me you were not! Here has been some mismanagement, *enfin* — do you not agree, Mr Brummell?'

'By a strange coincidence, I was just telling her ladyship that she is looking a little *mal soignée*,' he said with his funny little closed smile, and a droll look at Lucy.

297

Lucy drew Héloïse down onto the sopha beside her and said, 'Those were not his precise words, however. He has just finished roundly abusing me, so you, my dear Héloïse, must promise to leave me alone. Talk about anything but me, I beg you. What brings you to London?'

Héloïse explained about Mathilde's come-out.

'Is she old enough already? How time passes!'

'She's seventeen next month,' Héloïse said. 'I do so want her to do well! She is such a good girl, and has worked so hard at her lessons, and it would be the best way I can think of to fulfil my promise to her mother that I would look after her, if she were to make a good marriage.'

Lucy looked at her a little bleakly. 'A good marriage? What is that, I wonder?'

'You know perfectly well, ma'am,' Brummell said with a severe look. 'Pay no attention to her, Lady Strathord, but talk to me instead. Who is this young lady? Who are her people? If she is really presentable, you and I may make a success of her together.'

'You, Mr Brummell? What interest can you have?'

'Lady Aylesbury could tell you that, if she weren't deep in the dismals. My aim has always been to make London Society the most brilliant, the most polished, the most elegant, the world has ever seen. I mean, before I'm done, to have the last word on everything. If I have my way, no man or woman will be accepted in the best circles, unless *I* say so.'

Héloïse laughed. 'That would be power indeed! But one may trust your judgement, I am sure. How far have you got?'

He smiled enigmatically. 'How many men have you seen, since you arrived, ma'am, dressed like this?' He made a graceful gesture towards his own immaculate legs. 'And I have founded a new club — you must have heard about it? It is the old glee-club on the corner of Bolton Street. Oh, you look surprised, but when I tell you that the cook there is Jean-Baptiste Watier, formerly *chef de cuisine* to the Prince of Wales, and that the food is of unparalleled excellence, you will understand its attraction.'

'And you are obliged to sing for your supper?' Héloïse asked innocently.

'I am making some fundamental changes,' he conceded

298

with a smile. 'Not glees and catches, but deep play, macao and hazard, are to be the order of the day; and, more importantly, I shall be the arbiter in the matter of membership, dress, manners, the laws of play — everything.'

'But suppose no-one wants to be a member?'

'Leave me alone for that. Once I have refused a few eminent people, everyone will want to join.'

'You are very clever at understanding people, Mr Brummell,' Héloïse said. They exchanged a significant glance with each other, and Brummell rose to take his leave. He bowed formally over Lucy's hand, but held on to it for a moment longer than was merely polite, and looked into her face with real concern and affection. 'Come back to us soon, dear ma'am,' he said softly. 'It is not the same without you.'

When they were alone together, Héloïse said diffidently, 'I thought you might like to know how the baby goes on.'

Lucy's eyes met hers for the fraction of a second, and then moved away. 'I suppose you would have told me if there were anything amiss,' she said bleakly.

'I did not very much like to leave him, or my Sophie,' Héloïse went on. 'She is so fond of him — and he is the dearest little thing, always happy. They keep me amused all day long.' She paused, but still got no reaction from Lucy. 'In the summer, you must come up and visit us again. It would do you so much good, I am sure.'

'Perhaps,' Lucy said, and then, turning her face away, 'It was kind of you to visit me. But I am very tired now ...'

Héloïse stood up obediently. It was of no use, she knew, to push someone faster along the road to recovery than they could keep their feet; but her heart ached with pity for Lucy, shut away inside herself, suffering alone.

There was one other thing that needed to be said, however. 'Is it true that you are going into the country?'

'I thought I might,' Lucy said dully. 'I thought of going down to Wolvercote at the end of the week. It will be quieter there.'

'And your husband? Will he stay here?'

'I suppose so,' Lucy said without interest. 'He and Robert have plenty to keep them amused in Town this Season.'

'He is with him a great deal, this Robert, is he not?'

299

The ghost of a smile touched Lucy's lips. 'Where Chetwyn is, there you are sure to trip over Robert. I've got used to it now.'

'I think,' Héloïse said hesitantly, 'that you ought not to stay away too long from Town. Unless Lord Aylesbury comes down to the country too.'

Lucy moved her head with the irritation of weariness. 'I don't need him with me. I am perfectly all right on my own. I wish you would all stop fussing me.'

Héloïse said no more, picked up her muff, and moved towards the door, but as she reached it, Lucy called her back.

'Héloïse!'

She turned and looked back, and saw the real Lucy looking out from her eyes, lost, lonely, afraid.

'What is it, my Lucy?' Héloïse asked gently.

Lucy struggled for words. 'How do you bear it?' she asked at last.

'It gets better. In time it gets better.'

'I can't believe that.'

'I know. You feel that there can never be any gladness ever again, and it's of no use to tell you that you won't always feel like that. But it is true.'

'I feel as though — as though I've been left alone in the dark, and no-one even knows I'm here,' she said in a low, desperate voice.

'There are so many people who care about you, dear Lucy, and who want to help you.'

But Héloïse saw that she had turned in on herself again, and there was nothing she could say to comfort her. She took her leave, and her brow wore an anxious furrow as she went out to her carriage.

Chapter Sixteen

After so long in darkness, Chelmsford House was once again a blaze of light, with torches illuminating the whole street outside, a fringed awning over the great door, and a throng of carriages blocking Pall Mall and halting the traffic as far back as St Martin's. Everyone wanted to be there, not only because it was the first ball of the Season, and promised to be one of the biggest; but because the Dowager Lady Chelmsford was well liked and respected, and her son would one day be a very eligible *parti*.

Not so much was known about Lady Strathord. There were certainly some mysterious circumstances surrounding her, but on the other hand, she also had royal blood, and was received at St James's. Those ladies who had met her pronounced her charming and most elegant; and besides, she had the power to introduce to one's daughters the delightful Duo de Vesine d'Estienne, who was young, single, titled, and reputed to be rich. He might be unpronounceably French, but he was wanted for execution by Buonaparte, which made it quite all right to admire him.

On the whole, Society was prepared to find the unknown Miss Nordubois a sweet girl, and only wanted to discover that her fortune was not large, to think her a very eligible companion for their daughters.

The sweet girl in question stood very nervously at the top of the great staircase, up which the guests flowed like an unstaunchable tide. Each successive wave seemed to bear a dowager at its crest. Mathilde had never seen so many diamonds on so many puckered bosoms, so much gold and purple silk wound into turbans, so many pairs of sharply critical eyes, often reinforced by lorgnons which she felt to be completely superfluous. She was very glad of the comfortable presence to either side of her of dearest Madame, and dear Lady Chelmsford, who was not only lending her house and her countenance to Mathilde, but doing her the even greater kindness of being as tall as she.

A great deal of thought had gone into Mathilde's appearance for that evening, for besides the problem of achieving modesty and propriety without insipidity, there was also the question of how to make the best of her red hair.

Héloïse won the point in the end of not cropping. 'One must not look apologetic,' she said firmly. 'To crop is very well for those who have nothing to display, or those who are so pretty and golden, like you, dear Roberta, they may do as they please. But since everyone must notice Mathilde's hair, we must make them know we mean them to.'

As to the material of the gown, Roberta was for muslin. 'Nothing else becomes a young girl so well, and besides, she is so slender, it will drape to perfection on her.' The styles were all Greek and Roman that year, waistlines up under the bust, small, plain bodices with short sleeves, and straight skirts with long trains for evening-wear. 'But what colour? Pink is dangerous; blue is the safe choice, I suppose.'

'I always seem to wear blue,' Mathilde ventured to complain. 'I wish I could have something different.'

'White,' Héloïse said firmly. 'White muslin for her first appearance, with, yes, I have it, with gold trim. The gold will set off her hair so strikingly!'

Little ruffs around the neck were popular, but Héloïse spoke against them. 'She has a lovely neck, and such white skin. We must draw attention to it.'

'I have a very pretty topaz and gold necklace that would look very well,' Roberta said. 'Quite suitable for a young girl. And there are earrings to match.'

'No earrings,' Héloïse said. 'We shall have her hair up, so, and a gold fillet around it, very simple and à l'ancien. You see? Ciel, qu'elle sera ravissante!'

Mathilde felt more terrified than ravishing as she stood at the top of the stairs, despite the assurances not only of Marie and Mesdames that she looked quite as she should, but also of Colonel Taske that she looked exquisite, of Mr Firth that she looked lovely, and of Bobbie that she was entirely 'first rate!'

The gown was indeed very simple, quite plain except for the gold embroidered key-pattern around the neckline and sleeve-cuffs, and the gold fringe which edged the long train.

She wore the topaz necklace around her white throat, and her piled-up, burnished hair was bound with a gold ribbon supporting a white ostrich feather. Long white gloves, a bead reticule, and a handsome white ostrich fan completed her toilette. When she could stop being frightened for long enough, she was able to perceive that the looks given her by the other young women passing before her were not mocking, but envious.

The Duc arrived, looking heartbreakingly handsome and noble with his hair powdered and his arm in a sling; and when he had performed his greetings, he stood beside Héloïse chatting, quite unaware that he had rendered Mathilde incapable of speech simply by bowing over her hand and murmuring '*Enchanté, mademoiselle.*'

While he was still standing with them, the footman announced the Earl of Aylesbury and Mr Knaresborough, and they came up the stairs side by side. It was Lord Aylesbury who raised the all-important question.

'But who is to have the privilege of opening the ball with Miss Nordubois? I know Robert, here, is longing to ask her, but though he is very pretty, I'm afraid I outrank him, and that is everything, is it not? My dear Miss Nordubois, may I have the honour of your hand for the first dance?'

He performed a comic bow, and Mathilde glanced desperately at Héloïse, not in the least wanting to dance with Lord Aylesbury, even if he was an earl, and having hoped for a very different arrangement. The Duc, since he was standing on the other side of Héloïse and watching the scene with lazy amusement, could not help seeing the pleading look, and knowing how fond Héloïse was of her ward, he interposed smilingly.

'Ah, my lord earl, but I outrank *you*, and if Mademoiselle will not think it a disgrace to dance with a one-armed man, I hope to have the pleasure of leading her to the first set myself.'

Mathilde's face glowed, Héloïse accepted gratefully on her behalf, and Lord Aylesbury yielded laughingly, claiming the two second in compensation before he passed on with Mr Knaresborough into the anteroom in search of champagne.

Mathilde's highest hopes were fulfilled, and more, for she was a modest girl, and had hoped for no more than to be able to dance with the Duc; but when they reached the head of the set for the second time, he asked most charmingly to be allowed to take her in to supper. She danced, thereafter, as if on wings, and the glow of anticipation in her face made a mama or two remark sourly that Miss Nourdubois was really quite pretty after all.

The ball was a great success, and the crowd in the vast ballroom and noble old ante-chambers was so great that the hem of Mathilde's gown was trodden on during the supper recess and torn, which obliged her to retire for a few minutes before the dancing resumed to have it stitched. Then, remembering her promise to Bobbie, she slipped out and up the backstairs to the nursery to tell him how things were going.

She found him and Mr Firth enjoying their own supper, which the latter had smuggled upstairs on a tray.

'I say, 'Tilda, these lobster patties are simply first rate! Did you have some?' Bobbie cried as soon as he saw her.

'What they will do to our digestion, so late at night, I shudder to think,' Mr Firth murmured.

'But everyone else is eating the same things,' Bobbie said indignantly.

'That isn't champagne you're drinking, is it?' Mathilde asked, eyeing his glass doubtfully.

'No, only lemonade. M'tutor don't approve of champagne at my age,' Bobbie said with a sigh. 'I keep telling him and *telling* him, I need to get into practice for when I'm older, but he won't see it. I say, you do look pretty! I like having you here; I wish you could stay all the time. Is it a good dance? Who have you danced with?'

'Well, I danced the two first with the Duc,' Mathilde obliged, 'and then the two next with Lord Aylesbury. Then there was Lord Alvanley, and Mr Pierrepoint, and then Mr Knaresborough, and then Mr Charles Bagot. And then it was supper.'

'I like Mr Knaresborough,' Bobbie said, starting on a creamed-chicken boat. 'I think he's a trump. I saw him arrive out of the window, with Lord Aylesbury. Do you like him, 'Tilda? Nursey says you might do worse than marry him. She says he'd be a good match for you.'

Mathilde reddened. 'I don't like being called 'Tilda.

Anyway, I must go back now.'

'I'm sorry, I didn't mean to offend you,' Bobbie said meekly. 'Thank you for coming up and seeing me.'

'I promised I would,' Mathilde said.

'Yes, but grown-ups don't always remember their promises,' Bobbie said with the wisdom of experience.

Mathilde was amused at the idea of being a grown-up and then, catching Mr Firth's eye, realised that he was probably thinking just the same thing, and laughed.

'I'll see you at breakfast tomorrow,' she promised, 'and tell you everything then.'

'You won't,' Bobbie called after her. 'Ladies never get up until noon on the morning after a ball.'

'However can you know that?' Mr Firth asked, bemused.

Chetwyn and Robert found a charming house in Berkeley Square which only wanted completely redecorating and new-furnishing to be perfect for Robert's establishment. True, it did not have a ball-room, but there were some excellent stables just round the corner, off Hay Hill, for his new team of greys and a couple of Park hacks, and it was perfectly sited within reach of all the places where a gentleman naturally wanted to be seen. The two of them plunged into the delights of redecorating, and when they were not harrassing the builders or getting in the way of the painters, they were usually to be found in the various elegant shops around Bond Street, Piccadilly and St James's, poring over draperies, carpets, and furniture.

Chetwyn had never been happier in his life. He did not even much mind when Robert's mother came up from Bath, installed herself in Roberta's house, and continually turned up under their feet, poking about the house, criticising their taste and asking apparently unrelated questions about anything that came into her head. She would jump from the topic of Robert's bedroom furnishings to why Lady Aylesbury was still in the country, and thence to Chetwyn's plans for the summer. But he bore it all with enormous patience, and even offered to take Lady Serena driving in the Park to get her out of Robert's way for a few hours.

A rude awakening was preparing itself for him, however. Quite apart from the convenience of its location, Robert was eager to become a member of Brummell's new club, Watiers, because it seemed to be attracting the kind of dashing, elegant, witty young men amongst whom he would like to be numbered. Chetwyn had not yet bothered to join Watier's himself, but, happy to indulge Robert, he let it be known in White's that he wished Mr Knaresborough to be elected, and Sir Henry Mildmay, a distant cousin of Chetwyn's obliged by putting him up.

Chetwyn's sense of shock and outrage when Robert's application was turned down was the more extreme because it was so utterly unexpected. He cornered Brummell in Brooks's the following day, and demanded a private interview with him, to which Brummell, with outward calm, agreed.

'Well, sir?' Chetwyn said furiously as soon as they were alone. Brummell merely waited impassively, one eyebrow politely raised. The immaculateness of his attire, his high, starched neckcloth, his creaseless pantaloons, made Chetwyn want to hit him. 'I demand an explanation, Mr Brummell. What do you mean by it, sir?'

'Mean by what, my lord?'

'Don't trifle with me. You know very well. Robert — Mr Knaresborough has been refused membership of Watier's. Have you any conception how damaging that could be to his career?'

Brummell's face gave away nothing. 'I am sure the committee would be flattered by your high opinion of their consequence, my lord. Unhappily, their decision in the matter of membership is final, and does not admit of argument.'

'Humbug! Damn it, you *are* the committee! Everybody knows you are the final arbiter. It must have been you who turned him down, and I want to know why. I *mean* to know damn it, and I shall stay here until you give me satisfaction!'

Brummell did not answer at once. He stood quite still, looking at Chetwyn thoughtfully, as if deciding what to do about him, and a little of Chetwyn's fury began to leak away, to be replaced by apprehension. The younger man was so unmoved by Chetwyn's anger, it was unsettling.

'Very well,' Brummell said at last. 'You are right, of

course, that the final decision is mine. I refused Mr Knaresborough because I don't think he is the kind of young man we want.'

Chetwyn stared at him, aghast. 'But — good God, sir — he is *my friend*! What further recommendation can you want?'

'My lord, had you applied for membership, I would have refused you, too.'

Chetwyn reddened. 'You are impertinent, Mr Brummell!'

'I merely answered your question, my lord.'

'Then perhaps you'll have the goodness to explain yourself?'

Brummell looked at him steadily. 'I think you understand me very well,' he said quietly.

'By God, sir —!' Chetwyn began furiously, but Brummell cut him off. His face was still impassive, but his eye held a terrible pity.

'Come, now, my lord earl. Your wife is one of my dearest friends, and it is for that reason alone that I presume to speak to you as I do now. It is in everybody's interest that you listen to what I say. In London one may do a surprising number of things, and still be accepted, but this is not one of them. Give up your relationship with Mr Knaresborough before it is too late, for him and for you. Already people are talking. Send him away with his mother to Bath. He does not belong here. Let him sink back into the obscurity from which you should never have plucked him.'

Chetwyn whipped up his anger in defence against the fear newly-born in his soul. 'I won't, damn it! And I'll see you suffer for this, too, Brummell!'

Brummell looked at him with great sadness. 'No, I think not. I think it is you who will suffer, my lord, and I'm very sorry for it.'

The situation was intolerable. The story of Robert's being refused membership soon got around, and Chetwyn began to intercept odd looks from people who before were all too happy to fawn on him. The number of invitations on his chimney-piece thinned a little, and Chetwyn would not have cared for this, if it had not been that Robert minded. When

307

they walked down the street together, Robert's cheeks were perpetually crimson, and he held his head up not so much with pride but with defiance.

Chetwyn felt helpless. There was nothing he could do to force Brummell to change his decision. He could not even call him out, since it was well known that Brummell made a career of always refusing to go out, and a challenge would only have made Chetwyn ridiculous. Even Robert's mother began to eye him with suspicion, and treat him with a coldness very different from the obsequiousness which had always before marked her behaviour towards him.

Then one day just before Easter, he arrived at the house in Berkeley Street to find Robert and Lady Serena in the middle of a violent quarrel. They stopped as soon as he entered, but Robert was red-faced and his eyes were full of tears. Lady Serena's eyes were sparkling, and she faced Chetwyn with her mouth set in lines of grim triumph.

'Well, Lord Aylesbury,' she said coldly, 'I am come to tell you that Robert will not be spending Easter with you at Wolvercote after all. He will be joining me at a house party in Gloucestershire, at Lady Tewkesbury's, at the particular request of his *trustee*, Lord Ballincrea.' She emphasised the word triumphantly.

'And is this your decision, Robert?' Chetwyn asked quietly. Robert opened his mouth to speak, but Lady Serena forestalled him.

'Robert will do as his mother and his trustee tell him to. He is not of age yet, you know.'

'Mother, please —!'

'So you see, Lord Aylesbury, there is nothing more to say. And now I suggest you say goodbye. Robert will have a great deal to do if we are to leave tomorrow —'

'Tomorrow!' Chetwyn exclaimed, turning again to Robert. 'Robert, may I speak to you alone for a moment?'

'He has nothing to say to you!' Lady Serena cried shrilly, but Chetwyn continued to look steadily at his friend.

Robert returned his gaze, and then turned to his mother and said with as much firmness as he was capable of, 'Mother, I should like to speak to Lord Aylesbury in private for a moment. Will you excuse us, please?'

308

'I forbid it,' she cried furiously. 'I absolutely forbid it!'

'Please, Mother, don't excite yourself. I must speak to him, just for a minute,' Robert said, and led the way hastily out of the room before his resolve could be tested.

In the comparative privacy of the hallway they faced each other.

'I'm sorry, Rob,' Chetwyn said at last. 'I never meant to let you in for all this.'

'No, I'm sorry,' Robert said quickly. 'I don't want to go, but you see how Mother is, and with her poor health and her weak heart, I daren't defy her, or she'll make herself ill. But it won't be for long.'

'Won't it?'

'No, only a few weeks, over Easter and then I'll be back.' He raised his eyes to Chetwyn's face, and his innocence and hope and trust were heartbreaking.

'Rob, she won't let you come back,' Chetwyn said gently. 'She will always have the power to make you do what she wants.'

Robert's eyes filled with tears. 'I won't let her separate us,' he cried, and his lips trembled like a child's in his effort not to cry. Chetwyn stepped close and took him in his arms for a moment, his heart aching with love and sadness.

'It's all right,' he said. 'It's all right, Rob.'

'We'll see each other again, won't we, James?' Robert asked, his voice muffled by Chetwyn's shoulder. 'Please, we must. I can't live without you.'

'Of course we will, my dear,' Chetwyn said sadly. 'London's a small place.' He put him gently away from him, and knew he had to go at once, before his resolve failed him, before he broke down and howled like a dog for the misery and injustice of life. 'God bless you, Rob,' he said hurriedly, and went away.

He went down to Wolvercote that same day, arriving after dark, to the evident disapproval of Charlcott, who liked his employers to behave with proper ceremony.

'Where's her ladyship?' Chetwyn asked, stripping off his gloves and dropping them into the hat which the butler held with mute protest.

'Her ladyship is in her apartments, my lord. She never leaves them in the evening, and has left standing orders not to be disturbed.' This, his tone of voice implied was not at all what he was used to.

'I'll go up and see her,' said Chetwyn.

He had not seen her for six weeks, since she had retired to the country in February, and had not heard from her, nor expected to. When he entered the sitting-room which Robert had redesigned for her, she was sitting on the sopha sewing, while Docwra read to her — a very feminine and proper occupation, except that it was a broken brow-band that she was stitching, and not a silk shirt.

Docwra broke off when he entered, and rose to curtsey, but Lucy did not at once seem to notice the interruption. She had grown unbecomingly thin, he noticed, and he could see her collar-bones jutting out like a cow's hips above the neckline of her plain blue cambric dress, and her cheekbones seeming ready to break through the skin.

At last she looked up. 'Oh, hello, Chetwyn,' she said without surprise, and looking past him vaguely, said, 'Where's Robert?'

The automatic assumption, he thought: how it hurt him.

'He's gone to Gloucestershire. Can I speak to you alone, Lucy?'

'Yes, of course,' she said unemphatically, and waved a hand at her maid. 'Go away, Docwra. I'll ring when I want you.'

When they were alone, Chetwyn sat down opposite her, and waited for her attention. Her eyes were on her work, but after a while she glanced up at him briefly and said, 'What is it?'

'It's Robert's mother,' he said at last. 'He was supposed to come here with me for Easter, but she's made him go with her to join a house-party, along with Maurice Ballincrea.'

'She's a very silly woman,' Lucy commented unemphatically. 'But it doesn't matter, does it?'

'She will try to stop him coming back to London after Easter. She doesn't want him to associate with me any more.

Lucy looked up with a vague frown. 'Why should she do that?'

'She doesn't think I'm good for him,' Chetwyn said painfully.

'Oh, she'll soon change her mind,' Lucy said easily. 'She's a most dreadful snob, and you're an earl, while Ballincrea's only a viscount.'

'You don't understand. It isn't anything to do with rank.'

'Well, what then?' Her eyes had returned to her sewing.

Chetwyn hesitated; and yet she *was* his wife, and he had no-one else to confide in. 'Robert applied for membership to Watier's, and was refused. Your Mr Brummell turned him down.'

She looked up at that. 'But why would he do that? He knows Robert's your friend, doesn't he?'

'That was precisely the reason.'

'I don't understand.' He saw that she didn't. She was so innocent, and saw things so simply, very much in terms of animals. In the face of that daunting simplicity, he struggled for words.

'He — and Robert's mother — think that our friendship is — is — not wholesome.'

Lucy stared at him for a long moment, her brows drawn, and then she gave a little dismissive snort, and took another stitch. 'What nonsense!' she said. 'I should just ignore the whole thing, if I were you. I'm sure you're mistaken about Brummell: I expect it was someone else who was against Robert. Jealous, you know. People often are. And as for Lady Serena — well, her opinion is neither here nor there. She is the silliest woman I've ever encountered.'

Chetwyn stood up, looking down on his wife's bent head with sad affection. I was foolish, he thought, to expect her to understand, or to hope for sympathy from someone who doesn't even have pity on herself.

'I expect you're right,' he said. 'Goodnight, Lucy.'

'Goodnight.' She looked up at him for a moment, and was surprised to receive a fatherly kiss upon her forehead before he turned away and left her.

Chetwyn lingered as long as possible over his late and solitary breakfast the next day. Lucy had taken hers early and gone out riding with Parslow, Charlcott told him, as was her usual custom. Chetwyn toyed with the idea of visiting the children, but then reflected that if he appeared in the nursery, the first thing Rosamund and Roland would ask would be, 'Where's Robert?' He didn't think he could bear that, not yet. Roland would be devastated to be told that he would not be able to see his friend and hero again.

It was a fine day, warm, but with a little breeze, a day to be outdoors. Chetwyn decided to take a gun out after pigeons, and was just crossing the hall on his way to the gun-room, when, to his astonishment as much as his delight, Edward arrived from Morland Place.

'Ned! What a wonderful thing!' he cried. 'But I wasn't expecting you. Why didn't you tell me you were coming down? How long can you stay? A good, long time, I hope! Lord, how I've missed you, old fellow!'

Edward looked rather tired, but that was a natural consequence of the journey, Chetwyn thought. His spirits rose at the sight of that dear, familiar face. Of course, of all people who could comfort him, his oldest friend ought to have sprung at once to mind. Not that he would discuss the business with Edward, who in his way was even more innocent than Lucy, but just being with him would be balm to his bruised soul.

'How's Lucy?' Edward asked. He did not come forward to embrace Chetwyn, but Chetwyn was too delighted to see him to notice the omission.

'Oh, she's all right, I suppose. She's not much company, though. She keeps herself to herself, goes out riding with old Parslow, and sits in her room the rest of the time. I'm damned glad to see you, I can tell you. I was just on my way out to shoot some pigeons, for want of anything better to do, but now you are here, we can have a comfortable chat instead.' He thrust his arm through Edward's, and turned with him towards the octagon room. 'Charlcott, bring some refreshments, will you? And have Mr Morland's man unpack his things in the Blue Room. So what brings you here, old fellow? You can stay for Easter, can't you? How is everyone at home?'

When he had been installed in an armchair with dragons' heads for handrests, Edward let Chetwyn talk on, answering his queries about Morland Place and evading other questions until the footman had been and gone. Chetwyn poured him a glass of wine and set it on the black lacquer table at his elbow, before seeming to notice hs preoccupation and unsatisfactory answers. He filled his own glass, and then sat opposite Edward and looked at him enquiringly.

'So, what has brought you here?' he asked at last. 'Or was it just a very natural desire for my company?'

Edward drank some wine and put his glass down. 'Your young friend — Knaresborough — is he here?'

Chetwyn's heart sank with foreboding. 'No,' he said. 'No, he isn't here. He's gone down to Gloucestershire with his mother.' Edward did not speak, so Chetwyn elaborated. 'It's Lady Tewkesbury's house-party. Ballincrea is apparently to be there — the boy's trustee.' Still no reply. 'Ned, what is it, my dear?' Chetwyn said quietly. 'You'd better tell me.'

Edward looked down at his hands, embarrassed. 'I've had a letter from Lady Serena Knaresborough,' he said.

'Ah,' said Chetwyn wryly. 'Such a delightful woman, always so concerned in other people's affairs! And what had she to say?'

He looked up, frowning. 'She said — I'm not sure I understand it properly, Chet — but she said that people were talking about you, and that it was making Knaresborough — *notorious*, was the word she used, I think. She asked me to use my influence as your oldest friend and brother of your wife to make you stop — well, stop being his friend, I suppose.'

'Have you the letter here?' Chetwyn asked grimly.

Edward shook his head. He looked a little dazed. 'She said he was very young, and just starting out in life, and that your reputation was ruining his. Chet, what have you been *doing?*' he burst out.

'Go on — what else did she say?'

'She said — she said that it was common talk that your marriage was a marriage in name only, and that you were not the father of your children.'

'The poisonous bitch,' Chetwyn muttered. 'What else?'

'I think she was suggesting that your relationship with Knaresborough was improper,' Edward said, looking at him miserably. 'Is that true?'

313

'What else?' Chetwyn insisted, with murder in his heart.

'She seemed — I don't know, but it seemed to me that she was — trying to make me jealous. So that I would interfere between you and him.' Edward's voice was low, not with embarrassment, but with shame. Chetwyn could gladly at that moment have strangled Lady Serena for what she had done.

'Oh Ned,' he said painfully, contemplating the mess before him, disheartened, wondering if he could ever make things straight again.

'I don't know what to think,' Edward said. 'Ever since I got the letter, I've gone over and over things in my mind, wondering, asking myself questions, and I just don't know. So in the end, I thought the only thing to do was to come and find you, and ask you.'

'And what is it you want to know?'

Edward met his eyes, apprehensive and perplexed. 'I want to know — well, is she right?'

'About what?'

'Your relationship with Knaresborough. Was it — improper? Because if it was —'

'Yes, Ned, what then? Why do you feel you have to ask me these things? You and I have been friends almost all our lives. Can't you trust me? Has it come to this?'

'I don't know,' Edward said, looking away. 'I don't understand what's happening. I haven't seen you for such a long time. You don't come up to Morland Place any more, as you used to. You seem to spend all your time in London, or here with that young man. You seem to prefer his company —' He stopped, screwing up his face with misery.

'But now she has suggested to you that if you mind that, you must be feeling jealous, and that there is something unnatural in such a feeling.'

'Yes,' he said. 'And I can't help it, I am jealous! Why should you prefer the company of a callow boy like that to mine, your oldest friend — unless —?'

'Unless,' Chetwyn said, his mouth turned down with bitterness. 'Well, Ned, perhaps you had better answer the question for yourself. Was there ever anything improper in our relationship?'

'I don't know,' Edward said, very low. 'I've never thought of it before. I thought we just had a very special friendship. You took care of me when I was at Eton: I shouldn't have survived there without you. And since that time, I never loved anyone but you, but it was — just *love*, Chet, that's all!'

'Only that,' Chetwyn said. '*Love strong as death, jealousy cruel as the grave.* I have always loved you, too, though we've never needed to say it to each other before. But we've both grown up. Our lives are not simple any more, as they were when we were boys. Our needs are not the same. Robert was never meant as a replacement for you. He means something different to me.'

'But was he — is he —?'

Chetwyn held his eyes. 'Was there anything improper between you and me?' he countered.

'No! Never, not on my part; nor on yours, I always thought — but now I don't know.' He looked down at his hands. 'I feel so bad about it all, Chet. I don't know what to think. But I feel — I feel I don't want to see you any more. Not for a while, anyway.'

Chetwyn looked at his bent head with enormous sadness. 'Yes, I understand,' he said gently.

Edward couldn't look up. 'I'm sorry,' he said miserably. 'I feel I've let you down. But I can't help it.'

'It's all right,' Chetwyn said, remembering in a fragment of recollection how he had said the same words to Robert. His life was falling apart, but there was no-one to say it to him, no comfort anywhere. 'You'll stay a while, anyway, won't you? Lucy will want to see you, and the children.'

'Well, I don't know —'

'It's all right, I'll keep out of your way.'

Edward looked up. 'Oh Chet, I'm sorry!'

'You haven't failed me, my dear. Not failed in love — only in the joy of it.' He stood up, and the emptiness inside him where so recently he had a life was like the coldness of death.

'What will you do?' Ned asked him in a small voice.

'Oh, I have one or two things to do in my study,' he said, astonishing himself with the lightness he managed to put into his voice. 'And then I think I'll take a gun out after those pigeons. It's a lovely day for it, and my steward has been complaining about the damage they're doing.'

'I didn't mean that.'

'I know. Ned, my dear, do you remember your blessed mother, how she was always so full of good advice which we never used to pay heed to? She always used to say, that it is the height of bad manners not to know when to take your leave.'

'I can't help it,' Edward said miserably.

'I know. None of us can. That's the real tragedy of life.' He walked towards the door. 'Make yourself comfortable, Ned. Lucy will be home soon, and I know she'll be really glad to see you. I'll see you at dinner.' He was forty-eight years old, but his tread as he left the room was like that of an old man.

By the time Edward had refreshed himself and changed his coat, Lucy had returned, and as predicted was pleased to see him. She ordered a nuncheon to be brought for them both, and promised to take him up to see the children afterwards.

'Is his lordship in the house?' she asked Charlcott when she had ordered the food.

'No, my lady. His lordship took out his birding gun to Fowler's Copse. He said that he would not be back until dinner-time.'

'Very well.'

She and Edward had plenty of news to exchange, and were still sitting over the crumbs and rinds two hours later when a commotion was heard outside in the hall, followed at length by rapid footsteps, and the appearance of Charlcott, grim-faced, with one of the young keepers, Padgett, behind him.

'My lady, I'm afraid there's been an accident! His lord-ship —!'

'What!' cried Edward, and his glass fell from his fingers to the carpet, and rolled there unbroken.

'As he was getting over the stile in to the wood, my lady,' Padgett cried, twisting his cap violently in his hands. 'I can't think how he come to have his piece cocked! He's always so careful about such things.'

Lucy was on her feet. 'Is he badly hurt?' she said.

'Oh, my lady —' He met her eyes reluctantly, his face trembling with distress. 'His poor head, shot quite away, most dreadful! He's dead, my lady.'

To Edward, wandering like a lost soul in his shock and grief, the day seemed a year long, time stretching itself like a nightmare to accommodate an eternity of pain and horror. Into its grey expanse were embedded, sharp and deadly as shards of glass, fragmented images, out of sequence, unforgettable.

Two gardeners, bearing a hurdle between them, with something on it, a coat flung across the top half, the bottom half wearing Chetwyn's old, softly scuffed boots. A clog of leaf-mould adhered to the sole of one, and Edward could see the exact impression, ridges and veins, of a dead sycamore leaf, perfectly preserved.

Thorn, his lordship's groom, standing in the hallway, sobbing brokenly, his mouth shapeless with grief, turning his master's felt hat round and round in his hands.

Lucy, her face bleached of expression, sitting on the bottom stair as if she never meant to get up again.

A hand trailing over the side of the hurdle, the light catching fire in the great square emerald of the signet ring.

Docwra coming out from the bedchamber where they had taken him, her fingers pressed to her lips, her knuckles whitened.

Roland on the third-floor stairs, pressing his face to the banisters, looking down uncomprehendingly on the scene below until a hand came down from the shadows behind him to lead him away.

People came and went, asking questions, asking for decisions, and Edward wished he could have been prostrated like Lucy, led away and put to bed and dosed with laudanum. He did not in the least know what to do about anything, and caught himself again and again thinking that he ought to ask Chetwyn. Doctor, priest, lawyer, steward, carpenter, housekeeper, butler, they came in their endless, grisly parade, like a bizarre street carnival, passing and repassing, until his mind was blessedly numbed, and he could not feel anything, think anything, want, hope or remember anything.

Dusk came, and then dark. The candles were lit, but dinner had disappeared into the cavern of timelessness. Edward could not remember whether he had eaten or not. He could not even tell if he were hungry.

It was late when Parslow came to him, his face grave and intelligent, his eyes too probing, digging Edward out of his shell like a reluctant mollusc.

'Sir, there'll be an inquest,' he said. 'Has anyone been to his lordship's business-room?'

'I don't know. Why? Why should they?' Edward asked.

'Well, sir, somebody like yourself ought to go and see that everything is as it should be,' Parslow said carefully. 'There is just the possibility that there might be something there, something that could be open to misinterpretation.'

'What are you talking about?' Edward said, bewildered.

'His lordship's tragic accident, sir. It'll be brought in an accident, all right, but it would be as well to make sure there isn't anything . . .'

Images in his brain, memories of Chetwyn's last words to him, the way he had looked, the way he had walked away. Fresh and painful as new wounds. Comprehension was knocking at his consciousness, and he didn't want it, he did not want the new ideas Parslow was thrusting at him.

'No! Parslow, you don't think — you can't believe —'

'No, sir, of course not,' he said soothingly. 'I'd be happy to go for you, sir, if you was to give me the authority. I'd need your authority, sir, Mr Charlcott being the way he is.'

Don't make me think, Edward pleaded inwardly. In his mind Chetwyn walked away, endlessly walked away. How, then, could he see his face, his sad accusing eyes? 'Yes, yes, go. You have my authority. For God's sake, go!'

Parslow bowed slightly and left him, and Edward paced up and down the room, his thoughts revolving, and hitching at the same point each time like a crooked wheel. He went over Chetwyn's words to him. He said, I'll see you at dinner. He said, I have one or two things to do in my study. It was an accident. The keeper said it was an accident. He said — he said — but what if? Oh, dear God, what if? But it was an accident. It must have been an accident.

It seemed like hours before Parslow came back, and again

and again Edward was on the point of going himself to the business-room, to find out what was taking so long. But he never got further than the door, stopped in his tracks by a *what if* he didn't want to contemplate. At last there were footsteps outside, a discreet tap, and Parslow came in, his face impassive.

'What the devil took you so long?' Edward turned on him explosively.

'I beg your pardon, sir. I expect it seemed longer than it was.'

'And is everything all right?'

Parslow looked at him inscrutably. 'Everything is just as it should be, sir. His lordship's will is in his safe, where you'd expect it to be.'

Edward seized his arm, his fingers biting through the sleeve. 'What are you saying?' He shook the man in his urgency. 'Did you find anything?'

'Find anything? No, sir,' Parslow said gently. He unhitched the fingers carefully, one by one, as if afraid he might snap them. 'It was an accident, all right. A tragic accident. There's no doubt about it.'

Chapter Seventeen

It was not in Lucy's nature to think of asking anyone for help. It was fortunate, therefore, that she had two servants who cared very deeply for her, and who, in the course of an elliptical and sotto voce conversation outside her chamber door, determined that her ladyship ought not to be alone.

'Somebody ought to be sent for,' Docwra said with a significant nod.

'Lady Strathord?' said Parslow after a moment's thought.

'Her. It's best. But how?'

'Send a message,' Parslow said. 'You write it, I'll find someone to take it.'

'That Charlcott' — with a world of scorn — 'won't like it.'

'We won't ask him. The grooms look to Mr Thorn for their orders, and him and me get on very well. Leave me alone for the sending — you just do the writing.'

In consequence, Héloïse left Mathilde in Roberta's care, and hurried down to Wolvercote. She was received with open relief by everyone except the butler, who, though in truth extremely glad to have someone to take over the responsibility — for Edward was no more use in the present case than Lucy — felt it would diminish his standing to admit it.

Héloïse, however, had commanded servants since she was a small child, and was well able to cope with displays of temperament.

'I shall have to rely on you for everything, and ask you very many questions, I'm afraid,' she said, looking up at him with wide, sad eyes. 'I hope you will not mind it, for I know you are always very busy, and this will be so much extra work for you.'

Upon which Charlcott drew himself up and assured her magnificently that he had a good staff and would cope very well, my lady. She was so small and brown, like a little sparrow, and the sound of his name, rendered *Sharlco'* by her ladyship's pretty, broken accent, won all that served him for a

320

heart. His demeanour towards her never unbent, but he did later say to one of the footmen, whose report on the matter was not believed in the servants' hall, that the Comtesse was a very proper, agreeable lady indeed.

Chetwyn's death was a sad and horrifying business, and everyone in the house, each in his own way, turned to Héloïse for comfort and reassurance. It was a position and a duty for which she had been bred from the moment, like an infant princess at the age of five, she had been given her own household of a nurse, a maid, and a small negro boy. Her years in the convent had reinforced the lesson and given it the depth of a philosophical base, and her marriage at the age of fourteen, and all the subsequent troubles of her life had provided her with ample opportunity to practise and polish her skills.

So with apparent ease she took up the reins of the household. She ordered meals, listened to the housekeeper's daily report, gave the butler instructions about the reception or denial of visitors. She inspected the mourning-draperies, which had been stored away with herbs in cedar boxes in a remote attic since the death of the old earl, and gave orders for them to be beaten out, repaired where necessary and hung. She instructed Charlcott to put the livery servants into mourning, and the sewing-maids to sew weepers on to the sleeves of the lower servants.

She spoke with the estate carpenter about the construction and furnishing of the coffin, with the sexton about bells and vaults, with the priest of the church of St Mary about the funeral service, with the church-wardens about the proper arrangement of banners and the draping of pews, and with the head gardener about flowers. She interviewed his late lordship's secretary about the issuing of invitations, the housekeeper and the cook about funeral baked-meats, Charlcott about accommodation for the guests who had to travel a long distance, and the head groom about the accommodation of their horses, and the provision and furbishment of the funeral-car and black horses to convey the coffin to the church.

She spoke to the family lawyer about the reading of the will, the disposition of the estate, and the immediate provision of funds for its upkeep until the will was proved; and to the coroner, a local physician of great standing, about the inquest. She advised Miss Trotton and the nursery-maids about mourning-clothes for the children and the part they would have to play in the funeral. And in between, she found time to receive the more important of the stream of neighbours and tenants who arrived at all hours of the day to pay their respects and condolences.

But all these things were incidental to her primary task of comforting Lucy and Edward through the sad and exhausting business of the inquest, which was held in the great hall in order to accommodate as many of the villagers and tenants, who were all naturally anxious to be present, as possible; and then the funeral. The death of an earl, of old family and long-established estate, was not something that could be passed over lightly, and the funeral had to take place with all due ceremony. The local people expected it, the family demanded it, and the standing of the widow and the heir required it.

Though Chetwyn had had no immediate family, no family as ancient as his could be without a vast network of cousins, second-cousins, and connections-by-marriage, who closed in upon Wolvercote from the four corners of England, together with friends from various walks of society, representatives of the nobility, and neighbours from all over Oxfordshire and the five adjacent counties. When the day came, a mild day with a high, still, grey sky, an immensely long procession of carriages made its way at walking-pace down the long, winding drive from the house to the east gate.

The funeral car was drawn by six black horses, with beaded headdresses topped by black plumes, their long black saddle-cloths edged with swinging fringes almost to the ground. Each was led by a groom in mourning-livery, while behind the funeral-car Thorn led his late lordship's horse, saddled and bridled, to shew he had died in a sporting accident. In the first carriage behind rode Lucy, almost invisible under the weight and length of veils hanging from her black crape bonnet, and Roland, looking very small and bewildered and rather pinched about the face. He did not seem sure what to do with the black kid gloves and new black hat he had been given, and glanced from time to time at his mother, as though

322

he would have liked to ask her what was happening. But she was too far withdrawn from him to be approached, and he could only sigh and remember Trot's instruction not to fidget.

In the crowded, tiny church, hung with the achievements and banners of the Chetwyn family collected over the past three hundred years, every corner and ledge had been filled with flowers by the deeply-moved head gardener, Pole. He had known his late lordship from a boy, when he had been merely a gardener's boy himself. He had often saved him from a beating for stealing peaches from the hot-house, by pretending to have done it himself; and now performed the last service he would ever do him by denuding every bed, and annointing each bowl and vase of magnificent blooms with a helpless sprinkling of warm salt water.

In the front pew, the new little lord sat stiffly, his feet in tight new nankin boots dangling well clear of the floor, and raised a freckled face and round, Morland-blue eyes to the Rector, who spoke very long and very slowly from the pulpit, and occasionally addressed a stern and exhortative look towards the seventh earl when the words 'duty' or 'responsib ility' came into his peroration. The stern looks had the effect of making the seventh's earl's thumb, over which he still had lamentably little command, creep towards his mouth for comfort. The black kid gloves had been hastily dyed for the occasion, and the thumb tasted horrible, but for the moment, it was all there was to hold on to in a world grown unfamiliar.

The bell began to toll, the sexton's party took the strain, and the coffin was lowered into the family vault; and so James Cavendish Manvers Chetwyn, sixth Earl of Aylesbury, Viscount Calder, Baron Godstow, Knight of the Garter, and Hereditary Warden of the Port Meadow, was laid to rest amongst his ancestors.

At last the visitors were all gone, and the household was reduced to normal proportions. Héloïse sat with Lucy and Edward in the Countess's private sitting-room. Lucy, with Jeffrey dozing on her lap, stared into the fire, while Edward and Héloïse talked desultorily about the departed guests.

'So what will you do now?' Edward asked Héloïse when the

subject was exhausted. 'I suppose you must be eager to get back to London, to see how Mathilde goes on.'

'She will do very well with Roberta,' Héloïse said serenely. 'Of course, I must go back sooner or later, but there is no hurry.'

Lucy looked up at last. 'You needn't stay on my account, if that is what you are thinking,' she said. 'I'm grateful to you for coming — I couldn't have managed without you — but I shall be quite all right now.'

Héloïse looked at her doubtfully. 'I don't think you should be on your own.'

Lucy grimaced. 'On my own? With a houseful of servants cossetting me, and a nursery full of children?'

'That isn't the same thing,' Héloïse said.

'I know that,' said Lucy. 'But it's how you live.'

Héloïse did not reply. How could she point out to Lucy the essential difference, that she lived in intimate daily contact with her children and her servants, while Lucy saw only those whom she requested to see, and was wrapped around always with the distancing of rank?

'I don't think you ought to stay here, at any rate, Luce,' Edward said. 'I shall have to go back soon — there's so much to do at this time of year. Why don't you go to London? You'd have all your friends around you there, and things to do to keep your mind occupied.'

Lucy stroked Jeffrey's long ginger back, and thought of London, and of the house in Upper Grosvenor Street which she had shared first with Chetwyn and then with Weston. Its emptiness now would be intolerable, she thought. How could it be that in such a short time she had been bereft of the two closest companions of her life? What was there left for her? Where could she go now, to find a purpose, a direction?

It doesn't matter, she thought bitterly, to anyone or anything, what I do from now on. It doesn't matter if I live or die. Although she knew it was irrational, she felt she had been betrayed by those closest to her. They had died and gone away, and left her directionless, lost in the vast, featureless spaces of the rest of her life.

And since her adult life had betrayed her, she turned instinctively towards her childhood, which, at least in retro-

324

spect, had been happy and uncomplicated. I'll go home, she thought, and the idea seemed delightful and simple, and she wondered she had not thought of it before.

'No,' she said aloud, 'not London. I don't want to go to London. I have things to settle here first, and when all that's done, I shall come home to Morland Place. If you'll have me?'

She looked questioningly at her brother, and Edward's loneliness was warmed for a moment. He smiled and said, 'Oh yes, do come, Luce. It will be like old times, to have you back. We can go riding and have picnics and things, and be jolly.'

Héloïse, watching him, saw how the extraordinary innocence which had been both Edward's strength and his weakness still remained unchanged, despite trouble and sorrow. Just for an instant the eager face below the greying hair looked more like that of a boy of fourteen than a man of forty-four.

Héloïse returned to Chelmsford House, to be received joyfully by Mathilde, who was losing some of her shyness, and was longing to tell dearest Madame about the balls and routs and squeezes she had been at. Héloïse listened carefully for the mention of any young man's name more than another, but it seemed that though Mr Such-and-such had been an agreeable partner, and Lord What-you-may-call was very droll and had made her laugh a great deal, there was no-one who had either captured her heart, or shewn a particular interest in her.

'She is still very young,' Roberta said comfortingly to Héloïse when they were alone together, walking in the garden under the falling blossom of the cherry trees. 'You have only to see how she romps and plays with Bobbie, given the chance, to know that. She is the dearest girl,' she added with a warm smile, 'and Bobbie doats on her, and she will make someone a warm and loving wife one day.'

'But do you think she has taken well enough?' Héloïse asked anxiously.

'Oh yes,' Roberta said. 'The hostesses think her a pretty-behaved girl, and she gets asked to the right places. Other girls seem to get on with her, and she has partners enough at the balls, though her lack of fortune will prevent her from making a brilliant match —'

'Oh, but I never wanted that, only that she should marry well, and be happy,' Héloïse said quickly.

'I'm sure she will do that, given time,' Roberta said. 'But you know, at the moment she has the most dreadful crush upon the Duc.'

'Not really?' Héloïse said in amazement. 'But he is too old for her. I'm sure he has never even noticed her, except kindly.'

Roberta smiled. 'I did not say he had a crush upon her. He thinks of her as a child, of course. But she gazes at him in the most agonising way, and turns scarlet, poor child, if he speaks to her.'

'But this is very bad. I must take her away, where she will not see him,' Héloïse frowned.

'No, no, let it run its course. It won't do any harm. She will find a man of her own age to love sooner or later. I believe,' she added gravely, 'that every girl has to go through the stage of admiring an older man. In my case, of course, I was lucky enough to have married him.'

'Do you think, then, that you would have grown out of him, if he had not died?'

'Well, no,' Roberta admitted, 'but that was different.'

'How different?' Héloïse demanded.

'It was not a crush; it was love,' she said.

John Anstey came to visit, to find out from Héloïse how Lucy and Edward had coped with their bereavement, and was glad to hear that they were both going back to Morland Place.

'It will do them more good than anything else to go home,' he said. 'Yorkshire air and Yorkshire food will soon set them up.'

'Ah, but you Yorkshire people think that being there can cure anything,' Héloïse said. 'You wonder that anyone can ever bear to live anywhere else.'

'Quite true,' Anstey said cheerfully. 'I would not be in London if I did not have to be; but you, ma'am, I can't understand why you are here, when you might be at home in your snug cottage.'

'But you know very well, I am bringing Mathilde out,' Héloïse said, thinking it best to take him literally. 'How else shall she find herself a husband?'

'There are plenty of good lads in Yorkshire who would make excellent husbands,' Anstey said with a twinkling eye. 'You don't want her to marry a soft southerner, do you?'

'Don't dignify his nonsense with argument, Héloïse,' Roberta advised.

'I shall not,' she replied easily. 'I shall ask him instead what is so important as to keep him in London.'

'The peace negotiations, of course,' Anstey said promptly. 'Putting an end to this tiresome war.'

'I think it is a mistake,' Héloïse said doubtfully. 'This Napoleon is not one to trust. He will do anything and say anything to get his own way. The truth is not in him.'

'Well, Fox is a shrewd man, and he'll make sure we don't give anything away. He says he has two glorious things to do before he dies: to make peace with the French, and to abolish the slave-trade.'

'Ah, that would be very good,' Héloïse said. 'It is very abominable to sell the poor people's bodies so.'

'But will he succeed?' Roberta asked.

'I think so. It has foundered in Parliament before because those whose interest lay in maintaining the trade were in united opposition, but now the Government consists of so many different factions, there will be no impetus of resistance.'

He waited while Roberta poured him more sherry, and then went on, 'The other thing that has been occupying me in London is arranging the cartels of exchange for the prisoners taken at Trafalgar. It's very sad in some cases. Villeneuve, for instance, has no real wish to go back at all.'

'Ah, poor Villeneuve!' Héloïse exclaimed. 'It must be very hard for him.'

'Yes, indeed. He says he has been so kindly treated, and the glimpse he had of our ships made him believe that he could very happily have made his career in our navy. My boy John tells me that Collingwood said he was a very English sort of Frenchman.'

'He meant that for a compliment,' Roberta explained smilingly to Héloïse.

'So now he goes back to face Boney's anger —' Anstey resumed.

'Which will be very great,' Héloïse interposed.

'— and probably a court-martial for his failure to win the battle. But Villeneuve is not the only one who does not want to go back. I came across a curious case the other day. It's a young lad of about fifteen or sixteen who was picked up out of the water after the *Achille* blew up, and has quite a strange tale to tell.'

'Your French must have improved, my lord, if you understood it,' Roberta said genially.

'Normally, my dear Lady Chelmsford, I do not interview the common sailors myself,' he replied with dignity, 'but in this case I did go to see him, and though he speaks French, he mixes it in a most curious way with English and German and a vile patois they speak around the coast of Brittany. He seems able to make himself understood amongst sailors of both nationalities, and when you hear his story, you can see why.'

'Do tell us, then,' said Roberta.

'Well, it seems that the boy was working on a fishing-boat out of a small harbour near Brest, when the French authorities pressed him and sent him on board the *Achille*. But he did not come originally from Brittany. It seems that the owner of the fishing-boat on which he was working bought him in exchange for a case of brandy from the master of an English fishing-boat.'

'Bought him? Like a slave? How terrible,' Héloïse exclaimed.

'Yes, indeed, and it seems as though he was treated with great brutality by his previous owner, who kept him as a sort of cabin-boy, doing all the menial tasks aboard the boat, keeping him short of food, and punishing him harshly for anything or nothing. When the men got drunk, which they did regularly after a good catch, to celebrate, they would amuse themselves by tormenting the boy in various ways too beastly to mention here. Needless to say, he was very glad to be sold to a new master, and the French fisherman, though a coarse and uneducated man, was at least not such a brute, and treated him harshly, but fairly.'

'But how did he get into the hands of the wicked fisherman?' Héloïse asked. 'It was not his father, I think?'

Anstey looked at her intently. 'Here the story becomes even more interesting,' he said. 'The boy was in a shipwreck, of a fishing-boat which foundered during a storm on the Goodwin Sands, about seven or eight years ago.' Héloïse paled a little, and opened her mouth to speak, but Anstey lifted a hand. 'Wait, let me tell all. After the shipwreck he was taken to a foundling home, but he ran away from it to go back to the sea, which was all he knew. He made his way on foot, with, I imagine, great difficulty and hardship, to Hastings, and there he was picked up, starving and in rags, outside an alehouse by the man who was to treat him so brutally.'

'And before the shipwreck?' Héloïse asked in the thread of a voice.

'He does not remember anything clearly. He received a blow to the head when the ship foundered, and his memories of his previous life are merely unconnected fragments. But there are two indicators which, though insignificant on their own, make him rather more interesting to us. One is that, though he cannot remember anything about his origins, he undoubtedly speaks German as well as French. And the second is that his name is Charlie.'

'Charlie?' said Roberta. 'Is that all? But Charlie isn't a French name.'

'No surname. And of course, the French version would be *Charles*,' Anstey agreed.

'Karellie!' Héloïse breathed.

'That's what I wondered,' Anstey said quietly. 'If he had said to the English fisherman that his name was Karellie, he would probably have heard it as Charlie, and passed that on to his new master when he sold him.'

'If it should be the same!' Héloïse said in distress. 'That he should have suffered so, when I promised his mother I would look after him! *Oh ciel, je suis accablée de remords!*'

'You don't know that it is the same child,' Roberta pointed out, 'and even if it is, there is nothing you could have done to prevent any of it.'

'But it must be made right now,' Héloïse said firmly. 'Where is the boy, Lord Anstey? I must go and see him at once.'

'But wait,' Roberta interrupted with a frown, 'I don't understand why you said he doesn't want to go back with the other prisoners to France. If he has no memory of his origins, and the English captain treated him so cruelly, why should he want to stay?'

'That is rather the point,' Anstey said. 'He says he has nothing to go back to France for, and that if he does, he will probably be pressed again, either into the navy, or more likely into the army — Boney's plans seem to need more and more troops every year. All he knows is the sea, and fishing, and what he really wants is to be taken on board an English fishing-boat, where they will treat him kindly.'

'No, that shall not be,' Héloïse said at once. 'He shall come to me, and I shall take care of him, and feed him and clothe him and — oh, how excited Mathilde will be, to find her brother again! She always swore that he was still alive!'

'You don't know that it is he,' Roberta warned her, with an anxious glance at Anstey. Héloïse seemed to be going altogether too fast.

Anstey agreed. 'I must beg you not to say anything to Mathilde, and not to make any plans, until you have seen the boy. I should like you to meet him and talk to him, to see if he is the child you lost, but after that —'

'*Bien sûr*, he is the same! I can feel it in my bones!'

'After that,' Anstey continued firmly, 'we can decide what is best to be done with him. But I want you to promise me to withhold judgement until you have seen him.'

'Very well, whatever you say,' Héloïse said happily. 'Oh, my dear Lotti, at last I shall be able to fulfil my promise, and you will be able to rest in peace! When may I see the boy, my lord? Very soon, it must be very soon, so that we can begin to make up to him for all the horrible things that have happened.'

Anstey exchanged a glance and a sigh with Roberta, and said, 'I will take you to see him tomorrow, ma'am, but please, in the meantime, don't make any plans, or get too excited. He is not like any child you know.'

John Anstey did his best on the way down to prepare Héloïse

for disappointment; but nothing he could have said would have prepared her for the pathetic piece of human jetsam who was at last brought before her. She stared a moment, and then turned an appealing face to Anstey, begging quite plainly to be told that it was a mistake, that this was not the boy. But Anstey nodded grimly, and said, 'Charlie, this lady thinks she may know something of your past, before the shipwreck. Stand up straight, and answer her questions truthfully.'

It took Héloïse a while to restore order to her thoughts. The boy before her might well have been fifteen or sixteen, but he was puny and thin and small from malnourishment, with the pale, unhealthy skin and dull hair of poverty. On his face there were the marks of half-healed burns from the explosion which had flung him into the water, and when he moved his head, she saw to her horror and distress that where his left ear should be there was only a hole and puckered scar. She remembered the brutal captain, and prevented her mind from speculating on how he had lost it.

But worse than his appearance was the way he stood, his thin shoulders hunched as though against an expected blow, watching her with the sullen wariness of an ill-treated animal. And when she spoke to him, there was no light of intelligence or humanity in his eyes; he merely stared at her dully, with his mouth open.

She began to question him, speaking slowly and clearly in French, and at first there was no response at all from him, not even the flicker of comprehension in his face. Then, when at last he did speak, it was in a blurred, guttural voice, which ran words together, mispronounced them, and mixed in other languages almost at random, and a salting of coarse oaths which he evidently used as a matter of course, without, probably, knowing that they offended. It was very hard to understand his terse, jumbled answers, and what she did understand was not to the point. He remembered nothing before the shipwreck. He had never had a mother or father, that he knew of.

'But you must have had them once,' Héloïse persisted, 'Do you think you were French to begin with? When you were very little, did people talk to you in French? No answer. 'Or in

331

German?' She asked the same question in German, and again received no answer. 'Do you remember another shipwreck, apart from the one in England? When you were very little?'

'I was wrecked on the sands,' he said doggedly, seeing some response was essential, and not knowing what was wanted of him. 'They took me to a place for children, but I didn't like it. I ran away.'

'No, before that,' Héloïse insisted, and then decided to try to shock him into memory. 'Karellie,' she said sharply in German, 'where is Mathilde? What happened to your sister Mathilde?'

For an instant she thought that she might break through the fog in the boy's mind. He looked at her, not with the dull, uncomprehending patience he had shewn so far, but in bewilderment. Some struggle seemed to be going on inside him, and his lower lip quivered. Her heart was tugged with pity. She wondered how long it was since he had allowed himself to cry.

'You remember Mathilde, don't you, Karellie?' she asked, searching his face for understanding, and for some resemblance to her ward or to Lotti and her husband. But the boy only shook his head. He did not cry; the veil descended again, and his face hardened into its former lines. In them she could see nothing that could tell her certainly that this was Lotti's child.

She turned to look at Anstey, and he nodded and dismissed the boy with a kind but firm command, and he turned and shuffled away obediently.

When he had gone, Héloïse said, 'Oh, it is so terrible, so sad! The poor, poor child!'

'He really doesn't remember anything,' Anstey said, with the hint of a question in the statement, since he had not followed all of the conversation in French.

'Nothing at all. And yet I am sure it is he,' Héloïse said. 'The coincidence would be too great. I must take over responsibility for him at once. He shall not suffer again. I shall give him a loving home, at least.'

Anstey shook his head. 'My dear ma'am, you cannot take this child into your home. You see now why I wanted you to meet him before you made plans? He is not like Mathilde. He is a dirty, foul-spoken, ignorant, coarse boy. No amount of washing or feeding or new clothes would turn him into a fit specimen for your drawing-room.'

'But yet you wanted me to see him. Why should you do that, if you wish me to do nothing for him?' Héloïse said.

'I hoped you would wish to help him, but in the right way,' Anstey said. 'Help to place him in the way of keeping himself respectably, and in a place where he will not be ill-treated. That would be a true kindness.'

'If he were not Lotti's child, if it were certain he were not Karellie, I should want to do as much for him, now that I have seen him. I cannot tell you,' she added, with an unhappy look, 'how his story has appalled me. But what do you think we should do with him, my lord? Give me your advice.'

'The boy wants to go back at sea. If he were more intelligent, I would suggest placing him in the Naval College at Portsmouth, but you see how his mind is clouded, whether by the accident or by constant ill-treatment I don't know. Whatever the reason, such training would be far beyond his capacity.'

'Yes, I suppose so,' Héloïse sighed.

'I think the best, and the kindest thing, would be to find some kindly, respectable fisherman's family to take him in. If the family were paid a small amount regularly for his keep, and visited from time to time, it would ensure that they would do right by the boy. That way, he would be trained up to a useful trade, and protected from exploitation by unscrupulous people.'

'And you wish me to furnish the small amount?' Héloïse said. 'Well, it is little enough to do for him. But Lotti's child, to be an ignorant fisherboy! I do not think this is what she would have wanted.'

'Perhaps not, but what has happened was not in your power to alter, and I am sure this is the best thing to do for him now. You see for yourself how his mind is affected. Perhaps kind treatment and good food may begin to lift the cloud from his faculties, and if so, then you may wish to do more for him later. But for the moment —'

'Yes,' Héloïse said with a sigh, 'I see that you are right. And yet I feel so guilty about it.'

'That,' said Anstey firmly, 'is absurd.'

A week later, Héloïse travelled with John Anstey down to Folkestone, to interview the family that he had selected to receive the boy. Héloïse had insisted that she must see them for herself, to make sure they were suitable, and Anstey had thought it reasonable. He also thought that it would impress the family to see her in person, and make them more careful of their charge.

The cottage was very small, but looked neat and snug, the side which was towards the prevailing wind being faced with flints for protection, and the windows set deep in the walls. There was a strong smell of fish and tar and rotting weed in the air, and the bitter, sulphurous reek of cheap coal being burned. Inside, the cottage was sparsely furnished, but the floor was flagged and the walls decently whitewashed, and on the shelf over the fireplace were some pieces of pewter, well-polished.

The smell of fish permeated the air inside, too, but there was also a more agreeable smell of cooking issuing from a pot on the fire. The Upjohns were all there, ready to meet the visitor who was to make such a difference to their lives. Upjohn himself was a short, swarthy man, with massively powerful shoulders and blunt, scarred hands. His face was blue with bristles, but his eyes were quick and bright, and he looked at Héloïse directly and frankly, without either insolence or obsequiousness, which made her like him at once.

Mrs Upjohn was a thin, mousey woman, with shoulders bent from too much hard work, and hands red and flayed from being too often in water. Her clothes glittered strangely as she moved, and it took Héloïse a while to realise that they were spangled with fish-scales, like sequins. There were three small children: a squalling baby and a boy and girl of four and three.

'Now then, Upjohn,' Lord Anstey said heartily, 'this is the lady who wishes to place young Charlie Wood in a kind home.' This was the name they had decided to give the boy.

Mrs Upjohn brought forward a wooden chair and placed it by the fire. 'Would it please your grace to sit down?' she whispered, almost overcome with awe.

Héloïse sat, and surveyed the couple before her. 'You understand,' she said, 'that the boy has been badly treated in

334

the past, and that he is very rough in his manner. But he has worked for many years on fishing-boats, and knows the sea very well. I wish him to be useful to you, Mr Upjohn, and to learn his trade; and to be made a decent, honest man. You will need, I think, to be firm with him, for he has learned some bad ways from those who had charge of him before, but I wish him to be treated also with great kindness, for he has had very little of that in his life.'

'I think I understand you, ma'am,' Upjohn said, 'and I will say that I can't abide cruelty, to man nor beast. Anyone hereabouts will tell you that Ezra Upjohn is not the man to stand by and see a fellow human being suffer.'

'You understand that her ladyship will pay you a sum of money monthly for the boy's keep, as long as she is satisfied that he is being properly cared for?'

'I understand that, sir,' Upjohn said, 'and I won't deny that the money will come in very useful, for we've the little ones to care for, and though fishing is my life and I wouldn't want any other, there's no denying it's an uncertain living, up one day and down the next. Now that sum o' money, coming in regular, that will take a deal of worry off Mrs Upjohn's shoulders' — he gave his wife an affectionate glance, which she returned shyly — 'which I shall be glad to see done, for a better wife a man couldn't want, if he searched the whole of England. And I shall be glad, too, to have the help on the boat, until my Timmy is old enough to come out with me, which won't be for a long while yet, as you see, ma'am,' he said with a grin, 'for feed him how we may, he isn't but four years old, and won't grow any faster.'

Héloïse smiled, liking the fisherman more every moment. Her only doubts were as to how the quiet, mousey little woman would cope with Karellie's roughness. 'I hope your children will not be shocked by poor Charlie's manners,' she said. 'He has lived with a very low sort of people until now.'

'Don't you worry, ma'am,' Upjohn said quickly, divining her problem. 'Mrs Upjohn may look as though a gust of wind would blow her away, but there's steel underneath, and she'll soon bring the boy round her thumb. And having him out with me most of the day, I'll knock the corners off him in no time, never you fear. A boy will do a great deal to be like those he's with, and when he sees I don't cuss nor take the Name in vain, he'll stop doing it.'

When Héloïse and Anstey left the little house, and took their first deep breath of untainted air, Héloïse felt much happier about Karellie's future. 'I'm sure you have found just the right family to place him in,' she said as Anstey handed her into the carriage. 'I only hope that he does not corrupt those little children, or shock that poor woman. But the man will be very good for poor Karellie, and make a fisherman of him, if nothing else.'

'I'll have my agent keep an eye on them from time to time, to make sure all is well, but I'm sure you don't need to worry any more.' He hesitated delicately. 'You won't tell Mathilde, I suppose, about the business?'

'No,' Héloïse said. 'It is better for her not to know. If he really is Karellie, he is not the brother she remembers, and it would make her very unhappy to see him as he is now.'

'I'm sure you're right,' Anstey said, relieved.

At the end of May, when the weather began to be too hot for London, Roberta proposed going down to Brighton for a few weeks.

'It will be very gay down there this year. And with the camp nearby, there will be plenty of handsome young officers in scarlet regimentals to distract Mathilde's attention from the Duc.'

'I don't think a hundred officers all dying of love for her could do that,' said Héloïse, who had by now had sufficient opportunity to observe for herself her ward's secret passion for the French nobleman. 'But I suppose it would be a good thing to do, if there are eligible young men there.'

'In plenty,' Roberta said, amused. 'Should you like me to get her a pretty colonel with ten thousand a year? My Papa is sure to know of one. Or is it an admiral you want?'

'Don't tease,' Héloïse said with a sigh. 'And please don't talk of admirals. When I think of poor Pierre Villeneuve, murdered in that dreadful way, it almost breaks my heart!'

The report had recently reached England of the French admiral's mysterious death in an inn on the way to Paris. He had survived his dreaded return to France only by two days.

'But it said in the French papers that he killed himself,' Roberta said. 'There was a letter to his wife on the bedside table.'

'Pah!' said Héloïse crossly, becoming very French in her agitation. 'One does not believe such stupidness! A man killing himself does not stab himself ten times, and drag himself half out of bed in that way! That wicked monster Napoleon sent secret men to kill him, so that he could not tell the truth about Trafalgar, and shew the French people whose fault it really was. It was the assassins who wrote the letter, and a very vulgar letter it was, too, not what a gentleman would write to his wife.'

'Well, perhaps you are right,' Roberta said soothingly. 'We will never know the truth of it, I don't suppose. So now, shall we go to Brighton, or not? For myself, I should very much like a breath of sea air, and a little exploring in the pretty Sussex countryside.'

'To say the truth, dear Roberta,' Héloïse said wistfully, 'I long and long to go home and see my dear babies, and Flon, and my poor dog, and my dear little house, I have been away so very long!'

'If it seems so long, I have nothing more to say,' Roberta said with a smile. 'No, truly, I quite understand your wanting to see the children again. But why not leave Mathilde with me? I'm sure she would like to go to Brighton, since all her new friends will be there.'

'Oh, but I could not impose on you,' Héloïse said. 'You have been put to so much trouble already.'

'No trouble in the world,' Roberta said serenely. 'Mathilde is company for me, and I love to have an excuse to look at new gowns and bonnets, and go to balls. She is a dear girl, and I love having her,' she went on firmly as Héloïse tried to protest, 'and Bobbie would be quite heartbroken if she were to leave now. He wants her to stay with us for ever. His latest plan is for her to marry Mr Firth, so that she need not go away.'

'In that case,' Héloïse said, laughing, 'I have nothing more to say, but thank you. She shall stay with you until you tire of her, and if Bobbie cannot make her a match in that time I shall be very surprised!'

337

Chapter Eighteen

It was Kithra who reached Héloïse first when she stepped down from the carriage outside her house. Frantic with joy, he reared up on his hind legs, which made him about the same height as her, pinned her against the side of the chaise, and licked her face and pushed his cold nose into her ear until Stephen arrived to drag him off.

'I beg your pardon, my lady. He said it was you, and scratched at the door and whined like a mad thing, but I wouldn't have let him out if I'd thought it was. Welcome back, my lady.'

'Thank you, Stephen. I would have sent you notice, but it would not have arrived before me in any case. Is everything in order? Is everyone well?'

'Pretty much so, my lady. Here, you boy, be careful what you do with that box! Shall I pay the postboys, my lady?' Stephen said tactfully, since Héloïse seemed too preoccupied with gazing at her house to remember them.

'Oh, yes! of course — here is my purse. Oh Stephen, it is so good to be back! London was very pleasant, but so noisy and dirty and crowded. Here everything smells so good. Ah, here is my darling Flon at last!'

She picked up her skirts and ran to be embraced by her old friend, who first shed a tear or two, and then eyed her clothes keenly. 'That is a London pelisse, every line proclaims it! Very elegant, my love, and a killing colour!'

'It is the fashion this year,' Héloïse said. 'And what do you think of my hat?'

'Delightful, except that you sewed on that ribbon yourself, and did it very ill, as usual,' Flon said shrewdly. 'I shall take it off and do it for you before you wear it again.'

Héloïse laughed. 'Dear Flon, you always see everything! No-one in London noticed. But you are looking well, I am glad to say. Have the children been good?'

'Perfect angels,' Flon asserted, which was what Héloïse

338

knew she would say, whether they were or not. But now the news of her arrival had permeated the house, and here were the children running out to her, followed by the rest of the servants. Was that really her little Sophie, grown two inches at least since she went away?

'Maman, Maman, you've come at *last!*' Sophie cried passionately, flinging her arms round her mother's waist and gazing up at her with a face grown suddenly bony, and a gap in her smile that brought absurd tears to Héloïse's eyes. 'Kithra said you were never coming back again, and I told him and told him, but he wouldn't believe me.'

'Did he tell you so himself?' Héloïse laughed.

'Oh, yes. He talks to me all the time. Nobody else understands him.'

'You've lost a tooth.'

'Kithra wagged it out. But it was loose anyway. Flon shewed me how to bury it in the garden under a rose-bush, and in the morning there was a silver thimble there.' Sophie glanced sideways to see if Flon were listening and whispered importantly, 'She said the rose-fairy left it, but I think it was *her*. Was it, Maman?'

'I don't know, my love, I wasn't here,' Héloïse laughed, and unwound one of Sophie's arms to make room for Thomas, who was waiting for his turn, his light-brown forelock hanging over his brown eyes, like a patient pony. She picked him up and kissed his cheek, and he turned away in embarrassment, and then turned back to kiss her heartily on the ear, surprising both of them, and buried his face in her neck as everyone laughed.

The maids came forward to curtsey and smile, and last of all Monsieur Barnard came out, blinking like a cat in the sunshine, holding a wooden spoon upright in one hand like a sceptre.

'You were away far too long, my lady,' he said as Héloïse shook hands with him, and then added with a happy sigh, 'but the young carrots are perfect: you shall have them glazed, with a hint of nutmeg; and the strawberries are just ready. Roast duckling and strawberry tarts, and pink lamb cutlets, and syllabub.' His love always expressed itself in culinary terms.

'And what have you all been doing while I was away?'

Héloïse asked as she walked into the house, Sophie still wound round her waist and Thomas in her arms.

'I've been teaching Thomas to read,' Sophie said proudly, looking up with a proprietorial smile at her baby. 'He's very good, Maman. He has got nearly all the way through *The Little Lottery Book*, and he can read two pages of *The History of the Robins*, if I help him along a bit.'

'Well, that is very good indeed,' Héloïse said gravely. 'He must be very clever.'

Flon, coming up behind her, murmured. 'He doesn't really read it, you know. She's read the story to him so often, the little dear, he has learnt it off by heart, and recites it to her, and turns the page just at the right moment, from seeing her do it.'

'Maman, where is Mathilde? Isn't she coming home?'

'She's gone to Brighton with Lady Chelmsford, who very kindly invited her to stay with her all summer. She asked me, too, but I wanted to come home.'

'I'm glad you did,' Sophie said judiciously. 'It isn't the same without you. But isn't Mathilde married yet?'

'Not yet,' Héloïse said, suppressing a smile.

'She's getting very old,' Sophie said sadly. 'Didn't the gentlemen like her?'

'They liked her very much, and danced with her just as they ought, but none of them was just right. One must be very careful, my Sophie, when choosing a husband, for once chosen, one cannot change him, and he must last for ever.'

Sophie considered this. 'Yes,' she said at length, 'and she will have to find one that doesn't mind her having red hair. Because Alice said not every gentleman can fancy red hair, and Nan said *she* ought to know about gentlemen's fancies, because she had turned so many of them, so it must be true, musn't it, Maman?'

Héloïse laughed, and kissed Thomas and put him down. She pushed a lock of Sophie's hair off her brow, and said, 'When Mathilde meets the right man, my love, he won't even notice what colour her hair is.'

Sophie rejected this firmly. 'I don't think *anyone* could look at Mathilde and not notice,' she said.

Left alone at Wolvercote after the funeral, when both Héloïse and Edward had departed, Lucy had enough to do to keep her from sinking into a lethargy; for although the routines of the house and estate continued, uninterrupted by the death of a master who had always preferred to leave their running to hirelings, there always seemed to be someone asking for an interview with her. For the most part, they simply wanted confirmation from her that they were doing the right thing; others wanted an excuse to recount to her their own memories of the late lord. Lucy was surprised to find in how much affection his employees had held him. She had always assumed that as he had been a careless and largely absent landlord, he would be little missed; and this ability of his to inspire love in those who served him shed a new light on his character.

Others wanted her support for some long-delayed pet scheme to be introduced.

'His late lordship never cared for pineapples, my lady, but I always felt as how the glass house on the south wall of the west orchard would make an excellent pinery.'

'If you was thinking of putting any capital into the estate, my lady, there's that meadow down beyond the woods over to Pixey that ought to be drained and put under the plough. It's never been but sour grazing, and I mentioned it many a time to his late lordship, but he was such a one for tradition, begging your pardon, my lady, that he never would hear of it.'

There were also a great many visits from the family lawyer, and his business wearied Lucy most, for the arcane language of the law seemed to her to serve no other purpose than to make work for Mr Beguid and his like; and the number of documents involved in the simple transfer of title and estate from father to son only confirmed her view. Beguid himself was incapable of speaking plain English, and even when requested by Lucy to rephrase some obscurity so that she could understand it, it took many attempts before he could tell her that the capital settled on her in the will would provide her with an income more than equal to the allowance Chetwyn had made her during his lifetime; or that while she had been named as sole guardian of her children, the office of trustee was to be shared between her brother Edward and Chetwyn's cousin Cavendish, his nearest male relative.

From these importunities Lucy turned for relief to the undemanding company of her horses, and accompanied only by Parslow, she spent long hours in the saddle trying, as Parslow opined to Docwra, to tire herself out. Both Docwra and Miss Trotton tried to interest her in her children, who were bewildered and upset by the disappearance from their world, both of the father who, in the last two years, had made himself familiar and beloved, and their playmate Robert. But Lucy did not have anything in her to give the children. On the few occasions when she came face to face with them, the effort of speaking to them seemed to make her both restless and weary.

'She'll come to it in time,' Parslow said wisely. 'It's too soon yet. She still can't bear anyone near her.'

'She doesn't mind having *you* around,' Docwra said, with faint resentment that it was to her groom and not her maid that Lucy turned for comfort.

'That's because she knows she doesn't have to talk to me,' Parslow said. 'You women are always wanting to know how she feels, and whether she's all right, and whether she'd like a glass of wine or a warmer shawl. Always demanding.'

'We're naturally concerned for her,' Docwra said with dignity.

'I know that, Bessie, and she knows it; but you don't understand, she just can't bear questions. It's all she can do, just to keep her head up, without having to answer questions.'

'Well, what do you talk to her about?' Docwra asked. 'For I see you chatting away, all right, when you come in from a ride.'

Though he had never married, Parslow understood children very well, from having spent a lifetime with horses. He knew that what both wanted was certainties; and in her double bereavement, Lucy was very childlike. 'I just tell her things,' he said.

Despite what she had said to Héloïse and Edward, Lucy did go back to London before travelling to Yorkshire. The immediate reason was that Captain Haworth was going back to sea, and wanted to hand over Hippolyta, and London was more convenient for him than Wolvercote; but underneath was a desire, which she was faintly surprised to discover in herself, to see the house again.

Hicks was pathetically glad to receive her, and it was only after a day or two that she learned from Parslow that he was in fear of the house being given up, and himself and the rest of the London staff being turned off.

'But I should not have turned them off without making sure they had a place,' Lucy said, puzzled. 'Surely they must know that.'

'Yes, my lady,' Parslow said. 'They just don't want to leave your service.'

'Oh,' said Lucy. It was another new thing to think about, that her servants liked to serve her. 'Well, you may tell Hicks that I don't mean to give up the house.'

'Yes, my lady,' Parslow said neutrally, but with an inward hope that this might be a sign that deep down, below the layers of grief and loneliness, she had not despaired of life.

Captain Haworth arrived from Portsmouth with Polly and Africa, and the news that *Cetus* was all ready for sea again.

'I expect my orders will be waiting for me when I get back, but I know what they are,' he said. 'I'm to go back to Collingwood's squadron off Cadiz, to continue the blockade.'

'Poor Collingwood,' Lucy said with feeling. 'Not a day on shore, not a moment's rest since the battle.' After Trafalgar, fresh ships had been sent out from Gibraltar to reinforce the Cadiz fleet, and Collingwood had transferred his flag from *Euryalus* to the ninety-eight-gun *Queen.* One by one the ships damaged in the battle had been sent for refitting, giving their captains the opportunity to go on shore and rest and recuperate, to sleep in a bed and eat fresh food; but Collingwood had remained on station without a break.

'And there's no likelihood of his hauling down his flag in the immediate future, either,' Haworth said. 'Their Lordships have said they can't spare him, so it looks like another year on blockade, at least. The sweets of victory, you see,' he said with an ironic smile. 'We have nothing more to fear from the French by way of battle. Now we simply have to keep watch over their ports and choke off their sea-trade. Dull work!'

Lucy eyed him speculatively. 'It sounds as though you had

fallen out of love with the sea.'

'Oh, never that,' Haworth assured her, 'but I begin to think I may have reached the moment for coming ashore. I think of poor Collingwood, you know, and his daughters whom he loves and hasn't seen in so many years, and I don't want to go the same way myself.'

'You have Africa with you,' Lucy pointed out.

'Yes, but the time is coming when she ought to have a proper education and meet other young people of her own age, or she will grow up too strange to be able to make the adjustment later.'

'That's true,' Lucy said. 'What is it you plan to do, then?'

'I haven't got as far as making plans, yet,' he said, 'but I have my prize-money saved, and the award from Trafalgar, and there'd be my half-pay. If I were to give up my commission next spring, I think I could live snugly enough, in a small way, with my girls. Take a little house in Portsmouth or Southsea or somewhere like that. I shouldn't want to be too far from the sea.'

'Then you'd take Polly away from Flaminia?' Lucy said.

'I don't want to separate them entirely,' Haworth said. He smiled quizzically at Lucy. 'I was hoping that you wouldn't feel the friendship of a retired sea-officer beneath you, and that we might meet from time to time, for the children's sake, if nothing else.'

'Of course,' Lucy said briskly. 'Don't be a fool, Haworth. Do you think I'd have cared for your children all these years if I didn't like you? I hope we shall meet very often. You can come and stay at Wolvercote whenever you like, for as long as you like. I shall probably,' she added thoughtfully, 'be glad of your advice.'

'We'll help each other, then,' he said. 'Between us, we ought to be able to solve most of our problems.'

The prospect comforted Lucy a little. Kindly, sensible, practical, understanding, he was the sort of friend she most needed.

A friend of another kind came to visit her while she was still in Upper Grosvenor Street. Though she had not announced her arrival in Town, Mr Brummell left his card at once, and called on her a few days later. He eyed her black gown with sympathy, but shewed his understanding of her by forbearing to talk about her bereavement, and gave her instead the latest gossip.

'Lady Chelmsford is gone down to Brighton — rather early, but the best lodgings are so quickly taken. Did you know that the Prince has changed his mind about having the Pavilion rebuilt in the Chinese style? It seems that Porden — his architect, you know — has become interested in the Indian movement, so it's out with the mandarins and in with the nabobs! One can only wait with bated breath to see the result.'

'It will be perfectly hideous, whichever way they do it,' Lucy said with conviction, and Brummell's eyes twinkled.

'How deliciously rude you can be, ma'am! You ought to admire His Highness's taste more, since he is even now preparing to build a new stable for the Pavilion on your brother's model at Morland Place, only a great deal larger, of course. The cupola is to be twice as big, at least. Quite how they will get such an enormous dome to stay up, no-one has yet worked out.'

Lucy gave a faint smile, and Mr Brummell felt sufficiently encouraged to go on. 'And Mrs Fitz is in raptures over the result of the court case over little Minny Seymour,' he said.

Mary Seymour was the orphaned niece of the Marquess of Hertford, whom Mrs Fitzherbert had been looking after ever since the child's mother, her intimate friend, had died in July 1801. She adored the child, an engaging creature, who called her 'mama' and the prince 'Prinny'. Prinny and Minny were the greatest of friends; but the child's relatives had decided that Mrs Fitzherbert was not a fit person to have charge of her, and had taken a claim to court to have the child taken away from her.

'I had not heard it was concluded,' Lucy said. 'What did the court decide?'

'They found in favour of the Seymours, but ordered the child to be handed over to the Marquess as head of the family; and since Lady Hertford is a dear friend of Mrs Fitz's, the Marquess has given Minny back to her.'

'It seems a fair result for all concerned.'

'Quite so; and the Prince has discovered what an entirely delightful woman Lady Hertford is. Of course he has been thrown a great deal into her company during the negotiations.'

He watched to see if Lucy would pick up the hint, but she only nodded vaguely, and after a moment asked, 'How does your new club go on?'

'A *succès fou*, of course,' he said promptly; and then with a delicate hesitation, 'I am more than sorry that things happened as they did over young Mr Knaresborough. It was impossible for me to act otherwise; and yet if I had foreseen the consequences, I think I should have closed the club rather than precipitate them.'

Now Lucy was looking frankly puzzled. 'What consequences? What can you mean?'

Brummell shook his head, and gave her a fond smile. 'Nothing in the world. Dear Lady Aylesbury, life would not be the same without you! But they tell me you are going into the countryside — quite to Yorkshire, I believe?'

'For a little while,' she said. 'I shall come back when I feel —'

'Bored?' he supplied helpfully.

'Stronger,' she said. 'I believe I am very tired.'

'But you have many good friends in Yorkshire to take care of you,' he said. 'Lady Strathord has gone back — I suppose you knew that? She has given Miss Nordubois into Lady Chelmsford's care. A perfectly well-behaved young female, though her lack of family and fortune will prevent her from making a brilliant match. Lady Chelmsford seems to enjoy her company. It is odd, is it not, how all your ladies of fashion must have their little fondling about them, some unwanted waif to bring up and lavish affection upon?'

Lucy met his eyes doubtfully. Could he possibly be referring to Thomas? Surely he could not know about him? No-one was supposed to know that he existed, far less that there was any connection between him and Lucy. But there was something very knowing in Mr Brummell's satirical eye. It gave her something to think about after he had gone; for it had not until that moment occurred to her that, now Chetwyn was

346

dead, there was nothing to prevent her from having Thomas
to live with her. The idea was attractive. She had never
reared a child herself, having always been content to leave her
public children largely to Trotton's care. Perhaps, when she
was more settled, she might send for him. She needed something with which to occupy herself in the long years ahead.

Héloïse had only been back home a fortnight, and was returning one day from taking Sophie and Thomas for a ride in the
phaeton, when, drawing up in front of the house, she saw a
gentleman's horse tied up to the hitching-ring. Sophie saw it
at the same instant.

'A visitor! There's a visitor! Maman, why is your face all
red?'

'Because it's so warm. Help Thomas down, my love, and
take him in.'

Stephen came out to take Cygnus and Vega, and to tell her
that the Duc de Veslne-d'Estienne had arrived in her
absence. He pronounced the name without a stumble, having
had a great deal of practice since the first occasion.

A mixture of pleasure, disappointment and relief passed
almost instantaneously through her, and she said, 'But I
thought he had gone to Brighton for the summer, like everyone else. How strange that he should be here.' And she
hurried indoors to the parlour, where Flon was trying to
entertain the visitor, whose eyes would keep straying towards
the door, and whose attention had seemed very hard to
engage over the last fifteen minutes.

When Héloïse came in, he sprang to his feet, and a gladness
filled his eyes which told Flon a great deal, but posed even
more questions than it answered.

'Monsieur le Duc, what a pleasant surprise,' she said,
coming forward with her hand outstretched. He bowed, took
the hand and kissed it, and retained it for a moment as he
looked at her in a way that made her cheeks quite pink. 'What
brings you to Yorkshire?' she asked, a little breathlessly. 'I
had supposed you to be in Brighton.'

'I was there for a few days,' he said, releasing her hand at
last, as she drew it back firmly. 'But I had — I had business to

347

attend to, and then, since I was in the area, I thought I must call and see how you were. The journey home did not fatigue you, I hope?'

'Not the least bit,' Héloïse said, amused, taking a seat on the sopha. 'Have you seen Lady Chelmsford recently? Was she well?'

'I had the pleasure of seeing her ladyship at Lady Tonbridge's ball on Tuesday,' the Duc said. 'She seemed in good spirits.'

'On Tuesday? Oh, then you must only just have arrived in Yorkshire,' Héloïse said. The Duc looked unaccountably embarrassed.

'Oh — yes — just this morning.'

'I did not understand,' Héloïse said. 'It was kind of you to call on me so soon, especially if you have come to Yorkshire on business.' The Duc did not dissent from this view of his actions. 'And was Miss Nordubois at Lady Tonbridge's too?' she asked, aware of Flon's grave glance going from one of them to the other.

'Er — yes, I believe so. Yes, of course she was. She looked very handsome and danced with Major Ashton of the Ninth, I believe,' the Duc said, making an effort to be expansive. 'She seems to enjoy herself extremely. Lady Chelmsford was talking of arranging a picnic party to Rottingdene for Miss Nordubois and some other young ladies, with some of the officers.'

Héloïse smiled a little wickedly. 'And you did not feel compelled to delay your departure for such a temptation? Your business must be urgent indeed.' The Duc looked confused, and Flon gave a warning cough, and Héloïse felt she had teased him too far, and tried to make amends. 'I am sorry I was not here to greet you when you arrived,' she said politely. 'I was taking the children for a drive.'

'In your phaeton? What an elegant carriage that is, so delightfully light and balanced, and the horses so perfectly matched,' the Duc said with unexpected enthusiasm. 'How I wish I had been in time to go with you. But I suppose the horses are tired now?'

'No, not really. I did not drive them fast, nor far,' Héloïse said, a little puzzled, and then, as the Duc looked at her so expectantly, she felt obliged to add, 'Would you like to go for a short drive now?'

'If it would not fatigue you,' he said happily, standing up at once.

'Oh, I am never fatigued,' Héloïse said, and rang the bell to tell Stephen not to unharness the ponies. Not fatigued, but puzzled, she led the way out, wondering what it was that Flon was nodding to herself about so significantly.

Once in the phaeton, and driving at a leisurely pace along the lanes, the Duc seemed much more at his ease, although he did not seem to have as much to say for himself as usual, and kept silence in favour of staring alternately at the ponies' brown-tipped, cream ears, and at Héloïse's profile as she handled the reins. It was left to Héloïse to make conversation along the lines of how pleasant the weather was, what a profusion of wild flowers grew in the hedgerows, and what a good crop of lambs there seemed to have been that year.

By the time she reached Byland Abbey she had run out of conversation, so she pulled up the horses on the grass verge opposite the ruins, and said, 'Have you ever visited the ruins? They are really very interesting.'

'Should you like to walk a little, and look at them?' he asked eagerly. 'Will your horses stand?'

'For a little while, perhaps,' she said doubtfully, but he was already jumping down, and holding out his hand to help her out. They walked across the grass and stood looking at the tall west front with its vast broken circle of a rose window, reminder of what a magnificent church must once have stood there. 'It was a Cistercian house, you know,' she said, feeling the necessity to entertain him. 'Very rich, until it was destroyed at the Dissolution. It is not as big or as grand as Rievaulx, but I always think it is very charming, all the same, and the prospect over the fields is delightful.'

She received little response, and was racking her brain for something else to say about Byland Abbey, when the Duc suddenly found his tongue.

'Dear madame, won't you sit down? I have something most particular to say to you.'

He gestured towards a block of fallen masonry, dusted it with his hand, and gently but firmly obliged her to sit upon it.

Then he stood in front of her, and removed his hat. The sun shone on his glossy hair, and with his uncertain smile, he looked particularly young and handsome.

'It was not really on business that I came to Yorkshire,' he said abruptly. 'Or, at least, it was business of a sort, I suppose, but the thing was, dear madame, that I found Brighton most horribly flat and dull without you. If I had known you were not there, I would not have gone at all.'

Many things were suddenly plain to Héloïse. 'Monsieur le Duc,' she began in protest, but he flung himself suddenly upon his knees in front of her, and seizing her hand, said, 'Charles! Oh, won't you call me Charles, dearest, sweetest Héloïse — forgive me, but that is how I think of you! Yes, and I do think of you, every moment, ever since I first met you. The first time I saw your lovely face and sweet smile, I knew I had met my fate! I believe I loved you from that moment, but it was only when I arrived at Brighton and found you were not there that I realised how much I cared for you. Life without you was suddenly intolerable. I saw then what I must do. I must have been blind, not to see it before, but you will forgive me for that, I know, because you have the kindness of an angel! Forgive me that I have not asked you before, and let me ask you now: dearest Héloïse, will you marry me?'

Héloïse looked at him with astonishment not unmixed with dismay, perplexity mingled with pleasure, and was unable at once to answer him. She had known, of course, that he liked her — why else should he have spent such a flattering amount of time in her company over the last two years? And she liked him, too, and would have been mildly piqued to have seen him transfer his attentions to some other young woman. But she had never thought of those attentions as meaning anything in particular. For her, all thoughts of marriage had long since been folded up and put away.

The Duc took advantage of her silence. 'I see I have taken you by surprise. But you do not regard me, I think, with complete indifference? It is not disgusting to you, my offer?'

'Of course not,' she said weakly. 'How could I be other than flattered and grateful for your regard? But I had not thought —'

'Then please, oh please, dear Héloïse, do think now!

Though I have no royal blood, I am of good family — I have sixteen quarterings. My name is a venerable one, and my fortune, though diminished, is adequate, I believe, to support you in the style that becomes you. And we should suit each other admirably, I am convinced. We come from the same world, you and I, and we are both exiles for the same cause.'

'But you know that I am older than you? That I have been married? And what of the children? I have responsibilities, you see.'

'But of course I know these things. I am not a simpleton! The difference in our ages is nothing, and I adore the children. Here is no bar to our union! Sweet, lovely Héloïse, say yes, say yes quickly!'

He knelt before her, his handsome head framed by a romantic arch of ruined stonework and the blue sky beyond it, and she saw how marriage with him would be perfectly possible. He was sweet-tempered, amiable, well-educated, handsome, and French, and though his passion for her might not last, his good sense and good manners would never allow that to become apparent. After an initial period of fervour, they would settle down to a comfortable marriage in the French style, of mutual respect and affection, strengthened by common interests, and perhaps children of their own. And Sophie and Thomas would accept him very quickly, and though Mathilde might be upset at first, she would soon get over it, when she met someone of her own age to love.

Yes, it was quite devastatingly possible. She would have security for ever, a companion, someone to love and esteem her, the opportunity to have more children. But in the back of her mind was the thought, like the sad piping of a marsh-bird, that it would have been the most romantic and wonderful moment in her life, if only it had been James kneeling there.

James was married, and for ever out of reach. She ought not to think of him. She ought to put herself out of the temptation of thinking of him. She could never marry him, and now here was a kind, delightful, eligible man making the sort of offer for her that nine out of ten girls in London at this very moment would give their hair for.

'My dear — my dear Charles,' she said, using the name a little awkwardly. 'I am more grateful than I can say for your kindness. An offer from you is flattering indeed, and you are right, I am not indifferent to you. Far from it.'

'But you are going to refuse me, I can hear it in your voice!' he cried tragically, and she could not help laughing.

'No not that! But I must have time to think about it. The issue is not simple, you see; and though you may have known for a week that you were going to make me an offer, I have only just this minute heard about it.'

'Of course, I understand,' he said, relieved. 'It was thoughtless of me to expect you to answer at once. Naturally you must take time to consider.'

'Thank you. I shall try not to keep you waiting too long.'

'I can wait as long as you like, provided the answer is yes,' he said. He held out his hand and raised her to her feet, and then lifted her hand to his lips and kissed it with tender dedication. She had been lonely a long time; it was long since she had known the pleasure and security of strong arms around her; and something in her fluttered towards him in that instant, wanting to say yes, and be swept away. But too many things, not least his happiness, depended on her making the right decision. If she married him, she must be ready to give everything to him, everything she had kept back, wicked sinner that she was, for James.

Hot weather in July and al fresco parties naturally tend to come together in the human mind, and though James and Edward, left alone at Morland Place, might well have resisted the conjunction, the presence of Lucy and her children, and the arrival home from London of John Anstey in sociable mood, gave rise without too much struggle to a picnic party in Watermill Field.

Mary Ann was visiting her father as usual, and had taken Henry with her; Lousia Anstey, recovered now from the birth of her seventh, a female they had named Charlotte, came in a large and shabby barouche which had belonged to John's mother, with her other four surviving children, Alfred, Benjamin, Louisa and Mary; Little John was still at sea.

Another carriage brought the Morland Place children, and the other adults came on horseback.

It was the kind of party most likely to bring pleasure to everyone, for none were present but old friends, who preferred comfort to elegance, and companionship to wit. Rugs were laid down, and an enormous array of cold foods was spread out, and everyone ate and chatted at their ease. John Anstey, having recently come from London, had the best right as well as the best spirits for talking, and he entertained them with the latest London gossip, which was all about the so-called 'Delicate Investigation' into the conduct of the Princess of Wales.

'Though quite why they call it that, I don't know,' he said, 'for it really ought to be called the Indelicate Investigation.'

'John, dear,' Louisa said mildly, hesitating between cold ham and cold beef.

The Princess's behaviour, eccentric in youth, had become a greater scandal year by year, and her wild extravagance and uncouth manners had alienated most of Society, though there were still those who said she had been unfairly treated by both her husband and his father. But she was fond of male company, and very free with her male friends, and though the Prince had long ago repudiated her, and had not lived with her for many years, rumours had abounded both in 1801 and 1802 that she was pregnant.

The present crisis had arisen owing to the rivalry between the Princess and her neighbour in Blackheath, Lady Douglas, wife of Sir John Douglas.

'The Princess and Lady Douglas used to be great friends,' Anstey said, 'or at least, as much so as two such women could be. The Douglases were always in and out of Montague House, and it suited Lady Douglas's ambition to be seen to move in high circles.'

'Odious woman,' Lucy said. 'She tried to make up to me, once, at a ball at Cavendish House. Spiteful and showy, bold eyes and a mean mouth! I know the Princess is disgusting, but I'd prefer her of the two.'

Anstey smiled. 'It would be a hard choice to make,' he agreed. 'Well, to go on with the story, the Douglases have had Admiral Sir Sidney Smith living with them this long while, and it's well known that Lady D. and the Admiral are having an affair.'

'What, while her husband is there?' Louisa cried, staring at him. 'How shocking!'

'London is a shocking place, my love,' Anstey said mildly. Louisa's innocent outrage was less than tactful, considering the nature of Lucy's past entanglements, so he hurried on with the story. 'At any rate, with the Admiral visiting Montague House so often in the Douglases company, the Princess had ample opportunity to notice what a fascinating man he is, and she took a fancy to him. This led to rivalry between her and Lady D. I don't know who started it, but they began to blackguard each other behind each other's backs. The Princess told Lady Douglas that she was no longer welcome at Montague House, and sent letters and crude drawings to Sir John about his wife and the admiral. So Lady Douglas retaliated by accusing the Princess publicly of immoral behaviour with a number of people, including your old friend, Lucy, Captain Thomas Manby.'

'Hardly a friend. I met him once or twice, that's all,' Lucy said, waving a chicken-leg negatingly. 'He and the Princess were certainly friendly, from what I heard.'

'It's an edifying tale,' James said ironically, helping himself to cold veal and ham pie. 'What people you've been living among down there!'

'Not me, I promise you,' Anstey said. 'I live a life of hardworking respectability. Anyway, the whole thing got so out of hand that the Prince asked the Prime Minister what to do, and he felt obliged to lay it before the King; and the King, very reluctantly, as you may imagine, decided there must be an investigation. It was supposed to be kept secret, but a thing like that is bound to leak out, especially since they are taking evidence from the Princess's servants, about her evening parties, and who slept the night there, and so on.'

'It's being done for the sake of Princess Charlotte, I suppose,' Lucy said. 'The King doats on that child.'

'And she is the heiress presumptive to the throne,' Anstey said, 'and if the stories about the Princess having been pregnant were true, it might cause grave embarrassment, to say the least. There might be those to say the Prince was not her father either.'

'But surely it would be easy enough to disprove rumours about the supposed pregnancies?' Edward said. 'After all, where there is a pregnancy, there has to be a child.'

'Well, yes, but then the Princess does like to adopt little orphans and fondlings. There are several in her house, and in particular there's that little William Austin whom some people think needs explaining,' Anstey said.

'He's a nasty, spoiled little beast,' Lucy said. 'I don't know why the Princess keeps him.'

'She says she must have something to love,' Anstey said, 'and since she hates dogs and birds, and the Prince won't give her more babies of her own, she has to adopt them.'

'I can quite understand a woman wanting to have lots of children around her,' Louisa said, won over by this view. 'That seems natural to me.'

'The Prince ought to find it natural, at any rate,' Lucy said. 'He fought hard enough for Minny Seymour.'

'Well, the Commissioners are bound to find the Princess innocent, whether she is or not,' Anstey resumed, 'but I think they are going to have their work cut out to make it sound convincing.'

'She's a dreadful woman,' Lucy said, 'but then the Prince is a dreadful man. I always thought they deserved each other.'

'Why, Lucy!' You always say how charming he is to you,' James protested.

'So he is, but it doesn't mean I approve of his behaviour,' she retorted.

'He certainly isn't very popular at the moment,' Anstey said. 'He's been making very obvious advances to Lady Hertford ever since the Seymour case, and people are saying he means to make her his mistress.'

'Well, she's just the sort of matronly woman he likes,' Lucy said, wrinkling her nose, 'but it would be rather hard on Mrs Fitz after all this time.'

'The poor old King's health is being drunk with great fervour in the clubs at the moment,' Anstey said, 'and the wits have invented a new toast to the Prince: "The Prince of Wales *for ever!*"'

There was laughter at that, but Edward shook his head sadly. 'What a world it is,' he said, 'when the country is ruled by a madman, with a debauchee for an heir. What an example to us all!'

'We shall just have to look forward to the days of Queen Charlotte,' Louisa said soothingly. 'England always did well when she had a queen instead of a king. Look at Great Elizabeth and Great Anne.'

'And Great Mary?' her husband teased her. 'Don't forget her, my love.'

'That was different,' she said with dignity.

When the eating and drinking was over, the children, quite naturally, wanted to get up and run about, and the adults, just as naturally, wanted to recline and take their ease. John Anstey took himself off to a little distance to smoke a cigar, and James got up and went with him, and they strolled along the river-bank under the willows, chatting desultorily, while the fragrant smoke drifted up through the branches into the still, hot air. Edward, Louisa and Father Aislaby talked about local matters, and Lucy went to look at the horses.

The gold of the afternoon deepened, and time seemed to expand to accommodate an infinite number of permutations. John, forgetting his public status in a delightfully informal way, was now lying on his front on the river-bank, his coat off and his shirt-sleeves rolled up, shewing Arthur how to catch fish with his bare hands. Louisa watched them fondly from a distance for a while, until she felt driven to go over and warn them in a motherly way about dirt and wetness and the possibilities of drowning. Edward and Father Aislaby, despite the heat, went to organise a game of Kitcat for the rest of the children, which seemed the only way to prevent open warfare breaking out between Fanny and young Benjamin Anstey, who resented the way Fanny bullied his sisters.

James and Lucy, left alone, sat side by side on a rug under a tree and contemplated the scene before them in companionable silence, and after a while James got out his sketching-book, propped it on his knees, and attempted, without much conviction, to capture its essence in pencil. He paused and gazed more than he drew. It needed paint and colour to do the job properly, he thought. The countryside was at its best

356

at this time of year; but even if he had a palette of colours mixed by God's own seraphim, there were things he could never have captured.

The meadow, for instance, thick with wild flowers, had a deep rich July scent, a mixture of fragrance and promise and the underlying fruitcake solidity of the good earth. And a clever hand might set down the luminous quality of the great chestnut trees, spreading their beautiful, palmate leaves to the sun, but who could capture the dumb content of the carriage horses, dozing in the deep, well-water shade beneath them? Or the silent pleasure of the coachman, sitting at his ease on the box, puffing at his pipe, and occasionally sending a blue wreath of smoke in a companionable way about his horses' ears, to keep the flies off?

And what skill could ever quite represent the exact colour of the summer sky, the dense, creamy blue of it, which seemed close enough to touch until you stared into it for a while; and then it expanded away from you, further and further, until you felt that you were swimming upwards through an immensely deep ocean of air towards — who knew what?

At a little distance, the children defied the brilliant sun, their voices, high and clear, echoing on the still, hot air. Their calls of encouragement or enquiry were interrupted every now and then by the flat clack of a stick striking the wooden cat; then, like disturbed starlings, they would break into a flurry of movement and a shrill clamour of voices, as the in-team ran from post to post, counting breathlessly as they ran, and the fielding team shrieked at each other as they scrambled to retrieve the cat.

A particularly lucky strike by Hippolyta sent it flying almost to James's feet, and Fanny came scurrying, red-faced with heat and determination to scoop it up. The rivalry her elder cousin aroused in her seemed to intensify every time they met, despite the fact that Polly seemed not to have a competitive bone in her body, and gave in to Fanny on every whim. So determined was she on this occasion to get Polly out, she hadn't even a glance to spare for her father, only grabbed the cat up from the long grass and whirled away in a flurry of skirts, flying sash-ends, and tangled hair.

357

'Such energy,' Lucy murmured in disbelief. 'And in this heat, too!'

James turned his attention to her. It was odd to see her dressed in black, odder still to see her face so grave and lined, the bones standing out sharply, the mouth, even in relaxation, grim. What Weston's death began, Chetwyn's seemed to have completed: the merry child had gone for ever. And yet he remembered her so well, his little, rough-haired sister, it felt as though she must still be there, just below the surface, if only he could reach her.

'Do you remember the last picnic when we were all together?' he said suddenly. 'It was in this very field, just after Papa died.' Lucy was watching the children, and merely made an interrogative sound. 'You and I came in my curricle, and I let you drive my chestnuts. You were so excited, I thought you'd burst.'

She looked at him now, and recollection softened the lines of her mouth. 'They were a good pair,' she said. 'Bobbin and Sandlewood; nice action, except that Sandlewood had a tendency to scoop with his off-fore. You should have corrected that when he was a colt, but you left it too late.'

James laughed. 'What a memory you have for horses! You must have been about thirteen or fourteen then, and an extremely grubby child you were too, but you had the best hands I've ever seen, man or woman.'

'Thank you,' she said, and he could see she was pleased. She was watching the game again, but he saw some of the rigidity go out of her shoulders, and her hand reached out and plucked a stem of cocksfoot to chew, an unconscious gesture of ease. 'Edward was driving those blacks, do you remember?' she said. 'They simply wouldn't pull together, but he would have them because they looked good. It was all appearance with him in those days. That was Chetwyn's influence.' She sighed. 'He never was a horseman.'

'I remember, at that picnic, the three of you taking your shoes and stockings off, and sitting on the bank with your feet dabbling in the river,' James said, and watched her smile. Chetwyn and Edward, the inseparables, had admitted Lucy like a favoured younger brother to their company.

'Poor Edward,' she said after a moment.

James remembered how Ned had been when he returned after the funeral, and how many hours he had spent closeted with Father Aislaby, trying to expiate his guilt. What he felt he had to be guilty about, James had soon discovered, as the rumours sifted upwards, as rumours always did, from the servants' hall. 'I suppose it was an accident, wasn't it?' he asked tentatively. 'I don't mean to upset you, Luce, but there were rumours —'

'Of course it was,' Lucy said, and then turned to look at him. There was no concealment in her face. 'Of course it was. He would never have done a thing like that, even if he had reason, and what reason could he have?' James did not offer a suggestion. 'Besides,' Lucy added, 'Chetwyn always liked the easy life. If he had wanted to kill himself, he would have taken laudanum or something like that, and done it in the comfort of his own bed. No, Jamie, it was an accident all right. Poor Chetwyn!' She looked away. 'We've been unlucky, haven't we, in our marriages?'

'Perhaps because we always wanted too much,' James said. 'It would have been better to be single-minded like Mother, who just wanted an heir for Morland Place.'

'And now there's Fanny,' Lucy said, watching Fanny with sceptical eyes as the child bellowed furiously at Rosamund for dropping the cat. 'What would Mother think of her now, I wonder?'

'Fanny's all right,' James said irritably, jumping to defend his chick as he always did. 'She's only young. She'll settle down as she grows up.'

Lucy eyed him a moment, and then refrained from pointing out that he had been saying the same thing for the last six years at least. 'I wish Mother were here,' she said instead. 'Everything seemed to go wrong when she died. She would make things right again.'

'I wonder if everyone goes on feeling like that about their mother,' James said thoughtfully, 'or are we different? Is it unnatural still to feel more like her child, than like anyone's father?'

The point was too philosophical for Lucy. She threw away the chewed stem and picked a fresh one. 'We must make sure that they do better than we did,' she said, watching her own three establishing their place in the game. 'I mean to see mine are brought up properly, so that they don't make the same mistakes.'

'It sounds most uncomfortable,' he said. 'You don't mean to start now, this minute, do you?'

'Of course not, not until I get home,' she said, and then realised she was being teased. 'Don't be a fool, Jamie. You might do worse yourself than to take a pull on Fanny's reins now and then.'

Her mouth was more than ever grim at that moment, and James thought that it was a poor outlook for her children when they grew older. Her expression spoke volumes about rigid discipline and hard work, but very little about pleasure. But perhaps she was right. Everyone said he was too soft with Fanny. On the other hand, perhaps children would grow up the same way, whatever you did, turning into what was in them to be. How could one tell?

But thinking of his mother, which he did no less often as he grew older, he could not help feeling that Fanny, much as he loved her, was not the true heiress of Morland Place that Jemima had longed for. When his mother had died, he had felt that none of them who were left was big enough to fill her place; and he went on believing that the feeling he always had, of the house lacking its mistress, was not simply the effect of his longing for a certain person who remained unalterably twenty miles away.

Chapter Nineteen

Hobsbawn House presented a very different aspect to the world from the dusty, neglected look of a few years before. Now the elaborate furniture glowed with rubbing, the heavy drapes were freshly laundered, the rich carpets well-beaten. The air was filled with the scent of beeswax polish and pot-pourri, and bowls of flowers, tastefully arranged in corners, and on the multitude of side-tables, bureaux and commodes, spoke of a woman's presence in the house.

Mr Hobsbawn, too, wore the sleek air of content. His appearance had always been neat and proper, but without pretensions to finery. Now his hair was more elegantly dressed, his shirt-points stiffer, his neckcloths more elaborate, and his waistcoats more festive; and if he did not quite attain to pantaloons and Hessians, his breeches were certainly more stylishly cut, and his topboots bore a high gloss that no manservant of a careless dresser would ever have had the heart to work at.

A change had come over his behaviour, too, for while nothing could make him lie late abed, or be careless about his business, he began to leave more matters in the hands of his overseers, and unless there were an emergency or some special order to be put through, he left his mills in time to come home and dress for dinner in the evening. The fashionable of London Society might dine at three or four in the afternoon, but the hardworking millmasters of the industrial towns must wait until the day's work was done before taking their pleasure.

While Mary Anne was 'home', there were few evenings when they did not have guests at their dinner table, or an engagement abroad. There were dinner-parties, card-parties, and routs; and also public assemblies, balls, and concerts, for Manchester was becoming a very sociable town, and its public buildings were the envy of all Lancashire.

And whether walking with Mary Ann on his arm up the

grand staircase of some public building, or standing by the fireplace in his own drawing-room, watching her receiving his guests, Mr Hobsbawn's heart was filled with pride at the sight of his daughter so effortlessly leading society. Her manners were more polished, her clothes more elegant, her whole air so much more sophisticated than the other Manchester ladies that, despite his misgivings about his chick's worthless husband, he had to confess that being at Morland Place had given her something.

It had given her also little Henry; and if Mr Hobsbawn loved Mary Ann deeply, his adoration of his grandson reduced him quite frequently to tears. Not least among the reasons that he hurried home early from the mills was so that he could take part in the ceremony, which repetition had hallowed into tradition, of putting Henry to bed. This involved a pick-a-back up the stairs, a romp or a pillow-fight in the bed-chamber, and the reading of a story while Henry battled valiantly with his eyelids and the soporific quality of Mr Hobsbawn's voice.

If business delayed him, little Henry would be put to bed in tears by a nursemaid, and some special treat would have to be arranged in compensation, for Mr Hobsbawn's was no unrequited passion: Henry adored 'Granpa' quite as much as Granpa worshipped him. The happiest moments for both of them were on Sundays when, after church, they would go for a drive in the carriage in their best clothes along the principal lounges, and wave and bow to their acquaintance. Mr Hobsbawn rarely went to the mills on a Sunday, now, and when he was obliged to go, he usually took Henry with him, for the pleasure of hearing the extravagant praise his employees lavished on the boy, and of saying to him, 'One day all this will be yours.'

Mary Ann watched the progress of their love with fond eyes. It was right and proper that they should be close, and it seemed to her also the most natural thing in the world, for her father was the kindest and cleverest man, and Henry the most remarkable child, who ever lived. She was happy here in Manchester, and was able to banish for a while all thoughts of Morland Place and her other life, as though it were a recurrent dream, and being here at home was being awake. This was all she had ever wanted, a comfortable home, respectable acquaintance, a secure place in the world where she was valued for those things she valued in herself; a little sphere on which to impose order and symmetry. She had tried to bring order to the chaotic world of Morland Place, and had been baulked at every turn. Morland Place was not like home. She did not belong there.

It was the rational approach to life that the lower orders of Manchester were so signally lacking, and it was on this subject more than any other that she and Father Rathbone argued.

'You can't expect them to think rationally, when they are living in such misery,' he would say.

'But if they addressed their problems rationally,' she would argue, 'they would not be living in such misery. Look, for example, how the men spend their wages on strong drink, when their families are starving.'

'But their wages would not be enough to feed them properly, even if they didn't. So they drink to make themselves feel better.'

'But how can that help? Then they have even less to eat. And the ale is so adulterated, it makes them ill, and then they can't work. And the women — how often have we seen them just sitting around doing nothing, when they should be washing clothes or bathing their children? I know they have to fetch all the water from a common pump, but if they have time to do nothing, they have time to do that.'

Father Rathbone looked at her affectionately, knowing he could never make her understand that their sloth was a result of the hopelessness that went with continual poverty. The apathy of misery was something she had never experienced. Even when she had been personally acutely unhappy — and he had known her long enough by now to have understood something of her other life — it has always driven her to action. She knew nothing of that despair which he had seen in countless faces, in stinking, fly-teeming streets in India as well as in the dank, rotting cellars of Manchester, that made a man at last simply sit down and wait for death.

He couldn't, and didn't, expect her to understand. It was enough that she cared, and helped. This year he had persuaded her to try to involve some of the other ladies of position, and with the help of Mrs Pendlebury, who didn't mind what a committee was for, as long as she was at the head of it, they had formed the Committee for the Promotion of Health and Cleanliness amongst the Industrious Poor of Manchester.

It was not received with universal approval. There were many who thought that such things were not their business, and that it was not only unpleasant, but unseemly for ladies to concern themselves with dirt and disease amongst the lower orders. It was very difficult, however, when faced with Mrs Morland in person, in a burgundy velvet pelisse and a hat with a lace veil and long feathers that aroused one's deepest envy, when regarding the queenly purity of her profile or the exquisite elegance of her manners, to tell her that her notions bordered on the improper.

As Mrs Pendlebury and Mrs Morland, the undoubted leaders of society, were involved in it, most of the smart ladies of Manchester soon decided it would be too stupid to be left out of things altogether, and the public meetings, at least, became very popular. There were those held in the Exchange Hall or the Concert Room, when John Ferriar and Father Rathbone addressed the company with descriptions of housing conditions, and predictions of dreadful plagues to come, and gentlemen in the audience stood up and argued with them, and there would sometimes be thrilling altercations, to be discussed afterwards in excited whispers in drawing-rooms all over town. Even more popular were the meetings at the private houses of various leading members of the committee, with wine and cakes and usually only ladies present, when the conversation would quickly veer away from dull subjects like dirt and poverty, and the feathered hats would incline closer together and nod more animatedly over the favoured topics of new clothes, the iniquities of servants, and the astonishing talents of one's children.

Talking was one thing, subscribing money another, and taking action yet a third. Most of the ladies gave their husband's unwillingness as the reason for their inability to donate funds for the Relief of an Industrious Weaver Unable to Work after an Unfortunate Accident, or for the Provision of Soap to Twenty Families in Brock Street. So the committee got up a subscription concert for the first, and an extremely daring masquerade ball for the second, and the ladies had so much enjoyment from organising and attending the functions, that they were able quite to forget the charitable purpose underlying them.

But when it came to visiting the homes of the poor themselves, the ladies faded away like morning dew. Mrs Pendlebury was quite open about it. 'Imagine me, my dear Mrs Morland, walking about in those dreadful dirty streets, with dear-knows-what underfoot, to say nothing of going into the houses! I don't suppose I could even fit through the doors.' And Mary Ann, regarding her doubtfully, had to admit that it wasn't likely. She was so very large, and her draperies and turbans made her seem larger still.

Others like Mrs Ardwick fluttered in terror at the idea, and invoked their husbands again. 'Mr Ardwick would never, never allow it! Oh, dear Mrs Morland, pray do not mention it again! I feel such flutterings and spasms all over me, I am sure it will bring on the pains in my side!'

Mrs Spicer, whose youngest, about the same age as Henry, had fallen off his hobby-horse in the park last Sunday just as the Hobsbawn carriage was passing, and dirtied his lace collar in full view of Mr Hobsbawn and Henry, said, 'I wonder, dear Mrs Morland, if it is quite the *thing*, to go visiting these places, and with only dear Father Rathbone for company?' She leaned forward earnestly. 'I wonder Mr Hobsbawn should not give you the hint, ma'am, for I must say, it does present the most *peculiar* appearance, and your dear papa has always been so very careful not to do anything in the least *singular*.'

'I don't know what you mean, ma'am,' Mary Ann said, so sharply that the plums and cherries on Mrs Spicer's hat quivered and withdrew an inch or two.

'Why, ma'am, to be going to such places, such *low* places, accompanied only by a *man* —'

'Father Rathbone is a priest,' Mary Ann said, the tone of her voice descending like an axe on conversation's neck. Mrs Spicer mottled uncomfortably, and soon afterwards took her leave to go and visit Mrs Droylsden and explain to her with a sweet smile that, 'Dearest Mrs Morland was quite the most

365

unworldly creature, with a mind above such things as ordinary respectability.'

So Mary Ann was left alone in her philanthropy, and she found the visits very depressing. The smells in the streets were so abominable, especially on hot days, only surpassed by the smells inside the houses. The rows and courts of badly-built, mean, decaying tenements seemed to offer no comfort, barely any shelter, and no glimpse of beauty or propriety or order to raise the spirits of the wretches who lived in them. Dirt was everywhere, ground into the brick, the plaster, the clothes, the very faces of the people.

'How can they keep clean?' Father Rathbone would say. 'Even if you give them soap, they have no clean water.' The water-supply was his principal concern, the cause for which he used the platform of their public meetings, though with little success. The wealthy citizens said that it was the business of the Board of Health; the Board of Health said they had no funds, and that it was a matter for the wealthy citizens.

But the worst thing of all, as far as Mary Ann was concerned, was the ignorance and apathy of the people. They seemed to have no will to help themselves, and went on doing the wrong things, even after she had explained their error, because the mere effort of understanding seemed to be beyond them. She would come home angry, frustrated, and depressed, and sometimes not even Father Rathbone's tireless strength and patience could convince her they were doing any good. And then she would have to face her father's disapproval.

Mrs Spicer had underestimated Mr Hobsbawn. He was quite as well aware as she was of the odd appearance Mary Ann's activities amongst the millworkers presented, especially as he was a millmaster himself, although his labour force was largely drawn from pauper apprentices.

'But it reflects on me all the same, love,' he said. 'There are bound to be those who see it as a criticism of me; and besides, it isn't right for you to be going about to such places, what with dirt and disease and — and other things. I don't like it, and that's the truth.'

But Mary Ann stood firm by the rightness of what she was doing, and he had been too little accustomed to denying her anything she wanted, to insist on her abandoning her good works. Then came the day when she arrived home unexpectedly from the mill in the afternoon and found that not only had 'Mrs Morland gone out in the carriage to visit poor folk' but that she had taken Henry with her.

She returned at last, looking pale and fatigued, to find her father waiting for her in an obvious state of suppressed fury. Stripping off her soiled gloves, she touched Henry's cheek and told him, with a smile, but in a voice he would not disobey, to go straight upstairs for his bath. As soon as he had left the room, Mr Hobsbawn's anger boiled over.

'Bath? Aye, well may you tell him to bath! But will soap and water wash him clean of the taint of where he's been? Where *his mother* takes him behind my back? By God, Mary Ann, I never thought to see the day when my own daughter forgot herself and what's due to her family so far! To take my grandson to such places —!'

'You think them unfit for him, though I go there myself?' she asked quietly.

'You know my feelings about that, too!' he bellowed, 'so don't be putting on those mimsy airs with me, my girl! I should have nipped this lot in the bud from the first minute, and I would have, too, if I'd had a notion you'd be so foolhardy! Well, it's happened for the last time, I can tell you that. You'll not stir out of this house again, without I know where you're going, and if you won't abide by my rules, why, I'll have you locked in your bedchamber, until you come to your senses! And that's my last word on it!'

'Perhaps it may be,' she said, still with that devastating quietness, 'but it is not mine, Papa.' She took off her hat and laid it with her gloves on the nearest table, and stood where she had come to rest, like a leaf with no more volition to move until the wind should blow again. Neither of them at that moment had any conception of how tired she was. 'I cannot give up my work, and I will not. The condition of these people is beyond description. If you had seen it, Papa —'

'I don't want to see it! It's not my business to see it! And you would never have seen it, either, if it hadn't been for that damn' priest! Aye, and I tell you this, he'll not set foot in this house again, my word on it!'

'He will come when I invite him!' Mary Ann said, flaring up.

'Damn it, Mary,' he protested, a little pathetically, 'it's my house!'

She bent her head. 'I'm sorry Papa. I should not have spoken to you like that. You are my father, and I will obey you in everything that's right. But not in this. I cannot agree to stop doing what I am doing, because I am convinced that I must not. What little help there is for these people in this world comes from us. I cannot abandon them.'

'And what good do you think you do them?'

'Little enough, I suppose. I often feel discouraged, but that is no reason to give up. We do what we can.'

'But Mary, love,' he said pleadingly, 'can't you just send a servant with the food and the money, or whatever it is you take them? You don't need to go yourself.'

'It isn't food and money they need most, Papa, it's education. They need to be shown how to take care of themselves. Father Rathbone brings them spiritual teaching, and I — I try to teach them to be clean, and to care for their children properly.' She passed a hand wearily over her forehead, pushing back the fronds of her soft hair that had escaped around her brows. 'They don't learn very quickly,' she admitted with a faint smile.

'Well, well,' Mr Hobsbawn said, turning instantly to her defence, 'that's not your fault, love. They should be grateful you go at all, though I warrant it's little enough thanks you get from them, the dirty ignorant rabble.' His anger was whipping itself up again. 'But what in the name of perdition do you want to take our little lad with you for? What the heck do you think they can learn from him? You drag our little angel through all that dirt and muck and God knows what, and how's that supposed to help?'

'Oh, but it does, Papa,' she said earnestly. 'The women pay more heed to me when they see I am a mother too. They notice him, because he is so healthy and bonny, and they listen to me more closely because of him. He is my object lesson, he is the living proof that I am telling them the truth. And there is something else,' she said, hesitating, not sure if he would or could understand. 'He brings them something of himself, Papa, that I have no name for. These people, it's as though they live in perpetual darkness, like blind, caged animals. But Henry is so — so innocent and beautiful, he brings light to them. I've seen it again and again, their terrible, blind faces lighting up when they see him.'

Mr Hobsbawn's brow was corrugated with perplexity. 'But if they are blind, love, how the hangment can they see him?'

She looked at him with affection. 'Oh, Papa!' she said, with a tired smile. 'If only I could interest you in their plight, there is so much you could do. It needs you and others like you, men of substance, to do something for these people. Father Rathbone has fought and fought to try to get a decent water-supply established for them, but he can do nothing without the support of the wealthy families. If you would only help us! You can't think how terrible it is, and with the hot weather, Father Rathbone says there may well be plague, like there was in '96. I wasn't here then, but I'm sure you must remember it.'

'Remember it? I should think I do! I tell you what, young woman, if there's to be plague, you are not going down there again, not for anything!'

Mary Ann sighed. 'Only poor people catch the plague, Papa. Father Rathbone says so. He knows all about it. I must go and wash and change now. I'm very tired.'

'Aye, that's right, love, you go on up,' he said with tender concern. 'We'll talk about this later, when you're rested.'

She smiled a little, and went away, knowing that she left him firmly believing that he could persuade or bully her into giving up her work. She was glad, given his reaction, that she had not told him that there was already sickness in the courts surrounding Long Millergate: five cases today of a kind of fever which Father Rathbone had said, in a grim voice, that he had seen before.

Father Rathbone arrived at the house the following morning so early that he almost caught Mr Hobsbawn leaving it. Mrs Morland was still in her chamber, he was told, and he begged for a message to be taken up to her, and expected a long wait. But Mary Ann came down only five minutes later, neat as a pin from her cap to her shoes.

'What brings you here so early, Father?' she said, unaware

of how her face had lit up at the sight of him. He looked down at her, a little puzzled.

'When they said you were still in your chamber, I thought I had arrived before you were up.'

She smiled. 'I always rise early, and spend some time at my devotions,' she said without emphasis. 'Is something wrong?'

His face grew grave. 'I think there is. One of the women in Lob's Entry came to me early this morning with a sick baby, and told me that there are four others in her house alone.'

'The fever?'

He nodded. 'I'm afraid the plague I have been warning everyone about is here. Now they will have to listen to me. But can you help me? There is so much to do.'

'Of course,' she said briskly. 'I will come at once. What should I bring with me? What can be done for the sufferers?'

But he took her hand, and looked down at her penetratingly. 'Are you sure you want to do this? Do you know what you will face? I would not have you come with me unprepared.'

She looked up frankly into his face, light eyes into dark. She was so different in appearance from him, that they might have been two different species, not male and female of the same: she pale and curved and soft and cool, he hard and black and burning. Her small white hand was entirely engulfed by his, long-fingered, brown and strong, but she regarded him steadily as equal to equal; and if some of her strength came from her desire to please him, that did not diminish it.

'I understand. I am ready.'

He released her, now all urgency. 'Good, then prepare yourself quickly. Bring with you whatever medicines you have in the house. Have you laudanum? Quinine? Bring anything you have.'

She nodded and turned away to go and get ready. 'Bring your maid if she will come,' he called after her. 'She seems a sensible woman. And don't bring the boy.'

'I was not thinking of it,' she said.

It was a long day. The fever spread with frightening rapidity, and there seemed little that could be done for the victims. Diarrhoea and vomiting were rapidly followed by cramps in the stomach and limbs, and then collapse and death, the whole process happening sometimes within a matter of hours. Mary Ann, followed by Dakers, tight-lipped and disapproving but unshakeably loyal, went from house to house, able to do little more than persuade the healthy to isolate the sick, try to remove the children from the rooms of the infected, give a little laudanum to those in convulsions, bathe the faces of the dying.

They were not alone in their efforts to help. John Ferriar brought another physician and several nurses from the infirmary, and there were helpers, too, from the St Anthony mission; but in all, they were pitifully few. During the day they were joined by some women of the middle orders, tradesmen's and craftsmen's wives, upon whom Father Rathbone had worked his magic as on Mary Ann. They were the sort of people she never normally had anything to do with, and they looked at her with a certain suspicion; but by the end of the day there were no reserves left between the members of that small army. The enemy they had pitted themselves against was too terrifying.

By the late afternoon there were fifteen dead, and it was impossible to guess how many unknown victims might be suffering in windowless cellars they had not yet penetrated. Ferriar and Rathbone came together at the corner of Brock Street for a brief consultation.

'It's spreading,' Rathbone said abruptly. 'We shall never be able to contain it.'

'No,' said Ferriar. 'The time has come to make it public. We need more help than we can ever get from volunteers. We must call a public meeting.'

'Tonight?'

'Yes.'

'I think you're right,' Rathbone said, his mouth grim. 'I have seen this fever before, in India. We must tell them all about it, Ferriar, and spare no detail. We will never move them with pity, but by God, their self-interest will wake them up!'

The meeting was not well attended, for there had not been time to spread the word throughout the town, but there were enough people of importance there for decisions to be made, and to be sure that by the next day, everyone would know that the plague had come to Manchester. Mr Hobsbawn was there, torn between pride and outrage to see his daughter on the platform alongside the priest and the doctor, the superintendant of the Infirmary, the chairman of the Board of Health, and the baronet's daughter who owned the *Star*.

He waited at the end of the meeting to take her away with him, and when she came down from the platform he found himself face to face with Father Rathbone. The two men stared at each other inimically.

'Now then, sir, are you satisfied?' Hobsbawn demanded. 'Now that you've got your damned plague, and exposed my daughter to it, are you happy?'

'It is not my plague, sir,' Rathbone replied, his channelled fury more searing than Hobsbawn's undirected fire. 'It is yours. It belongs to you and everyone like you in this city who would not listen to my warnings, who were content to allow these people, who make your wealth for you, to live in conditions that none of you would willingly condemn a dog to.'

'Make my wealth? Make my wealth? God damn it, sir, I tell you here and now I make my own wealth! I got where I am today by my own efforts, by the labour of these hands, sir, and I've never been afraid of hard work! No-one in my mills works longer hours than I do!'

'But what do they go home to, Mr Hobsbawn?' Father Rathbone demanded. 'A comfortable house and nourishing food? Or a dank cell full of pestilence?'

'You talk like one of those damned French revolutionaries,' Hobsbawn growled in fury. 'Aye, and you look like one! We don't want your sort here, making the lower orders discontented, telling them they are as good as their masters!'

'Papa, Father Rathbone didn't say that. But hasn't every creature that lives the right to enough to eat, and a dry floor to lie down on?'

'Well, and my 'prentices get all that, and more. I pay for it out of my own pocket. It's not my workers as are spreading this plague, so don't you come laying it at my door! Aye, and don't be looking to my daughter to be helping you out of this mess, either. It's not fitting for a lady to be exposing herself to things like that. I said all along it was wrong, and now you see I was right.'

Mary Ann and Father Rathbone exchanged a look which agreed quite clearly that further argument was useless. The priest bowed formally to Mary Ann.

'Mrs Morland, good night, and thank you for your invaluable help.'

'Good night, Father,' Mary Ann said as Hobsbawn tugged importunately at her arm, and dragged her away. Outside the carriage was waiting, and Hobsbawn's rage turned swiftly to concern as Mary Ann stumbled a little, and had to be helped up the steps.

'Eh, love, you're not sick?' he cried in alarm.

'No, Papa,' she said, 'only tired.'

'And hungry too,' Dakers said sourly from the depths of the carriage. 'For if you've eaten a crust today, madam, it's more than I'll compound for.'

The thought of food sickened Mary Ann, but she said calmly, 'Yes, I believe I am hungry. I'll have some supper when we get home.'

'Aye, you will. I'll see to that, ' Mr Hobsbawn said eagerly.

When they arrived home, he fussed over her like a mother, obliging her to sit down in his own armchair while he removed her hat and shoes, ordering a vast supper and standing over her while she struggled to eat enough of it to satisfy him, pouring with his own hands a glass of brandy which he insisted she drink 'to ward off the fever'.

'And you'll not go off tomorrow visiting those sick folk,' he said, half command and half plea, when she finally stood up to go to bed.

'I'm tired, Papa,' she said. 'We'll talk about it tomorrow.'

'Aye, well, but you've no need to go, now they've made it public. They'll have all the help they need. You'll only be in the way, love.'

'That's true. Good night, Papa.' She smiled and kissed his cheek, and went away, leaving him with the uneasy feeling that she had not said quite all he had wanted. Mary Ann climbed the stairs, longing for hot water and her own bed, but stopped first at Henry's chamber, for she had not seen him at all that day. He was asleep in his bed, sprawled on his back in his usual untidy way, so at odds with the controlled neatness of his waking self. She straightened the covers he had flung off, and smoothed the hair from his brow with a loving hand. He was so lovely, so perfect, her precious son. She bent to kiss his warm velvet cheek, and he murmured and turned his head restlessly on the pillow, but did not wake.

Exhaustion made Mary Ann sleep later the next morning than usual.

'Why didn't you wake me?' she asked crossly as Dakers drew the curtains. Her maid looked stubborn.

'There was no need that I could see,' she said. 'You wanted the sleep.'

'Nonsense. I must get up at once. You had better put out the brown cambric, and my strong shoes.'

'Nay, madam, you're not going down to Long Millergate again,' Dakers said. 'The master left orders before he went out this morning that you were not to go on any account.'

'And who is to stop me?' Mary Ann asked grimly as she swung her legs out of bed.

'Well, madam,' Dakers said cunningly, 'Mr Bowles has orders not to let you take the carriage out.'

Mary Ann's nostrils flared with fury — she was not her father's daughter for nothing — but she controlled herself. 'Very well, I shall deal with that question later. And now, lay out my clothes, if you please.'

'Not the brown gown, madam,' Dakers said, half stubborn, half frightened.

Mary Ann turned a cold fury on her. 'If you do not do as I say, Dakers, I shall dress myself, and you will pack your bags and leave this house within the hour.'

Dakers wilted. 'Yes, madam,' she said unhappily.

Bowles, the butler, proved harder to shift. He had known Mary Ann from infancy, but he was dedicated to his master, and feared the consequences of obeying her more than he feared her odium. Seeing he was adamant, Mary Ann bade him order her a hack-coach, and when he demurred, she told him that the alternative was that she walked out in the street and found one for herself, upon which he could only yield.

The carriage came, and Mary Ann stepped in, her basket on her arm, and Dakers, furious and sullen, climbed up after her. She disliked everything about the business, but if her mistress insisted on going, then she should not go alone.

The hack dropped them at the corner of Long Millergate and Water Lane, and as they turned off Water Lane into the courts, the first thing that assailed them was a sulphurous stench. Following it, they came upon a scene of activity that was very different from the previous day. In the middle of Brook's Entry was a barrel of burning tar, whose acrid smoke at least drowned the usual smell of putrefaction and filth in the teeming court, and, it was therefore to be hoped, would kill the evil miasmas. Beyond the tar barrel was a bonfire, and male helpers were dragging mattresses and pathetic scraps of furniture out of the tenements and flinging them on the fire, while others staggered in with barrels of limewash to paint the walls of the dingy rooms.

Father Rathbone was co-ordinating the efforts of his small army, and turned to greet Mary Ann with a glad smile that lifted her heart. He wiped the sweat from his brow with the back of his arm. It was a hot day, and the heat in the court was intensified by the bonfire and made intolerable by the acrid stench of the tar-barrel.

He took her hand and pressed it briefly. 'I knew you would not fail me,' he said.

'What has happened here?' she asked.

'All dead,' he said, with a jerk of the head towards the house being limewashed.

'Every one?' she asked in horror. There had been twenty people in that house, at least.

'We found it empty this morning, except of the dead or the dying. Some may have run away, of course,' he said with a shrug. 'But at least we can purge this house of the infection. If only we could do the same in every house! In Lob's Entry, for instance, or Grey's Court, where half the people are sick already. But of course they will not have their poor little scraps burned, and who can blame them? It's all they have.'

'You have more help today,' she said.

'And there will be more still by tomorrow. Did you see the *Star*? It's on the front page. There's to be another meeting tonight. We must have money as well as helpers, if we are to purge these hellish places.'

'What shall I do?' Mary Ann asked practically.

He thought for a moment. 'Can you go and help Ferriar in Thomas Court? He has moved everyone that can be moved out of the Infirmary, and we are sending the sick people there, making it into a plague hospital. The sooner we can separate the sick and the healthy, the better. But some of them don't want to go — the Infirmary has a bad reputation amongst these people — and some are unwilling to part with their relatives. That's where you can help: persuade the mothers to let their sick children go, for instance.'

'Very well,' she said, and was turning away to obey him when he caught her back to press her hand, and flash her his vivid smile.

'Thank you,' he said. 'If there were more like you in the world!'

It was another long, hard day, filled with the sights and sounds and smells of distress, as the band of helpers tried to drag order out of the chaos. Mary Ann went only once to the Infirmary, accompanying a sick woman and her three children who would not go without her. As Father Rathbone had said, the Infirmary had a bad name, amongst the ignorant poor. Only those who could not help themselves would go there.

One visit was enough to convince Mary Ann that in their place, she would have felt the same. The big, drab building, grey and grim like a prison, was filled to overflowing with the old and sick, and smelled like death. Harrassed physicians and nurses did what they could for the flood of victims being brought in, but it was obvious that few, if any, of them would live. They were being isolated from the healthy, that was all. At the back of the hospital carts were being assembled to take the dead to a plague-pit, even then being dug outside the limits of the town.

She came to recognise the look of those beginning the disease, the pinched, anxious face, the sunken eyes, the cold, clammy skin. With her small store of laudanum gone, she had nothing with which to ease their suffering. In the dark cellars and cramped rooms she found them lying helpless in their own filth, often without so much as a bowl to vomit into. They were tormented with violent thirst, which nothing seemed to slake, and often the one thing she could do for them was to trot back and forth from the communal pump with jugs or bowls of water. It was vile stuff, cloudy and brackish, sometimes green with living things, but the fever-victims gulped it as eagerly as though it were iced champagne, though often they brought it up again after a few minutes.

Working all day in the gloom of the tenements, or the unnatural twilight caused by the smoke outside, she did not notice dusk coming on, and had no idea of the passage of time until Father Rathbone came to find her, in a tiny house at the end of Brock Street where she was kneeling beside a dying woman who would not let go of her hand.

He knelt too, on the other side of the rag mattress on which the woman lay, and spoke the words of absolution over her, and after a few minutes the dark, sunken face grew still, and Mary Ann freed her hand and got wearily to her feet. The priest looked at her intently.

'Have you eaten today?' he asked accusingly.

'I don't remember,' she said, and then returned his look defiantly. 'Have you?'

He grinned. She wondered where he found the strength. 'A fair question,' he said. 'Come, then, we will go and find food, and then we must go to the meeting.'

'What, is it so late?' she exclaimed, and then looking about her vaguely, 'But we cannot go. There is too much to do.'

'Listen to me, Mrs Morland! You will be of much more use to me at the meeting than you are here. There are others who can do what you are doing here, but no others can impress the town folks as you do. So as your general, my gallant, gentle soldier, I order you to come with me and eat. You must recruit your strength before we go to the Exchange to rouse the consciences of the people.'

She nodded, too tired to smile or resist. 'Very well,' she said, glad to have someone tell her what to do, and take the responsibility from her.

'Where's your maid?' he asked as he led her outside.

'I don't know. We got separated some time ago. There was too much to do for her to dance attendance on me.'

'Never mind, we'll leave word for her to meet you at the Exchange later. Come, now, come, we'll have to walk, but it isn't far.' He encouraged her along kindly, and she followed him obediently, not caring enough where they were going to ask. They left the teeming courts, crossed Long Millergate, and through one narrow lane after another made their way into a poor but respectable neighbourhood, where printers and 'prentices lived. Finally they halted in front of what had once been a shop, but now sported in black capitals on the impenetrably dirty window the words, 'St Anthony's Mission'.

Mary Ann looked up at the priest in dumb enquiry. He reached into a pocket for a key, and opened the small door next to the shop door, saying, 'I have living quarters upstairs, over the mission. Small, but comfortable, and at least I can give you something to eat and drink.' He turned back to look at her as she hesitated. 'You aren't afraid to come in with me?'

She shook her head, and he smiled and went in, holding the door for her and saying, 'Be careful on the stairs. They are rather uneven. Wait, stand still until I have lit the lamp. There, now, come up, come up.'

At the top of the stairs was a doorway with a curtain over it, which he held aside for her, and she entered a small room, spare and neat like a monk's cell. There was a narrow bed covered with a grey blanket, a bare wooden table and two wooden chairs, a small cupboard in the corner, and a chest pushed up against the wall. The only touch of luxury was a battered armchair covered in soiled red velvet standing beside the fire, and a rag rug before the hearth, and the only ornament a wooden-and-ivory crucifix on the wall over the bed.

Father Rathbone placed the lamp on the table, and knelt before the fire to rake up the embers and put on more fuel.

'Now then, you come and sit down here, by the fire,' he said, 'and we'll soon make you comfortable.' The fire blazed up, and he pushed the kettle on its crane over the flames. 'I'll make you some hot tea when it boils,' he said, 'but first ...'

She watched him in silence and he went over to the

cupboard and brought things out and laid them on the table. A loaf of bread on a board, two cups, two plates, a piece of bacon wrapped in gauze, a tea-caddy and teapot, and finally, with the air of coming to the best last, a tall black bottle. He grinned at her, and pulled out the cork with his teeth like a pirate in a story, and poured some of the contents into the two cups.

'There,' he said, handing her one. 'Now, don't be looking at me like that! Do you think I'd give you anything harmful? It's the best port wine money can buy, and will put heart into you. A rich gentleman gave it me, and its eleven brothers, for the saving of his soul after a particularly sinful debauch. That is to say, he had been doing the sinning, not I.'

She laughed, and drank, and felt the warm, powerful redness stealing through her veins and glowing in the pit of her stomach.

'That's better,' he said approvingly, busying himself at the table. 'I like to see you smile.'

'Do you?'

'I do indeed. I love all God's works of beauty, but a beautiful woman is the finest of all his creations. There, now, and is the colour that's come stealing to your cheeks because of the wine, I wonder, or my fine words? You are not much used to receiving compliments, I think.'

'Not so. Papa is always telling me I am beautiful,' she countered.

'Papa is a wise man. But has no other man told you so? God save us, was every man you ever met but myself stone blind, then?'

She turned her face away from his teasing and said nothing. He brought two plates, bearing slices of bacon and a thick piece of bread, gave her one, and sat disarmingly on the floor at her feet with the other.

'There, my lovely girl, poor stuff it is, I know, but it'll give you strength. Eat now, eat. Pay no heed to me, or to manners. You must be as hungry as the north wind.'

She had thought, before the port wine, that she could not face food, but now she found that she was savagely hungry. For a few moments she tried to eat politely, then she saw how the priest was devouring his portion ravenously, and gave in

379

to her own appetite. She cleared the plate, accepted a second helping, finished her port, and asked for a drink of water, for she was very thirsty. Then he cleared the plates away, and made tea, and when it was poured out, he sat again at her feet, and they sipped in companionable silence for a while.

'It is strange to be here,' she said after a while, looking round the room. 'That is, this room is strange.'

'How, strange?'

She hesitated. 'I'm not sure. I've never tried to imagine how you lived, but if I had, it would not have been like this, I think.'

'What, then?' he asked, looking up at her in amusement, the jumping flames reflecting in his dark eyes.

'It's so ordinary,' she said. 'Like the kitchen of one of the estate-workers back in Yorkshire. I should have expected ...' She hesitated, frowning, not sure what she would have expected.

'Something more exotic?' he suggested. 'Strange trophies from my travels, rich hangings, jewelled caskets?'

She laughed. 'Yes, I suppose so. But now I am getting used to it, I see that this is much more like you.'

'Getting used to it, are you?' he murmured. 'And what does it tell you?'

She licked her dry lips. 'I should know,' she said hesitantly, 'that no woman lived here.'

'Since I have lived here,' he said, 'no woman has ever crossed the threshold until now.' He put his cup aside and looked up at her intently. 'But I wanted to bring you here. I've often thought about it, imagined you sitting in that very chair by that very fire. So many times I've lain awake in my bed over there, imagining what you would look like, sitting here.'

'But — why?' she asked. Her heart seemed to be beating too fast, and she thought vaguely that she was too close to the fire, and ought to move back from it. The heat was too much for her. She began to feel a little faint.

He took her cup from her nerveless fingers. 'Why?' he repeated, as though it were an outrageous question. 'Why?' he knelt up, and faced her, put his hands on her knees, and looked into her eyes, which were now on a level with his. 'My sweet, lovely girl,' he said, 'I don't know what kind of a man it is you have married, but I tell you he isn't near good enough for you, or he would long ago have kissed that half-awake look out of your eyes! Priest that I am, I would do better than that by you, if you were mine. Has he never taken you in arms, like this — or kissed you, like this —?'

Her eyes closed and her mouth tilted, her lips parted for his as though it were what she had been born for. One part of her mind stood aside and protested at what she was doing, but it was a small, distant voice, beside the thundering torrent of feeling that filled all the rest of her, sweeping away her resistance like a flood scouring a dry gully. No, James had never done that, had never roused in her any response that came near to this. She felt as though her blood were on fire. She felt as though her heart would burst with the violence of its beating.

He was the one who pulled away, sat back from her, panting, regarding her with those burning coals of eyes. 'Ah, God,' he said softly, 'how the touch of you stirs me to madness, my lovely girl! It would take only the smallest push to send me over the edge.' He lifted one of her hands and turned it over and kissed the palm, and then folded down her fingers one by one. 'Don't look at me like that,' he said tenderly, 'or I shall forget myself entirely. You are a dangerous woman, Mrs Morland, did you know that?'

His last words brought her back to reality, and her cheeks suddenly burned with shame at what she had done. A priest of the Holy Church! And she a married woman! And yet her mind was still cleanly halved, like an apple, and the dark, abandoned half of it was crying, I don't care, I don't care! I want it to go on! I want much, much more!

'Father —' she whispered. 'I — I d-don't know what to say —'

'Then don't say anything,' he said, in a comfortable voice, taking command of the situation. He replaced her hand in his lap, and got to his feet. 'Nothing has happened that needs a comment. Sure, a general has the right to salute his soldier, hasn't he? And talking of which, we have to remember that the campaign's but just beginning. We have a meeting to go to, Mrs Morland, if it has slipped your mind. Are you ready, now?'

He was making it easy for her. She stood up, smoothing her skirt and hair with automatic gestures, looking round for her gloves. He held the curtain aside for her, and she was careful not to look up into his face as she passed him in the confined space; and when they were out in the lane and walking towards the main street, she made sure she kept far enough from him for no part of her to brush against him as they walked.

The second meeting was not like the first. The hall was crowded, and the faces looking up were not bored, or belligerent, but worried, even frightened. Their sins had come home to them: one of the horsemen of the apocalypse had got loose, and was galloping down on them, and they were eager now to listen, wanting only to know what to do to propitiate him.

Mary Ann sat on the platform, lending her presence and authority, but she could not concentrate on what was being said. She felt flushed and strange, her heart-beat seemed erratic, beating now too close and too loudly, thundering in her ears, now too far off and faint, fluttering away from her so that she felt weak and dizzy. Her eyes strayed again and again to Father Rathbone's dark, vivid face as he harangued the assembly. Why had he done it? What had he meant by it? Why had she responded to him as she had? And, most of all, how far had they been accomplices in the crime? Had she really believed, as she had told herself all along, that he was a priest and therefore not a man? Or had she followed him into battle not as a soldier, but a camp-follower?

Her thoughts tumbled about chaotically, and the serried faces below her seemed very clear and far off, as though seen through a perspective-glass. It was so hot, she thought, and she was so thirsty. She put her hands up to her cheeks and they felt burning hot — or was it that her hands were cold? She thought longingly of her bed. If only the meeting were over. Why did they have to go on talking and talking?

Her wish was answered. There was a disturbance at the back of the hall, and the latest speaker faltered and then stopped as heads began inexorably to turn; and then with a sense of foreknowledge Mary Ann saw Simon, her father's elderly manservant, advancing down the central aisle as fast as his bowed legs would carry him, with Dakers, whom he must have collected on his way in, scurrying behind him.

Mary Ann's legs got her to her feet without her knowledge, and carried her to the steps and down from the platform. Simon reached her first, turned his white-whiskered face up to her and cried, 'Missus, you're to come at once! Master's sent me wi' coach for you. It's the little lad, missus — he's not well.'

She met Dakers's eyes across his shoulder, heard her own voice ask, 'What is it? Has the physician been sent for?'

Simon's face wrinkled with vicarious pain. He's been ailing all day, but now he's fluxin' and wraxin' something cruel, missus. We sent for Doctor Foley. He should be there by now.'

Dakers's expression was unfathomable. 'You'd best come, madam,' were her words, but Mary Ann felt as seared by them as if she had said, 'It's a judgement on you.' She flung a look backwards towards Father Rathbone, and hurried behind the servants past the staring, whispering multitude and out of the hall.

Outside the coach was waiting at the foot of the steps, and Simon hobbled ahead to open the door and let down the steps, and it was only when she faltered at the foot of them, as though they were a steep hillside, that Dakers said in a voice that mingled forgiveness and concern, 'Are you all right, madam? You look so flushed and strange.'

'Yes, yes,' she muttered, climbing in with a great effort. 'Only tired. Hurry! I must get to him.' There were many things it could be. Children often had these little ailments. He may have eaten something that disagreed with him. In this hot weather, food turned more quickly, and the cook may have given him something not quite right. Her mind offered her these facile comforts, but the dark, atavistic instinct of motherhood gripped her with sharp claws of dread.

The door was shut, the coach lurched forward, and she sank back against the cushions and closed her eyes in exhaustion, and her head swam sickeningly. She hadn't realised she was so tired. She could hear Dakers's voice talking to her, but it was too far away for her to understand what she was saying.

'It's all right, it's just fatigue,' she said, and her voice was as small and clear as an ice crystal, and made no sound at all. She turned to look at Father Rathbone, and he smiled and brushed the beech leaves from her hair. They were in a boat, floating down a river in the bright sunshine, and she knew that a great deal of that didn't make any sense, but the floating sensation was so pleasant she didn't care.

'It will take us all the way to the sea,' he said. There were ladies in white muslin dresses and white parasols strolling along the bank, who waved to them as they drifted past.

Chapter Twenty

There were lights shining out from the windows of Hobsbawn House, and strange horses in the courtyard. Simon and Dakers between them half-dragged, half-carried Mary Ann into the hall. All the servants were there, the butler and footman whispering together, the maids weeping, and the cook wringing her hands and moaning.

They all surged towards Dakers. The footman, John, took her place to support the mistress, while the maids cried out like disturbed birds.

'Oh, Mrs Dakers, what's come of the mistress? Is she sick too?'

'Our little lad is so sick! Doctor's with him now.'

'Is it the plague? Do you think it's the plague? Lord save us!'

'It is, I know it is!' the cook wailed abandonedly. 'We shall all catch it now! We're all going to die!'

'Nobody's going to die,' Dakers said sharply, cutting across the clamour, 'but plenty of people are going to get smacked heads if they don't stop their noise and look to their duties.' A quick glance had told her that the butler, pale and shaking, was not going to take charge of the situation, and the mistress was already beyond giving orders. 'Hannah, run up ahead and turn down my mistress's bed, and you, Becky, go with cook and fill hot water bottles and bring them up. Now John, Simon, take her upstairs, gently now! Mr Bowles, where is the master?'

'He's with the doctor, and the little boy,' the butler replied quaveringly. 'Eh, he's so sick, poor little mite! I don't know what's coming to us! I never saw such carryings-on in all my days. It's a judgement on us, that's what it is!'

'Never mind that now, Mr Bowles. Just run upstairs and tell the doctor the mistress is sick, and he must come and see her at once.'

Between them, she and Hannah got Mary Ann undressed

and into bed. The mistress's face was pinched and wan, and her eyes seemed sunken, their orbits darkened. As soon as they had got her into bed, nausea overcame her, and Dakers had to hold the bedroom basin while she vomited. Dakers had no doubt what the sickness was, and when she turned to hand Hannah the clothes she had taken off Mary Ann, she saw that Hannah had no doubts either. The woman shrank back wide-eyed from the clothing, putting her hands behind her defensively, and said in a whisper, 'It's the plague! She brought it home with her! Now we shall all catch it. Oh, dear God!'

Dakers advanced on her fiercely. 'Shut your mouth! And take these clothes away!'

'I dursn't! I dursn't! Nay, Missus Dakers, I dursn't come near you! You've been with them sick folk all day.'

Dakers's mouth turned down bitterly. 'Then get out of here!' she snapped. 'I'll tend her myself, you ignorant, ungrateful slut!'

Hannah turned and ran, collided with the doctor in the doorway, recoiled from him, and scuttered away down the passage, batting off the walls like a panicking bird.

Mr Hobsbawn came in hard on the doctor's heels. His fleshy, high-coloured face seemed to have been stretched flat and drained of colour. His eyes met Dakers's, but he had nothing to say. Horror had taken his voice away.

The doctor came quickly to the bedside and reached for Mary Ann's wrist, laying his other hand on her forehead. Her eyes opened and stared at him. 'Doctor Foley?' she whispered.

'How do you feel?' he asked her.

'Thirsty. So thirsty,' she whispered, and the tip of a dry tongue came out in a vain attempt to moisten her lips. Water.'

'I'll get it,' Mr Hobsbawn said, his voice cracking with anxiety, and he stumbled round the bed to the table where the bedroom jug stood, and filled a glass. Dakers took it from him and supported Mary Ann's head while she drank. Mary Ann looked at her father across the rim, and love and sympathy passed between them.

'I'm sorry, Papa,' she whispered.

'Eh, love,' he said miserably. 'You'll be better soon. You're just tired.'

'Yes. Just tired,' she said. A spasm racked her, and she

turned pleadingly to Dakers and the doctor, her eyes suddenly wide with urgency.

'You'll have to go out for a minute or two, Mr Hobsbawn,' the doctor said calmly. 'Quickly, please,' he added, as the old man hesitated. Dakers abandoned etiquette and took his arm and hustled him to the door, propelled him gently out into the passage, and closed it behind him. He turned outside and stood facing the door, his head a little tilted, his large, work-hardened hands hanging useless by his side. After a while, Bowles appeared beside him, and they watched the door in numb silence, like two old dogs shut out from the fire.

It was a long time before the doctor came out. Beyond him they could see Dakers by the bedside, a black shape cut out from the nimbus-light of the candles. Already the room had the smell of sickness about it. The doctor halted before them, and they looked at him with pathetic hope, wanting a miracle, wanting him to tell them it was not what they knew it was. Their dependence irritated him.

'Well, it's the plague all right,' he said sharply. 'She and the boy must be isolated, and you had better send the servants away. Mrs Dakers is willing to do the nursing. You had better go away yourself. The fewer people who are exposed to this thing the better.'

'Go away?' Mr Hobsbawn cried, as if that were the only part he had understood.

'It's very infectious,' Doctor Foley said irritably. 'Can't you understand that?'

'Aye, I understand all right,' Mr Hobsbawn said, his voice regaining some of its normal boom. 'All them as wants to can go, but nothing will take me from my daughter's side or my little grandson's. What sort of a man you take me for?'

'You understand the risk you will run? And for what? There is nothing you can do for them.'

'Never say it!' he cried in a frightened voice. 'They'll come through! They've got Hobsbawn blood in their veins, and Hobsbawns are fighters. We'll bring them through. You just tell us what to do.'

'There is very little anyone can do,' the doctor said wearily. 'Keep them warm. Give them plenty to drink. Champagne is best — iced if possible — as much as they want. Brandy for

387

the stomach cramps. That's all.'

'And what are you going to be doing?' Hobsbawn demanded.

'There is nothing I can do. We saw this kind of plague before, back in '96, and we don't know any more about it now than we did then. The strong sometimes recover by their own will, if they are carefully nursed. Otherwise . . .' He shrugged. 'I must go now. I have other calls to make.'

'But you'll come back?'

'Don't you understand, this is an epidemic? By tomorrow morning, the fever will be all over the town, and I shan't have time to come back to anyone. Nurse them well — that's their only chance.'

He thrust past them and went away down the stairs, followed by the two pairs of frightened eyes. Then Hobsbawn turned to his butler. 'Well, Bowles, are you going to desert us?'

Bowles had to swallow several times before he could find a voice. 'Nay, master,' he said, without great conviction. 'You've been a good master to me. I'll stay.'

'Right, then what are you waiting for? Go and get some champagne, and send John out for ice. Sir Toby Rummage has got an ice-house. He's a good man at a pinch; he'll let us have some. John'd better take the carriage, for quickness. Cook and the maids had better be sent away.'

'Yes, sir. Cook's got a cousin in the country —'

'Then they can go there. Go on, man, bustle about!'

There was a world of thirst, a torment of thirst. Mary Ann cried for drink, drink, and Dakers held her head while she gulped water and champagne, and then held the bowl while she vomited it up again. And the thirst was not slaked, only grew, until it was no longer inside her, but she was inside it. She was a speck of sand in a universe of desert; nothing existed but the thirst, and her.

And the pain, and the diarrhoea. After the first time, she was too weak to get out of bed, and she lay weeping with shame in the mess she had made, except that there were no tears to her weeping: she had not moisture enough. Dakers petted her and tended her, grim old Dakers, whose mouth was set in a harder line than ever. But that was comforting: it was her strength. Mary Ann clung to her, her granite-faced, disapproving old nurse. Twice her father came in, and she hated that. She didn't want him to see her like this, and she she didn't want to see his loud, bounding strength conquered, quivering with misery at the sight of her.

The candles burned down, and Dakers lit fresh ones, and their burning was the only thing that told Mary Ann time was passing, for to her it seemed that they were locked in a timelessness of pain and misery. In delirium she drifted through a confused and fever-parched consciousness, populated with strange and menacing shapes and colours, and voices that buckled and twisted so that she could not understand them.

From time to time she drifted back to the single point of reality which was Dakers's hand holding hers. It was the pivot of consciousness to which she must return; but as time passed and she grew weaker, the moments of return grew shorter and further apart.

John did not come back with the ice, and when Bowles went outside to see if there were any sign of him, he discovered that the carriage had not been taken out, and the coachman had locked himself in his room over the coach-house and refused to come out. John had evidently simply run away. The butler went back inside and closed and bolted the door, and returned to the kitchen, where he and Simon had been sitting at the table in silence, waiting.

Bowles did not blame John, or the maids. There was nothing to be done here. If he and Simon were young men, and had somewhere to go, they would probably have gone, too. But after a lifetime of service, this was their only home, and Hobsbawn and his daughter their only family. So they sat and waited, their sense of unreality increasing with every hour that passed.

From time to time the people upstairs would ring for fresh candles or water or towels, and one of them would take them up, and hover at the door of the sickroom, peering in uncomprehendingly but hopefully, before returning, disappointed, to their silent vigil below. They did not discuss the situation because they could not believe that it was happening. All they could do was to wait for something they understood to come and reclaim them to service.

Henry died in the early hours of the morning, still holding Granpa's hand. Mr Hobsbawn had been sitting so long, watching the pinched, damp face, listening for the faint, shallow breathing, that he did not at once understand that the boy was gone, and even when he did, he remained motionless, unable to believe it, hoping and hoping with the dumb faith of love that the breathing would begin again, that the eyes would open and his little boy would smile at him in that way that had so lit up his life.

But at last the comprehension began to seep into his brain, and he felt a blind misery rising in him like water, filling him to drowning, and he began to moan, rocking his great body back and forth, clutching the small cold hand that would never again reach up, warm and trusting and alive, for his.

'No,' he cried. 'No-o-o!' His eyes brimmed and flowed over, and the tears ran over his cheeks, and he rocked and moaned in his inarticulate, animal grief, for his stolen child, the precious child of old age, the irreplaceable.

It began to grow light, and Dakers came to with a start, to discover that she had drifted off, not quite to sleep, but to a state of half-consciousness close to it. Mary Ann was quiet, the voiding and the spasms and cramps over, but not even the eyes of love could believe that she was better. Her skin was dark, cold and clammy, and her breathing was shallow. She seemed to be in a state of collapse.

Dakers got up, feeling her old bones creak in painful protest at having remained so long in one position. She opened the bedroom door, smelling from the contrast with the air outside how the room must stink, and walked along the passage to Henry's room. The first glance from the doorway told her the story. The boy was dead, and Mr Hobsbawn was slumped in the chair by the bedside, sleeping the uneasy sleep of exhaustion. It was hard to wake him, and she disliked doing it, seeing the agony of recollection gradually returning

390

to him, but it must be done.

'Sir, I think someone ought to go for the priest. I don't think it will be long.'

He got to his feet with difficulty and stumbled to the door, like a wounded bear, and she followed him, turning as she reached it to look back once at the silent figure in the bed. There was so little of him, he barely made a shape under the bedclothes. Her mouth turned down bitterly. She had nursed Mary Ann from babyhood, and this was the end of it.

She followed her master into Mary Ann's room, and found him standing by the bed staring down, and seeing that he was incapable of any further effort, she left him there and went down to the kitchen. The two old men were sitting to either side of the table, motionless as a pair of fire dogs, and they looked up without expression as she came in. She told Bowles that he must go for the priest, and he went without demur. It was no time for servants' hall etiquette; he was quicker on his feet than old Simon.

It was half an hour before he returned alone, to climb the stairs to the bedchamber and tell them that the priest was not in his house.

'I asked the neighbours, but no-one seemed to know where he was,' Bowles said. 'Some of them thought he had gone to the Infirmary; so I left a message that he was to come at once when he got back. I hope I did right, sir. I didn't know what else to do.'

'You did right,' Dakers answered for her master, who seemed as far beyond speech as action. Bowles hovered, looking past her towards the bed.

'She's not ...? She will be all right, won't she? I mean —'

'You'd better go downstairs and wait,' Dakers said brusquely. 'If the priest comes, bring him here at once.'

The light was growing stronger outside the windows, and Dakers drew the curtains and snuffed the candles, and went back to the bed to look at her mistress. Mary Ann's unconsciousness seemed a little less profound. Dakers poured a little brandy into a glass, and lifting the heavy head, tried to trickle the liquid into her mouth. After a moment the tongue moved to touch the cracked lips, and then she choked a little, and opened her eyes.

She looked blankly at Dakers, seeming not to know where she was, and then her eyes moved to her father's face, and gradually awareness entered them. Dakers put her head back on the pillow and smoothed the hair from her brow. Mary Ann still looked at her father, and her lips moved, but no sound came from them.

Hobsbawn leaned forward. 'What is it, love?' he asked, and his voice sounded rusty with long disuse.

Mary Ann tried again. 'Henry?' she whispered at last.

Dakers spoke before her master could summon any words. 'He's all right, madam, sleeping quietly.'

Hobsbawn stared at her in perplexity, but Mary Ann did not see. Her eyes were fixed on her maid's face beseechingly. 'Then — it wasn't —?'

'No, madam,' Dakers said firmly. 'It wasn't the plague. Just something he ate.'

Mary Ann closed her eyes in relief, and her lips moved silently in thanks. Dakers caught her master's eyes and glared him to silence, and before he could recover himself enough to speak, there was the sound of a violent banging on the house door below, and the sound of someone shouting to be let in.

'It must be the priest,' Hobsbawn said. 'Thank God!'

Bowles must have opened the door, for the banging ceased, but there was a sound of voices raised in altercation, and Dakers got up and went to the bedroom door, and opening it, saw Father Rathbone running up the stairs, his face drawn and white, with Bowles hurrying after him, protesting and waving his hands ineffectually.

Dakers barred the door, her eyes spitting fury. 'What do you want?' she demanded fiercely. 'Haven't you done enough? How dare you come here! Get out of this house at once!'

'How is she?' Rathbone said as if she had not spoken. 'I must see her! Foley at the Infirmary said she was sick, but I couldn't believe it. I thought she — for God's sake, woman, how is she?'

'She's dying,' Dakers said in a vicious hiss. 'The boy's dead, and she's dying, and now perhaps you'll be satisfied!'

She saw something go out of him, and for a moment, if she had not hated him so much, she would have pitied him. He stood quite still for a moment, his eyes wide and unseeing, taking the new knowledge and the new feelings into himself. Then he said in a different voice, so gentle that it hurt her, because it made anger hard to hold on to, 'Has she had Extreme Unction?' She didn't want to answer, but he saw from her face that she had not. 'You must let me in. You must let me do that for her.'

Hobsbawn came up behind her, and saw who was there. His face darkened, but before he could bellow his rage, Rathbone spoke again, softly. 'She has not had the rites. You must let me in, sir, to do what has to be done. Come, now, whatever you think of me, I speak now as a priest of Holy Mother Church. Do you want her to die without unction?'

The power of his presence forced them to yield, they stepped back reluctantly before him, and he crossed to the bed and knelt beside it, and took Mary Ann's hand. She opened her eyes, and saw his dark, narrow face before her, strong and shining and dangerous like a blade, and her cracked lips curved into a feeble smile.

'You came,' she whispered.

He held her hand tightly, tightly, trying to pass his strength into her. 'Yes, I came. I have come to prepare you for your journey. Are you ready?' There was no weakness in his voice, no fear, no sorrow. The other two stood back, watching in silence. There was no place for them there, and though they hated him, they could not resist him. The murmur of his voice came to them, though not her replies; they saw him take out the wool and mark her forehead with the chrism, and make the sign of the cross, heard the familiar rhythm of the benediction though they could not discern the words. Hobsbawn, like a performing bear trained too young ever to forget, went down automatically, but with painful difficulty, on to his knees, but Dakers resisted, stood aloof, holding back from everything she might feel except the anger which sustained her.

At last the priest stood up, and came over to her and said in a low voice, 'You had better let me see the boy now.'

'I told you, he's dead. You're too late,' she said harshly.

'No, it's not too late. I can still perform the ceremony while his soul is hovering near. Let me go to him. Let me help him.'

His eyes were filled with understanding and pity, and she turned away from them.

'Do what you please,' she said, and pushed past him to go back to her mistress. The absolution had taken the last of her strength. She was unconscious again, her breathing barely stirring her. Her flesh had shrunk back against her bones, and her nose seemed strangely prominent beneath the smear of the holy oil on her brow.

Hobsbawn got to his feet and shuffled across to the bed. He looked at his daughter, and then at Dakers. 'She's going,' he said, and he sounded bewildered, as though the words did not make sense. 'I thought she'd get better. She was strong and healthy. How can she die just like that?'

Dakers didn't know what to say. 'Maybe she won't,' she said. 'We must pray.'

A little while later, Rathbone came back into the room. 'It's done,' he said quietly. Hobsbawn turned on him, goaded, rose to his feet and drove him back to the door in a desperation of grief.

'Aye, it's done, and you know who did it! You killed them, both of them, with your meddling schemes, and now you've done your worst, you can get out of this house, before I break your neck with my own hands! Get out of here, I say, and don't ever let me clap eyes on you again, damn you, or I swear by this hand I'll kill you!'

Rathbone looked at him for a moment with that same enormous pity, and then he left without another word.

The raised voice had stirred Mary Ann's feeble consciousness, and in the silence that followed, he heard her call out faintly, 'Papa!' He hurried to her side, and took hold of her hand.

'Yes, my darling? Yes, Mary, my love? What is it? Papa's here!'

But she did not speak again, or seem to know he was there, only sank further into the cold darkness.

Some time later Dakers stood up. 'Well, she's gone,' she said in a flat, bitter voice. A world of love, a lifetime of care, and it came to this. She needed anger, to make sense of her pain. 'And you know who's to blame for it.'

Hobsbawn raised a haggard face. Her anger would sustain

her; she would feed on it, and it on her, and it would keep the grief at bay and make her strong. But he did not want to be sustained. He wanted to lay his head down and die, because all the warm brightness of his life lay there before him, cold and empty and dead, and there was nothing to get up for, ever again.

But Dakers held his eyes with her bitter, brooding stare.

'I told him,' he said feebly, defensively. 'I sent him away.'

'Not him,' Dakers said fiercely. 'Not the priest. She wanted to please him, and that's what did the harm, but she never would have run after him in the first place if that husband of hers had treated her right. *He's* the one that's to blame. *He* killed her, as sure as if he stabbed her with a knife! I wish to God she'd never set eyes on him!'

Given the hot weather and the nature of the disease, there could be no waiting while an elaborate funeral was arranged. The bodies of Hobsbawn's daughter and grandson were conveyed to their hastily-dug grave as soon as darkness fell, with only the three servants to carry torches and walk with the old man behind the coffins. On their return to the house, Hobsbawn reached the end of his endurance, and had to be helped to his bed by Simon and Bowles.

Dakers went to her late mistress's chamber and sat down at the desk, facing the empty bed, and began to write a letter to James Morland. If the pen had been dipped in acid instead of ink, the words could hardly have seared the paper more; but before she could finish the letter, exhaustion overcame her, and when Bowles came looking for her, after seeing his master comfortable, he found her asleep with her head on her arms. He shook her awake and helped her to her room, and since he could hardly help her undress, he persuaded her to lie down as she was, fully-clothed, and she was asleep before he had had time to draw the counterpane over her.

The news first reached Morland Place in a letter from Father Rathbone to his friend Aislaby. It was the week after race-week, and Lucy was still at Morland Place. She and Edward were breakfasting with James — their second breakfast, and his first — and talking over last week's successes and failures, when Aislaby came in with the letter in his hand.

'Ah, I wondered where you had got to, Father,' James said. 'Come and try some of these mutton cutlets! I think Danvers is at last beginning to understand how to dress mutton. That's the trouble with a cook who wasn't brought up in sheep country. They think a sheep and a cow are the same animal, only different sizes.'

'Shut up, Jamie,' Edward said, noticing the priest's expression. 'Are you all right, Father? You don't look quite the thing.'

'I'm afraid I have some very grave news,' he said. 'I hardly know how to begin to tell you.' He stood by his chair looking round at them, the letter open in his hand. 'I've had a letter from my friend Rathbone, in Manchester. There has been a serious outbreak of fever amongst the poor people who work in the mills — a particularly virulent kind of fever. They are talking of an epidemic.' He stopped, and handed the letter to Edward. 'I think you had better read it.'

James stared. 'For God's sake, what's happened? Is my wife ill? Is that what you're trying to say?'

Edward had taken the letter, and his eyes skimming the page jumped at once to Mary Ann's name half way down. 'Oh, dear Lord,' he said, looking up at his brother.

'What is it?' James asked again, his eyes wide, now, with anxiety. 'Ned, for God's sake!'

'It's the fever,' Edward said reluctantly. 'She and the boy .'

'Both of them?'

Edward met his eyes. 'He says there was nothing anyone could do.'

James stared, comprehension coming to him slowly. 'They're dead?' he whispered incredulously.

Edward nodded, and bowing his head away from his brother's eyes, read on down the letter. 'They don't know what this fever is, but it's very infectious, and it carries people off very quickly, in a matter of hours. Because of the epidemic, they had to bury them immediately. There wouldn't have been time to send for you.'

James shook his head as if trying to clear it. 'Dead?' he said again. 'Dead and buried? Both of them? I can't believe it.'

Edward looked at him unhappily. 'It must have been very quick,' he said, trying to offer comfort. 'They were taken ill at night, and died the next morning. They couldn't have suffered much.'

'My son,' Aislaby said, watching James's face, 'let me offer you the consolation of faith. Father Rathbone was there at the end, and gave them absolution. Prayer can comfort you, too.'

Only Lucy said nothing, knowing from her own experience that nothing could help.

'But — a fever amongst the poor people — how could she and the boy catch it? Hobsbawn is not ill? I don't understand,' James said.

Aislaby answered. 'She was engaged in charitable work amongst the poor. When the fever began, she helped to nurse them —'

James stood up abruptly, pushing his chair away so violently that it fell over backwards. 'Why didn't they send for me?' he said, 'My wife and son! Why didn't Hobsbawn send for me?'

'There wasn't time,' Edward said, gesturing with the letter. 'It says here —'

'I don't believe it!' James cried. 'The old man wanted them to himself. It's what she wanted too. Why else did she spend half of every year there? I don't know why she ever bothered to come back. She always thought Morland Place wasn't a patch on her precious Hobsbawn House!'

'Jamie!' Edward protested, but James rushed from the room, and when Edward made to follow him, Lucy caught his eye and shook her head.

'Leave him alone,' she said. 'He won't want anyone with him just yet.'

Edward's face creased. 'That poor, poor woman! And poor little Henry! It's so hard to believe. Alive one day, dead and buried the next! And she had such an unhappy life, poor creature. James treated her very badly.'

'I don't suppose he meant to,' Lucy said with a shrug. 'She just wasn't one of us. She didn't fit in.'

'We didn't give her much help,' Edward said.

Lucy shook her head. 'She didn't want help. Jamie was right, you know — she always thought herself superior to us: that's why she wouldn't adapt to our ways. She just wanted to make this house as much like her father's as possible.'

'Surely this is a moment for thinking forgiving thoughts,' Aislaby reproved her gently.

But Lucy faced him robustly. 'I'm sorry, Father, but her being dead doesn't change the facts. I never much liked her, and I certainly didn't like the way she changed things here. That doesn't excuse Jamie for the way he treated her, of course, but she got her own way in the end and went off to stay with her father, and now she's died there, so she'll never need to come back.'

'Oh Lucy,' Edward said reproachfully. 'You're so hard. Don't you feel any pity for that poor little boy, at least? And what about Fanny? How ever are we going to tell Fanny?'

'Fanny won't care two straws,' Lucy said, 'though I dare say she'll pretend to, if she thinks it will get her treats.' Father Aislaby refrained from comment, knowing that Lucy was right about that, at least. 'As to Henry, well, he was a nice child enough, as far as it went, but one can't feel the same sort of regret about a child's death as about an adult's. There's simply less to them. You're just being sentimental, Ned.'

'You're just being provoking,' Edward retorted. 'I think someone ought to go after Jamie. He was obviously really upset. She was his wife, after all, and Henry was his only son.'

'I wonder how old Mr Hobsbawn will leave his property now,' Lucy said. 'He always said he wouldn't leave the mills to Fanny, but now Mary Ann's gone he may change his mind. Fanny's his only kin now.'

'Don't be so mercenary,' Edward snapped. 'Anyone would think —'

Father Aislaby decided the sibling quarrel had gone far enough, and intervened to say, 'We ought to hold a requiem mass for them in the chapel as soon as possible. May I talk to you about the arrangements, Mr Morland? I doubt whether I ought to trouble Mr James with the details at the moment.'

'A requiem mass! Yes, that's the thing to do,' Edward said,

glad to be brought back into the paths of right thinking. 'And we must write our condolences to Mr Hobsbawn. The poor old thing must be heartbroken. He thought the world of his daughter.'

Aislaby sat down, and he and Edward began to discuss letters, mourning clothes and masses with proper solemnity, and Lucy went on eating toast, her face impassive. She really could not care about Mary Ann, or the child. She had had so little to do with them of recent years, that their deaths seemed quite remote from her, unreal. Her thoughts were with her brother, whom she really did love, wondering what he was feeling, and how he was going to conduct his life from now on.

When James ran from the unwelcome attention of his family, he turned instinctively towards the one accessible friend he had in the world. He crossed the inner court and went out through the bakehouse passage and the back door, skirted the orchard wall and came up to the rails of the home paddock, where Nez Carré was turned out.

The old horse was twenty now, but apart from the salt-cellars over his eyes, and the grey hairs in his mane, he didn't look any different to the eyes of love. He lifted his head from his grazing at James's whistle, and came at once, breaking into a graceful trot as he neared the fence. James climbed over, and Nez Carré whickered, his ears pricked and his eyes shining with welcome, and as he reached his master he thrust his nose under James's arm, a gesture remembered from foalhood, his greatest act of love.

'There, old fellow! Good old boy!' James murmured, pulling the long ears, while Nez Carré nudged further under his arm, his eyes closed with content. Here was perfect accord, James thought. He did not ride the old horse much any more, except for a gentle amble around the estate, but he never let a day pass without coming to see him, and bringing him a carrot or a handful of oats. He reached into his pocket, and Nez Carré felt the gesture and jerked his head back, and was mumbling with his lips at James's arm before he had even got his hand out of his pocket.

'Greedy, that's what you are,' James laughed, and extracted the carrot, holding it by one end. Nez Carré's lips felt their way half way down it, and then he bit it through, and crunched contentedly, nodding his head up and down and blowing with pleasure. James gave him the other half, and watched him eat, enjoying the horse's simple, concentrated pleasure. Then he stood still while Nez Carré investigated both his hands and pockets to make sure there was nothing else good to eat, and then felt with his lips all over James's face, and finally took hold of his hair and gave it an affectionate tug. James stroked the smooth neck and cheeks, and finally allowed himself to think about what he was feeling.

Guilt; shame; remorse. These were the sensations that crowded in on him when he thought of his wife and child dead. Sadness, yes, on their behalf, the sadness he might have felt for any young life cut off untimely; but more than that, most of all, guilt, that he had never valued her, or made her happy. He had brought her humiliation and sadness; he had condemned her for so many years to loneliness; he had treated her so badly, that she had been driven to take refuge from the hostile world he had created around her, in the home of her childhood.

Well, she had been happy there, he had no doubt, but it did not assuage his self-blame. He was aware, too, of a painful regret that now it was too late ever to make amends to her, or to come to know her. She had good qualities, of that he had always been sure, and if he had taken the trouble to try to understand her, he might have held her in sufficient esteem for their marriage to have been more than an emptiness with a name.

He tried to think of Henry, tried to attach to him the feelings that ought to go with the words 'my son', but he could not find them in him. He found himself thinking of the other boy he had begotten, Mary Skelwith's son, who was twenty now, a boy no longer, but a grown man. James saw him from time to time about the city, where he was taking up the reins of his father's business: a good-looking young man, well-grown and sensible, if rather solemn. James saw him without a pang. To beget a child is not to be its father: that was a lesson he had learned long ago, with the pain that betokens true self-knowledge. And in that sense he was not Henry's father. He had quite deliberately shut himself away from Henry, refused to love him or know him, left him to his mother; and she, of course, had been happy enough to consent to the division. And having refused the loving part of fatherhood, he was not now entitled to its grief.

It was as well, perhaps, that Henry had died. As a little boy, he was happy enough with his mother's love and attention; but as he grew older, he would have begun to look towards James, would have wanted fatherhood from him; and when it was denied, he would probably, seeing Fanny loved, have decided that the fault lay in him, that he was in some way unloveable. James would not have wanted that for him.

Perhaps, he thought, I ought only to have daughters. The thought stirred up a new pain. He rested his face against Nez Carré's broad cheek, felt the warmth of him under the smooth, hard hair, smelled the good, sweet horse-smell of his skin. He loved this horse. There was in him, as in every horse, the holiness of a creature which could only be as God made it, moved by simple hungers and simple loves to do what it was made for and nothing else, to praise God and know Him in its innocence.

He remembered the day Fanny was born, how he felt when she was first placed in his arms, pearly and tender and damp like a rose-petal just that instant unfurled. He remembered how in that moment he had felt her completeness and unsullied perfection, and wanted to protect her. I have spoiled Fanny, he thought with a sudden, searing understanding. I have loved her unwisely, and too well, and I have spoiled her, and changed her from that perfect, innocent thing into a copy of all my worst faults. A father of daughters? There was Fanny and there was Sophie, and what had he ever done for either that they might thank him for?

Nez Carré sighed with content and let the weight of his great head rest on James's shoulder, and James blinked away the tears of remorse, which were perilously close to self-pity, and thought, but I can make amends, to both of them. Guilt and shame are wasteful. The thing is to put matters right. And that brought him to the place he had been avoiding in his thoughts, that he had been circling not from fear or distaste, but because it was too beautiful.

Héloïse. Admitted at last, the thought of her flooded him with joy, like brilliant sunshine. Now at last he could marry her and bring her back to Morland Place, her and Sophie, put right what had gone horribly, stupidly wrong all those years ago. He thought of being married to her, loving her openly and honestly, without shadow, without guilt, being with her as of right, never having to part from her, seeing her and touching her every day of his life. He imagined the unique joy and contentment of requited love, and thought, surely this is what we were made for?

The pain in his shoulder from the weight of Nez Carré's head brought him down to earth from his raptures. He pushed the horse off him, and Nez Carré woke with a snort. 'Everything is going to be all right,' James told him. 'There will have to be a period of mourning first, but what is a few months of waiting, with the certainty of happiness at the end of it?' Nez Carré nudged him in agreement. 'How shall I tell her? Write to her? No, that won't do. I shall have to go up there and tell her myself. Perhaps I should go down on one knee and propose to her again, do the thing properly?'

Nez Carré had no opinion on the matter. He was beginning to feel hungry again. He lowered his head and nibbled first at James's shoe so as not to hurt his feelings, and then began to nose casually at the grass around it.

James's first instinct was to go at once, today, not to waste an instant of the time they might be happy in. But he thought again of Mary Ann, and restrained himself. It would not do. It must not be said that he went rushing off the moment he heard she was dead. Some respect was due to her. He would wait a few days, and then ride quietly over to Coxwold and tell Héloïse the news, and ask her to wait until the mourning period was over. He must do everything properly this time, make no mistakes. It would be all right. There could be no more misunderstandings between them now.

Nez Carré was beginning to move away, grazing as he went, and James gave him one last affectionate slap on the rump and climbed back over the fence, and began to walk towards the house. It was going to be difficult to get through the next few days, to do what was expected of him, to offend no-one, to keep up appearances. But he must do it. He wanted nothing in his present behaviour to be able to cast a shadow over the happiness of the future.

I'm sorry, Mary Ann, he addressed her in his mind, for all the wrongs I did you. I wish I had behaved better by you, and I'm not glad you're dead, truly I'm not. I can honestly say I never wished for your death, even in the depths of my heart; and I will pay you the respect the world demands. So forgive me, now, if I am glad that I can marry Héloïse. I can't help it.

Chapter Twenty-One

Dakers's letter to James came the following day, and brought home to him for the first time the reality of his wife's death, and with it, the reality of her life. Here was another view of the calm, polite, neatly-dressed woman who had shared a roof and a name with him, but little else. She had been Dakers's nurseling, Mr Hobsbawn's daughter, the darling of Hobsbawn House; and firmly as they had loved her, they had hated and despised him.

The strength of the animosity towards him shook him badly. It was unpleasant to discover all that hatred in a woman who had been living under his roof, like finding scorpions nesting in one's mattress. He felt threatened by it, but he felt also misjudged, misunderstood. I am not like this, he thought, reading the letter again, his eyes screwed up defensively as though the words might jump off the page and attack him. It was a caricature of James Morland, this black-hearted villain of Dakers's pen. He was foolish, selfish, careless of others, but he was not worth so much bitter hatred.

He wondered if Dakers really did, as she claimed, speak for Mr Hobsbawn too, and then decided that hatred of this order was a woman-thing, and that Mary Ann's father must be feeling far more grief than bitterness. It was not James's fault, by any stretching of the facts, that Mary Ann had gone sick-visiting against advice. Every mistress of Morland Place since it was first built had visited the sick: it was a duty laid down by long tradition; and if Mary Ann had resembled her predecessors in nothing else, she had had a stern sense of duty. As for this priest about whom Dakers hinted such dark complications, that was obviously the fantasy of an embittered virgin. Mary Ann hadn't enough hot blood in her to feel passion for any man, least of all an ordained priest of Holy Mother Church!

A letter of condolence had been dispatched at once, on

receipt of Rathbone's letter, but this epistle of Dakers's resolved a doubt which had been growing in James's mind, as to whether or not he ought to visit Mr Hobsbawn. He knew he had not been a favourite with his father-in-law, even before he had run away to Héloïse, and that since that episode his name had probably been unmentionable at Hobsbawn House; but now that Mary Ann was dead, he must shew that he knew what was proper, at least. Mr Hobsbawn might not receive much pleasure from a visit, might even misinterpret James's concern, but he would regard the lack of a visit as a cold-hearted neglect of duty which only confirmed his bad opinion of his son-in-law.

Father Aislaby, appealed to to confirm James's judgement, obliged.

'Doing the right thing may not always win approbation, but not doing it can never make one feel easy. It is an attention you ought to pay. Whether or not Mr Hobsbawn will receive you is a matter for his own conscience, but I think he will. From what little I know of him, I would say he is hasty-tempered, but a good man underneath.'

'Good,' James said. 'I'm glad you approve. Then if I had better go, I had better go at once. And,' he said as the idea struck him. 'I'll take Fanny with me!'

Aislaby was not quite quick enough to conceal his dismay, and when James frowned at him, hastened to say, 'Perhaps it may not be safe to take her, with the plague about.'

'Nonsense,' said James. 'Only poor people catch the plague; and besides, Fanny is as a strong as a horse. I shall not take *her* sick visiting, you know.'

Still Aislaby hesitated, and James went on, 'Now what? Don't you think it's a good idea? If it is right for me to pay Mr Hobsbawn the attention, it must be right for Fanny, too. And having lost little Henry, he will surely welcome a visit from his own granddaughter — his only grandchild now.'

Aislaby struggled to recover himself. 'Oh — yes, yes. I'm only afraid it might be too much for him. Fanny is not a quiet, gentle child. Her noisiness might be too much for his nerves at a time like this.'

James looked wounded. 'Fanny will behave herself. You underestimate her, you know. She will understand what is expected of her on an occasion like this.'

Aislaby, who had been privileged to witness in the nursery some of Fanny's reactions to her orphanhood which James had not, doubted it, but he could not tell James that. He sought for another explanation. 'There is the possibility, too, that Mr Hobsbawn might misunderstand your reasons for taking Fanny with you,' he said desperately. 'He may think you are only concerned with persuading him to change his will in Fanny's favour. After all, she has never visited him before.'

James considered this, and rejected it. 'He may think so, of course, but then we have already decided that he may think my purpose in coming is a mercenary one. It can't be made worse by Fanny, and might be made better. If the thing is right in itself, it ought to be done, and the consequences must look after themselves. Fanny's quite an heiress in her own right, as Mr Hobsbawn knows. He must know that she doesn't need his money.'

Aislaby, seeing James's mind was made up, had nothing more to say.

Fanny had been far more intrigued by her new status as orphan, than upset by her mother's death. Ever since Henry had been born, Mary Ann had removed from her daughter even the scant attention she had previously paid her, and if they met at all in recent years, it was only by accident, because they happened to be in the same room at the same time. When they did meet, her mother would look at Fanny with indifferent eyes, caring too little for her even to scold her, as some of the older servants still dared to do. Fanny didn't mind their scolds, because she knew how to win them round. She had use only for people who admired her, or whom she could manipulate, and as Mary Ann was in neither category, her indifference towards her daughter was more than equalled by Fanny's towards her.

So when James had come in person to tell her that her mama and little brother were dead, the news did not distress her in any way. She considered first of all what her reaction ought to be, and seeing that James expected her to be upset, and that the nursery-maids were inching forward already, preparing to comfort her, she decided not to disappoint them, and cried very prettily for ten minutes or so. It was an accomplishment she had developed over the years, and had found very useful on those occasions when she had driven her attendants to the point where their exasperation with her outweighed their fear of her temper. She had often heard Sarah say to Lotty that the crying proved that Miss Fanny was really a good girl underneath, in spite of everything.

So she cried first of all, and was petted and comforted, and listened to the underlying approval in the voices around her. James in particular was impressed by her sensibility, for though he defended her against every criticism, it was sometimes with the wistfulness of hope rather than the firmness of conviction. Fanny's tender tears brought such emotion welling up into his voice as he told her she was his good little girl, that she was quite overcome by her own performance, and cried in good earnest for some minutes.

When the first transports were over, she began to be aware that her bereavement could be put to good use, as everyone around her seemed prepared to treat her as though she were made of some fragile material, and told her cousins quite sharply that they must be particularly kind to poor Miss Fanny, who had lost not only her dear mama but her dearest little brother too. At dinner time, when they asked her in tones of tender concern if she could fancy anything to eat, she began to perceive the possibilities of the situation. She sighed sadly, and said in a faint and quavering voice that she couldn't eat a thing, and then allowed them to persuade her gradually into all her favourite foods, cold chicken, currant tarts, syllabub, orange cream, and jellies.

For the rest of the day, she had her own way in everything simply for the lifting of a finger. Her cousins' toys, which normally she had to bully them into letting her play with, were handed over eagerly. She was begged to choose the games they played, given the leading part in everything, and allowed to win without even having to cheat. At supper she was regaled again with everything she had ever expressed a preference for, was allowed to sit up as long as she liked, and brought Jenny to speechlessness with reading aloud her favourite stories by the hour.

She went to bed at last well pleased with her new status. Previously she had flaunted her possession of two live parents over her cousins, who had all lost one, but secretly she had been jealous of the distinction of their orphanhood, particularly that of Flaminia, Rosamund and Roland, as being so recent. Now she was not only to join them, but to outstrip them, with a double bereavement as recent as yesterday. She looked forward to putting on mourning clothes the following day, aware from whispers she had overheard that the sewing maids had been working on them all day in secret, downstairs in the laundry-room. Lucy's children had recently gone into half-mourning, their papa having been dead for six months now, so Fanny would have no rival to her interesting appearance in stark black. She would be the centre of attention, just as she ought.

So when James came to ask her if she would like to go and visit grandpapa with him, he was working on more malleable clay than he might have expected. Fanny had spent a good deal of the morning admiring her reflection in every glass she passed, for the black of her mourning-gown made her look interestingly pale, and the purple ribbon in her hair made her curls look darker and more lustrous. She was beginning, however, to crave a larger audience, having come near to exhausting the possibilities of the nursery. She was used to a more vigorous life, and having everything she wanted for the asking was proving a little insipid. She wanted new worlds to conquer, and the idea of a grief-stricken grandfather was appealing.

She saw the scene in her mind's eye: the old man, his grey head resting in his hand, weeps into a black-bordered handkerchief; Fanny enters, looking fragile in black, runs to him crying, I will comfort you, Grandpapa. He looks up; he starts; she is the image of her mother; an angel come to comfort me, he cries, enfolds her in his embrace, and sends for the lawyer to change his will. Not for nothing had Fanny stolen Jenny's circulating-library novels and read them under the bedclothes; and listening to the servants' gossip when they thought she was otherwise engaged had given her a very clear understanding of her grandfather's financial potentialities.

And quite apart from all that, there was the prospect of a trip in the carriage with her father, having his attention all to herself for hours and hours, travelling across country she had never seen before, stopping and perhaps even eating at inns, staying away from home, everything novel, everything delightful. It would have been worth it for that alone; so when James asked her tentatively if she would like to go, she gave him a brave, sweet smile, and said that if Papa said it was the right thing to do, to go and comfort Grandpapa, then they ought to do it.

James looked at her with surprise and relief and gratification. 'And you will be good, won't you, Fanny?' he said coaxingly.

Fanny looked a little hurt. 'Good, Papa? Of course I will.'

James smiled hastily. 'Of course you will, my pigeon, I know that. It's just that your grandpapa will be very upset, and he may not seem very pleased to see us, just at first, and so we must be careful what we say and do, not to upset him even more.'

Fanny smiled her prettiest smile. 'Grandpapa will be pleased to see *me*,' she asserted, 'I'm his only grandchild now, and his heiress. I shall make him love me, too. It will be all right, Papa.'

He gathered her in and kissed her tenderly. 'I'm sure it will, chick. Who could help loving you?'

Fanny, gathering this to be in the nature of a rhetorical question, merely snuggled closer, and forebore to mention Father Aislaby and Aunt Lucy, to say nothing of her departed mother, her mother's personal maid, and Farmer Ramsgill of Eastfields Farm, whose heifers she had chased on horseback last week.

Setting off very early the following morning, they arrived at Hobsbawn House in the late afternoon, after a journey that was a series of delights to Fanny. James was glad for his own sake that he had brought her, for as they neared their destination, he began to feel apprehensive about their reception, and then suffered a resurgence of remorse and guilt. Fanny's spirits sustained him, and he hoped, too, that her presence would deflect some of the hostility that might otherwise be aimed at him.

The blinds were down on the windows of Hobsbawn House, and the doorknocker was wreathed in black crape, and these sights brought home to James abruptly the genuine mourning that must be going on inside. Fanny was still bubbling with excitement, and he took a moment before descending from the carriage to warn her to be quiet and modest when they went in, and not to speak loudly or laugh or ask questions.

'They will all be very sad about your mama, and you mustn't upset them. Be a good girl, and don't speak unless you are spoken to.'

'I know,' Fanny said impatiently, peering out of the carriage window. 'Is this where Mama was born? It's a nice house, isn't it? Will it be mine one day?'

James felt a brief spasm of doubt about the wisdom of having brought her after all, but the steps were being let down, and it was too late to turn back now. His knock upon the door was a long time answering, but at last there was a sound of drawing bolts, and the old butler stood there, blinking in the light after the twilit gloom of the hall. He did not at once seem to know who James was, and stared at him blankly.

'Bowles, isn't it?' James said. 'Is your master at home? We've come to pay our condolences, Miss Fanny and I. A terrible business, this. I know how much you must feel it. You've been with the family a long time, haven't you?'

Gradually recognition had been dawning on the butler's grey face, and James was not surprised when it was followed not by welcome but by anxiety. He could hardly expect the old servant to receive him joyfully.

'Mr Morland,' he said at last. 'And Miss Fanny. Why — I don't know what to say. You've come to see master?'

'Yes, that's right. May we come in?'

At the gentle reminder, Bowles stepped back automatically, and they had entered the hall before he remembered to say, 'I don't know if he'll see you. He's seen no-one yet.' he sounded dazed, and talked on in a monotone as he shuffled after them. 'Not that people are visiting much. It's the plague, you see. It's gone beyond the poor people this time: there's cases all over town. Folk are stopping home, now, afraid of catching it.'

'Well, I'm not afraid,' James said, restraining Fanny with a glare from hopping from one foot to the other as she stared around the hall in frank curiosity. 'Will you be so kind as to go and tell your master we are here, and want to pay our respects?'

'Aye, well, I'll tell him,' Bowles said doubtfully, and went slowly away. The house was unnaturally quiet. The ticking of the long-case clock by the stairs was the only sound. James occupied the time by paying off the postboys and carrying in their bags. He was puzzled that there was no footman to do it for him. Had the servants run away, he wondered? The reality of the plague which had killed his wife was in this silence.

Fanny had noticed it too. 'Papa, where is everyone?' she asked, tugging his sleeve. 'Doesn't Grandpapa have any servants?'

'Of course he has,' James said automatically.

'Then why doesn't someone come? I don't like it here. I want to go home,' Fanny said.

Someone had come. Out of the shadows behind the stairs, silent and menacing, Dakers appeared, so unexpectedly that Fanny let out a little scream. The woman had hardly eaten for days, and her face had taken on a skull-like appearance which made her glittering eyes and hard mouth all the more frightening and sinister. Even James had to take a firm hold of his senses and tell himself that she was only a harmless old woman.

'So,' she hissed, 'it is you! I thought I heard your voice. Have you come here to gloat? I should have thought you'd have more sense than to come to this house, after what you've done. But no — there isn't an ounce of proper feeling in you, is there?'

James swallowed. 'Now, Dakers,' he said, 'I know you're upset, but that's no excuse for insolence. I've come to see Mr Hobsbawn, not you, so just you go away and get on with whatever you were doing.'

'I don't take orders from you,' she said. 'I'm not your servant. I'm nobody's servant now, since you killed my mistress, God rest her poor sweet soul. A misery you made

411

her life, and you drove her to her death. And you have the gall to come here, and bring that hell-bound imp with you!' She flung out an accusing finger at Fanny, who jumped with a creditable speed of reaction to hide behind her father, holding on tightly to his coat-tails, in case the old madwoman was a witch and could spirit her away.

'How dare you speak to me like that?' James began angrily, but Dakers advanced another step towards him and cut him off.

'I've wanted to say that and more to you for many a long year, but I never did while my mistress was alive, and not because I didn't dare, either. But she wouldn't allow it. She defended you, poor deluded soul. She would have you treated with proper respect, though you shewed her none, and so I held my tongue. But there's nothing to stop me now. I watched her die, and I'd give my life to watch you go the same way, only slower.'

James was stunned anew by the depth of her hatred, by the black venom that gushed out of her The anger left him. 'Dakers, I didn't kill her! You don't know what you're talking about. It wasn't my fault,' he cried.

She came another step forward, and Fanny screamed, and then a voice from the top of the stairs broke through the tension below.

'Dakers! That's enough! Go back to your room.'

She turned her head a little, but did not unfix her eyes from James's. 'Nay, master,' she said, 'I've not finished.'

'Yes, you have,' Hobsbawn said, and his voice had the old ring of authority. 'I'll deal with this. Go to your room at once, and stay there until I send for you.'

She went, gliding reluctantly and by inches across the marble squares of the hall, and disappeared into the shadows from which she had emerged. James lifted a grateful face to Hobsbawn, feeling behind him to detach Fanny from his coat.

'Thank you, sir,' he said. 'I'm afraid that poor woman's grief has unbalanced her.'

'She's not herself,' Hobsbawn said abruptly. 'Come up.'

James mounted the stairs, holding Fanny's hand, and came face to face at last with his father-in-law. Hobsbawn seemed in some curious way to have shrunk, for though his body was

412

as massive, he seemed not to fit it. His face was haggard, and he moved painfully, like a very old man, but his eyes were steady as they regarded James, without either welcome or hostility, and James felt that the power was still in him, and that it was for him to receive or reject, not for James to give, comfort.

'Well,' Hobsbawn said at last. 'You've come, then. You'd best come in to the drawing-room. Bowles, bring something up. Wine or something.'

James followed the old man into the room. Because the blinds were half way down, it was gloomy, and there was already an air of dusty neglect about it. Hobsbawn sat down in a chair beside the unlit fire, and James sat down on the sopha opposite him, placing Fanny beside him. One good thing about Dakers's outburst was that it had so frightened Fanny that she was on her very best behaviour, and sat quite still where she was put, with her hands in her lap, her eyes large as she surveyed the dim room and the dour old man before her.

'Well, then,' Hobsbawn said at last, 'what have you to say for yourself?'

It was not a welcoming sentence, but then James had hardly expected welcome. 'I am come, sir, to pay my condolences,' he said. 'I received a letter — a bitter, accusing letter — from that poor woman, purporting to represent your feelings too. I couldn't believe that that was true; but whether it was or not, I could not neglect to come at such a time.'

'Could you not?' Hobsbawn asked in a flat voice.

'She was my wife,' James said quietly.

'Aye, but you never loved her!' Hobsbawn cried resentfully.

James turned his hands over in a little helpless gesture. 'Sir, that was not in the bargain.'

Hobsbawn was silent a long while, the struggle evident in his face. 'Nay, you're right. It wasn't. But all the same, you didn't expect me to forgive you for the way you treated her, just for the making of one visit did you?'

'No, sir. I didn't think you would like me more because I paid this visit; but you would have liked me less if I failed to pay it.'

Another silence; and then Hobsbawn raised his head a little

413

and looked directly into James's eyes. 'I like plain speaking,' he said. 'And you're right. I don't like you, and I can't forgive you, but you did the proper thing by coming, and it must have taken some courage on your part. And you brought the little lass, too.' His eyes moved to Fanny. 'Come here, child,' he said.

James felt her reluctance rooting itself into the seat of the sopha, and he had to push her very firmly to make her go over and stand before her grandfather. The old man surveyed her gravely, looking, James guessed, for some likeness to Mary Ann. Presumably, he found it, for at last he smiled a little, and said, 'Well, then Fanny, what have you to say for yourself? Do you know who I am?'

'Yes, Grandpapa,' she said in subdued tones.

'I've seen nothing of you, since your little brother was born. You're grown quite a young lady. How old are you?'

'I'm nearly eleven, Grandpapa,' Fanny said, and even her present uneasiness could not keep the pride out of her voice. Hobsbawn's grim old face softened a little.

'Nearly eleven? Aye, your birthday's in October, I remember that well enough. Well, if you are a good girl, I shall give you a sovereign before you go, to buy ribbons for your birthday.' Fanny beamed. This was more familiar territory. Hobsbawn reached out and fingered the black material of Fanny's gown, and she flinched only a very little. 'I suppose you dislike very much to wear black, don't you?' he asked neutrally.

Five minutes ago, Fanny might have been caught by the question, but the promise of the sovereign had given her back her wits, and she tilted her head a little in a disarming gesture James knew very well. 'I shouldn't like to wear any other colour just now, Grandpapa,' she said sweetly, 'for mama and my little brother are dead.'

James held his breath for a moment, and released it in a soundless sigh as Hobsbawn reached up a heavy paw and patted Fanny's cheek affectionately, which Fanny endured very well.

'Aye, you're a good little puss, I see that,' he said, 'and you've a look of your mother about you after all, when you smile. She could always wind me round her finger. Well, you and I must be friends, Fanny, for I've no-one left in the world but you. One day you shall come and stay with me, but not now. You mustn't stay long now, with the plague about. Manchester isn't a healthy place for little folk to be.'

'I'm not afraid, Grandpapa,' Fanny said promptly. 'I'm never ill.'

'Aye, aye, well,' Hobsbawn said, visibly impressed. 'We won't take the risk, any road. But before you go home, we'll go and visit your mother's grave. You'd like that, wouldn't you, puss?'

It didn't sound enjoyable at all, but Fanny was still revelling in her new conquest, and said, 'Oh yes, Grandpapa,' as if it were the greatest treat in the world.

There was nothing yet to mark the graves, just two poor mounds of earth side by side, one long and one short. The sight of them subdued even Fanny, who had begun to grow regrettably uppish again, and there was something so pathetic about the smaller one, that she lifted a pale face to her father for reassurance and there was a hint of uncontrived moisture in the wide eyes.

'I haven't done anything yet about headstones,' Hobsbawn said. 'I haven't had the heart for it. But they shall have the best that money can buy, you may depend upon it. Her mother is buried just over there, and I've my own place kept for me, beside her. She was a good woman, and I never wanted another, though I could have married again, a dozen times, if I'd wanted. If I'd known how this would end, maybe I would have. I thought I'd leave everything to Mary Ann, and to her sons.' He sighed, and his face looked colourless in the dusk. 'It's a hard thing to work all your life to build up your fortune, and have no-one to leave it to at the end.'

At that moment, by some miracle, Fanny did not say anything, only slipped her hand into her grandfather's. James could not tell if it were a spontaneous gesture or not, but Hobsbawn started, and then looked down at her, and some of the pain left his face. James was glad. It did not matter to him whether Hobsbawn changed his will in Fanny's favour or not; he was honestly indifferent to the Hobsbawn fortune; but he saw that Fanny had brought her grandfather comfort, and that removed a great deal of his sense of guilt and unease. The visit had answered better than he hoped; he had done his duty, and the way was thus left clear for him to follow his heart, and secure his future to Héloïse.

A fine day with a pleasant breeze had taken Héloïse and her family up to Sutton Bank for a kite-flying expedition. A hired carriage took Flon, Marie and the children, together with the enormous picnic basket carefully packed by Monsieur Barnard, while Héloïse and her suitor drove in the phaeton, with Kithra making a smiling, panting, and to the Duc, unwelcome third between them.

It was a perfect day, and a perfect place, for kites. The blue sky, touched here and there with purely decorative wisps of white cloud, veined with a light but steady breeze, seemed to reach down almost to touch the green top of the sheer cliff. From the foot of it the land undulated gently away, patch-worked into green and golden fields and dense, full-leafed woods, sprinkled with grazing animals, buttoned down here and there with a snug, slate-roofed farm and its cluster of outbuildings.

Héloïse could have stood for hours just gazing across the unique landscape, so different from anything she had ever known in France. England was so complete, she thought, everything one could want all drawn close around one, nothing wasted, nothing out of reach. She wondered for a moment whether she ought to feel guilty about loving it so much; but then, she thought, as she had often told other people, I am only *half* French. The rest of my blood is Yorkshire blood. I ought to feel at home here.

The Duc, standing beside her, for once was not in accord with her thoughts. 'It is pretty,' he sighed, 'but it is not France.'

Héloïse drew in a breath of clean air. 'It is more than pretty,' she said. 'I was just contemplating what it is about England that is so different, and I think it is a kind of magic. From here, everything looks so tiny and neat, but it is only pretending to be small. As soon as you come to any place, poof! the magic begins, and it grows bigger and bigger around you even as you look.'

'You sound as though you were in love with it,' the Duc said with a puzzled air. 'Don't you long to go back to France?'

'Beautiful France,' Héloïse said. 'Of course, something stirs in me when I say the words. I love my country, and grieve for her. And yet I have been in England now for almost as long as I lived in France. My life has been divided between them — and I think my heart is, too.'

Her own words gave her pause, but before she could follow up the train of thought, her attention was claimed by Sophie and Thomas, who had come here to fly kites, not to gaze at the view. They had already run as far as the outcrop and back, with Kithra bouncing hugely between them, and had determined the best place to begin.

'Oh, please come, Maman, monsieur,' Sophie begged with the urgency of childhood. 'I'm sure the wind will die away if we don't begin *now*!' Héloïse could remember being just as convinced about the evanescent quality of pleasure when she was that age, and with a smile at her companion, allowed her hand to be seized and herself towed along, back to the second carriage where Flon and Marie were unpacking the impedimenta and looking about for the best place to set out the picnic.

'Just over there, I should think, by that thorn tree,' Héloïse answered the unasked question. 'Have you the kite there? The children are anxious to begin.'

It was handed out, a handsome thing, as tall as Thomas and a little more, painted in yellow and blue and red, with a goggling dragon's face and a long tail. It was a most satisfying kite, purchased at the Lammas Fair in Thirsk by the Duc himself, and if he had done it in the hope of purchasing the children's favour, he had spent his money wisely.

He and Sophie and Thomas set off along the cliff to the place Sophie told them anxiously that she had 'chosen *specially*' for the launch. Héloïse lingered a moment to direct an enquiring look towards the large number of empty bowls and baskets which were appearing from under the carriage seat.

'For the bilberries, my lady,' Marie explained. 'They're just about ready, and this is a famous place for them. Monsieur

Barnard was very anxious we should get as many as possible.'

Héloïse laughed. 'Oh, then I need not worry about your having something to amuse yourselves for the next hour. Crawling about the bilberry bushes on hands and knees will be such fun for you!'

She hurried after the children, and for the next hour, as she watched the three of them take turns at flying the kite, she reflected that there was no pastime so utterly innocent, nor any man so grown-up that a kite would not cause the boy in him to step out and take over. She watched them contentedly, seeing how happily they played together. Thomas was a little young for sustained attention, and wandered off now and then with Kithra to investigate a rustle in the bracken or to examine a particularly interesting beetle, but Sophie and the Duc were enraptured by the kite, and could not have enough of it. They let Héloïse take a turn once, and she was transported back instantly to her childhood as she felt the importunate tug at the string in her hand, the exhilaration of its power. She and her papa had flown a kite many times on the terrace at St Germain. She squinted up into the dazzling sky and smiled, remembering, and then yielded her place to Sophie.

Another family had appeared on the same errand, the father and two little boys preparing to put up a clown-faced kite with all the solemnity of engineers preparing for a balloon ascent. After a while the two groups joined forces, the two men discussing technical matters such as air-drag and the correct length for a tail, while the children went through the ritual of exchanging names and ages. Héloïse found herself quite superfluous, and with a private smile left them to it, and walked back to the carriages.

Flon had found herself a scrap of shade, and was sitting peacefully with her hands in her lap, watching the distant scene. She smiled as Héloïse sat down beside her.

'They've found some friends,' Héloïse said.

'So I see. It is a good spot for kites.'

'I expect they think he's their father,' Héloïse said, watching the distant figures running about.

'A natural assumption,' Flon said neutrally.

'I suppose so. He's very good with the children. I think Sophie likes him.'

'Sophie likes everyone,' Flon said unhelpfully, and when Héloïse gave a little exasperated sigh, she added, 'You must make up your own mind, child. You can't expect me or the children to do it for you.'

Héloïse smiled ruefully. 'Of course, you're right. It's just that I am finding it so difficult to decide. I wish you would give me your opinion, dear Flon. It might help me to understand my own thoughts.'

'I thought you could have guessed my opinion,' Flon said. 'It is an excellent match for you, such as your father would have been happy to make, if he had been spared. A young man of ancient family and good character, titled, wealthy, and devoted to you. Personable, too, not that that matters so much, but it is more agreeable to have handsome children, and I believe his children would be very handsome.'

'Very,' sighed Héloïse.

Flon eyed her shrewdly. 'He is French, too, which is very important. Foreigners have different ideas about marriage, and it can be difficult to adjust to them. A woman should always marry a man from her own background, if she can; then she and her husband will understand each others' ways.'

'True. All these things are very true.'

'Then, my dear, what is your difficulty? Why do you keep this good young man waiting for an answer?'

'Because — oh, because of my foolishness,' Héloïse said, looking down at her hands. 'Because my first marriage was so unhappy, and because I have known love. I am afraid I would not be able to give myself wholeheartedly, and that I would not make Charles happy.'

'Romantic ideas are all very well for the English, my love,' Flon said carefully, 'but you and I know how dangerous they can be. Love is all very pleasant, where the other qualities exist as well, but it is no basis for a marriage on its own; and where everything proper and respectable is offered, a young woman ought not to refuse just because she does not think she feels all she ought.'

Kithra came running up to thrust his muzzle into Héloïse's face and make sure she was all right, and she caught his head in her hands and shook it affectionately, and pulled his ears, and he groaned with pleasure and flopped down on his side,

419

dropping his heavy head into her lap in a sudden access of love.

Flon, watching her face, divined her thoughts and went on, 'I know you still think of him, my dear, and I know also that *you* know you ought not to. He is another woman's husband, and beyond your reach.' Héloïse turned her face. 'I would not say these things, except that you asked for my opinion,' Flon added gently.

Héloïse turned back, and smiled at her apologetically. 'Yes, I know. I did ask, and you are right, of course, except —'

'If the choice lay between the Duc and him, I would not think of urging you. I know which you would choose, and whether or not it was the right choice in my opinion, would be nothing to the point. But the choice lies between the Duc, and remaining as you are, and you were not made for the single state, my love. You are wasted so. There is so much in you to give, and much that cannot be given to your servants and your children and your dog. You need a husband.'

Héloïse sighed, and pushed Kithra gently away, and he got up and went nosing off amongst the bushes. 'You may be right,' she said. 'At least I know that I ought not to keep him waiting any longer. It isn't fair to him.' They were coming back now, Sophie and Thomas running ahead, while the Duc strolled behind them with the kite under his arm, still rolling up the string. 'Here they come. They must be hungry. I wonder what dear Barnard has put up for us?' She met Flon's eye and smiled. 'Don't worry, I will make up my mind soon. Perhaps today.'

'It's a good day for it,' Flon said.

'Good day for what?' the Duc asked, reaching them just at that moment.

'Picnics and kites and other things,' Héloïse said, patting the ground beside her.

'Especially other things,' he said, kissing her hand and smiling into her eyes. He sat down beside her and looked around him contentedly. 'It is so pleasant to have a family around me. I little thought when I left France that I would ever have so many people to care about again.'

Sophie sat down by Marie, to give a running commentary as she helped unpack the basket. Thomas came and leaned solemnly on Héloïse's shoulder, already a little drowsy with the heat, and blue about the mouth where he, too, had discovered the bilberries. Kithra nosed here and there and finally flopped down beside Sophie, to be pushed away with loud protests that he was too hot and dribbled on her, and the Duc caught Héloïse's eye and grinned. It was all very, very pleasant, she thought, and there was no reason in the world why that thought should have such a wistful quality to it.

After the meal, a certain somnolence settled over the party, and the thorn-tree's shade circled over a group content to sit and stare at nothing in particular, and think private thoughts. Kithra stretched out and snored softly in his sleep, his flank twitching as the occasional fly landed on it, and after a while Flon snored too, her back resting against the tree trunk and her chin sunk on her chest. Marie was chatting quietly to the hired coachman, and the murmur of their voices was like the sound of the bees harvesting amongst the clover.

Héloïse sat with her knees drawn up and her arms around them, a childlike pose that the Duc found very appealing. He leaned back on one elbow, chewing a grass blade and gazing at her as she pursued her thoughts. Only when he saw her draw a deep sigh, as though she had completed a chain, did he reach out and take her hand and murmur, 'Shall we go for a walk?'

She got up at once, and he waited while she brushed her skirts and retied the ribbon of her broad straw hat, and then offered her his arm, and they walked off together, taking, by unspoken consent, the path which led down into the shade of the wood. Under the trees the light was dim and dappled as the leafy tops moved in the light breeze. The earth under their feet was springy with centuries of leaf-mould, and there was a rich, peppery, green smell of fern and moss and foxglove and fool's parsley which took Héloïse back to the woods around Chenonceau where she had ridden as a child, and where she had met her first husband.

The Duc, of course, knew Chenonceau well, having been brought up on the neighbouring estate. Héloïse introduced the topic, and they chatted pleasantly as they walked along, encouraging each other's memories to yield up new details of places they had both known. Here in the wood, there was less immediately to remind them that they were in England, and for a while they were transported back to their native land, forgetting as they talked that they were in exile, and would probably never see it again.

'Do you remember,' they said, and 'Do you remember?' The smooth-sliding green glass of the River Cher, and the flat, reedy smell of it; the sun shining on blue-slated turrets and roofs, and the spicy, evocative smell of box which always seemed to go with the crunching of gravel underfoot; the wide empty roads white in the sunshine, and the rich smell of dust hanging in the air; the hazy blue smudge of Paris seen from the top of Montmartre, pierced with a hundred church spires; cats and concierges sunning in courtyards, and the smell of coffee and new bread that haunted the early streets; the sound of bells in a country town on Sunday morning, falling together for a stroke or two and then tumbling apart again; the creaking wheels of an ox-cart bringing a farmer and his family in to church, stiff in their best clothes, and clutching a great, black bible between them.

And suddenly the Duc turned to her and took both her hands, his eager face looking down on hers, his eyes alight with passion.

'Oh, dearest Héloïse, you see how much in accord we are! Won't you please marry me? We will be so happy together, and talk of France every night, to keep our memory green.'

Héloïse smiled at him. 'Dear Charles, what a reason to be married!'

He kissed her hands one after the other. 'I can give you other reasons in plenty, if you want them! Oh, I know I promised to be patient, and I have tried to be, but it is very hard. Don't you think you might decide now?'

'Yes, you are right to ask. I have been wrong in keeping you waiting so long,' she said contritely. 'Thank you for being so patient with me, Charles. I will give you my answer now.'

Chapter Twenty-Two

On Monday 1 September, 1806, James rose early and rang for Durban, and told him to bring Nez Carré in, give him a good feed, and groom and saddle him.

'Very good, sir. Shall you require me to accompany you?' Durban asked of his master's back, as James craned his head to look out of the window at the sky.

'No, I shan't need you,' said James, trying to sound casual. Durban bowed and turned to leave. 'Make sure he's well groomed,' James called after him. 'I want him to look his best.'

'Yes, sir.' There was nothing odd in the request itself, and James usually did ride alone when he took Nez Carré out for an amble about the estate, but there was something almost of boyish eagerness about his master's demeanour this morning which told Durban that today was an important day. The servants' hall had been speculating ever since the news of Mrs James's death how long it would be before he brought home a new wife, and Durban, who had always kept himself to himself, might have made a number of new friends over the past three weeks if he had cared to. But he had served Mr James in the army, and remained a soldier at heart, and gossip was anathema to him. He shrugged off the other servants' overtures with his usual brusqueness, and let them conjecture for themselves.

Durban went down the backstairs to the servants' hall, warned Ottershaw to lay an extra cover for early breakfast, and crossed the inner court and went out the back way into the dewy morning to catch Nez Carré and bring him in. The old horse came eagerly when he called, pricking his ears and snorting with pleasure at the prospect of an outing. Durban had no need to hold his headcollar as they walked back along the track towards the barbican: Nez Carré nodded along beside him as though his head were fastened to Durban's shoulder.

'It'll be a long day for you, old 'un,' he said conversationally. 'I hope he remembers to give you another feed when you get there. But I reckon he couldn't do it without you. You've always been there, when anything important happened, haven't you?' Nez Carré blew in Durban's ear by way of answer. 'Maybe you'll even have to do the asking for him.' He stopped talking as they reached the drawbridge and he saw the gatekeeper standing under the arch smoking his first pipe of the morning.

'Mr James going out, then?' the keeper said indistinctly between puffs. Durban nodded curtly, catching Nez Carré's headcollar in case he should shy away from the smoke. 'Aye, well, he's got a nice day for it,' the keeper went on, reaching out to pat Nez Carré's shoulder as he passed. 'Reckon t'old 'oss could put 'is own saddle on by now, eh, Mr Durban? Knowing old devil! Where's young master off to, then?'

But Durban was past him and entitled to ignore the question. He put Nez Carré into an empty stall and went off to mix him a feed, and the boy doing the watering, who passed him in the yard, could not have guessed from the impassivity of his face that his thoughts were far from calm. I hope to God she doesn't turn him down this time, he was thinking anxiously.

Nez Carré was so glad to be out that he would have dashed off at a canter had James let him, and in spite of his years, he gave his master no easy ride until he settled down into his long, comfortable stride. What Durban had said was true — Nez Carré had been there at all the important moments of James's life, and to have left him behind, today of all days, would have been unthinkable. James's spirits were high, and he sang aloud as he rode across the fields, and the horse's long ears flicked back and forth, listening to him.

It was only when they reached Oulston, the next village before Coxwold, that James began to feel nervous. Twice before they had been prevented from marrying, and it seemed almost too good to be true that there was now nothing to come between them. His over-heated mind began to tease him with dire possibilities. Supposing something had happened to her? A runaway horse, a mad bull, a rabid dog, a lightning-struck tree, a cliff-fall, an earthquake? Or any one of fifty fatal diseases? Nez Carré, sensing his mood, began to sweat, fidgeting and trying to break into a trot, and James forced himself to be calm, eased his hands and let the horse walk out and stretch his neck. This was the purest folly, he told himself, and deliberately shut his mind to speculation. He would have his answer in a few minutes, so why torment himself?

Now here at last was the village, the main street with its ancient church and pretty inn and modern fronts added to old houses; and here was the turning at the end of the street, and there the white paling fence, and the neat house of mellow brick which he remembered as well as if had been his childhood home. The creeper had grown a good deal since he had seen it last, and the white roses climbing over the face of the house were nodding in at the open bedroom windows. She still had not begun the building of the new wing, he thought with a smile. Well, she never would, now.

Nez Carré was still moving freely, not even tired by the leisurely journey. With rest in the shade, water and a feed, he would be as fresh as ever for the journey back later today. James jumped down and led him into the shade of the chest-nut tree, and was running up the stirrups when a movement at the door of the house called his eye. He expected it to be Stephen, coming out to take his horse, but it was Héloïse.

She had come out alone to meet him. In his mind's eye he saw her for an instant as she had been that first time he had seen her here, in a brown cambric dress and blue apron, with her hair tumbled and a smut on her nose; nine years ago, he realised in astonishment. She hadn't changed much: she was not one who would ever look very different. Today she was wearing a long-sleeved dress of spotted muslin, very soft and flowing, with her hair in Roman curls on top of her head, bound with a blue ribbon. She looked like any lady of fashion, cool and elegant and languid, until you noticed the narrow vivid face and the great black Stuart eyes, and the lips parted in a troubled smile.

Of course, she had seen his mourning-clothes, and knew someone must be dead. She was waiting, apprehensively, to know the worst, anticipating no pleasure from his visit, but simply that of seeing him again. The dog he had given her came thrusting past, head low and tail swinging, to investigate him, jabbed its muzzle against his leg and stared up at him with its yellow wolf-eyes. Nez Carré snorted and pawed the ground warningly, and Héloïse called sharply, and the dog ran back to stand beside her.

'I'd forgotten you had called him Kithra,' James said.

'Did you ever know?' she said. 'James, who it is? Who has died?'

He had to reach inside himself for the words. It was strange how shy and uncertain he felt. Whenever he had imagined this moment, he had always seen himself rushing to her, claiming her joyfully and unhesitatingly; but the reality was not like that. He was too conscious of her as a separate person, and suddenly as he stood looking at her, he could not think of any reason why she should accept him, after all this time, after all he had done and not done, all the failures of his life.

He had a very strong impulse to jump back on Nez Carré and ride away without speaking, which he resisted as too absurd. Behind her he saw movement at one of the windows, and guessed she had forbidden anyone to come out until she called them. Anyone was having difficulty in restraining herself, and the thought made him smile inwardly. He crossed the distance between them and stood before her, grave and undefended.

'My wife and son,' he said. 'Last month, in Manchester, of a fever. She had been visiting the sick, and took the boy with her, God knows why. They took ill and died the same night.'

She did not speak; her eyes were wide with apprehension. It was impossible that she, intelligent as she was, did not draw the same conclusion from the news as he had, but she betrayed no faint glimmer of pleasure that he was now free to marry her. James had heard from Marie, how Héloïse had danced around the room when her husband was dead, how she had refused to mourn him. But that was different, of course, he had been an evil man, and only her fierce sense of honour had made her take care of him in his illness. The fear of being glad that Mary Ann was dead must be so strong in

426

her that it quite extinguished any spark of happiness she might have in his presence. Well, he thought grimly, whatever pleasure I have ever brought her, there has always been pain mixed in with it.

'I thought you might have heard already,' he said.

'No,' she said, and had to moisten her lips before she could continue. 'No, I had not heard — I suppose — James, what can I say?'

'Don't say anything. I won't play the hypocrite with you. You know how I felt about her. There was a time when I might have been glad of her death — thank God, that was a long time ago! But still, when I first heard, I felt guilty and remorseful. Well, I've gone through that, and there's no need to trouble you with it. It was one of the reasons I did not come to you at once.'

'One of the reasons?' she said. He was surprised at how upset she seemed. Even her lips were pale. He had not expected it to be so great a shock.

'Of course, I thought of you at once — that was natural. But I wanted to do everything properly this time, to make sure we got it right. Marmoset, when you sent me away before, I didn't entirely understand — well, you know that. Left to myself I should not have gone, and though I don't think we should ever have stopped loving each other, I think I see now that we would not have been happy.' He frowned with the effort of putting it all into words. 'I always came to you before like a noisy, heedless child, demanding what I wanted as if I had a right to it, and leaving you to pay the price. If you had not sent me back that time, I would have stayed that child. I would never have grown up.'

'Oh James,' she began, and he waited, but she didn't seem to be able to go on.

'I'm different now,' he resumed with a little, crooked smile. 'You see, I don't come to you demanding: in fact, I'm as nervous as a colt. I come, not as an equal, because I know I can never be your equal, but at least as one who is free to ask, who has something to offer you, in exchange for all your great goodness. I am a widower, Marmoset. I love you with every living part of me, and I am come to ask you to marry me.'

He hardly knew what he expected her reaction to be, but

he had not expected that little, fluttering movement of the hands, or the tears. He took her in his arms at last, not to kiss or caress, but to comfort.

'My dear, what is it?' he asked gently as she wept into his waistcoat. The words came in fits and starts, and painfully.

'Oh James, first my husband came back, and we could not marry, and then when he died, I came to find you, and you had married. It was as if God were against us, so that it should never be. I gave up hope at last, and I tried to stop loving you, but I could not.'

'I'm glad of that, at any rate,' he said gently, stroking the back of her neck while she clung to him with little hooked hands like a bird's claws. She lifted a hot, wet face at last to look up at him in distress.

'But you don't understand! Now your wife has died, and Charles — the Duc, you know — has been asking me for so long to marry him, and only last week I gave him my answer.'

It was James's turn to feel shock. He had not imagined this, blind idiot that he was! He had never thought there could be anyone else for her.

'You — you've accepted him? Dear God, Héloïse!'

The fingers gripped harder. 'No, no, I refused him! But James, I almost said yes! Just think what might have happened!'

And suddenly he was laughing, so violently that she thought at first he was ill. 'Oh Marmoset, you *fool*!' he crowed. He doubled over with laughter, almost choking with it, while she watched him at first with puzzlement and then with disapproval.

'James, stop it at once! Have you gone mad? Oh, do stop, it is not funny at all!'

And at last he drew a long, gasping breath, and straightened up, and took her into his arms, and looked down, wet-eyed and shaking, into her adored face. 'My dear love, never, never, never, will I let you go again! Once I have married you, I won't let you out of my sight.'

She looked demure. 'I have not said I will have you, yet.'

He kissed her forehead and folded her in against him. 'I don't propose to give you the chance to refuse me. To think you almost accepted that block of a duke!'

'He is not a block!' she said indignantly, pulling back from him. 'He is a charming young man, handsome and clever and —'
He silenced the rest of the sentence by kissing her, and when she could speak again it was with a joyful smile.

'We must go and tell the children, and Flon and the servants,' she said happily.

'I think they will have guessed already,' James said with a glance at the windows.

'Oh, were they watching? The villains! But they will be so pleased, James.'

'I certainly hope so; but I give you fair warning, that if anyone disapproves, they had better keep it to themselves. I don't propose to change my plans for anyone this time.'

'And what are the plans?' she asked. 'When shall we marry?'

'In my heart,' he said, 'this very instant; but publicly, I feel I ought to wait a little while, at least until I have completed three months' mourning.'

She nodded. 'Yes, that is proper. It ought to be more, but I am so afraid' — with a little, anxious frown — 'that something will happen to prevent us.'

'I know,' he said. 'So am I.' And he placed his arm over her shoulder, and she wound hers round his waist, and they walked towards the house to tell the news.

'Monsieur Barnard will be so glad to go home,' she said.

It was well after dark when James reached Morland Place, but there was enough moon for Nez Carré to find his way over such familiar ground. It was well that he could pick his own ground, for James had too much to think about to do it for him. His mind was crowded with the images of the day, of the joy and clamour of the little house. It was so different from Morland Place, where everyone went alone about his own business, and the servants were remote, well-schooled figures who served but did not intrude. At Plaisir everyone knew where everyone else was, what they were doing, how they felt, all they hoped and feared and thought. When Nan got a splinter from the logbasket, she howled at the top of her voice, and everyone else came running to expostulate, examine, and comfort. Bernard the cook flung saucepans about the kitchen in a rage, Stephen quarrelled with Alice about some point of etiquette, Marie sang at the top of her voice because it was her day off tomorrow, the children ran in and out, and everyone a hundred times a day went to find Héloïse. The only silent creature in the house was Kithra, but his hard, wet nose and his lashing tail more than made up for his lack of bark in making his presence felt. They lived on top of each other like puppies in a basket, and there was no room to be ignorant of or indifferent about each others' concerns.

It had all left James feeling rather bemused; and of course, there had been the children to get used to. It was almost an insult calling Mathilde a child; for she was evidently quite a sophisticated young lady. She had been full of her experiences in Brighton, where the genial attention of so many young officers had begun to place her passion for the Duc in a proper perspective in her mind. Héloïse had warned James that she had not told Mathilde about his offer of marriage. Since her disappointed lover had gone back to London before Mathilde had arrived at Plaisir, there seemed no reason to upset her by mentioning it; but James, having listened four times to a description of the perfections of a Major Ashton of the Ninth, thought that Héloïse's delicacy came a little after the event.

The children were very disturbing to James. Thomas, to his eyes, had already a great look of Weston about him, and brought home strongly to James's mind the whole tragedy of his sister's sad life. Lucy's love for Weston had been as strong as his for Héloïse, but even he could hardly begin to guess at what she must be suffering from her appalling loss. His own emotions, tangled as they had always been, from his childhood loneliness, his youthful passion for Mary Skelwith, his growing understanding and love for his mother, ripening at last into what he felt for Héloïse, gave him little insight into the feelings of a single-minded creature like Lucy. She loved with a simple, unquestioning directness like an animal, and like an animal would be unable to rationalise her loss.

All this went through his mind when he saw Thomas; but Sophie dazzled him into wordless humility. Thomas might be a symbol of many things, but Sophie was a real, human child, bones and flesh and skin that smelled like fresh wood-shavings, a missing tooth and a smile like sudden sunshine, arms like twigs and scarred elbows, overflowing with high spirits and a geniality too large for her small frame, constantly spilling over into hugs. She hugged her mother and Thomas and the dog, she hugged the servants and the handsome china baby that the Duc had bought for her; she even, perilously, hugged Monsieur Barnard, and he would smile sidelong at her, and annoint her forehead with whatever was on the wooden spoon he happened to be holding at the time.

She would have hugged James, too, but for her perfectly natural shyness, for if he had to get used to the fact of her being his daughter, she had to get used to having a father. They treated each other with a certain grave formality at the moment, through which willingness to like each other shone so patently that it needed only the right occasion for affection to begin. James could never have enough of looking at her, and had to be careful not to stare unless her attention were occupied elsewhere. Héloïse said she looked like him, but he could not see it. Certainly she had his soft, reddish dark hair, and there was something of him in the shape of her face, which was broader than her mother's and more regularly featured. But James could only see that the warm olive skin and the great dark eyes were her mother's; and that most of all, Sophie looked like Sophie.

'How could we have made her?' he murmured to Héloïse at one point when they were all in the garden, and Sophie was pretending to be Mathilde dancing at her coming-out ball, which had Thomas in fits of giggles.

'We didn't,' Héloïse said serenely. 'God made her.' And then she had turned to meet his eyes, and the same thought had occurred to both of them, and her cheeks had grown a little pink. When they were married, they could have others — not like Sophie, for who could be like Sophie? — but others as wonderful and precious. James thought of the Morland Place nurseries full again, and could almost feel his mother's spirit smiling approvingly at him.

So the contrast between the two households struck him very forcibly when he arrived back at Morland Place. Edward and Father Aislaby were in the drawing-room, where a fire had been lit against the cool of the evening. The sight of the two men sitting in silence to either side of the fire struck him as somehow pathetic. We have been three old bachelors, for all that Mary Ann lived here, he thought.

They looked up enquiringly as he came in, and seeing James's expression, Edward said, 'It's all settled, then? Congratulations.'

'You know where I've been?'

'Durban told me. Oh, it wasn't his fault: when you were gone so long, I was worried that you had had an accident, so I made him tell me.'

James grinned. 'But I hadn't told him! I suppose it's foolish to think you can ever keep anything from your own servant. Yes, I went to Coxwold and asked Héloïse to marry me. I hope you approve?'

'Of course I do. I know how much you care for her. And I think it's the best thing that could happen for all of us,' Edward said. 'She'll put things right again. It will be almost like having Mother back.'

James was deeply moved that Ned, from the depths of his own loneliness, could be so generously pleased for his brother. 'Thank you for that,' he said. 'I know Mother would have wanted . . .' He had to stop and clear his throat.

'Have you made any arrangements?' Father Aislaby supplied the silence.

'Not in detail, only that we shall wait until I have done three month's mourning before we marry. It ought to be longer, I suppose, but neither of us can bear any more delay.'

'You'll be married here, in the chapel?'

'Oh yes,' James smiled. 'I wouldn't feel married otherwise. I hope that as trustee of the estate, Ned, you will approve my installing a new wife and her household? You have the final say; if you disapprove, we'll have to go and live somewhere else.'

'Don't be silly,' Edward said vaguely, his mind elsewhere. 'I say, Jamie, have you thought how you're going to break this to Fanny?'

James looked puzzled. 'Break it to her? Why should you think it will be bad news? She never cared about her own mother, so why should she mind a new one?'

'I don't know *why* she should,' Edward said, 'but I'll wager the crown of England to a bent nail that she will.'

James saw from Aislaby's expression that he agreed with Edward. He frowned. 'She doesn't know where I went today?'

'No,' said Aislaby. 'She asked, of course, but I just said that you had gone out on business.'

James shrugged it aside. 'Oh well, I'll face that problem when I come to it. I expect she'll get used to the idea quite quickly.'

Happiness made James wake early the next morning, and he lay for a while savouring the unfamiliar feeling of looking foward to his life with delight. Everything would be different from now on, he thought. He would cast out his old, bad habits, lying late abed, missing morning mass, getting drunk at the Maccabees and coming home in the middle of the night. He would sleep every night with Héloïse in his arms, and wake to joy and companionship. He looked back over his life and was appalled at the loneliness in which he had lived almost all of it. Well, that was all over now. He would have a companion with whom to share every moment and every thought.

He couldn't lie still. He had to share his happiness with someone, and decided that it ought to be Fanny first of all. She was still sleeping in the nursery, having it to herself again now that Lucy had gone back to Wolvercote with her children, and James dressed himself, padded the short distance to the night-nursery, and went in.

Fanny was up, kneeling on the window seat in her night-gown and looking out of the window. She turned as James came in, and her face lit, until she remembered she was cross with him, and then she settled a scowl over her features.

'Lord, Fanny, what's that for?' James blinked.

'You went out all day yesterday, and you didn't even come and say goodbye. And you didn't come up and say goodnight when you got back, either, and I was still awake, because I heard one of the maids knock at your door and tell Durban.'

James sat down on the window-seat beside her and pushed

some of her night-tangled hair off her face. 'I'm sorry, my love. If I'd known you were awake I'd have come up, but I had a lot of things to discuss with Uncle Ned and Father Aislaby.'

'Did you bring me a present?'

'No, but I have got some wonderful news for you.'

'Is it about where you went yesterday?' Fanny asked suspiciously.

'Yes. Do you know where that was?'

'No,' Fanny said pouting. 'Sarah and Lizzie were whispering last night after I was in bed, but I couldn't hear what they were saying. Where *did* you go, Papa? I asked Durban, but he wouldn't tell, nasty cross thing.'

James laughed. 'Fanny, my darling, how would you like a new mother, and two new sisters, and a little brother? Well, a sort of brother, at any rate.'

He offered it like a great treat, but there was no answering pleasure in Fanny's face. 'No thank you,' she said firmly. 'Is that where you went?'

'I went to see a lady whom I've known for a very long time, since before you were born, or I even met your mama. I wanted to marry her long ago, but there were reasons why we couldn't. But now I've asked her to marry me, and she's said yes.' Fanny's scowl grew fearsome. 'Aren't you pleased?'

'No,' said Fanny at once. 'I don't want you to get married. I like you like this. I don't like this lady. I don't want her here.'

'Fan, you don't know her. She's the nicest lady in the world. Wouldn't you like to have a new mother, to tuck you up in bed, and buy you pretty clothes, and take you out in the carriage?'

'No,' said Fanny furiously.

'And two nice new sisters to play with?' James tried with waning hope.

'No. I hate them! I won't have them! This is my house, everyone says so, and if it's my house I won't have this horrible lady. You're my papa, and they shan't have you!'

James tried coaxing, but Fanny put paid to that by bursting into tears, and when he went on trying to persuade her of the pleasures of a new mama, she increased the volume and quickly managed to cry herself into hysterics. The maids came running, and after a while James crept out, crestfallen, followed by a hostile, red-eyed glare from his whooping daugher. Outside in the passage he found Durban waiting for him.

'She'll get used to the idea,' James said hopefully. 'It was just the shock, coming so soon after her mother's death.'

Durban had no need to reply. For once, his opinion was there to be read in his expression.

For Héloïse, there was no dissenting voice in her household. Once the maids had been assured that they were to remain in her service, they could only be happy for her, and Barnard looked forward with relish to returning to his own kitchen, and having the scope of a large household on which to exercise his skills. Stephen was a little doubtful as to whether the change would be for the better for him, for in a large household he would not have the single authority he had at Plaisir, but Héloïse assured him that they would find some suitable position for him, which would not be beneath his dignity, and he had to accept that.

Mathilde was transported by the romance of it all. Dear Madame was to marry her childhood sweetheart, and they were all to go and live in a real castle, with a moat and drawbridge and a ghost and everything! It was like something in a novel. Of course, Madame and the gentleman in question were both widowed and quite elderly, but in spite of that, they were so much in love it was quite pretty to see. And they were to live close to York, which, to one who had recently discovered the pleasures of dancing, could only be a benefit. Lizzie Spencer went to assemblies in York, and she said that all the best people attended them, and lots of officers from the barracks at Fulford.

Sophie was a little sad at the thought of leaving Plaisir, which was the only home she had ever known, but the promise that she should be a bridesmaid and Thomas a page at Maman's wedding, and that they should both have ponies and learn to ride when they went to the new house, did a great deal to put it in its proper perspective.

'I keep being glad about such absurd things,' James said to Héloïse on one of his frequent visits to discuss plans. 'This morning when I woke up, I found myself thinking that your park phaeton and ponies would at last be used for the purpose they were intended for — driving about the Morland estate.'

'I know,' Héloïse smiled. 'I mean, I understand how you feel. I was telling Mathilde the other day about the swans on the moat, and I suddenly heard myself, how enthusiastic I was being about them. Oh, but I shall be so glad to be at Morland Place again! I keep thinking that I am going home.'

'I'm glad you feel like that about it. There are quite a few of the old servants still there, who remember you. You should see their faces light up when they talk about you.'

'It is so lucky that your cook — what is his name? Danvers, yes — so lucky that you could find him a place. I could not imagine Barnard serving under anyone else.'

'Oh, John Anstey's delighted! He's had one bad cook after another, and he's always envied us Danvers, and Danvers is delighted to be moving to a new house, with a modern kitchen, and to be able to spend his off-duty time in the city, instead of having nothing but fields around him. So everything works out very well. I shall be glad to have Barnard back at Morland Place, though I don't know what he'll think of the Rumford Mary Ann installed. She and Barnard never got on together.'

Some of the light in her face faded at the mention of Mary Ann, and by an understandable connection of ideas she said, 'Is Fanny still against it?'

'I'm afraid so,' he said. 'I thought she'd come round to the idea in a day or two, but she still sulks and scowls and bursts into tears if I try to talk about you.'

'It is very bad,' Héloïse frowned. 'I don't know what we should do. Do you think perhaps I ought to come and meet her, so that she can see I am not an ogre?'

James looked doubtful. 'I'm only afraid it may put you off the whole idea if she is unpleasant to you. She can be very bad when she really puts her mind to it.'

Héloïse laughed at that. 'Oh, you foolish, do you think *anything* could make me want not to marry you? I'm only afraid that something will happen to stop us.' She clutched his hand.

'I can't tell you, James, what terrible, stupid fears I have.'

He put his arms round her. 'You don't need to tell me. I have them too, all the time. But everything will be all right, you'll see.'

As Fanny continued intransigent, it was decided that Héloïse should come to Morland Place one Sunday and spend the day there, so that Fanny could be introduced to her and, it was hoped, discover her to be no threat. The fifth of October was chosen, and dawned a delightful, sunny, Indian-summer day after several wet weeks, and everything seemed set fair for Héloïse's first visit to Morland Place in ten years, except that Fanny refused to get out of bed.

The baffled maids at last were forced to call upon James to solve the problem, and he went up to the nursery and tried to coax her.

'Come on, Fanny, don't be silly. I promise you you'll like her. Everybody does. She's so very pleasant and good-tempered; and I want you to make a good impression on her. You can be such a good girl, and I want you and her to love each other.'

'I won't love her. I hate her!' Fanny cried into her pillow.

'You're just being silly,' James said, beginning to feel irritable. 'Now get up this instant and let Sarah dress you. Madame will be here soon, and I want you to be downstairs ready to greet her when she arrives.'

'I won't! I won't have her here! I hate her! If she comes here, I'll kill her!'

James grabbed her by the shoulders and shook her roughly. 'Now that's enough! I won't have you talking like that! I've tried to be patient with you, God knows. Get up this instant, and get dressed, and come downstairs, and I warn you, Fanny, if you don't behave yourself today I shall be very angry indeed.'

Fanny eyed him cautiously, aware that this time he was serious. Her tantrums had reached the limit of their effectiveness. She burst instead into unhappy rather than angry tears.

'You don't love me any more!' she wailed pitifully. 'You love this other lady instead, and when she comes you won't want me, and you'll send me away!'

James took her in his arms. 'Oh Fanny, sweetheart, is that what's the matter? Of course I love you! My getting married won't make any difference. You'll always be my darling little girl.'

'Promise me! Promise you won't love her more than me!'

'Of course not. I love her differently from you. Don't be silly, Fan.'

'Say you love me best!' she cried passionately, and James obliged.

'I love you best of all, Fanny. Now will you be a good girl and get up, and be nice to Madame when she comes?'

Fanny nodded into his shoulder, and allowed herself to be detached inch by inch. James handed her over to Sarah, who had been waiting all the while with her clothes, and went out, and Fanny, still hiccoughing and wet-cheeked, watched him go thoughtfully. She knew how far she could push her father, and though that was a very long way indeed, she was aware that she had come to the end of his tether at last on this matter. She would have to change her tactics.

When Héloïse arrived for her visit, therefore, she found a subdued and outwardly polite Fanny waiting in the great hall to say how-do-you-do and curtsey.

'How do you do, my dear,' Héloïse said pleasantly. 'I hope we shall be friends.'

'Yes, madame,' Fanny said demurely, as she had been instructed, and James, standing behind her, felt a surge of relief. He did not see, as Héloïse did, the burning look of hostility in the eyes she lifted briefly to her rival's face as she rose from her curstey.

It was a pleasant day. After taking some light refreshment, they all went for a walk around the gardens while the sun was high, and James produced some bread for Héloïse to feed the swans, which made her laugh. Then Father Aislaby went away to his duties and Fanny to her dinner, and the other three looked over the house together, and made plans.

'I thought we'd sleep in the great bedchamber when we're married,' James said. 'It needs new hangings, but we can get that done before the day. My mother and father slept there, you see, and they were so happy, I feel it would be appropriate.'

438

Héloïse smiled. 'Thank you. I should like that. And what of the others? Mathilde is too old to sleep in the nursery. She ought to have a room of her own.'

'The west bedroom is the prettiest,' Edward said. 'Our sister Mary always used to have it. It's a nice bedroom for a young lady.'

Héloïse hesitated. 'I wonder, if it is the best bedroom, shouldn't Fanny have it? She is the young lady of the house, and the heiress, too.'

'Fanny sleeps in the nursery,' James said.

'But I think she will not like to share it with my children,' Héloïse said carefully, forbearing to add that she did not like the idea of Fanny, in her present mood, having free access to Sophie and Thomas. 'If the occasion of our marriage is also the occasion of Fanny's being given her own room, like a grown-up girl, it might help to reconcile her.'

'That's a good idea,' Edward said. 'I think you ought to do that, Jamie.'

James shrugged. 'All right, if you think it will help. Then Mathilde had better have the red room, I suppose — not that it's very red now, but I can't get out of the habit of calling it that.'

They continued their stroll, talking about redecoration and new hangings and china and linen. They wandered into the long saloon and Héloïse stopped in front of the portrait of Arabella Morland and stared at it thoughtfully.

'I wonder what Mathilde will think of it when she sees it — but probably it will not strike her. One can never see the likeness of oneself in other faces. I told you, did I not, James, how your mama and I were sure that this lady is Mathilde's ancestress? There will be a kind of rightness, after all this time, in Mathilde's coming to live here. As if a loose end has been tied.'

James put his arm around her. 'Everything about your coming here is right,' he said. 'And Mathilde's is not the only loose end. You should have been mistress of Morland Place long ago, when we first meant to marry; and now you will be.'

'For a little while only,' Héloïse reminded him with a faint smile. 'Don't forget it is Fanny's inheritance. And when she comes of age, we may find ourselves turned out.'

James laughed. 'Oh, she'll have got over her sulks by then, my darling, I promise you. And if she doesn't, we can always go back and live at Plaisir.'

'You're keeping that, then?' Edward said.

'Certainly,' James answered for her. 'We shall use it to get away together, when having all these people around us becomes too much.'

'Oh, but I like to have lots of people around me, James,' Héloïse objected. 'It is what I have looked forward to most.'

'Not most, darling,' James prompted, but she gave him a wicked smile, and refused to yield.

The offer of the new bedroom did something to placate Fanny, though at first she was suspicious about why the unknown Mathilde was being given the red room, which was bigger. She thought that perhaps she was being fobbed off with second best, but Edward told her quite sharply that the west room was indisputably the best, and prettiest, and that the Countess Annunciata when she was mistress of Morland Place would sleep in no other, and James added that Mathilde would later have to share the larger room with Sophie, when she became too big for the nursery.

Still Fanny was not convinced, until finally James said, 'For heaven's sake, Fanny, you can have the red room if you really prefer it. I just thought you'd like the blue room best.' And then she smiled graciously and accepted.

The other placatory treat that was offered her was to be a bridesmaid at the wedding, which she refused sulkily until she learned that 'that woman's' children were to be so honoured, and then she changed her mind, provided she could be first and best, and have a better gown than her step-sisters.

The question of clothes was a vexed one to Héloïse, who doubted whether Flon's fingers would be capable of the work involved, and yet who did not want to hurt her feelings by engaging an outsider. Flon herself solved the problem by addressing it one evening at Plaisir.

'I should like to make all your wedding clothes, my love, but I fear my poor old hands are too stiff now. With Marie's help, I could still make your wedding-gown, at least, but for the rest I think you will have to engage a mantuamaker. I'm sorry to let you down so, but it's best to be honest.'

As Fanny insisted that her gown must be made by the leading mantuamaker in York, it was decided to let her make all the other clothes. Héloïse did not want an extensive new wardrobe: she felt absurdly superstitious, for one thing, that if they made too many plans, something would go wrong; and for another, the wedding would have to be small and quiet, and the wedding visits would be circumscribed by the recentness of bereavement. But Flon was adamant that her gown for the wedding itself would be the most beautiful thing she had ever seen. 'For this occasion, you must dazzle everyone,' she said.

There was a sadness in packing up and leaving Plaisir, which had been a home and a haven to them all. Even Barnard, who was to go on ahead to Morland Place in order to settle in and prepare the wedding feast, was a little sorry to go; but his mind was much more on what changes he would find to his kitchens, and how long it would take to train the other servants to his ways. When he arrived at Morland Place, he found his reputation had gone ahead of him, and the servants who did not already know him were so much in awe of him that there was an almost cathedral-like hush in the servants' hall that first day. It put him in such a good humour that he quite forgot to object to the Rumford, and even found himself using the slow hob for a particularly temperamental sauce. Fortunately no-one noticed, and as soon as it was smooth, he was able to put it to one side and hasten back to his usual place, between the open fire and the enormous, scrubbed table.

Marie's sadness in leaving was more particular, and gave her several sleepless nights. Her friendship with Kexby, the carrier, had begun casually, and she had enjoyed the convenience of having him to take her out on her days off as much as his company. He was not the sort of man even a middle-aged woman dreams of; but his tireless kindness and good-humour had recommended him more and more to her affections, and now the thought of never seeing him again quite overset her.

Kexby himself, without ever in his life having meant to cause anyone pain, her least of all, brought her unhappiness to a peak by asking her to marry him.

'I'm not much of a catch, I know,' he said humbly, 'and I wouldn't have presumed to ask you, except that you was so kind as to say you'd be sorry to go and not see me namore. But I've a little house, and my business, and my bit saved, which you could have every penny to make the house nice, just as you wanted, and I'd see you never wanted for anything. I think you must know by now how much I think to you, Mary love, and it would break my heart never to see you again.'

Marie hastened to disclaim his humility, to assure him that she was honoured by his regard and flattered by his offer. It took her a great deal of heart-searching and many tears before she could turn him down. But how could she leave Madame? Particularly at a time like this. She had been maid to Madame's aunt, had known her since she was a child, and more than that, had fled France with her when her life was in danger, had gone through peril, shipwreck, poverty, exile, joy and misery with her. How could she leave her now, on the brink of a new life, and the fulfilment of all her dreams?

Had Marie asked Héloïse the same question, she might have received a different answer, but Kexby only nodded humbly, and said he quite understood.

'But York isn't so very far away,' he said hesitantly. 'Mebbe if I was to make a trip down there once in a while with my cart, you p'raps wouldn't be against seeing me again? I wouldn't make a nuisance of myself,' he added hastily.

Marie's lip trembled, and she placed her hands impulsively in his, making his ears grow quite pink and hot. 'I should be so happy if you would come,' she said. 'And perhaps, in a year or two, when Madame is settled, if you still felt the same way, you might ask me that other question again.'

'By!' Kexby said fervently. 'You just give me the nod, and I'll ask you right enough!'

The wedding was to be a quiet one, attended only by the family, servants, and estate workers. Lucy travelled to

Morland Place for the ceremony, but without the children, and there were no guests except for John and Louisa Anstey. Louisa, of course, was like a sister to the Morlands, and John had agreed, in the absence of any suitable male relative, to give Héloïse away.

She was to sleep the night before the wedding at Morland Place, in the great bedchamber, with its new hangings of crimson brocade, in the elaborately carved bed of age-blackened oak, where Morlands had been born and died generation after generation since the house was first built. James would sleep in his room in the bachelor wing for the last time that night, and they would be married the next morning in the chapel.

All the servants were lined up in the hall, including the servants from Plaisir who had come on ahead, when Héloïse finally came home to Morland Place on All Souls Day, 1806. It was an occasion which might well have given Fanny cause for jealousy, for there could hardly have been a person present, except herself, who did not regard the ceremony in the light of welcoming home the Mistress to her own; and seeing the joyful faces all around her as Héloïse went along the line shaking hands and exchanging words with the household, Fanny vowed that the very instant she came of age and the trust was ended, 'that woman' would be sent away.

For now, however, she must bide her time, and look about her for other ways of taking her revenge. The tall, red-headed Mathilde she regarded as no threat. She was quite old, a grown-up really, and no-one, Fanny was convinced, could care two straws about a thin, freckled creature with hair that colour. But the sight of Sophie had raised all her bristles. Here was a real potential rival, and the smile her father had bestowed upon the child had made Fanny cold with fury. She did not know who or what Thomas was, except that Sophie evidently adored him, and Fanny was glad, because it made Sophie vulnerable. She could be got at through Thomas, if it became necessary.

All evening the house seethed as the newcomers settled in, and there was more noise and movement than Morland Place had heard for a long time. The Plaisir household might be small, but they were very vocal, and chattering and calling to each other in a mixture of French and English, pattering up and down stairs, unpacking bags, mislaying and searching for things, and coming into the drawing-room to ask questions and receive instructions, they made their presence felt.

Father Aislaby held a special service in place of vespers, and after it, Héloïse, worn out with excitement and emotion, decided to go straight to bed. James said goodnight to her at the foot of the chapel stairs.

'When you come down those stairs tomorrow morning, it will be to marry me,' he said, holding both her hands and looking down into her eyes. She did not smile. She looked very tired, and rather subdued. 'What is it, Marmoset? Are you having second thoughts?'

'Oh no!' she said at once. 'Not that, my James! Only — I am still a little afraid. It seems too much happiness to be possible.'

'Foolish,' he said. 'What can happen now?'

She placed her fingers against his lips. 'Don't say it. The gods may be listening.'

He kissed the fingers and returned them to her. 'Go to bed, my superstitious little pagan, and sleep. Tomorrow we will be man and wife at last, and nothing can prevent that now.'

She went up the spiral stairs, and James went away to prepare himself for a sleepless night; for whatever he might say to comfort her, he knew all the same superstitious fears. When Durban came to wake him the next morning, he found his master wide awake, and wanting to be reassured like a child that Madame had not died in the night.

Morning came to the great bedchamber too, and Marie woke her mistress and helped her into her wrapper, ready for Father Aislaby's visit. Héloïse had arranged with him the night before that he should come at dawn and hear her confession and shrive her, and give her his blessing. When that was done and he had gone away, Marie came back with Flon, and when they saw how white she was, Flon said, 'This will never do. You can't go to your wedding looking like that.'

'I feel sick,' Héloïse confessed.

'It is no wonder,' Marie said severely. 'She ate nothing at

444

supper last night, and hardly anything at dinner, either.'

'Well then, she must eat breakfast,' Flon decreed. Héloïse protested, but Flon only said, 'I won't have you fainting at your wedding and shaming me. There is plenty of time. Marie shall run down and fetch you something while I see to your bath. I can hear the maids next door now with the water.'

When she had bathed, Héloïse was obliged to sit down at the dressing-table and confront a tray of fresh bread, fruit, and hot chocolate. Knowing it was of no use to protest, she began reluctantly to force something down, and then almost at once began to feel better. When the tray had been cleared, the unpleasant swooping sensation inside her died down to a distant fluttering, which she now felt strong enough to cope with.

'And now all you have to do is stand quietly while we dress you,' Flon told her. She stood in front of the looking-glass, and the image that faced her seemed remote and unreal. She thought suddenly of James, probably at that very moment being dressed by Durban in his wedding clothes, and it seemed both absurd and beautiful that they, who knew each other better than anyone in the world, should be going through this strange ceremony to establish the fact. She wished for one passionate moment that she could be tall and fair and handsome for him, and looked with disfavour at her tiny, child-sized body, dark skin, and long-nosed, wide-mouthed face. Make me beautiful, she wanted to cry to Flon and Marie, as they lifted the wedding-gown over her head and settled it about her.

Flon's last piece of work was indisputably her best. It was the most expensive thing Héloïse had ever worn, a long-sleeved gown of soft, exquisite, Chantilly lace. Even the best warehouse in York could not supply material so costly: it had had to be sent up from London, with Roberta's help. It was cream-coloured, which better suited Héloïse's dark complexion, over a plain satin slip, with a close-fitting bodice, high waist, and long, flowing skirt. The rest of her toilette was as simple: her dark hair was dressed with white roses, the last fragile blooms of the Indian summer, and around her throat she wore the priceless collar of diamonds Jemima had left her.

The two women stepped back at last to view their handiwork, and even they were left breathless by what they saw. The love that had gone into the making of the magnificent gown, and the joy in Héloïse's face, had performed a kind of alchemy. On this day, the happiest day of her life, she was beautiful, with a beauty that seemed almost more than human.

Flon could not speak, and Marie only said, 'I wish your papa could have seen you,' but their eyes said everything. Héloïse opened her arms to them for a loving embrace, and then the last Stuart princess turned and went down the chapel stairs to her wedding.

At the foot of the stairs the rest of the party was waiting, Fanny, Mathilde, Sophie and Thomas in their new dresses, and kind John Anstey, smiling reassuringly. She smiled at them, but she didn't really see them, and Anstey had to lift her hand and place it on his arm, where it rested, trembling lightly. Inside the chapel the voices of the boys lifted in the anthem, joyful, but clear and pure and inhuman, and she thought it was like the sound stars would make, if stars could sing. Two of the footmen pushed the doors back for her, and she walked forward into the central aisle.

There were candles everywhere, competing with the late autumn sunshine pouring in through the windows, and faces, row upon row, turning to look at her, all smiles, as she went past. She did not see them, either. Her eyes were fixed on the one dear, familiar form, waiting for her at the end of the aisle before the altar. Edward was beside him as his groomsman, and they both turned as she reached them. John Anstey released her and stepped back, and she came to rest beside her lover.

They had reached it at last, this goal that had seemed so unattainable, all troubles past, all hazards survived. It hardly seemed possible. He looked down at her, and his lips curved in a smile that made her throat ache. It seemed almost frightening to be loved so much.

Father Aislaby stepped forward. 'Dearly beloved,' he began, and at the sound of the familiar words, James's shoulders relaxed in a long sigh of relief. His hand down by his side reached for hers, closed round her slim, cold fingers and squeezed them reassuringly. I've got you, he thought, safe at last; and the smile with which he faced Father Aislaby was nothing short of triumphant.